THE SMUGGLERS' FINGERS

THE SMUGGLERS' FINGERS

PAUL WEBB

YOUCAXTON PUBLICATIONS

OXFORD & SHREWSBURY

ISBN 978-1-912419-08-1
Printed and bound in Great Britain.
Published by YouCaxton Publications 2019

YouCaxton Publications
enquiries@youcaxton.co.uk

This book is dedicated to
Ruth
without whose love and support it would never have happened.

Thanks are due to Ralph and Rosie Guilor and Martyn and Jacqui Cohen for getting me drunk on an Algarve balcony and making it seem like a good idea, and special thanks go to Stephen and Christine Hugh-Jones - they know why.

AUTHOR'S NOTE.

This book was started at a time when battles between would-be wind farm developers and rural communities were raging across the country.

A system that granted ludicrously generous subsidies had encouraged landowners big and small, and not all particularly scrupulous, to try and claim their slice of the pie. Most local authorities and political parties of all hues were desperate to burnish their 'Green' credentials so there was often a presumption in favour of the developments, regardless of local feelings. The turbines at the time were hopelessly inefficient, noisy and expensive, and remain to this day blots on our landscape.

It could be argued that some of these failings and criticisms have since been addressed; the subsidy regime has effectively been stopped, which, coincidentally, coincided with a huge drop in turbine costs, and local politicians woke up to the fact that wind farms were more likely to be vote *losers* than winners and so councils were instructed to pay more attention to residents. Manufacturers claim, that although getting bigger, the turbines are becoming ever quieter and less intrusive - the former is debateable the latter obviously nonsense - that much has not changed.

The events and characters in this book are of course wholly fictional but the story, whilst a little outrageous in places for the sake of local colour, could have occurred in any one of a hundred locations across the country.

But *Smugglers' Fingers* is not to be approached or read as a polemic focussed wholly on the 'wind farm wars'. Despite the tone of the above it is meant to be fun, a laugh, a satirical and irreverant swipe at the establishment and many of its institutions. No political party is spared, nor are the politically correct, and organisations from every area of life, from the WI to the EU get the piss taken.

Be warned: the book also contains reams of bad language, numerous references to drunkeness, some substance abuse (class B only) and plenty of casual sex. It's probably best kept out of the hands of the impressionable and to paraphrase one of the barristers at the *Lady Chatterley* obscenity trial: '...not a book you would wish your wife or servants to read'. Most wives these days are probably a bit more broad-minded but you might still want to keep my humble effort out of the hands of your housemaids and junior footmen.

Everyone else... enjoy!

PW

CHAPTER ONE

One day the answer to the question of whether all parties need to be present for an orgasm to qualify as simultaneous will no doubt be found, probably under a hairdryer in the crumpled pages of a once glossy magazine. But for the moment the question was rhetorical.

Within the last few minutes there had in fact been three orgasms, and two of them had indeed been simultaneous, albeit separated by nearly eighty acres, three hedges and several hundred disinterested sheep. The third had occurred some moments earlier but although presumably aware, George had not changed her deceptively lazy rhythm and had ridden serenely if soggily onto her own climax. Now, still wearing the half smile that had remained unchanged during the love making she slowly relaxed her arched back and glanced dreamily each way up and down the grassy sunken lane where the car nestled discreetly into the landscape. Through the open window she could see her bike and the trug of early mushrooms lying on the bank where she'd left them. They would have provided an alibi - should it have occurred to her to need one.

Half a mile away Sir George Hoggit, panting heavily, straightened up stiffly, took half a step backwards and gave a resounding slap to the plump pink buttocks that appeared from under his bulging waistcoat.

'Right oh, that'll do, off you go.'

The abruptness of the dismissal was not unusual for anyone Sir George considered in his employ, however temporary and regardless of whether they were serving him a drink, ploughing one of his fields or submitting to semi-consensual sex. The owner of the buttocks was neither surprised nor disappointed at her own lack of satisfaction. She straightened from the bonnet of the Range Rover and threaded a wispy piece of black string between her flushed cheeks. Sir George watched with interest, some form of underwear he presumed. The girl glanced over her shoulder with blank bovine eyes as stained jodhpurs followed the thong. Sir George lost interest and fumbled stickily under his protruding belly.

'Well go on then!' he snapped, 'back to the yard.'

Still astride, George modestly rearranged her billowing skirt and smiled down at the flushed face on the car seat beneath her. The face smiled back. It was weathered and mature but its owner had once been told, and never forgotten, that the smile was 'boyish'. Now in his fifties he was happy to believe it, grateful for the implication of youth and he used the smile often, especially with women. With George though he suspected the effect was minimal, and anyway unnecessary. She was the most extraordinary creature apparently occupying her own gentle world oblivious to the realities of her surroundings. Floating harmlessly and unharmed through village life she somehow managed to combine an incontrovertible innocence with an unconscious eroticism. Donald McCruddy knew he'd never really know her. Even their lovemaking had a vague surrealism and it had occurred to him that he probably wasn't her only lover. But their relationship had proved uncomplicated and undemanding and as far as he could tell it suited them both.

Without a word and almost unnoticed George had slipped from the back of the car. Having rearranged her skirts again, she'd collected the little wooden basket and bike and set off under the overhanging blackthorn blossom down the green lane towards the village - and the vicarage. After a few yards, almost as an afterthought, she turned and with the same distracted smile fluttered a few fingers in Donald McCruddy's direction. He wondered idly whether she ever wore underwear.

Still struggling to regain his breath Sir George had eventually shooed away his mount. The girl had used the big car as a mounting block before settling gingerly into her saddle and tugging the horse's head round. For reasons that hadn't been explained she'd been instructed to return to the stables by an indirect route that avoided the usual track, so as she swung the horse's head away and urged it into a tentative trot she didn't notice the sleek silver car appear in the opposite distance. Slowly it started making its way along the ridge-way track.

Sir George retrieved his jacket and cap from the front seat. He was a big man, always had been, but recent undisciplined years of self-indulgence and a complete lack of interest in any form of exercise had, according to his 'idiot' doctor, now rendered him technically obese. His oversized frame was not flattered by the inevitable rural uniform of sagging tan cords, large checked shirt and stained waistcoat, all subject to strains they weren't designed for. The enormous patched tweed jacket he was now struggling into completed the ensemble. His recent vertical exertions had flushed and mottled the heavy jowls and lumpen nose. Small porcine eyes glistened with rheumy malevolence and his thinning grey hair stood up in wispy tufts waiting to be tamed by the cap.

The silver car was still half a mile away and moving slower than ever. Sir George grunted impatiently, fished a large hip flask out of the door pocket of the Range Rover and after trying and failing to mount the recently vacated bonnet, settled uncomfortably on the front bumper. He took a large swig. The concoction had been introduced to him at some long forgotten shoot - whisky and Drambuie mixed in no particular proportions - and the familiar spirit-burn was a sensation he never failed to enjoy. He up ended the flask again, settled back as comfortably as he could and studied the landscape. It wasn't the aesthetics that appealed to Sir George it was the sharp proprietorial rush that this critical inspection always gave him. Almost everything he surveyed, at least in the foreground, he owned. It was an exercise that he'd repeated many times but it never failed to fill him with a grim, triumphant satisfaction; he'd worked bloody hard to get here. Anybody watching would have seen Sir George grimace painfully - it was in fact a smile.

From this vantage point the elevated ridge offered truly stunning all-round views of what many urbanite calendar buyers would consider quintessential English countryside. The gradually blurring folds of retreating hillsides with their interlocking shades of pasture and woodland were scored by lines of hedges and walls interrupted only by sharply defined monochrome trees of every shape and size. It could have been a 1930s poster for Great Western Railways. By contrast the foreground was startling in its bleakness; there were no trees and the only hedges and walls formed the boundaries with the distant roads or were lost below the steep flanks of the ridge, it was in effect one enormous field. Sir George was proud of this, he owned and contracted some of the biggest machines in the county and without hedges and walls to interrupt their mechanised courses they could move straighter, faster and more efficiently. The tree-hugging lot hadn't liked it of course and some of the locals had cut up a bit rough; there'd been some silly question over the ownership of some of the doomed hedgerows but that had soon been satisfactorily resolved - at least from Sir George's point of view. And it hadn't been cheap getting the contractors to work over a bank holiday either, but aided and protected by a group of traveling types Sir George had recruited from a lay-by outside Bartford, they'd moved the machines in after dark on the Friday and got to work. By the time some irate locals had tracked down a seriously hung-over council conservation officer late on Tuesday morning all that remained was a field of prairie proportions and a few gently smoldering piles of ash. In the meantime Sir George and a reluctant Lady Arabella had quietly slipped off to the farmhouse in Tuscany for a couple of weeks. By the time they returned the ash piles had more or less gone out and although one or two locals still smoldered belligerently the worst was over.

Sir George later learnt that this episode had earned him the local soubriquet of 'Hedgegrubber Hoggit', which to his intense annoyance had apparently caught on. He wasn't exactly sure how, but like every other bit of local gossip, scandal or libel it had no doubt been started in the village pub. And he had his suspicions by whom. The public schoolboy humour bore all the hallmarks of his despised neighbour and 'professional' Scotsman, Donald McCruddy. Sir George was convinced that McCruddy was no more a Scot than he was, and it irritated him to watch the idiot trying to play the part of the Scottish laird in this most English corner of the country, strutting around with the obligatory Labradors 'oching' and 'ayeing' with his suspiciously unreliable accent. McCruddy had even turned up in the pub one night in a kilt of an extremely dubious tartan, which had attracted much ribaldry from the corner of the bar where the youngsters tended to gather. There'd been a lot of giggling and suppressed shrieks, which McCruddy had pretended to ignore, until suddenly a buxom young thing had dashed up behind him and whipped up the kilt to reveal a pair of rather grubby boxer shorts emblazoned with characters from *The Simpsons*. A huge cheer had gone up from round the room, the reputation of Scotsmen everywhere was irreparably damaged and McCruddy was never seen in the pub again wearing anything but long trousers. Sir George smirked to himself at the memory, he didn't't go to the pub very often but he was glad he'd been there that evening. He'd even slipped McCruddy's nemesis a ten pound note when he'd met her later on his way to the gents - curiously she'd been coming out.

Sir George Hoggit and Donald McCruddy's mutual animosity went back a long way. Rooted in a long-forgotten boundary dispute and nurtured by fee-hunting lawyers it had become almost violently acrimonious before settling down into a smoldering feud. McCruddy owned slightly less land than his neighbour but it was better quality, more valuable and crucially at the moment, it held the key to Sir George's latest moneymaking scheme. His consultants in the very earliest stages had identified the only feasible route for the vast outsized vehicles that were going to be required as being along the line of the ancient green road, the sunken grassed lane once rumoured to have been a contraband route that ran straight up from the nearest useable highway to the windswept ridge. And it belonged to Donald McCruddy. It was the one part of Sir George's whole cunningly constructed plan that he had yet to find an answer to: how to get McCruddy to co-operate?

Sir George wouldn't even contemplate a direct approach, apart from forcing him to prematurely reveal his plans it would immediately expose a vulnerability in his scheme that McCruddy would gleefully exploit. Hard cash would usually have been Sir George's next approach but strangely, at least to Sir George, money didn't seem to be a McCruddy priority. 'And calls himself a Scot!' he muttered and allowed himself another twisted smile. He knew what his neighbour really wanted of course - a title. When plain Mr George Hoggit had discreetly leaked the news of his own forthcoming honour most of his neighbours and associates had been appalled but not altogether surprised. But McCruddy had developed an almost pathological envy, and having never shown much inclination towards social climbing in the past now made no secret of his ambition to catch up with his preening neighbour in the title stakes. Sir George sipped from his flask and thought, he was nothing if not a realist, and knew that even if he'd wanted to, engineering the award of any sort of honour would be almost impossible - he just didn't't have that sort of influence. God knows he'd used every contact, lever and wile he possessed in pursuit of his own knighthood. He'd spread favours and cash liberally with every political party and not a few individuals benefiting considerably. Others had not faired quite so well, but in due course a mixture of bribery, manipulation and bullying had got him onto the influential quango the chairmanship of which, he was assured, would bring an automatic 'K'. After a discreet interval.

'Not a bloody OBE, definitely a knighthood?' he'd demanded of the appalled civil servant.

Discreetly reassured, he gracelessly accepted. 'All right then, I suppose I'll take it. I know bugger all about it of course,' he'd added. 'I'm a businessman not a farmer, but never mind that.'

He'd duly taken the chair of his quasi non-governmental panel of spongers and professional committee sitters and then for several years spent a few hours a month in an irresistibly soporific committee room in the bowels of Whitehall where he dozed through dreary discussions on matters agricultural. Apart from the promised title there had of course been other benefits; he'd enjoyed the deference his position seemed to demand, it was something that as *Sir* George Hoggit he was looking forward to getting used to. The sixty thousand pounds a year stipend had not been unwelcome and the foot-and-mouth outbreak had gone particularly well; he'd been expected in London *twice* a month during the panic with a resultant doubling of his remuneration. And with the responsible department understandably over-stretched, not least by militant demands for compensation and the threat of mass suicide by dairy farmers, officials hadn't had time to question the multiple expenses claims that the future Sir George had submitted by the bundle. Yes, it had all been most satisfactory. And then in due course the promised and impatiently awaited knighthood had been bestowed. Most satisfactory indeed.

No, even if he'd been in a position to swing something for McCruddy, he wouldn't. It would be too high a price to pay. Apart from having married well, at least in the opinion of those not party to the arrangement, his title was the only social advantage he had over his neighbour and he fully intended to carry on enjoying all the advantages his superior position gave him - especially McCruddy's discomfiture.

Sir George shifted uncomfortably on the cold metal and eyed the approaching car. Taking a last swig from the hip flask he set about reviewing McCruddy's weaknesses and his own options: the knighthood was clearly a non-starter, money he was fairly sure wouldn't do the trick and a direct negotiated approach was just too risky and unpalatable. He reached under his belly and scratched irritably at his crotch. Girls, women, *there* was a possibility. Although McCruddy was inconveniently un-married - no blackmail opportunities there - he had in the past been linked to several fairly messy indiscretions. Nothing had ever reached court or the tabloids but the alleged seduction of one society hostess who happened to be the wife of a local magistrate had caused a particular stir locally. The matter would probably have gone relatively unnoticed - except by the judge who had to revoke his own shotgun licence for threatening to shoot his rival - but it then emerged that McCruddy had also been sniffing round the JP's two daughters. The eldest, a recently presented 'deb' was promptly 'disengaged' by the young titled landowner patiently ensnared for her by her mother, whilst the younger, still at Cheltenham Ladies College, had inexplicably failed every one of her GCSEs. The cuckolded husband and father had immediately taken early retirement from the bench and re-applied for his shotgun licence, whilst McCruddy had hastily appointed a farm manager and disappeared abroad on business for a month or so. Rumours from village sources, mainly female, hinted at a villa of some substance and time-share developments on one of the less salubrious *costas*.

Yes, the sex scandal angle had definite possibilities. The bastard had screwed up before and it was only a matter of time before he did again. And the Honours Committee were bound to hear of it - Sir George would make sure of that - unless of course...

He stood up stiffly, reluctantly returned the hip flask to the car and made a mental note to put out a few urgent feelers in the village about his neighbour's current 'activities'.

Despite himself Sir George was impressed by the car but he was damned if he was going to show it. He'd no idea what it was but it was clearly an expensive model. It also occurred to him that minor public servants would not in the normal course of things be able to afford such an indulgence. It would certainly raise a few eyebrows, but not, however, Sir George's. That this particular Bartford planning officer owned such a car came as no surprise to him, what did surprise him was that the council employee should be so indiscreet about it.

'Nice car,' he sneered, 'very subtle, very understated, must blend in really well with all the old bangers in the staff car park.'

The driver didn't answer, he knew he wasn't expected to. A hidden button slid the smoked glass window shut and the man got out, a gangling figure in an ill-fitting suit with thinning dishevelled hair and an uneven shave. His smile was uncertain, nervous and revealed predictably bad teeth, but the pale watery eyes were cold and calculating and there was an unexpected confidence, almost an arrogance about his body language. The overall impression was of hard-core seediness. The advertising people at Mercedes would undoubtedly have been disappointed; their Sunday supplement advertisements clearly anticipated their sleek, silver status symbols in somewhat more glamorous hands. Only a marketing man with a well-developed sense of irony would have chosen Clive Hallibut to try and project that image.

'Sir George, how are you?' The voice was hoarse and slightly hesitant.

His often intimidated and bullied colleagues at the office wouldn't have recognised this anxious slightly apologetic figure. He looked around him as if suddenly realising where he was, slowly turned full circle and looked closely at Sir George.

'Lovely view.' It was almost a question.

They both looked, Sir George for once beyond his own boundaries. The blue sky was giving way to occasional clumps of fluffy cumulus but the early summer sunshine still bathed most of the surrounding hills, fields and wooded outcrops with a crisp light. Most trees were now in leaf and with any man-made structures tucked into sheltering folds of the landscape, there was little evidence of humankind. Neither of them realised it but if the world had been flat the sea would have been visible on the southern horizon. The natural beauty of the scene wasn't completely wasted on Hallibut.

'Beautiful,' he said.

'Well don't get too used to it.'

Hallibut shot Sir George a wary glance. 'Here it comes,' he thought. He hadn't been summoned all the way out from Bartford just to admire the view, and although Sir George had always arranged their meetings where they would be unobserved, clearly today's choice of location was about more than discretion. It seemed that Sir George was in a hurry too, there were none of the usual pointed reminders of past 'co-operations' and sly references to the planning officer's personal finances, or lack of them. Today, to Hallibut's surprise, it looked as if it was to be straight down to business, but then he wasn't aware of the increasingly uncomfortable state of Sir George's underwear. Hallibut glanced ruefully at the tufts of fresh grass tangled round the number plate of the low slung car and swallowed his apprehension.

'What have you got in mind, Sir George?' he prompted. There was no response and he hurried on, 'The business park looks like it's coming on well. Nearly finished. Plenty sold and let too judging by the agent's boards. Went well didn't it?'

There was at last a grunted response, 'Hmph. No thanks to you.'

9

'Sir George...' Hallibut's voice was whiny but his eyes had narrowed, '... you know the problems that gave me. I'm still not quite sure how we got away with - managed - to negotiate it through committee. It *is* on a flood plain *and* Green belt.' He shook his head as if marveling at his own ingenuity.

Sir George's looked at him contemptuously and there was another long pause before he said quietly, 'The family enjoying the pool in this fine weather?'

When Sir George changed from bullying bombast to quiet sarcasm Hallibut knew he was at his most dangerous; he looked into the distance at nothing in particular and said nothing.

'I've had a little idea Sir George said. You're going to like this one... *and so will the council.*'

The planning officer doubted it somehow.

'We're going to build a wind farm.'

The use of the inclusive pronoun was not lost on Hallibut. 'Where?'

'Here of course.'

Hallibut had already known the answer; he didn't really know why he'd even bothered asking the question... disbelief, hope perhaps? He looked back along the ridge. 'What *right* here?'

Sir George impatiently stabbed his arm along the ridge. 'Well, there, there, there and there and then...' He thrust out his other arm, '...there, there...'

'Christ, how many are we talking about?'

'...there and there.' Sir George dropped his arm and skewered Hallibut with a challenging scowl. 'Eight.'

'Christ!' The planning officer slowly went through a full circle again as if just checking where he actually was, then took a deep breath. 'It won't work ... can't be done.' He shook his head apologetically, almost sadly.

Sir George ignored him. 'They'll be the latest models, about 100m high, in a straight line along the ridge.' His arm was up again. 'All on my land of course,' he added.

'Of course.'

'Shouldn't be too many objections, people are getting to quite like them.'

Hallibut looked at him incredulously. 'Not too many objections! Christ!' His voice became more assertive and with it louder. 'Where shall we start? There!' It was his turn to start stabbing the horizons. 'A listed ancient monument, that's the National Trust pissed off for a start. Over there! The wetlands bird sanctuary; apparently geese don't get on with big noisy, whirly things that dice them up, and the RSPB have got a lot of clout these days, half the cabinet are bloody twitchers.' He paused for breath, 'Just over there, the Gresham estates, grade one listed... even the folly. And he's a fucking lord!'

The outranked *Sir* George Hoggit gave a contemptuous snort.

'And then down there, that guy that screwed the judge's family, the Scots guy, he won't be happy.'

This was one objection too far for Sir George and he exploded with a bellowed 'Bollocks!'

Hallibut hesitated for a moment, appalled at the enormity of what he knew he was going to be asked to do, and only too aware that he'd long ago put himself in a position where he couldn't refuse. But he tried anyway. 'And then... then... all of it ...' He swept the horizons, '...everywhere ... wherever ...' He was starting to splutter, 'footpaths ... bridleways ... horse riders, bloody ramblers. The cycling lot ... tourists. Oh God! The fucking Tourist Board!' He shook his head grimly, 'no, no I'm sorry, it's just not...' he floundered for a word, '...on' he added lamely.

'Finished? Good, lets get down to a bit of detail then.' It was as if Hallibut had never spoken. 'The consultants have got a fairly detailed scheme together already: plans, reports, photos and all the other nonsense. They'll soon cobble together all the usual environmental bollocks and they've had someone have a quick look round for newts and bats and things and reckon there's nothing here that can't be dealt with - one way or the other.'

Hallibut looked at him suspiciously.

'We've got one of these energy companies on board as partners - well that's what they think anyway - Ref Watt Green Renewables, heard of them?'

Hallibut shook his head.

Sir George rubbed his hands together. 'Yes, it's all coming together quite well.' He paused and scowled down the hill. 'We're going to need a bit of local co-operation for the access roads and the cabling...' There was just the slightest of hesitations, '...but we'll soon get that sorted out. Oh yes, and we'll need a retrospective planning consent.'

'What the hell for?'

'The mast.'

'What fucking mast?'

Sir George looked at him with distaste. 'It's for measuring the wind or something. Bloody nuisance ... bloody expensive too.'

Hallibut looked quickly along the ridge. 'Where is it?'

'It's not up yet,' Sir George snapped. 'Sometime later today probably, maybe tomorrow. Shouldn't need it for long. We'll tell any nosey locals it's for the Met Office. Something to do with global warming and all that bollocks. It's only about sixty metres high and...'

'Sixty metres! Christ!'

'Anyway just talk to my people and get the paperwork sorted out will you?' It was an order not a question. 'Now, apart from that, what we need you to do at this stage is to start softening them up at the town hall. You know the sort of thing: Green energy, saving the planet, good for the community, maybe a few jobs in it for some of the local layabouts, the usual old bollocks. There must be a government policy somewhere you can say we're implementing. The parish council won't be a problem, we'll bung them a few bob for a new kiddie's playground or something, and anyway the chairman needs a bit of a favour from me,' he smirked unpleasantly. 'Get on with it then.' Sir George turned towards the Range Rover.

Hallibut looked after him. 'Oh Christ.'

'Oh, by the way,' Sir George stood at the open door of the car. 'A little bird tells me that *chez* Hallibut is due to get a bit bigger in the near future, quite a lot bigger from what I hear. Going to be expensive no doubt. Be nice not to have to take on more mortgage I'm sure ... don't want too much debt hanging over you with that young family.' He paused slyly, 'Always the risk of redundancy too I suppose ...'

Sir George left the ambiguous cloud of promises and threats hanging in the air and drove away.

Hallibut looked worriedly after the car. Sir George's information, as ever, was unnervingly accurate. Hallibut's father had died about a year earlier, inconveniently and in Mrs Hallibut's opinion, selfishly, intestate. Once the financial and legal wreckage had been cleared up only son Clive found that his inheritance amounted to the bill for the funeral expenses and a full-sized professional's snooker table. The young Hallibut had been brought up playing the game and in adulthood had always coveted the table. But now he had it, he had to house it - hence the new extension.

The planning was the easy bit; he'd knocked up some sketchy plans one morning and dumped them on the desk of one of his more cowed colleagues who'd duly made up a single-paragraph report of recommendation, surreptitiously rubber-stamped the whole lot and Hallibut had his approval by the end of that afternoon. In due course his wife would pacify their incensed neighbours and the resident's association dust would soon settle. But Sir George was right, paying for the huge new room and the two extra en-suite bedrooms he'd slipped on top for good measure was indeed going to be a challenge to his finances - to say the least.

Hallibut walked thoughtfully back across the hillside towards his incongruous car.

At the noise of Sir George's car Lady Arabella Hoggit turned from the huge chestnut horse she was grooming and with hands on hips waited for Sir George to appear. She was a handsome woman in the accepted county way; ash blonde hair, bobbed and lacquered to helmeted perfection, framing what was naturally an open, friendly and cheerful face. Not, however, in the presence of her husband, then a pinched hard-eyed mask of pursed mouth and frowning wrinkles would replace her normally pleasant features. Without Sir George's presence a casual observer would probably place Lady Arabella in her early forties, but a closer study and allowance for cleverly applied make-up would perhaps suggest ten years older. Well toned from an active largely outdoor life her figure was naturally firm and shapely making her a favourite grope at the numerous hunt balls and charity dances she attended. She was undeniably attractive, albeit with a curious indefinable masculinity; something only vaguely sensed by even the closest of her county friends but increasingly a topic of lively gossip amongst a growing number of the prettier and more knowing stable girls.

Sir George didn't like the look of the body language. He opened the car door and both feet weren't on the ground before a throaty roar confirmed his fears.

'George! Have you been shagging my staff again?'

There was a crash as a bucket hit the cobbles, dropped by the youngest and newest stable girl who'd not yet been fully inducted into the Hoggit ways. Lady Arabella ignored her and the suppressed sniggers and knowing glances of more seasoned employees and continued at the same volume, 'Poor little Becky can hardly sit down, she certainly won't be able to ride out this evening.' Lady Arabella tossed her hair and gave an unladylike snort before turning back to the chestnut.

Sir George's mottled cheeks coloured further, he hadn't much liked the vague insinuation that the girl might not have been an altogether willing participant. He nervously smoothed his hair replaced his cap and ignoring the surreptitious glances headed for the stable-yard office at a brisk lumber. And he'd almost made it, when the plump face of 'little Becky' suddenly bobbed up over the last stable door and for the second time that morning considered him with bovine disinterest. Startled and put off his stride Sir George grimaced back at her before quickly turning again towards the chipped green door. But the delay had been enough, and there was another throaty snarl from across the yard.

'There was a call for you.' Her tone combined aggression with suspicion, which immediately made Sir George's ears prick up. Anything that made his wife suspicious was normally, by definition, to his advantage.

He stopped, his hand on the latch, and turned to meet her as she marched across the yard viciously tugging long hairs from the grooming brush. At least the next part of their exchange was apparently to be in private.

'It was that slimy little weasel that you've had here before. Your so-called consultant,' she sneered. 'I recognised the voice. He didn't want to give me his name but I soon got it out of him,' she added triumphantly.

Sir George could imagine. 'Did he leave a message?'

'Just said to ring. Apparently you know the number.' Her voice lowered to a rasping hiss. 'What are you up to now? The last time that little shit was round here was when you were fiddling that so-called business park.' Her voice was starting to resume its normal volume and Sir George glanced round nervously.

'I don't want to see him round here, George. If you insist on dealing with lowlife you can do it somewhere else.'

'Bella, it's just a bit of busin...'

'I don't want to know, George. And don't call me that!' She stalked away.

He sighed heavily and depressed the latch.

'And the last time he was in the house...' she'd spun round again '... that little silver statuette disappeared. I wouldn't put sneak-thieving past him, he looks the type. I still don't know why you wouldn't let me call the police.'

Sir George shifted uncomfortably. It was in fact him who'd removed the miniature silver horse from a drawing room cabinet where through the window it had been much admired and coveted by one of Becky's prettier predecessors. She'd been delighted with the gift and with only a little coaxing had been lured to a distant Travel Lodge to show her appreciation during a champagne soaked afternoon of imaginative, and sometimes painful, role play. The corners of Sir George's mouth twitched at the memory.

'I'm warning you George...'

He was snapped back to the present.

'...if I see that little turd round here again he'll get both barrels!'

Lady Arabella didn't wait for a reply and strode back to the giant brown horse waiting patiently on the far side of the yard. There was a flurry of activity as sweeping, shovelling and grooming resumed around the yard and heads ducked guiltily back down behind stable doors.

Sir George made good his escape and slipped hurriedly into the small quarry-tiled office. He ignored the piles of rancid tangled leather tack piled in the corners, brushed quickly past the walls of out-of-date racing calendars and headed for the crisp white-painted door that led exclusively to the main and strictly private accommodation of Hoggit Hall. None of the stable staff, male or female, conquest past or potential, was allowed to cross this threshold.

Once in his oaken office Sir George poured himself a drink ... a splash from the whiskey decanter, a contemplative pause... then another larger splash. He grunted approvingly as he eyed the crystalline two inches of amber liquid, adjusted his crotch and slumped into the large leather chair. After a moment, which included a large swig, he swung round to his desk and reached for the phone.

CHAPTER TWO

The pub was generally known as 'The Smugglers', or 'The Finger' to those amused by the crude Americanism. It was small by modern standards but then it wasn't modern. Like many of its ilk the origins and history of the building were as vague as its name. It boasted the obligatory oak beams, which were more or less honest in their appearance of supporting the building and over the smoky years had acquired a rich dark patina, and of course a collection of horse brasses. The lowness of the ceiling was more than an illusion for anyone over six foot two. A few years earlier a little gentle social engineering had been attempted and the dividing wall between the lounge and the public bar had been removed. Neither group of patrons, both happy in their self-imposed drinking apartheid had wanted the change, but the demolition went ahead anyway. The missing wall made no difference, each group of drinkers continued to refer to the two ends of the room by their previous designations and treated them as such, retreating to their chosen habitat and cheerfully ignoring those occupying the other. There was a large inglenook-type open fire at the lounge end, which Sid could rarely be bothered to lay and light, and a log burner in the bar, which involved less work and was therefore more likely to be burning. Sometimes bolder occupants of the lounge took things into their own hands and raided the log store by the outside gents and made their own fire.

Simon Cassady was sitting in a lesser-favoured corner of what had been the bar. It was in fact a small alcove just off the main area, stone-flagged, in sight of the log burner and rather optimistically known as 'the snug'. As a recent incomer Simon had chosen his spot carefully, wary of any drinker's hierarchy that might have existed in the pub and keen to avoid a trespass. As usual he'd been joined by Sid, foul-mouthed Londoner and landlord of the Smuggler's Finger.

'That's a bit of a bugger,' Sid said cheerfully, nodding at Simon's elbow, which was resting in a puddle of beer. It didn't seem to occur to him that a landlord's duties might include wiping up these puddles before they achieved the adhesive qualities of discarded chewing gum. Simon peeled his right elbow off the table and reached for his glass. In truth a pint of bitter wasn't really his drink of choice but if he was to fit in with the local pub crowd he'd realised that he was limited to either a long glass of cloudy cider or a dimpled tankard of flat bitter. He'd started by trying one of the scrumpy ciders, as recommended by Sid, but it had tasted foul, just two pints had given him a splitting head-ache and he'd been overtaken by the most appalling diarrhoea before he'd even left the pub. Bitter, he'd decided, was the lesser of the two locally acceptable evils.

'It's quiet today.' It wasn't particularly but Simon felt the need to say something.

Sid looked round in surprise. 'Not really,' he said, glancing at the un-served customers waiting impatiently at the bar. This wasn't unusual. Once Sid was settled on his stool opposite Simon and nursing his ever-present half-pint pot he'd usually ignore any customers until he'd put the world to rights, or at least poured vitriol on that day's targets. These nearly always included his customers, his bank manager, the weather, the brewery, and then anything that had caught his eye in that morning's paper. He seemed to like Simon though, which despite Simon's attempts to disguise his recent metropolitan past he assumed was because of their mutual London connection. The only other person Simon had never heard insulted, belittled or scorned was Sid's wife, the heavily made up, cheerfully blousy and now mysteriously missing Beryl. Despite her obviously unscheduled departure and prolonged absence Sid remained touchingly loyal.

How and why Sid and Beryl had ended up in Plompley owning and running the Smuggler's Finger was something of a local mystery in itself. Certainly no one could describe Sid as a dreamer, the 'mine host' type with illusions of easing through retirement behind his polished oak bar dispensing real ale, home-cooked food and bonhomie to a pub full of amiable locals. The speculation had been predictably mischievous and at times lurid, particularly with the abrupt disappearance of the landlady;

there had been dark mutterings of false identities, outstanding debt and even London gangsters prowling the neighbourhood - all completely unfounded. The truth was much more mundane; perusing a trade magazine Sid had spotted a small advert for the Smuggler's Finger at what appeared to be a laughably low price and concluding that some naïve yokel was ripe for the plucking had quickly moved in for the kill. In fact while Sid was still busy making impossible promises to his bank manager the gormless yokel in question was also moving quickly, eager to take possession of his new restaurant in one of the more fashionable streets of Pimlico where he soon came to the attention of the Michelin organisation. He got his first star round about the same time that his imaginative cooking skills also came to Sid's attention - the last three years' books for the Smuggler's Finger to be exact.

Beryl in particular seemed to feel the pressures of running a new rural venture, particularly one with financial feet of clay and despite a brassy amiability had soon managed to alienate most of the locals and regularly upset visitors. Matters came to a head late one evening with a wine-flinging incident involving the wife of the chairman of the local Round Table and shortly after this Beryl announced she was going home to her mother - and promptly decamped to Lytham St Annes where she resumed a close friendship with an estate agent friend of long acquaintance. The rumour-mongers had had a field day for a few weeks, until the post mistress who was Plompley's gossip-in-chief and Beryl's only friend in the village, reported receiving a cheerful post card from her. It was of Blackpool Tower, which had puzzled Sid as Beryl's mother lived in Bexhill, but reluctantly the chatteratti had had to accept simple desertion as the explanation for her sudden disappearance and they soon lost interest.

The ambiguous postcard did little for Sid's mood. Never the most gracious of hosts his behaviour and manners now slipped below the accepted norms of common courtesy and settled somewhere between unpleasantly rude and outright offensive. His customers dealt with it in different ways. Startled strangers and visitors shocked by the landlord's behaviour simply made a note never to return, whilst the locals watched in amused fascination as Sid's rudeness reached near satirical levels. Therefore, despite and because of Sid, the pub stayed busy and popular.

For the moment the landlord was silent, slouched moodily across from Simon elbows placed carefully to avoid the adhesive puddles. Simon again felt the need to break the silence: 'I was wondering Sid, someone asked me the other day, why's it called the Smuggler's Finger? It's an odd name.'

Sid looked up without interest and licked his lips. 'Dunno. No one seems to know.' He flicked his head over to the opposite corner of the bar. 'They say one of them old farts does ... but they wont tell' he added loudly.

The two crusty but un-ageable locals in question ignored their host and continued to peer into their respective glasses, the levels identical. After years of drinking together they'd unconsciously synchronised their drinking speeds, both reaching the last dribble on precisely the same sip. They made their pints last far too long for Sid's liking but he tolerated them because they looked like a couple of extras from a rural soap opera, something Sid was shrewdly aware of when tourists were in town. They were known jointly, if not exactly with affection but with no malice either, as *'Aaright,'* a composite of the respective pronouncements they made on just about any subject.

'I wanted to change the bloody name,' Sid continued, 'But Ber ... the missus, said it would piss off the locals. Probably right,' he concluded. ''Ad a bit of fun with the new sign though.' He cheered visibly remembering the appalled reaction of most of the villagers at the unveiling of the crudely unambiguous artwork.

The large swinging board portrayed the inevitable 18th century nautical figure, more pirate than smuggler, and at Sid's insistence the artist had reluctantly incorporated every literary piratical cliché available to him: the leering one-eyed rogue wore the obligatory black tricorn hat and eye patch, he brandished a hook in place of his left hand, a parrot of extremely dubious lineage perched on one shoulder and the butt of a crutch protruding from the same armpit suggested a wooden leg somewhere down below. Inevitably the character was unshaven, ruddily flushed - no doubt by a surfeit of rum - and sported the usual brass buckles and buttons in regulation pirate style. The small area of background appeared to be a beach piled with crude wooden barrels and crates, presumably recently landed contraband.

The protesting artist had then been persuaded (on the promise of an increased fee and anonymity) to add a few whimsical 21st century twists: the parrot's expression of concentrated satisfaction was explained by a large puddle of guano graphically dribbling from the smuggler's epaulette; the character was smoking, but instead of the traditional clay pipe or cheroot an obviously modern, filter-tipped cigarette dangled from his lower lip; in his right hand he raucously waved, not a foaming leather tankard or pewter goblet but a slim green bottle familiar to any modern-day lager drinker. The whole appalling joke was rounded off quite literally with a finger up to Sid's customers. The artist had managed, reasonably convincingly, to arrange the pirate/smuggler's hand so it gripped the lager bottle with just the middle finger prominently and rigidly in view. A blackened fingernail drew further attention to the single digit and left the observer in absolutely no doubt as to the board's message. 'The Finger' crowd had loved it, presumably not realising that Sid spread his contempt equally between both ends of the bar, but the customers who resolutely referred to the pub as 'The Smugglers' or by its whole title were predictably appalled - much to Sid's satisfaction and delight.

He allowed himself a smile at the memory of the consternation in the lounge end of the bar that evening. Of course it had been Beryl who'd taken most of the stick, and Sid had to admit that that evening might just have been one of the last straws that broke the peroxide camel's back before she launched herself at that stuck-up Round-Table bitch.

'So what was the old sign like Sid?'

'Eh?' Sid started and one elbow slid into the spilt beer. 'Shit! The what, the old sign? Oh, fuckin' boring.' The scowl had returned and Beryl was already forgotten. 'Hills, cliffs, stuff like that. Bunch of blokes with lanterns, few donkeys, barrels and things. All standing around by this cave scratchin' their arses.' He chuckled unpleasantly, pleased with his critique.

'I chucked it in the log shed. I'll get round to breaking it up for the burner one of these days.'

A distant phone rang. 'Oh, bleedin' 'ell, who's that now?'

Sid grunted to his feet and headed for the bar, kicking his stool roughly at the table but Simon had learnt from past dousings and his glass was already hovering several inches above the sticky surface.

'It's for you. Probably not coming,' Sid said spitefully and tossed the cordless phone to Simon.

Simon sighed heavily. 'Hello?'

'Cassie, darlink!' It was her baby voice, which Simon hated almost as much as the feminine diminutive of his surname. 'You're not answering your mobile,' whiny baby now.

'No.'

'Why not?'

'Because it's half a mile away.'

There was a long pause. 'Oh!'

Not having at least one mobile phone within reach at all times was anathema to Sophie. She was Simon's country-weekend girlfriend, or at least that had been the idea when he'd first slunk away from London. During the week she would be married to the advertising agency she claimed to hate so much ('But the money's so good darling ... and I do meet some incredible people, even publishers, you never know darling...') and every Friday afternoon she was to point the little yellow sports car west for another weekend of misty country walks, log fires, hearty meals, and of course Simon. That had been the plan, at least as Simon had understood it. But the urgency to escape the pressures of the metropolis had apparently soon dwindled. Simon had become increasingly resigned to the breathless, sometimes slurred, late Thursday night calls when he'd listen with increasing cynicism to that week's excuse plucked from Sophie's professionally honed imagination. She wasn't working so hard at it these days, there'd even been the odd repetition: the 'impossible deadline' had been used at least twice, there'd been several variations of the 'unreasonable client', the malfunctioning lift had been pretty feeble and the heavy period was just pathetic.

'What's up?' he asked coolly.

She was ready for him. 'Oh, this account manager, he's just so...' She giggled, '...unmanageable.'

'So are you coming down?'

'Cassie, darlink, if only I could. It's just so...'

He cut short the baby babble. 'Oh well, no matter, I've got some work I need to finish too so that suits me quite well actually.'

'Work?'

'Yes, work. Writing, remember?'

'Oh yes, your writing.' There was the suspicion of a giggle in her voice again and Simon had the odd feeling that she was sharing a joke with someone.

'Your writing, of course, how's it going at the moment?'

'Oh pretty well actually.'

Simon had long harboured a vague ambition to write, or at least to see himself in print, and when it became clear that the corporate writing was on the wall at the bank it had seemed like the ideal opportunity to take a rural sabbatical and give it a go. 'Sabbatical' sounded so much better than 'redundancy'. In fact the timing had been quite opportune; the redundancy pay-off had been more than he'd expected, the bonus pool had paid out, despite the bank facing multi-billion pound losses and fines and so far the web of obscure passwords and cyber booby traps he'd left behind seemed to have kept buried any past indiscretions or cock-ups. Even so it had been a relief to get out. The financial authorities were now rampaging through the industry, a small but influential group of rabidly left-wing MPs were addressing their committees in froth-flecked indignation, and public opinion, if *The Daily Mirror* was to be believed, would have anyone caught in pin-stripe within half a mile of a bank strung up from the nearest lamp post by his testicles ... or presumably some female equivalent.

In fact now was a good time *not* to be 'something in The City.'

'Simon, are you there?'

'Er, yes, sorry, mind wandered for a minute. Um, it gets like that sometimes when you're hooked into a really good theme or plot line.' He hoped he sounded suitably intense and creatively distracted.

'What, something you're writing?' There was just that suspicion of a giggle again.

'Well yes, of course...' There was a yelp from the handset. 'Are you all right, where are you?'

Sophie pushed the probing tanned hand back down towards her knee and rolled defensively onto her front. 'Oh, in the office as usual,' she sighed, 'I'm not going anywhere soon the way these clients keep changing their minds.' She stretched out a slim arm and got her fingertips to the champagne flute.

'I thought it was an account manager causing the trouble. And what was that noise?'

'I was just sipping a coffee.'

'No, that... squawk.'

'I do not *squawk*!'

'Well you did then.'

'Simon! I will not be interrogated. I'm in the office, I've got a problem with one of our accounts and now I've spilt coffee on my keyboard. All right?'

Simon decided to change the subject. ' If you're interested...'

'Of course I am, darling. So go on, what *are* you writing at the moment?'

'Well, I've had a bit of a change in direction.'

Simon's writing had yet to make an impact, even on him. Whilst still in London he'd managed the occasional rambling observational essay, usually penned in a state of over-stimulated sleeplessness following a vodka session in a West End bar and the use of any convenient flat surface in its cloakroom. Witty and erudite at the time they were invariably rendered dull and contrived by the cold light of day.

Once established in his writing 'studio' in the smaller of the cottage's two bedrooms he'd decided that his first serious attempt to get into print would be a series of short stories. He'd spent nearly an hour perusing the magazine shelves of the village post office, studiously ignoring the range of surprisingly hardcore pornography, before eventually deciding that the readers of *Country Tales for Gentlefolk* should be the first to enjoy his literary outpourings. He'd set to work and in due course ground out three truly appalling short stories. The rejection of the first story he took philosophically, the second he would admit was a disappointment but the refusal of the third story, re-written to include a few less Labradors and a bit of heavy petting and mild drunkeness, had left him embittered. His mood wasn't improved when he noticed that all three rejection letters were identical and the returned manuscripts bore not a coffee ring, a wine stain nor a cigarette burn, not even a crease at the stapled corners - they'd clearly not been read.

'So go on, what's this change of direction? Ooh ...'

'Eh? Oh yes, sorry, I was off again.'

'Yes me too. Go on, yes, go on.'

'Are you sure you're ok?'

'Umm, yes, fine.'

'Well don't laugh, but its nature.'

'Ooh, I love nature ...' the giggle was clear, throaty ... masculine.

Simon ignored it. 'Yes me too, animals and things. I was quite good at biology actually...' There was a smothered snort from the receiver. '... well, anyway the local rag down here runs a few pieces; you know, country notes, diaries, farming bits, that sort of thing. So I thought, how hard can it be? I've done a bit of research...'

In fact Simon had spent a happy morning working his way round the Bartford charity shops putting together a collection of discarded coffee-table books covering birds, mammals (large), butterflies, native amphibians, mammals (small), and forests' worth of trees and plants. He'd even spent 25p on *Big Cats of Africa,* just in case the rumours of a local 'Beast' turned out to be true. But his best investment was undoubtedly the 10p spent on *The Ladybird Guide to the Seasons.* Although a bit dated and clearly aimed at a younger readership it guided Simon to what *should* be going on in the gardens, fields and hedgerows of Bartfordhire. Under its guidance and regardless of what was actually happening outside, Simon had 'referenced' large chunks of text from the appropriate book, introduced the first person, a few local details for authenticity and then sent the finished articles off to *The Bartford Bugle*. He'd entitled his column 'Musings of a Countryman' and was still waiting for a response but he had high hopes.

'...so I'm still waiting, but a thing I did on swallows was quite good actually.' He paused, listening intently. 'Are you there?'

Sophie hadn't pushed away the stroking hand this time. Her arched spine encouraging the insistent finger that caressed the crease at the base of her spine. She smothered an involuntary moan with a breathless: 'So... ooh, darling, have those magazine people, ooh...' She broke off, '...er sorry, have they...aah, seen sense... I mean agreed to print anything yet?' she finished in a rush.

Simon took a deep breath. 'You haven't heard a word I've said have you?'

The arms stretched above her head accentuated the flattened stomach encouraging the champagne to trickle down between her breasts to puddle in her dimpled navel before overflowing onwards and downwards. A tousled head bent to meet the flow. Her outstretched hand let the handset slip softly to the floor. 'I think he's gone,' she murmured.

'Not coming eh?' Sid rescued the phone from the spilt beer.

'Nope.' In the past Simon would have replied with a breezy: 'There's always next weekend', or something equally optimistic, but now he couldn't be bothered. He tasted his beer without enthusiasm and leant back into the corner.

'And do you know Sid,' he said thoughtfully, 'I think she was on the job.'

Sid slouched back across the room to serve two new customers who had appeared at the lounge end of the bar. Simon could only see their backs but they struck a comical contrast, the one tall and enormous in straining tweed and obviously in charge - even his body language blustered - the other, short and slight with a furtive demeanour like a diminutive rodent in greasy dark pinstripe. For some reason they made Simon think of *Wind in the Willows*. This was definitely Mr Toad out with one of the other animals, perhaps Ratty... or was it Mole? No not Moley, that would be unkind to one of the book's most loveable characters. Simon looked down the room again. Perhaps Moley has a distant cousin he mused, one who sells second-hand cars or something, that would explain his shifty manner and why he was in an empty pub at closing time with Mr Toad. He was trying to flog him a dodgy car - or perhaps it was just one of the weasels. Simon smiled to himself at this little flight of fancy, took a reluctant sip of his beer and watched the characters disappear round the corner of the bar.

Sid, having greeted the late arrivals with his customary rudeness and got a satisfactory reaction had disappeared triumphantly into the bowels of the pub. Simon picked up his glass and moodily swirled the murky remains around until a half-hearted foam appeared. When Sid came back he'd get himself a last drink, a lager. The pub was almost empty now, the only sounds a murmur of conversation coming from the latecomers secreted in their corner and a gentle wheezing from the Aarights. They tended to show few signs of life at this stage of the lunchtime session but would become reanimate shortly after six o'clock when they'd set up their monosyllabic chorus again for a few hours.

For the first time in many months Simon twitched for a cigarette. The beer wasn't doing anything for him and all of sudden he felt just a little bit alone and in need of ... something. He wasn't quite sure what exactly but ... something. There was no doubt in his mind that he and Sophie were finished. A shame - he supposed. She was a bitch of course, but the sex had been good and if he was to avoid developing nasty monastic tendencies other arrangements would have to be made, and soon. He cheered at the prospect. As it happened, over the last few days and without any premeditation he'd found himself repeatedly crossing paths with a strangely attractive woman. She wore a long floating skirt, a dreamy half smile and rode a bike - after a fashion. Two days before, he'd rescued her, the bike and a little wooden basket when for no apparent reason she'd veered onto the village green, slithered across the wet grass into a low bank and cartwheeled spectacularly into a flower-bed. Amazingly she'd not been hurt, and even as Simon helped her to her feet an enigmatic smile had remained on her lips. It was a thing of beauty Simon decided, as was the pert little bottom that had flashed before his eyes at the heart of an airborne Laura Ashley whirl on its way into the sweet peas. This lady wore very brief underwear. She was certainly older than Simon's twenty seven years but attractive in that ageless way that some women have and others can only envy. Her thanks had been casual but strangely intimate in a voice that was soft and sensual. Simon had been fascinated and beguiled.

He was brought out of this slightly erotic reverie by the sound of scraping stools and an increase in the volume of murmurs from the lounge, the sounds of people getting ready to leave. There was a flurry of loud harrumphing and hawing punctuated by the odd obsequious squeak; Mr Toad was dismissing the Mole - or weasel.

Simon heard the door rattle shut and swirled his beer again but it was not to be revived. He made his way to the bar, and since Sid had disappeared for the duration to do whatever mysterious things it was that landlords did mid-afternoon, Simon quietly lifted the heavy sticky hatch, slipped behind the bar and helped himself to a green foil-topped bottle from the chiller. He put two pound coins by the till and ducked back under the lowered hatch. As he emerged, still stooped, his eyes caught an orange flash from under the table opposite. Still bent double he crossed the chipped quarry tiles reached into the shadows and hooked out what turned out to be a tightly folded map.

Back in his private corner Simon delighted at the first fizzing chill of the icy lager, sucked guiltily from the neck of the bottle. Even the metallic flecks of foil were a treat. He glanced at his find. It appeared to be brand new and was one of those large-scale national maps designed for walkers and other outdoor types. Closer inspection of the stylised cover showed that Plompley village was near the centre of the sheet, surrounded by a large area of rural Bartfordshire that stretched nearly as far as the outskirts of Bartford itself. Simon sucked thoughtfully at his lager. He was pleased with his find; the map might prove useful for his newly adopted rural interests. Trying to avoid the spilt beer he wrestled the stiff creases until he'd managed to re-fold the sheet to a manageable size with Plompley more or less central and started to study the detail. It looked very different from an elevated two-dimensional perspective but Simon started to recognise features and slowly became orientated. There were bends in the roads that he'd never noticed as he hurried around the countryside; buildings were revealed, houses and farms that gave no clue of their presence from the ground, and there were ponds and streams, some apparently quite large, lying unsuspected in corners of fields and concealing coppices. Simon easily identified the pub, the distinct PH helped, and having established this benchmark moved on to his cottage. He was intrigued to find that it warranted its own tiny white box and noticed that one of the secretive streams seemed to run along the hedgerow at the back of his small garden. He traced the gossamer-thin blue line through a series of convolutions defying the normal rules of hydrogeology and followed it uphill into open countryside. Eventually the blue line disappeared into a random collection of squiggly lines and little wispy fans or tufts. He guessed the little tufts probably indicated some sort of marshy area and this was presumably where his stream rose, its source. He wasn't sure about the squiggles, he'd look at the key later.

Curiously, he was starting to feel a sort of proprietorial pride in this little trickle of water and taken by a metropolitan's spirit of adventure decided that he should take to the wilds and try to trek to its source, try to retrace the route his finger had just so effortlessly taken. In fact he'd go further, he'd make the whole journey and seek out those sunny uplands and climb the hill that bore forth his stream. Walking was good for you - he should do it more. He'd be able to think and create as he strode out across the countryside; he'd observe, note, absorb the natural beauty and allow it to take root in his artist's soul there to germinate into ideas and inspirations for stories and novels, perhaps even poetry ... if nothing else it might at least give him some idea of which book to plagiarise next for *A Countryman's Musings*. He looked at the map more closely and found that the contour lines looped around to join themselves in a long flattened sausage shape enclosing what he knew must be the top of the hill or ridge. Within the smallest loop the words 'Spout Hill' were neatly printed and close to one end was a black dot and the printed figure '329'. This must be the highest point, presumably in metres, about a thousand feet. That was impressive; this was no hill, this was practically a mountain. There seemed to be some sort of track or path running along the ridge, which was bound to offer views and would be ideal for poetic striding.

It was then that he noticed the faint pencilled cross 'Aha, treasure!' He smiled to himself and moved his finger along the parallel dashed lines marking the track. There was another neat little cross an inch or two along. And then another similarly spaced, and then a fourth. Intriguing. There was something worth noting along this track, at least as far as the previous owner of the map was concerned, presumably Mr Toad. Another reason to go exploring. The combination of flat bitter and chilled lager reinforced Simon's resolve; he would trace *his* stream, discover the source, conquer Spout Hill and dig up Mr Toad's treasure. He belched gently, 'parp parp'. Lager finished, he re-folded the map, placed the empty bottle on a different table and without a glance at the two petrified Aarights hunched by the unlit log burner slipped out of the door.

Once the clatter of the dropped latch had been absorbed there was silence in the pub for a full five minutes.

'That were George 'Oggit earlier.'

'Aar.'

The two old men leant forward and peered hopefully into their beer glasses.

'Or should I say, *Sir* George 'Oggit, right?' he snorted.

'Aar.'

'They calls 'im 'edgegrubber now.'

'Aar.'

They both thought about this for a few frozen minutes.

'No idea why.'

'Aar. Who were the little feller with 'im?'

This too was considered for some moments.

'Dunno.'

The other nodded sagely. 'Aar. Looked dodgy though. 'E 'ad a map.'

'Right.'

'Bound to be up to no good, that George 'Oggit.'

'Right.'

'Young feller's got the map now.'

Without any word or signal they both raised their glasses and drained the last inches of cloudy liquid.

'Expect 'e's up to no good too.'

The other nodded his head sadly, 'Aar.'

They both sat in mournful silence for a few minutes.

''Ome.' It was a statement not a question and they both straightened and started their coat-gathering, lace-tying, chair-scraping leaving ritual.

CHAPTER THREE

Bartford was an architecturally ambiguous town but with a prevalence of unexciting but nicely proportioned Edwardian and Victorian buildings designed to accommodate all, from artisan to aristocrat. Here and there the townscape was punctuated with an odd Georgian or even Elizabethan gem that had somehow resisted the 20th century appetite for cleared real estate. With a cobbled square for its curious open-sided market, some rather overstated castle ruins and a reasonable selection of independent shops and pubs the town was considered desirable - in fact so desirable that any genuine local earning less than fifty thousand pounds a year could no longer afford to live there. Tourists were slowly discovering the town helped by the recent proliferation of property and rural-escape television programmes, no matter how appallingly researched and presented. Recently, one such programme had spent twenty minutes espousing the delights of Bartford when in fact it had all been filmed in neighbouring Bogdownton Heath, a misconceived 'garden city' thrown up on slippery piles of industrial spoil back in the 1950s. The producers had only realised their mistake when the accounts department queried the address of the hotel on their expenses claims, but after a hurried rewrite of the commentary and some imaginative editing the programme had gone out anyway.

There was really only one architectural bone of contention in Bartford and that was the council offices. Thrusting skyward from the otherwise generally pleasing townscape the offices towered over the neighbouring buildings casting much resented shadows on different areas and sections of the population depending on the time of day and the season. Today, as the late morning, early June sun was high in the sky the corporate gloom cast by the building was restricted largely to the market square and one or two neighbouring streets. That the building occupied one of the most desirable town-centre positions was also controversial to say the least. The land had originally been occupied by several rows of rather dilapidated almshouses and a large two-room building that had been purpose built in the 17th century as the grammar school. A committee of well-meaning but naive trustees had somehow kept the whole affair ticking over until eventually the joint demands of outrageously inflated repair bills and similarly disproportionate accountancy fees had brought their ancient trust to its creaking knees.

Things had had to change and a new more worldly board was appointed with a brief to continue the philanthropic ideal but to make the project self-funding, and without feathering too many local nests. A plan was devised for a tasteful three-storey building, which would include community facilities, some highly lettable offices to provide income and a floor of flats, which were to be made available to the less fortunate of the town. The plan was innovative and popular so naturally the council turned it down. The demoralised trustees then allowed the matter to stagnate and were caught completely unawares by a sudden council-sponsored compulsory purchase order, which was quickly followed by a self-granted planning consent for the present concrete edifice. The new council offices were duly declared open by a rather sheepish county sheriff and with all due ceremony named Cockburn House. Claude Cockburn ('...it's pronounced 'Co'burn') was the councillor who'd paved the way for acquiring the site by overseeing the compulsory purchase order and ensuring it completely wrong-footed the trustees. He was now leader of the council.

In acknowledgement of their cooperation the planning department had been allocated prime floor space for their office requirements. Perched on the seventh floor, those lucky enough to have their work hutch at the outer edge of the open-plan space, away from the neon-lit hub and not straddling a pillar, had spectacular views over the town and what was generally held to be some of the prettiest countryside in south-west England. The ideology of the architect and management consultant who had dreamt up this noisy, stuffy and impersonal office was to create 'an egalitarian production environment with no perceivable hierarchy or preconceived areas of superiority', which the head of Human Resources had helpfully translated as: 'Everyone sit where they like'. In reality the more senior staff had bagged most of the favoured window cubicles at an early stage and even those with seniority who'd been a bit slow off the mark soon bullied or cajoled their way to a prime spot. It wasn't unheard of for a lesser-ranked employee to return from holiday to find that he or she had been ousted in their absence and was now condemned to a cell opposite the lift doors, far removed from a coveted window. Or even worse, within full view of the dreaded public desk where there was always the risk of catching the eye of some awkward member of the public. Without exception, any hapless citizen who managed to run the gauntlet of bag scanners, non-English speaking doormen and deliberately ambiguous signage and made it to the seventh floor *Outreach & Public Engagement Servery* was considered 'a bloody nuisance'.

Senior planning officer Hallibut had what was arguably the best spot on the floor. He'd managed to back himself into a corner that enjoyed a dual aspect and also the best views, looking south and west over the town. He'd further enhanced his personal space with a considerable increase in floor area after quietly spending a Saturday morning in the otherwise deserted building re-arranging the padded partition panels of his unfortunate neighbours.

It was here late on a Monday morning that the head of the *Integrated Community Resources & Social Infrastructure Policy Development Unit* - the planning department - found Hallibut. He was tilted back precariously in an oversized *executive* chair, his stockinged feet crossed on a crumpled pile of papers and plans on the corner of the desk. *The Daily Mail* was open on his lap. As the bald head of his immediate superior appeared over the beige partition Hallibut flicked out a hand to click his computer mouse, but Tom Gander still had time to involuntarily register a fleeting image of clipped blonde hair and glistening pink. He blinked several times to erase the retinal image, cleared his throat and looked for somewhere to sit.

Hallibut took his time looking up. 'Oh, hello Tom.' He lazily slid his feet off the desk and waved a hand at a chair, which like most surfaces in the cubicle was covered in a disorderly mess of papers. Tom Gander hesitated before scooping up the pile, then added it carefully to the stack on a nearby filing cabinet and turned to sit. The whole pile slid to the floor covering what little carpet had still been visible.

'Leave it!'

Tom Gander eyed the mess and sat down. 'What can I do for you, Clive?' He sounded nervous, but then he always did, particularly when he was in the presence of Hallibut. Theirs was an uncomfortable relationship. Hallibut, the senior man in both years and experience was the logical superior, but his expected course of promotion had been disrupted by one of those unexpected and unfortunate social coincidences, when the new secretary to the council's head of HR turned out to be an old friend of Maxine Hallibut's. She had duly been invited to one of the Hallibut's weekend barbecue parties and returning blearily to the office on Monday morning had chattered away innocently about the swimming pool, the luxury cars parked casually outside their garages, the Scandinavian multi-media system and the seemingly endless flow of champagne. The head of HR, a suspicious ex-detective, was already aware of jealous rumours circulating about the planning officer's inexplicably lavish lifestyle and he decided to make a few enquiries. A few words at the lodge and a couple of pints with some of the local boys and he soon got confirmation of what he'd already suspected, even though it was un-provable. He'd duly reported to the chairman of the appointments committee and within weeks it was announced, to most people's amazement and not least his own, that the ineffectual and wholly un-ambitious Tom Gander was to get a leapfrog promotion. The new head of the Integrated Community Resources & Social Infrastructure Policy Development Unit had never quite shaken off the feeling that he and Clive Hallibut had somehow ended up in the wrong roles. Like babies accidentally switched at birth.

'So what can I do for you Clive?' he repeated tentatively.

'I've got a little proposal... well *I* haven't,' Hallibut added quickly, '...a major local figure and landowner has made an informal approach with a ... proposition.'

'Oh yes?'

'Yes, I think it's something we should look at, and subject to the usual procedures...' Tom Gander allowed himself a wry smile. '...and after proper consultation, of course...'

'Of course.'

'...I think we could probably run with it.' Hallibut lifted himself up on the arms of his chair and glanced around the vast office. There were the usual ranks of bowed heads, flickering computer screens and here and there the pathetic attempts at personalisation: dying pot plants, faded photos of gurning children and photocopied witticisms encouraging the incumbent nail painter or nose picker to 'Keep Calm and Carry On' or do something, presumably sexual, standing up. It was a normal lethargic office morning. Hallibut was about to resume his seat when a stooped figure rose to its feet in the adjoining hutch and stood gazing out of the window. The figure gave every appearance of not being aware of his neighbour's presence but Hallibut knew better. This unprepossessing dandruff-flecked figure with its tufts of greasy grey hair, bottle-bottom glasses and nicotine-stained moustache possessed legendary eavesdropping abilities. Delighting in dripping any poisonous gossip he acquired into just the right ear he'd been the cause of more resignations, sackings, divorces, and in one case a messy suicide attempt, than the most vicious of gossip columnists. Hallibut signalled Tom Gander to stay silent and leant his elbows on the neighbouring partition.

'Radar!'

'What? Yes? Oh hello, Clive, didn't know you were there.'

'Bollocks. Sod off for a smoke or something will you?'

There was no hesitation or obvious resentment, the shabby figure was quite used to this form of address from all his colleagues, from the humblest post-room school-leaver to the head of department. He slotted an unlit cigarette under the moustache, thrust his hands deep into the pockets of his cardigan, stretching it almost to his knees, and ambled towards the lift. Hallibut resumed his seat with a satisfied grunt.

Tom Gander had passed the time idly shuffling some of the papers on the floor with his foot. Once Hallibut was seated again and without looking up Gander said quietly, 'How is George Hoggit?' As a matter of principle he refused to use the man's proper title. He remembered *Mr* Hoggit trying to address a council agricultural sub-committee during the foot and mouth problem. Hoggit had been so drunk he'd dropped his notes and when he'd tried to retrieve them couldn't get up again. The meeting had never been concluded. Tom Gander was himself more or less teetotal.

Hallibut frowned at the mention of Sir George. 'Yes, well you're quite right, he is involved in this but I think what he has in mind has real merit, very much in line with the national agenda. Should be acceptable to our political masters,' Hallibut smirked, 'and could probably expect cross-party support. Well thought out as far as it goes ...' He petered out.

'Go on.'

'Well, I think before we get the scoping consultation it might be as well to breech the subject with Co'burn.'

Now Tom Gander knew it was serious. To involve Claude Cockburn, the ruthless and politically ambitious council leader at this early stage meant that whatever Hallibut and Hoggit were up to it was big, and undoubtedly controversial. Big trouble.

'So?'

'So what?'

'So what are we talking about this time? Another bloody business park on a piece of flooded Green Belt?'

Hallibut ignored the implied accusation and the sarcasm. He'd got away with that; and anyway, who was it now with the swimming pool, the Bang & Olufsen and the Mercedes? He adopted his best committee-addressing voice:

'Sir George Hoggit is proposing that Bartfordshire makes its contribution to the national targets and EU requirements on climate change, carbon reduction and the provision of renewable energy by...' He paused and glanced at Gander who'd fixed him with an unblinking pale blue stare. '...by erecting an eight turbine wind farm...' Tom Gander blinked. '...on Spout Hill,' Hallibut finished quickly.

Tom Gander gave up trying to hold the stare and looked up at the ceiling for several moments. Snapping his head down he caught Hallibut apparently sneering at him.

'Fuck!'

Tom Gander swore almost as rarely as he drank alcohol but this was even worse than he'd expected. 'Spout Hill,' he repeated slowly. He knew it well, it was a favourite Sunday morning walk for the family. He rapidly ran through a mental list of some of the wealthy, powerful and influential individuals who'd be affected and who were certain to howl their protests from the back of every hunter, ruthlessly bully every councillor and bombard the letters pages of every newspaper - some of which they owned.

'Can't be done, Clive.'

'I thought you'd say that.'

'For very good reason.'

'Ah yes, well, Sir George and I...' Hallibut stopped abruptly, conscious that he'd slipped into close association again. 'Hoggit and his people have already outlined a very good case and are currently padding it out. I think you'll be impressed.'

'It's not me you've got to worry about, it's the councillors, the committee ... Co'burn. They're going to take some convincing.' He paused. 'And have you thought about local interests?'

'What local interests?'

The contempt in Hallibut's reply infuriated Tom Gander.

'Lord Portly for instance, the conservation people, the tourist board, ramblers, horse riders and, oh yes, the odd resident, you know the people who actually *live* up there. They may not be too keen on having eight fucking great windmills in their back gardens either.' Tom Gander was shocked by his own outburst; two 'fucks', one 'bloody' and one 'hell' in one conversation. It was not the first time the appalling Hallibut had had this effect on his vocabulary. He stood up to leave.

'We need to get to Co'burn,' said Hallibut quickly.

'We?' Tom Gander could feel another expletive bubbling up.

'I think we… er, Sir George …has one or two ideas that might appeal to our beloved leader.'

'I bet he has.'

'Just set up a meeting for the three of us. You look supportive and I'll do the rest. This could be good for everyone.'

'Humph.' Tom Gander was almost round the screen. 'When?'

'As soon as.' Hallibut couldn't keep the impatience out of his voice. 'End of the week latest.'

Left alone, Hallibut spun round in his huge chair and gazed thoughtfully at the distant greening hills. This was not going to be easy but it was a start.

'Bloody Hell! You frightened me to death. Who the hell are you?' The shock had made Simon sound aggressive although his body language said otherwise as he quickly backed away from the extraordinary figure that had lurched out from the low hanging hawthorns. From a safe distance he studied the small, dense and clearly mobile bush that had just tried to ambush him. '*What* the hell are you?'

The bush seemed to be a mixture of both living and dead foliage consisting mainly of last season's bracken with the occasional sprig of drooping conifer, but a closer inspection also revealed a just discernible human form. Simon could make out military camouflage, muddy canvas boots, a crushed bush hat and what appeared to be a ragged string vest round the lower face. Two excitable dark brown eyes peered out from the paint-streaked face. The whole ensemble seemed to be held together by a complicated arrangement of straps and belts hung with various pouches and several alarmingly large scabbards, which presumably sheathed equally large knives.

After this rapid appraisal Simon took another precautionary step back and rather apologetically repeated his question: 'Er, what are you … I mean, what are you doing?'

'Surviving,' came the confident reply.

'Oh.' Simon risked taking his eyes off the bush and glanced around.

'Surviving what?'

'The holocaust.'

'Oh, right. I didn't know there'd been one.'

There was no immediate reply and Simon found the hesitation reassuring.

'Well... there hasn't been one ... not yet,' said the bush.

'Oh, right.'

'But there will be. Nuclear probably.'

'Oh, right. When do you think?'

'Soon, very soon.'

'Oh, right ... bummer.'

The bush rustled, presumably in agreement.

Simon studied it further and deciding its inhabitant was probably harmless started to enjoy himself. 'What's your name? If you don't mind me asking,' he added.

'Warren.'

'Well, nice to meet you, Warren.' Simon held out his hand, which after a pause was hesitantly taken in a fingerless, black leather-gloved grip. It was a disappointingly weak handshake.

'They call me Bunny,' the bush said. 'It's better than Godfrey.'

'Yes, yes, I suppose it is. But *Bunny*? Oh I see, yes, Bunny *Warren*! Right.'

The bush rustled again: 'Or Bugs.'

'Bugs?'

'As in Bunny, like the...'

'Yes, yes I can see that one. Which do you prefer?'

'Well ... the lads in the Scouts call me "Rambo",' the bush said brightly, 'but I think they're probably taking the piss.'

Simon considered this for a moment and asked kindly, 'What does your wife call you?' He very much doubted that Bunny/Bugs/Rambo was in a long-term meaningful relationship, let alone had a wife, but to his surprise the reply was a prompt:

'Oh, always Bunny.' There was a flash of grinning teeth through the grease paint and string vest, 'or "gerroff!"' the bush sniggered.

Simon chuckled obligingly, 'Yes, right.'

'God, I'm knackered.' The uppermost clump of foliage was removed, presumably with the hat somewhere in it, to reveal a shock of brown hair and a round face plumply pink through the green and brown streaks. The remains of the bush eased stiffly down onto a convenient rock and started shedding equipment; several pouches were followed by a small rucksack then what appeared to be a camera bag.

'A camera?'

'Yep. Surveillance purposes.'

'Right. Christ, what's that?'

'Crossbow. *The Silent Killer*,' 'Bunny' said proudly.

'Is it loaded?'

'Certainly is.' He aimed the sinister matt-black weapon at a nearby tree and pulled the trigger. There was a hollow twang - and nothing else. 'Bugger. The bolt must have fallen out somewhere.'

Relieved that Bunny had effectively been disarmed, Simon thought he'd change the subject. 'What do you watch?' he asked nodding at the camera case.

Bunny looked sly. 'Anything or *anyone* that may be of interest.'

'What sort of interest.'

'Just of interest.'

Simon was none the wiser but decided his new friend was probably a practising peeping Tom.

'You'd be surprised.' Bunny couldn't resist. 'All sorts going on round here. And coming off!' he sniggered.

Simon nodded knowingly and tried to look impressed.

Bunny was suddenly on his feet again busily re-draping his equipment and moulting showers of dead ferns and pine needles. Eventually, satisfied with the remains of his camouflage he reached for the boltless crossbow and with a brisk 'Right I'm off,' ducked into the nearest bit of undergrowth, presumably intending to melt wraithlike into his background. Simon watched with interest as the depleted bush ricocheted off a couple of low branches and crashed through a hazel thicket before letting out a startled yelp and dropping abruptly out of sight. There was a muttered: 'Shit!' and the sound of increasingly frantic thrashings in the undergrowth. Then a moment later: 'Fucking barbed wire!'

'Are you OK?'

The thrashing stopped and there was a long pause.

'Yep.'

It was clearly a dismissal. Simon shrugged and set off down the sunken road towards the village and the pub.

Simon had set off that morning to trace the source of his stream as described on the map. He'd spent the previous evening armed with a bottle of Merlot, the map and a broken compass, sprawled on his hearthrug planning the expedition. Simon spent a lot of time on the floor of his sitting room, it was the only place he could breathe when the little coal fire was lit, forcing him ever lower as the room filled with choking smoke. It was one of the concessions he'd been forced to make by cottage life, along with remembering not to straighten up under the skull-cracking beams and having to eat at the pub when the ancient AGA refused to cooperate. The fire coughed smokily and spat a hot ember somewhere across the room. Simon didn't bother to pursue it, he'd long given up on his rental deposit, but he did risk a quick visit up to the coffee table to refill his glass before ducking back below the smoke and back to the map. He'd all ready taken the time it took to down two glasses to study the key in some detail; the squiggles at the source of his stream were apparently 'outcrops'. What's more, he could now tell the difference between a bridleway and a European parliamentary constituency boundary. One, he'd alcoholically mused, was a thoughtfully aligned right-of-way, purposefully and logically established by common use and historical precedent - the other was an arbitrary, illogical and meaningless bureaucratic invention imposed by an organisation that could be similarly described. The comparison and analysis amused Simon. It was quite clever really he decided; he would write it down and see if he could somehow work it into his next

Countryman's musings. No harm in introducing a bit of politics, *The Bugle* might like that. At this point a combination of red wine and mild carbon monoxide poisoning had overtaken him and he'd dozed comfortably like a dog on a mat, only waking when the smoke alarm on the landing belatedly reacted to the fug.

Next morning he woke later than intended and was feeling the effects of the previous evening but a rare cloudless sky, the gleaming new walking boots by the back door and black coffee soon dispelled the lingering tastes and effects of stale wine and soot. The great outdoors beckoned. But then, having beckoned it promptly started being awkward. The hedge at the bottom of the garden proved to be the first obstacle, serving notice that features on the ground had no intention of behaving like the neat lines and symbols on the map. Simon was used to the precise concrete definitions of the London *A to Z* faithfully replicating the ordered streets and squares of the obliging capital. The blurred overgrown realities of the countryside with its unexpected and often painful obstacles came as an unpleasant surprise and he soon realised that this was not going to be as straightforward as his crisp new map had suggested.

An hour later, apart from wet feet where deceptively dry clumps of marsh grass had lured him into ankle-deep slurry, and a few scratches collected from brambles and barbed wire, Simon was pleased with his progress. Admittedly the tumbling, sparkling brook that he'd hoped was going to lead him to the sunny uplands of Spout Hill had proved something of a disappointment. Most of the time he'd found himself following an indistinct muddy trickle, which sometimes couldn't even be bothered to stay above ground, soaking spongily into one of the treacherous moss cushions that dotted the hillside. But Simon was enjoying the challenge. He took particular satisfaction from knowing that the route was of his own invention and he was making his own rugged way across the landscape independent of the path diviners. It didn't occur to him that other land-users, and particularly owners, might not appreciate this pioneering spirit as he forced gaps through their hedges, dislodged stones from their walls and sagged their fences. His insistence on virtuously shutting every gate he came across - regardless of how he'd found it - was also to prove irksome later in the day when unsuspecting farmers came to herd their confused cattle along unexpectedly blocked tracks.

Simon had just decided that the bog currently enveloping his boots was indeed the tufted source of his stream, a fact confirmed by the overgrown outcrop of crags and modest cliffs that cradled the little marsh, when there was a shout from a neighbouring field. He turned to see a large figure standing astride a mud-splattered quad bike waving wildly at him. Simon tentatively waved back. This got the figure even more excited and it produced a large stick from somewhere, which it started to wave around its head. Simon didn't bother to wave back this time and as two curiously marked dogs leapt from behind the rider and streaked towards him he set off at a fast squelching trot in the opposite direction. He knew from the map that beyond the nearest stone wall, where he could already make out a mossy gate, lay the sanctuary of an indisputably public highway. Minutes later, gasping desperately and only yards ahead of the dogs, he flung himself over the rotting gate dislodging the top rail in the process. Stumbling to his feet again he set off up the tarmacked hill at a laboured jog, panting with exhaustion and panic. It was several breathless minutes before there was a shrill whistle from down the hill, the dogs obediently disappeared and Simon felt he could risk slowing to a walk.

He was nearer the top than he'd realised and suddenly found he could go no higher. A whole new gently contoured panoply of jumbled greens, yellows and browns spread itself out before him. Simon checked the map, looked to the right along the ridge and eyed the next planned stage of his walk without enthusiasm. With his personal safety now reasonably assured, exhaustion, wet boots and clammy trousers had become the issues. But the track looked easy and was well defined, several vehicles had obviously used it recently, and to Simon's relief there was a weathered wooden sign that made clear that the public were also entitled to use it. About half a mile along the track he could see a skeletal mast or aerial towering incongruously over the landscape - a useful landmark. He re-consulted the map and although he picked up on a couple more faint pencil crosses - just along the ridge if he was right - the mast didn't get a mention. Simon knew a map symbol existed for such a structure; it was odd that the map-makers had ignored it. There also appeared to be a path from near the mast, which went straight down the hill to the main road. This would definitely be a quicker way back to the village and with less chance of meeting the quad-bike-riding hellhounds too. Simon cheered at the thought and having assured himself he was also entitled to use the downhill path without risk of being savaged by man or beast set off wearily. Passing both points where he thought the subject of the crosses ought to be he could see no signs of anything on the ground, no markers, no diggings, nothing to distinguish these points from anywhere else on the hillside. He was too tired to investigate further, for the moment they would have to remain a mystery.

Meanwhile the mast loomed larger and larger. A network of guys and supporting cables became visible and although Simon couldn't even guess at the height he could make out something moving at the top catching the sunlight stroboscopically. Closer up it was obvious there was some sort of control box set about six foot above the ground, which on closer inspection proved to be an apparently random and constantly changing digital read out. He gazed up at the flickering tip for a moment and decided it was time for the pub. He quickly found the homeward path, helpfully and reassuringly sign-posted, and set off downhill following this new track with ease. It appeared to be a sort of sunken road, which from the top quickly scored about six foot into the hillside and was flanked by intermittent rough stone walls with occasional outcrops of flaking natural rock, grassy banks and mossy mounds. Unfamiliar stunted trees covered in white blossom were profuse, there was an occasional holly, which Simon recognised, and what he thought might be a species of rather wizened and gnarled oak. An almost solid wall of ferns, bracken and heather added depth to the enclosing banks. He was intrigued; was this track some curious geological anomaly or could it have been man-made? It appeared to be almost straight making no concessions to the gradient; perhaps it was Roman, created by the passing of many thousand sandalled feet and the occasional chariot. He'd been happily developing this theme, lost in increasingly romantic and unlikely scenarios when Bunny Warren had tripped over a root and tumbled leafily into his path.

CHAPTER FOUR

Sid was quite busy for a midweek lunchtime. 'Fuck! What 'appened to you?' he bellowed, as a dishevelled Simon squelched wearily into the pub. A chintzy group of ladies lunching in the bay window of the lounge went suddenly silent... then all started to talk at once, rather louder than before. The honorary secretary of the Bartford Baptist Ladies Bowls Club unilaterally decided there and then that their next AGM would not be in The Smuggler's Finger, however good the lasagne.

Simon was relieved to see that his usual niche was vacant and flopped down damply. Sid managed to serve one or two more customers before his curiosity got the better of him and he wandered over to watch with amused disgust as Simon eased off his sodden boots.

'Couldn't get me a drink could you, Sid?' Simon asked peering up from under the table. Sid started as though stung. 'I'll pay for it,' Simon added hastily. Sid relaxed, shambled over to the bar and ignoring several obviously waiting customers sloshed a dark frothy brew into a pint pot.

'Thought you looked like you needed a bit of body.' He slid the glass carelessly across the puddled table. 'Mild. That'll put some 'air on yer bollocks.' There was a synchronised wince from the lady Baptist bowlers. 'So come on then, what yer been up to?'

'Spout Hill, I've been up to Spout Hill. On foot,' Simon added unnecessarily.

'Where's that then?' Sid demanded, 'and anyway what for?'

'Oh, I enjoy a good walk.'

Sid was visibly sceptical but Simon unfolded the now slightly battered map, found Spout Hill and with a muddy finger traced his route, leaving out the reason for the detour via the lane to the top.

'Bleedin' silly way to spend a morning,' Sid muttered. 'What're the little windmills all about?'

'Windmills?'

'Yeah, why've you made them little crosses with stalks? What 'appens there then, buried treasure?' He chuckled at his own wit.

Simon peered carefully at the map and remembering that the only reliable feature on his 'broken' compass was the tiny magnifying glass, got it out, slid it over the creases and squinted again at the faint pencil marks. Sid was right they had got stalks. They were windmills. Simon told him about the mast and to his surprise, Sid was suddenly interested.

'The thing on the top, spinning you said? Was it like two little cup things whizzin' round?'

'It could have been, it was a long way up.'

'Anemometer,' Sid puffed with casual authority.

'An what?'

'Anemometer. Measures the wind. That's what the digital bit would 'ave been and why it kept changing. It was a read-out showin' the speed of the wind. Probably the direction too if you'd looked.'

Simon was surprised and just a little suspicious. 'How do you know all this Sid?'

'I was in the navy, merchant, haven't always spent the bleedin' day...' he raised his voice provocatively, '...sellin' tossers watered down beer.'

The Baptist bowlers reached for their handbags and coats.

Simon carried on quickly: 'It didn't look like it'd been there long, there were tyre marks everywhere.' He rubbed some mud off the map. 'So someone wants to know how fast and where the wind comes from on Spout Hill,' he mused.

Sid looked at him pityingly and spoke with slow patronising sarcasm. 'To see how fast their windmills'll go round, 's obvious.'

Simon looked at the smirking unshaven face. 'It's about wind power isn't it? Wind turbines.'

'Oh give the man a bleedin' coconut! Course it is.'

'But it's beautiful up there, you can see for miles, in fact you can almost see the sea.'

'So? When did that ever stop 'em? It's big money, very big money, bugger the view!' This was Sid's parting shot as he and his empty half-pint glass headed reluctantly back to the bar to deal with a delegation of the more worldly Baptist lady bowlers and their bill.

Simon eyed the lustreless dark liquid in his glass without enthusiasm. Eight wind turbines on Spout Hill - that was how many marks he'd eventually found - it was bound to be controversial. It could be big news, very big news locally, countywide probably ... perhaps even nationally. This would set *The Bartford Bugle* on fire. Whoever broke this story would definitely see their name in print ... assuming it was true. Some niggling doubts bubbled to the surface of his mind. Was he jumping to the right conclusions? After all most of this was on Sid's, say-so. Sid of all people. What if he started a false controversy and none of it was true? But then did it matter? He thought about some of the headlines that had themselves made headlines over the years: did comedians really eat people's hamsters, had that bus really been on the moon, did Elvis really serve fish and chips in Barnsley? No, it was all nonsense and no real harm done.

He would write his article with authority as if he *knew* that a wind farm was going to be built on this local beauty spot. He'd claim to have *sources* - which he couldn't possibly reveal - and if he was wrong, well, he had a journalistic responsibility to report his suspicions and if it turned out he'd been mistaken, misinformed, then hey, no harm done.

The meeting with council leader and aspiring parliamentarian Claude Cockburn had gone surprisingly well. At least Hallibut thought so.

'Well gentleman what have you got for me?' Cockburn had been expansive but wary. It would never have occurred to him to ask what he could do for a visitor to his ludicrously pompous office, as far as Cockburn was concerned anybody crossing its threshold was there to advance the interests of its occupant, preferably by helping him edge a little further up the greasy political pole. The currency of Cockburn's life was votes: as a teenager he'd first cut his teeth garnering them for a parish council seat, before moving smoothly on to an uncontested seat on the town council and from there to the county council. This last move had taken a bit more effort and imagination and he'd had to resort to a campaign of scandalous rumours and libel to neuter his nearest rival. However, the experience had proved useful and the newly elected councillor had then set about taking control of the more influential committees using similar tactics, before trampling over every convention and launching an audacious coup to secure the leadership. In a literal sense the coup had been bloodless, but it was by no means victimless. Using off-the-record briefings Cockburn had launched a ruthless and effective campaign of character assassination against political rivals and intransigent 'colleagues' - with some of his slurs uncomfortably close to the mark. This had prompted a remarkably high number of resignations within a very brief period - something duly noted by the local press - and suddenly, previously unknown and unremarkable councillors found their finances and private lives being gleefully and very publically raked over. Some fared even worse; the wife of the chairman of the ways and means committee was granted the quickest of 'quickie' divorces on grounds the judge insisted were kept secret to protect the children. Apparently some of the chairman's *ways* were verging on the depraved and all his *means* were definitely illegal.

Cockburn had duly become leader of Bartfordshire Council and established himself as a man not to be trifled with. He was of course almost universally loathed and feared in equal measure throughout the council - and that's how he liked it. If ever questioned on the specifics of his ideology or politics he would either sidestep the question completely or serve up a well-mixed cocktail of policies drawn from across the political spectrum, which was contradictory, utterly meaningless and thus unchallengeable.

Hallibut knew the man reasonably well and knew the type even better. He expected the interview to be short; despite his political ambiguousness Cockburn liked to present an image of decisiveness and Hallibut knew he'd only get one chance. His challenge was two-fold: to offer a scheme with supporting policies that would appear not only politically responsible, but perhaps more importantly, would also appeal to Cockburn as a vote winner on the doorstep.

Hallibut was helped in the first of these objectives by the policy-makers. All central government policies and directives were written in a well-practised form that meant if it became politically expedient to reverse the policy it could still be claimed that the original and obvious purpose was still being fulfilled. In this way any policy could be interpreted and applied in any way, thus minimising political embarrassment and accusations of 'U' turns. Most regional authorities adopted the same approach when distilling central government policy down to local level and they drafted their local plans and *Community Mission Statements* in such a way that they too could be applied to either end of the argument.

Hallibut had had no problem finding a government policy and its local counterpart that he could conveniently interpret and present in support of Sir George's scheme. He'd be able to confidently assure Councillor Cockburn that by adopting and applying *Government Directive RE07/1376/W* Bartfordshire council (and by implication its leader) would gain credit and kudos for so diligently implementing Westminster's will. The second part of his pitch was at a more private level and aimed solely at feeding the fires of Cockburn's personal political ambitions. Anyone enhancing or advancing this cause could count on some reciprocal favours. In Sir George's name Hallibut intended to indicate that one of the most influential personages in the county was in a position to give Prospective Parliamentary Candidate Cockburn a platform complete with large captive audience to address, whilst also considering a generous and carefully camouflaged contribution to the Cockburn campaign fund. Hallibut had two immediate problems with this strategy: firstly, he'd not consulted Sir George specifically on these points, and secondly, and more immediately, he didn't want Tom Gander present when he introduced this aspect of his proposal.

As Hallibut had anticipated, his interpretation of the government's renewable energy policy went down well. Cockburn's political antennae had immediately picked up on the opportunities for personal credit without Hallibut having to spell it out and within minutes it had been adopted as council policy.

'Do we have a site in mind?'

'Well as a matter of fact we have been approached with an outline proposal.'

'I see.'

'Yes, it's a well thought out plan and would certainly comply with policy.'

The one you made up this morning and we adopted five minutes ago, Tom Gander thought.

'It's also being put forward by one of the larger landowners and leading county figures.'

'Oh yes?'

Hallibut saw the gleam in Cockburn's eyes and knew he'd hit a chord. 'Tom, why don't I quickly brief Councillor Co'burn on a few of the details, no point us both being away from the office. Cockburn shuffled impatiently in his chair. 'It shouldn't take long,' Hallibut added quickly.

Tom Gander gratefully left the room, with the minimum of courtesies.

Left alone, Cockburn looked piercingly at Hallibut but said nothing. His eyes asked all the questions.

'Sir George Hoggit of Hoggit Hall...' Hallibut thought the grand address might help. '...has come to me, us, with the idea.'

'I thought it might be,' Cockburn said quietly.

'He's got some good people behind him and it's a well thought...'

'So you said. Where's he proposing to put these things?'

'Oh, on his own land.'

'Naturally.'

The sarcasm wasn't wasted on Hallibut. 'At a place called Spout Hill.'

'Never heard of it. Many voters... residents... nearby?'

'Very few. And they tend to vote *UKIP*.' It was a brazen acknowledgement that Hallibut knew where Cockburn's priorities lay and it also took the discussion in the direction he wanted. He hurried to capitalise. 'Er, Sir George has indicated that he thinks it may be useful for you and he to meet. I believe that apart from explaining his plans...' Cockburn looked bored. '...he's planning a large county event, a fund raiser, and he would appreciate your thoughts on a worthy local cause.' Cockburn looked up sharply and Hallibut wondered whether he'd pushed it too far. 'And he hasn't decided on a guest speaker yet,' Hallibut added.

Cockburn smiled thinly. 'I think I see, Clive. Thank you.'

Hallibut didn't think it could really have gone much better. All he had to do now was to break the news of his unilateral promises to Sir George. Tricky.

Sir George was in a pensive mood. He'd taken refuge in his study, as he often did when things around the house, especially Lady Arabella, became a bit trying. He usually made himself wait until after 11 o'clock but this morning he'd distractedly reached for the decanter shortly after ten thirty and was now slumped behind his desk deep in thought. There was a half-full tumbler balanced on his expansive waist-coated belly. Apart from Arabella's obvious suspicions things were going fairly well he decided: Wormold was performing - and so he bloody should at his rates - the RefWatt crowd seemed to know their stuff, and a bland but imaginatively supportive *Environmental Statement* was in the advanced stages of preparation. The bland bits had been lifted directly from the *Friends of the Earth* website, whilst the more imaginative elements had been dreamt up by Wormold's team of post-graduate interns during pot and alcohol-fuelled brainstorming sessions. The conclusion of the report had been prepared well in advance and was a superbly contrived piece of Green doublespeak; illogical, impenetrable and totally irrefutable, but unquestionably and emphatically in favour of the construction of the Spout Hill Wind Farm. Sir George was reasonably confident that Hallibut would secure the required support of the council - he'd better - and despite the ludicrously expensive *Meccano* tower Wormold had insisted on erecting none of the locals seemed to have got wind of his plans so far. Sir George had argued long and hard against the cost of the meteorology mast, pointing out that all the wind data required to prove the viability of the scheme had long since been prepared anyway. But the consultant was adamant, they should at least be seen going through the motions of genuine monitoring and data collection he said. The telephone rang.

'You want me to WHAT?' he bellowed a few seconds later.

At the other end of the line Hallibut took a deep breath and tentatively put the phone back to his ear. 'It would more or less guarantee the support of the council,' he mumbled. Adding rashly, 'without question.'

There was a long pause. 'You do realise that this is Arabella's... Lady Hoggit's *do* you're talking about here? *Her* fete, *her baby*. Anyone trying to...' He interrupted himself. 'Anyway how do you and this Co'burn know so much about it?' There was some muttering from the handset. 'Yes I suppose so, it has been going on for bloody years,' Sir George said bitterly. There was more muttering. 'Christ, are they on about it all ready? I never read the rag, but yes, she does like maximum publicity. I suppose it will have been in there. Bloody press!'

Sir George thought about the implications of Hallibut's suggestion for a moment. 'This council leader, at the end of the day he's only one person, one vote, how much difference can he make? Has he really got that sort of influence?'

'Oh believe me he has,' Hallibut said with feeling. 'What he says goes, no question. Everyone here, officers, councillors, committee chairman, they all toe his line. He's going places in the bigger political world too, utterly ruthless. Believe me, this guy could've had Stalin for breakfast.'

'What, he's a Communist?'

'Eh? No, he's just that ruthless, rules by terror.'

Sir George thought that sounded a bit over the top but let it go.

'Actually he's a sort of Liberal.'

'A Liberal! I hate fucking Liberals! You mean to say you want me to sit through some bloody dreary speech and *then* make a bloody great donation for the privilege ... to a Liberal?'

'Well ... yes.' The directness of the answer took Sir George aback. 'He's not a proper Liberal, not in a Paddy Ashdown sort of way.'

'Well what sort of bloody way then?'

'Well, he sort of looks at ideas as they come along. It can get a bit muddled but he sort of takes policies from here and there.'

'Here and there?'

'Well, sort of ... whatever fits at the time.'

'Sounds like a *proper* bloody Liberal to me,' Sir George snorted. 'I suppose he's all for bloody Europe?'

'Well, bits of it I gather.'

'Bits of it! I suppose he wants to bugger around with our farming subsidies like the rest of them?'

As far as Sir George was concerned the only thing the European Union was any good for was subsidies. A bureaucracy designed to provide unearned income via huge handouts rewarding the inactivity of the all ready rich was always going to appeal to someone of Sir George's instincts. He also liked the undeniable whiff of corruption that clung about the whole organisation, which somehow added a certain frisson to the endless form filling. Having thoroughly exploited the EU model it was almost inevitable that Sir George would be drawn towards the newly fashionable and fast-approaching gravy train that was renewable energy - and of course its attendant culture of subsidies. He'd also quickly realised that wind power, despite its glaringly obvious limitations, was going to become the darling of fickle politicians and campaigners and would therefore lend itself particularly well to exploitation.

'Right, so what about renewable energy? Has your man managed to decide where he stands on that one?' Sir George demanded.

'Well, actually this might work rather well for us... you.'

'What do you mean "might"? What's their bloody policy? Yes or no?'

'Well, it all depends.'

'What d'you mean it bloody *depends*? Depends on what?'

'Well, quite a few things really.'

Sir George took a deep breath. He had a suspicion that Hallibut was being deliberately obtuse and he wasn't going to play this game any more. 'Right,' he said quietly, 'arrange a meeting.'

Hallibut, alerted by the change in tone came back hurriedly. 'Perhaps not just yet, but I think *we* ought to meet. There are a few... pointers that Councillor Co'burn has given me that perhaps we ought to explore before you meet him.'

'Pointers?' The tone was still measured but also suspicious.

'Just a few ideas that will help oil the wheels and get things moving.' Oiling wheels was something Sir George understood. 'Right, usual place, six o'clock.' He put the phone down and reached thoughtfully for his glass. It was already empty.

Up in his lofty office Hallibut was left with a whining handset. He shrugged and flicked the cradle to get an outside line, dialled his home number and left a message for his wife explaining that he'd be late home and reminded her that the pool people were coming round to check the filters.

The meeting had been predictably short although Sir George had still managed to gulp down two double whiskeys. The first while Hallibut was still at the bar waiting for his frothy lager to settle. Sir George looked around the grim little pub in mild disgust. It was something of an oddity, squeezed onto the thin end of a wedge-shaped Victorian terrace and designed as little more than a wide corridor with a street door at each end and a bar running the whole length of one side. It was dirty, run down and smelt slightly of urine but had the distinct advantage of never being likely to attract anyone who knew Sir George, or for that matter Hallibut. In fact at this early stage of the evening there were very few customers at all: a couple of estate agents were stood at the bar muttering valuations and prodding half-heartedly at *The Daily Telegraph* crossword, a sullen youth fed a pyrotechnic fruit machine and a heavily made up woman of indeterminate age sat nursing a white wine and watching both doors hopefully. She knew she'd have younger and more attractive competition later when the evening girls came out and the toilets filled with dealers. Sir George and Hallibut were always long gone before the regulars appeared.

Sir George had not been altogether surprised by Hallibut's 'pointers'. They were largely what he'd expected a pushy politician to want in return for a bit of influence and patronage: a platform from which to con and cajole the voters and some hard but legitimate cash to spend on whatever it was politicians squandered money on in the run-up to an election. What had surprised and slightly alarmed Sir George, however, was that Hallibut and this character Cockburn appeared to have quite detailed knowledge of the forthcoming Hoggit Hall Fete and were already planning how to harness it as some sort of campaign vehicle for the council leader.

The summer fete was, and always had been, Lady Arabella's pet project. It was her annual charitable fundraiser for the great and good of 'The County', or at least those whose names appeared on a fabled approved list. And there was always a supporting cast of worthy villagers, a few of the more presentable farming families and members of selected local clubs and organisations to make up the numbers. It was something Lady Arabella had proudly nurtured and developed over the years and Sir George was uncomfortably aware that any perceived attempt to interfere with her showcase would be fiercely, probably viciously, resisted.

'There should be more *gravitas*. Some respectability. You need someone with authority that people can take seriously, someone with something sensible to say.' After devising and dismissing several oblique schemes for tackling Lady Arabella on the subject, Sir George had decided on the direct approach. A frontal attack. 'It should be someone of standing,' he continued, 'a local dignitary, perhaps.'

'We've got Mickey Moyst,' Lady Arabella interrupted, and bent back to the plans spread over the wrought-iron table.

They were standing outside the full-length drawing room windows on the raised, honey-stoned terrace looking out over the grounds that stepped away from the handsome house in carefully designed tiers. Immediately below the terrace was an area of formal beds and gravelled paths. These led onto the extensive lawns, which in turn merged into carefully neglected areas of wild flowers and grasses which continued over a carefully dredged stream, complete with stone bridge, before eventually merging into the undisciplined natural beauty of mature woods.

Lady Arabella stabbed a finger at the plans then straightened up and stabbed again, down the garden, letting out a bellow: 'You! Yes you there. More to the right, yes the right ... no *my* right! Yes, your left.' She dropped her arm. 'Idiot.'

The lawn was a mass of chaotic inactivity with crumpled heaps of creased, off-white canvas, stacks of green-painted poles and nests of tangled hemp ropes spread to all corners. There were probably about twenty workmen dotted around in various states of undress and lethargy. Only one seemed to be showing any real sense of urgency; he was wearing a hard-hat and luminous tabard and darted from pile to pile waving a clipboard , to no obvious effect.

'Mickey Moyst!' Sir George snorted, 'some juvenile so-called celebrity from... what's it called, *Fun Radio Bartford*, or something? For goodness sake! What you should...'

'Get that bloody tractor off that bed!'

Sir George winced.

'Mind that Statue! For God's sake! You! Yes you with the hat, are you in charge?' Lady Arabella didn't wait for a reply. 'Get a grip man can't you? Idiot!' She hadn't bothered to lower her voice this time and with that, dismissed the garden and everyone in it to turn impatiently to a visibly nervous Sir George. 'What exactly is it you want, George?'

'Er, well...' Her sudden attention had caught him off guard, '...you're going to so much trouble, so much work, as you always do, I think it would be a shame not to set the right tone. The fete, *your* fete, is so important to the county. He was back on script now but thought he might be overdoing it. 'Well, I strongly feel that we should have a serious pillar of the local community here on the day to acknowledge all your hard work, to give credit where it's due and to open the event.'

'I told you, we've got Mickey Moyst. He's booked and paid for.' Lady Arabella turned back to the marquee plan and Sir George knew he had to think fast:

'Well, of course we could have him as well. For the younger crowd I suppose,' he added.

'As well as who?' There was a suspicious edge to Lady Arabella's voice that Sir George had hoped not to hear during this discussion.

'Claude Co'burn.'

'Who the hell is he?'

'*Claude Co'burn*? Oh come, Arabella, you know perfectly well that he's the head of the council. The County Council, *Bartfordshire County Council*.'

'I know which bloody county I live in, George! And now you mention it I think I have heard the name. Spelt "cock" isn't it? Cock by name cock by nature from what I've heard.'

'Oh really!' Sir George snorted. 'Silly political sniping that's all. He's a good man, very probably our next MP, very community spirited, does a lot for charity... including *Riding For The Disabled*. Could be a great help to your causes.'

Lady Arabella looked at him calculatingly; this was the main charity she supported, indeed all the proceeds from the fete would be going in that direction. Sir George sensed the hesitation. 'I'm sure Mr Moyst wouldn't mind sharing the... er, honour, with Councillor Co'burn. Moyst could go first of course.' Lady Arabella glanced at him, surprised at this concession and murmured something that Sir George didn't catch. 'What was that dear?'

'Don't call me *dear*!' she snapped automatically.

'No, no, sorry Bell... er, Arabella.'

'What's in this for you George, what's it all about?'

Sir George had prepared for this one: 'As I said, Councillor Co'burn is very up and coming, both in the political world and in the wider community, and I think it's important that we support, and are seen to support, the worthier members of the establishment who genuinely have the interests of those they represent at heart, whilst at the same time their support and patronage gives back to society and can give extra exposure to the modest efforts of others trying to make a difference - such as you and your fete - and ensure that you receive the right sort of publicity and a reflected glow of...'

'George! Bollocks! As you would say.'

Sir George immediately and wisely shut up. Lady Arabella looked at him closely. 'I don't know what you're up to George but as it happens, on this occasion, you might just be right. Perhaps we should have a slightly more serious tone, as well as Mickey Moyst's poppy drivel.' She turned away and looked down the garden. 'All right George I'll go with you on this one, not without reservations mind you.'

Sir George rubbed his hands together vigorously. Lady Arabella knew the sign and realised that although she didn't know what it was yet, her husband was celebrating some sort of victory.

'Now about the fete proceeds.' Sir George was all business again.

'What about them?'

'Well obviously now we have two... er, personalities for the fete it makes sense that the funds we raise should be split between causes too.'

'And just who, or whom had you in mind as a worthy recipient of *my* largesse George?'

Sir George failed to read the signs. 'Well obviously Councillor Co'burn should be involved. I think we should put half of the proceeds at his disposal, for causes close to his heart and...'

'Such as?'

Still Sir George failed to register the danger signals. 'Well...' he looked thoughtful, '...in order to fully engage with the community and help it realise its aspirations it makes sense for him to be able to represent us all at the highest possible level. So getting elected to parliament would...'

'Using *my* money?' Sir George saw the danger at last. His wife's voice was getting louder by the word and one or two interested heads on the lawn had already turned their way. 'You are seriously proposing that we take thousands of pounds away from disabled kids and their ponies and give it to some jumped up little town-hall Jonnie who fancies playing big-boy's politics. NO... WAY... GEORGE!'

'But think what he could do for...'

'NO! Bloody NO George!'

'But... but... he *is* a Liberal.'

'A Liberal! They're the bloody worst, that's what you've always said. Your bloody words George! What's happened to all those Tory-supporting years eh? What about Dennis?'

'He's in prison,' Sir George said sulkily, 'Not much good to us there.'

'And who's fault is that?' she flung back.

Sir George said nothing. He wasn't prepared to re-open that particular can of worms, not while his quango expenses were still a matter of public record.

'NO! I don't care if he's a Liberal or a bloody *Monster Raving Loony,* not a penny, not a bloody chance!' Lady Arabella stormed to the edge of the terrace and bellowed some unnecessary orders at a couple of hapless tent-erectors having a quiet smoke on a pile of sacking. Turning round suddenly, she leant casually against the weathered balustrade, arms outstretched along the mossy coping, and studied Sir George critically. 'If you really want to give the sod some pocket money to play with you could always sell some of those shares of yours in *Nigeria Mining & Chemicals.* Then you could write him a big fat cheque on that nice discreet little Isle of Man account you manage so quietly.'

Sir George was stunned. He gasped and mouthed like an ailing fish. God! How did she know about those? No one knew. Not even his accountants, *especially* not his accountants. He struggled to compose himself, desperately trying to think what else his wife might have discovered while searching his office - that was the only way she could know about his *Bank of Douglas* account and the extremely profitable but ethically debateable shareholding in the embargoed West African company. Lady Arabella was looking at him with an expression of contemptuous satisfaction and Sir George knew he'd pushed his case, and his luck, as far as it was going. 'Right...' he said briskly, '...so that's agreed. The fete funds go to the riding people and I'll take care of Co'burn's... er, causes. Your Moyst moron can give the crowds a bit of patter for a few minutes and then we'll have a few civilised words of welcome from our future member of parliament and the formal opening. Excellent.' He turned to go.

'George.' It was her ominous hiss. She walked over to him. 'I *know* you're up to something, I don't know what yet but I smell a very big rat.' She leant slowly forward until their noses were inches apart. 'If you fuck up my fete...'

CHAPTER FIVE

Her hand was cool and firm in his, confident and unselfconscious. Simon willingly let himself be led down the narrow leaf-mulched path weaving between untended hazel thickets and clumps of drooping deflowered bluebells. It was all rather surreal and he still wasn't quite sure how he'd got here.

Their meeting had presumably been accidental; he'd spotted her a few hundred yards up the lane, unmistakeable in the billowing floral skirts and perched childlike on the stile. She had the air of somebody who didn't need a reason to sit on a stile, apparently lost in her own thoughts and smiling gently at nothing in particular. She certainly hadn't given the impression of someone waiting for anyone.

Simon had been unenthusiastically ambling towards Hoggit Hall, a begrudging reporter's notebook in his pocket. He was sure Plompley could probably offer bigger journalistic challenges, like the Spout Hill wind farm to start with, but in the meantime a village fete seemed an obvious subject for his *musing countryman* column. Unconsciously his pace had quickened when he recognised her in the distance. Their initial exchange had been conventional, smiles and small talk, but under her amused gaze he'd inexplicably found himself reduced to stuttering inanities. She, by contrast, was relaxed, her manner unaffected, somehow seductive and Simon had found her surprisingly and delightfully tactile. Bewitched again he'd readily accepted the suggestion of a woodland walk and wordlessly followed her over the stile.

Simon now became vaguely aware of an amplified voice somewhere ahead of them. The woodland was thinning to reveal slivers of what was clearly a grand, honey-coloured house. The upper parts of grubby, sag-backed marquees could be made out over the thickening undergrowth. Simon felt a surge of disappointment; they'd presumably arrived at the Hoggit Hall fete and he'd clearly misread the signals, having dared to hope.

The brushed cheek, the stroked arm, the hand holding, they'd all been just platonic gestures and her intangible eroticism was going to remain just that - untouched.

Distracted by his disappointment and the signs of activity through the undergrowth Simon stumbled with a sudden change of direction and gradient, wincing as small branches whipped his face and tugged at his clothes. His hand was released and he opened his eyes to find himself in a curious sylvan hollow thickly surrounded by towering undergrowth and with no visible entrance or exit. The privacy was immediately obvious and Simon turned quickly looking for confirmation of his newly aroused optimism. He was not disappointed. His guide was lying back on the grassy side of the hollow with one knee lifted under the voluminous skirt and her arms lying loosely by her sides. The simple white blouse had been unbuttoned and eased back onto bare shoulders exposing small firm breasts with startlingly pink nipples, their prominent tightness the only obvious sign of arousal. The enigmatic smile seemed unchanged but had somehow become unambiguously sexual. Simon watched transfixed as this nymph, smoky grey eyes fixed dreamily on his face, reached slowly down to the hem of her skirt, gathered and rucked it in careful handfuls and lifted the folds to her waist. Replacing her hands softly by her sides she gently parted her legs and with the hint of a sigh raised her hips slightly offering up her exposed pudenda and more. Simon gazed in awe at the tiny manicured triangle of honey-coloured pelt and thought it was the most erotic thing he'd ever seen. He started to unbuckle his belt and wondered whether he should ask her name.

A series of echoing taps was followed by the inevitable high-pitched shriek and Sir George jumped back from the microphone stand.

'Don't stand so close, man.' The patronising estuary drawl was efficiently picked up by the sound system and duly relayed around the gardens and assorted tents, marquees and stalls of the annual Hoggit Hall Fete.

Sir George glanced frostily over his shoulder but didn't lean quite so close for his next pronouncement. 'Er, yes... well, good afternoon everybody... er, can everyone hear me?' There was a faint 'No!' from near the back of the crowd and a few muffled giggles from nearer the front. As usual the PA system had been set up at the edge of the raised drawing-room terrace, which served as the stage for the fete, and it was here at two o'clock sharp that the hosts and their VIP guests had gathered to make the obligatory speeches of welcome and formally announce the proceedings open. Thus they would unleash an orgy of coconut bashing, rubber-duck hooking, bonny-baby judging, swinging, sliding and slithering; jumble rummaging, target shooting, out-sized vegetable skulduggery and various nausea-inducing rides. Many of the fast-food stalls would probably have a similar effect, particularly the hot-dog concessionary whose deep freeze had been on the blink and who was hoping to off load a batch of out-of-date and partially defrosted frankfurters.

But first the assembled throng were expected to listen to the great and the good. On the 'stage', apart from Sir George, looking uncomfortable and uncharacteristically nervous, was Lady Arabella, predictably immaculate and radiating her customary charm, Councillor Claude Cockburn clad in dark suit, purple tie and just a bit too much matching hanky, and finally a slight youth of indeterminate age sporting vertical bleached hair, huge sun glasses and chewing vigorously. This was Mickey Moyst, breakfast show DJ at *Radio Bartford FM*: catchphrase (to be bellowed): 'Yo ... oohh, c'mon! Moysten yer morning with Mickey!'

Sir George gulped and pressed on. 'We are very pleased and, er, honoured to have two special guests here to open this year's fete. In particular we would like to thank Councillor...' He got no further.

'Yo ... oohh! Way to go! Lets moisten it with Mickey! Yo, oh, ... ooh!' As Sir George had turned to wave a welcoming arm at Cockburn the diminutive DJ had slipped under his elbow got between him and the microphone and was now in full flow. Cockburn did what all politicians do when embarrassed; he smiled grimly and pretended he was enjoying himself, but Sir George, face swollen and flushed was obviously livid and poised to make a counter-attack, when he caught a look from Lady

Arabella. He retired muttering and wincing at the whoops and bellows echoing around the garden.

He wasn't the only one. The large and increasingly impatient crowd were mainly of more mature years and more likely to have *Terry Wogan* or *John Humphries* joining them over breakfast. Most had never heard of Mickey, moist or otherwise, and were more interested in getting their hands on the choice bits of jumble, picking up a rosette for their marrow or getting their bonny baby judged while it still smelt reasonably sweet. Others were already eyeing up the hot dog van where the cunning operator was laying ground bait with an early batch of frying onions.

In fact the only encouragement Mickey Moyst got was from a small group of teenage girls collected self-consciously at the foot of the terrace steps. But even they seemed to be tiring of the innuendoes, plugs and desperately repeated catchphrase. DJ Mickey decided to play his trump card. 'Autographs!' he bellowed, 'I'll be signing autographs for all you lucky...' There was a squawk from the scattered speakers and the system died again leaving little Mickey Moyst squeaking like a choirboy whose balls have inconveniently dropped in the middle of Evensong. The only people who could hear him now were the stage party and the schoolgirl coven - and they weren't listening anyway. Sir George saw his chance and grabbing Cockburn roughly by the arm he charged the vainly mouthing DJ to one side and thrust the microphone stand into the councillor's hand. 'Don't move,' he hissed. There was another squawk and the crowd was treated to a muttered but electronically amplified, 'What the fuck...?' from their startled council leader. There was a cheer from a group at the back who had temporarily and unsteadily abandoned the beer tent - Sid hadn't waited for the official two o'clock start. Mickey Moyst, conceding defeat, produced a large black marker pen and headed hopefully towards the gang of schoolgirls, who with arms crossed protectively over pubescent breasts promptly scurried away pouting and giggling towards the beer tent.

Realising he'd never finished his introduction of Cockburn, Sir George once more took possession of the microphone and decided to start again with some humour. 'As I was saying before I was so rudely interrupted...' he paused and grimaced his best smile. No one laughed. He looked hopefully over the sea of faces and gave up. '...er, I would like to introduce Councillor Claude Co'burn.' He paused for dramatic effect, 'our parliamentary candidate who...'

'*Prospective.*'

'Eh, what?' Sir George looked irritably over his left shoulder at Cockburn.

'Prospective, I'm the *prospective* parliamentary candidate. It's important legally,' Cockburn whispered.

'Oh, yes, right.' Sir George turned impatiently back to the microphone. God he could do with a drink. 'Our *prospective* parliamentary candidate, Councillor Claude *Cock*burn.' He turned and thrust a welcoming arm at Cockburn to be greeted by a livid scowl and realised what he'd just said, Oh bollocks! He needed a drink.

Cockburn rearranged his face and took the microphone from a cringing Sir George, who backed hastily towards the full-length windows and the sanctuary of the house. Cockburn cleared his throat noisily prompting audible groans and a distinct fraying round the edges of the restless crowd as people started to move hopefully towards the stalls and stands. Undaunted, their councillor launched into a well-practised spiel employing the authoritative and hectoring tone that worked so well in the council chamber. In the thronged garden of Hoggit Hall, however, it just came over as a patronising drone and the crowd were in no mood for a drone. Few were listening and those that were got a jumbled account of 'unavoidable' council tax increases, 're-scheduled' rubbish collections and bookless and staffless libraries that unfortunately needed to be 're-defined'. But it was to be understood that none of this was Councillor Cockburn's fault. It was all ... 'unavoidable' ... 'historical profligacy' ... 'the previous administration' and so on... and on. After about ten minutes most of the crowd had drifted away and the pressures for a start to proceedings were becoming irresistible. Many stallholders, envious of business being poached by their more impatient rivals, had already dropped any pretence of waiting for the official off and were now selling hard. The level of wailing from the bonny baby marquee was reaching its pre-judging crescendo and the *WI* were struggling to hold back a pack of garrulous women who were determined to get in some early designer-label pillaging at the jumble-sale tent. Meanwhile Sid was doing brisk business in the beer tent and watched approvingly as the sky darkened and those intent on making an afternoon of it jockeyed for a stool or comfortable corner within easy reach of his bar. Elsewhere the odd shout or cheer echoed off the ash trees as a coconut was tumbled, a duck hooked or a tin target slain.

Cockburn droned doggedly on, but when he noticed Sir George slipping unsteadily back onto the terrace he decided this was the time for his rousing climax.

'And so finally...' There was a muted cheer from the beer tent, '...our thanks to our ever-generous hosts, Lord and Lady Hoggit...'

There was a snort from over his right shoulder followed by a reptilian hiss, '*Sir George* and Lady Hoggit, idiot!' Lady Arabella had clearly had enough.

'Er... apologies, of course...' Cockburn hurried on, keen to make amends. 'But apart from our thanks we should also congratulate our hosts on their forward thinking, their sense of community and their ready acceptance of social and environmental responsibilities. They set a fine example.'

Lady Arabella tried to look gracious but she'd heard it all before and knew from the chorus of wailing babies, cheering drunks and shrieking bargain hunters that the fete would soon be out of her control - something she hated. Sir George did his best to beam and tried to look benevolent but only succeeded in looking blearily smug.

Cockburn built to his finale. 'In particular they should be congratulated on taking the lead locally in the fight against the very real threat of global warming and carbon, er, pollution, no...' he fumbled for the word, '... emissions. A very real threat indeed and we all have our part to play.' He looked stern, paused dramatically and then waved an arm towards the grand house. 'Here in Bartfordshire we are rising to this challenge and I am delighted, no more than that, delighted and *proud,* that our hosts are taking the lead on all of our behalves.'

Lady Arabella's eyes narrowed and she was suddenly listening very closely.

Cockburn continued. 'Allowing their land to be used for a significant Green energy development, as I say, sets a fine example and where Lord and Lady Hoggit and the *Spout Hill Wind Farm* lead undoubtedly others will follow!' This last, delivered in rousing tones that boomed from the speakers and re-echoed round the garden. 'Oh... and I now declare this fete open,' he added.

There was a stunned silence. Enough people had heard the pronouncement to quickly inform or confirm for inattentive neighbours that they had heard right and everyone was now absorbing the information. Cockburn remained standing on the terrace beaming uncertainly and still flanked by his uncomprehending hostess and florid, gawping host. The only noises for a few moments came from some of the not-so-bonny babies and muffled and slurred bellows of 'Moisten it with Mickey!' from the beer-tent where the up-staged Mickey Moyst was plying some of the more receptive teenage girls with vodka and *Redbull*.

As the level of conversation around the gardens returned to normal levels Lady Arabella mentally re-ran what she thought she'd just heard. Ignoring the bewildered Cockburn she swung round to her husband - or at least to the spot where he'd been a split second earlier - just in time to see his bulky tweed back disappearing into the house. Elbowing aside Cockburn she stormed after him, then hesitated, took a deep breath and turned back to the garden. Generations of *noblesse oblige* kicked in and Lady Arabella fixing, on her most charming smile, descended the worn stone steps to the main lawn to reclaim her fete.

By the time Simon and George had made their separate ways across the ancient stone bridge and appeared amongst the tents the hubbub had returned to the levels one would expect at a neighbourhood gathering. But there were no cheers or shouts of laughter, this was not the sound of people enjoying themselves. Many of the villagers had drifted into the groups and cliques they occupied in other walks of village life and their conversations were intense and grim, some animated and angry. There was an underlying rumble of dissent. Many of the stalls were being ignored, their only customers the parents of demanding children and the screechy and now obviously drunk gang of schoolgirls. They had soon bored of Mickey Moyst, leaving him wobbling precariously on a bar stool in the beer tent.

With the babies all judged, the less bonny specimens already en-buggied and slinking home the winners triumphantly suckling bottle or proud blue-veined breast, the loudest noise for the moment was coming from the jumble sale where a pitched battle was taking place between the women from two neighbouring streets with the hapless WI organisers stuck in the middle. The noise levels in the beer tent were also steadily rising. With more stalls being abandoned and disappointed traders dismantling their stands in disgust people were instinctively heading for where there were still sounds of life, and that was the bar. Sid was delighted and reacted predictably by quietly putting up all his prices.

Lady Arabella had bustled around hospitably for a while, increasingly giving the appearance of a surviving general inspecting the site of a recently lost battle. Eventually, no longer trusting herself to engage civilly with the remaining villagers and not yet ready to launch an assault on her husband, she gave up and quietly slipped away towards the stables and the comforting reliability of her equine charges and their minders.

'Hello, dear, had a nice walk? You're a bit late you know.' There was no reproach in Richard Devine's voice and as George floated to his side he smiled gently down at her.

'Yes thank you, dear, very nice. Yes, I suppose I'm rather late but it was so lovely.'

'Oh good,' he said vaguely and ran a finger round the inside of his dog collar.

'It all seems a little... subdued. Is everything all right? People seem to be leaving already. I do hope the jumble sale went well.'

Richard Devine winced. He'd finally been unable to ignore the screaming, not to mention the bad language, coming from the sale tent and had felt obliged to enter the fray as a blessed peacemaker. The image of the redoubtable *WI* chairwoman, wild-haired and blouse ripped to the waist, repeatedly head butting Mrs Sponge the school dinner lady was one that would stay with him for a very long time.

'Yes, well, I think everyone's had a bit of a shock,' he said. 'Not least poor Lady Arabella, I suspect.' As a popular and uncontroversial local vicar he was a regular recipient of Lady Arabella's charming attention and he genuinely liked her. 'It would seem that the council, with Sir George's co-operation, intend to build one of these wind farms on Spout Hill. It slipped out during that council chap's speech. I don't think it was meant to.'

'Good Lord!'

'Quite,' Richard Devine said dryly. 'There's quite a gathering over in the beer tent and only one topic of conversation. They're getting quite steamed up. From what I gather not a soul likes the idea.' He looked thoughtful then added quietly, 'I can't say I do either.' George looked at him. She wasn't used to him holding strong views on anything - even God. He glanced towards the beer tent. 'Quite frankly I wish it would rain or something and we could wind this whole thing up, it really has been rather trying... disappointing.' George took his hand sympathetically and it duly started to rain.

Flushed with post-coital satisfaction Simon had strolled casually across the gardens oblivious to the deserted stalls and partially dismantled stands. He slipped into the back bar area of the beer tent where he found Sid cursing cheerfully as he changed a barrel.

'Looks busy in here,' Simon said. Then picking up on the bad tempered atmosphere and distinctly un-festive mood added, 'What's going on?'

'Your fucking wind farm, that's what's going on!'

'Ah,' Simon glanced at his watch, 'is *The Bugle* out already?'

'*The Bugle*, what the fuck's it got to do with *The Bugle*?'

'My article, they said they'd print it,' Simon said with casual pride.

'Nothing to do with you,' Sid said dismissively, 'it was that council pratt who came out with it in 'is speech.' The barrel Sid was wrestling with hissed ominously. 'They went spare,' he chuckled, tossing his head towards the crowd of belligerent and increasingly drunk villagers on the other side of the bar. 'And now it's raining too,' he gloated, rubbing his hands together delightedly.

'Oh.' Simon was disappointed, but then he felt again the bullet hardness of George's nipples in his mouth. 'Oh well,' he said, 'it'll probably come out soon.'

Simon was right. Councillor Cockburn may indeed have stolen his thunder but only just, in fact only by a matter of hours.

As the sub-editor with responsibility for environmental stories and religious affairs had failed to return from her holiday in Thailand - the authorities still insisting that the white powder found in her luggage wrapped in a pair of soiled knickers was cocaine and not as she claimed *Andrew's Liver Salts* - Simon's laboured 1,500 words headed *Wind Farms Blowing Our Way,* had landed straight on the editor's desk. The name of Plompley had caught his eye and after just a few minutes scan reading, ignoring the appalling syntax and grammar, his journalistic antennae had started twitching. He put down the last crumpled sheet and looked up as his assistant appeared in the doorway.

'Any news of Rebecca?'

'She may be shot apparently.'

'Excellent!'

'You what?'

'Great story, right on our doorstep. We should be able to...'

'Hang on a minute! We're talking about our religious affairs correspondent being publicly executed for drug smuggling here. It doesn't exactly reflect well on the paper does it?'

'Only if she's guilty.'

'Well they won't shoot her if she's not guilty.'

'Not necessarily.'

'And that doesn't worry you I suppose? As long as we get a story.'

'Oh don't go all pious on me, Mattie. I don't remember you being so bloody holy when you pretended to be a stress councillor to get that rape victim's story. Eh? All I'm saying is, start building up a bit of background; talk to the family, get a few old photos in school uniform, maybe with a family pet or something, you know the sort of thing.' He looked thoughtful. 'No chance of finding out what sort of guns they'll use I suppose?'

Mattie looked at her editor coldly. She'd always rather liked Rebecca. 'Anything else?' she asked.

'Yeah, maybe.' He waved the wad of close-typed A4 sheets, 'Who's this Simon Cassady, have we run anything by him before?'

'Umm, name rings a bell. Is he the nature-notes guy? He didn't call it "Nature Notes", it was some other God-awful corny title, "Musings" or something like that. Yes, I remember now, it was crap. Half of it had probably been lifted straight from *Reader's Digest* and the rest wasn't exactly rivetting; I don't think many of our readers were surprised to learn that swallows appear around May and then disappear again in September. What about him?'

'Well he may have something here.' The editor tossed the sheath of paper across his desk. 'Don't bother checking it out for the moment, just rewrite it in plain English and pep it up a bit. Get the *NIMBYs* going, you know, a bit alarmist. Not for the lawyers though,' he added hastily.

Mattie sighed, reluctantly scooped up the bundle and headed for the door.

'Get it back to me later will you, I think we'll get it out a bit sharpish. It can only be a matter of time before someone else spots a bloody great sixty-metre mast and puts two and two together.'

Now Mattie was intrigued.

Sir George was slumped defensively behind his expansive desk listening irritably to the muted sounds of the dying fete outside. God, what a cock-up! To save repeated trips to the sideboard he'd brought the whiskey decanter with him and it was now planted firmly in the middle of the blotter. He hadn't bothered with the soda. From time to time he shot wary glances at the door, which he'd taken the precaution of locking. Sir George knew he had to start preparing his defences and had been urgently turning over in his mind every Green or environmentally friendly argument he'd ever heard or article he'd ever read. There weren't many. He needed time and a clear head and knew he had neither. He gulped down the contents of his glass and headed for the window in search of the compliant Becky.

Bunny was drunk. He was also stoned and in the early stages of what promised to be an appalling hangover. Having spent the morning helping Sid to set up the outside bar he'd taken full advantage of the landlord's uncharacteristic appreciation and made an early start. Then, before the crowds had arrived Bunny had wandered off round the house looking for a quiet spot to smoke the joint he'd furtively scored the evening before from the youngsters behind the scout hut. It wasn't something he did very often but it made him feel subversive. Unfortunately on top of four pints of Sid's roughest cider it also made him feel sick, so he'd spent the last hour slumped in the corner of a little-used hay store in a state of sweaty semi-consciousness.

Now, more-or-less awake but still disorientated and slightly nauseous, he was tottering back towards the beer tent determined to postpone the threatened hangover. Hunched in his customary combat jacket, tightly buttoned to conceal the shoulder-holstered hunting knife, and clutching the ever-present camera, Bunny stumbled round the corner of an outbuilding and straight into an equally unsteady Sir George.

'Bloody Hell! Who the Devil are you?' Sir George didn't wait for an answer. 'And what are you doing here?' He caught sight of the enormous camera, 'You're not press are you?' he snarled.

Bunny quite liked the idea but admitted he wasn't. Adding: 'So who are *you*?'

Sir George was momentarily taken aback but in best *Mr Toad* style drew himself up and pronounced, 'I am *Sir* George Hoggit.'

Bunny let this sink in. 'Well I,' he announced, 'am *Mr* Godfrey Warren - *Esquire*.' They looked at each other for a moment and then Bunny grasped the initiative. 'So what are *you* doing here?'

Caught out by the temerity of the question Sir George blurted out, 'Er, I live here. Now look here...'

'Well *I* don't,' Bunny interrupted. Adding formally, 'actually, I'm visiting.'

Sir George peered at him closely, 'Aren't you the caravan-site chap?'

'I am the joint owner, yes,' Bunny said proudly.

Sir George relaxed, more comfortable dealing with a known quantity, albeit a curiously garbed one. 'So exactly what *are* you doing?' His tone was slightly less aggressive and he indicated the large camera. 'Are you birding or twitching or whatever it's called?'

'I observe,' Bunny said.

Sir George was again taken aback. 'Oh, I see,' he said, but clearly didn't. 'Anything in particular?'

'Goings-on.' Bunny tried to look important. 'For security reasons.'

'What here?'

'Everywhere. It's the moral decline you see.'

Sir George nodded uncomprehendingly.

'All sorts going on,' Bunny continued. 'You'd be surprised.'

'I doubt it.'

Bunny fingered his camera. 'People who should know better, pillars of the community.'

'What, and you take photographs of them?' Sir George was intrigued.

Bunny, flattered by the interest of his illustrious host and with a bravado fuelled by a mixture of scrumpy and marijuana, warmed to his theme. 'Only if I consider they might present a future threat. I've got it all here.' He patted his telephoto lens affectionately.

'Well I trust you'll respect my privacy,' Sir George snapped, reverting to *Mr Toad* pomposity.

'Oh of course not your Lor... er, Sir. Oh no, you're definitely not a suspect. No question.'

Sir George nodded sternly.

Bunny looked sly, 'More than can be said for some of your neighbours though.'

There was a ripple under Sir George's tweed. 'Oh yes?'

Bunny's chemically rearranged senses weren't so confused that he didn't pick up the change in tone. He glanced melodramatically over his shoulder and edged forward conspiratorially. Sir George, who'd also bent forward was treated to a moist, warm blast of Bunny's curiously sweet and sour breath as he whispered: 'The vicar's wife!'

'Oh.' Sir George reeled back from the fumes disappointed. 'Don't know the woman.'

'Oh yes,' Bunny said with relish. 'Shocking!'

'Quite,' Sir George muttered, but was clearly losing interest. He adjusted his crotch and turned to resume his hunt for the stable-girl.

'And you'd have thought that Scottish bloke would have learnt his lesson wouldn't you?'

Sir George froze mid-turn, instantly sober. After the briefest of hesitations he turned slowly back, casually slipped his hands into his pockets and feigned casual ignorance. 'I'm not sure I know whom you mean.'

'Yes you do! You know ... your neighbour.'

'Oh that chap, yes, of course. Mac something ... McCruddy, that's it, er, Donald I think. My, what *has* he been up to now?'

'That's the one.' Bunny licked his lips. 'At it like bloody rabbits! And the vicar's wife too!' He shook his head in delighted, disgusted disbelief.

Sir George was stunned. He carefully repeated Bunny's phrases, '"At it like bloody rabbits," "...the vicar's wife too." Donald McCruddy!' Sir George was unaware of his surroundings for a moment, his mind whirling.

'Yep. If you don't believe me it's all here.' Bunny brandished the telephoto lens. 'The camera never lies.'

'Fuck!'

'Eh?'

'Oh sorry, I'm just a little shocked I suppose,' Sir George recovered. He was working hard to keep the smirk off his face whilst marvelling at his good fortune and wondering how best to utilise this remarkable information. Firstly, he obviously needed to play along this grubby little voyeur now fidgeting in front of him. 'Well it's been nice chatting,' he said, 'I do hope you're enjoying the fete.' He nodded politely and turned away.

Bunny looked after him a little disappointed. It wasn't often he had such an attentive audience and he'd been hoping to explain some of his local conspiracy theories, particularly the ones about the scoutmaster being a de-frocked vicar - which was in fact true - and having links with a Columbian drugs ring, which had yet to be proved.

'I've just had a lovely idea.' Sir George turned casually back towards Bunny who brightened at the renewed attention. 'Wouldn't it be fun...' Sir George gushed, '...to play a little joke on my old friend Donald? You know, make him blush a bit!' Eager to please and still chemically befuddled Bunny didn't register the sudden change in Donald McCruddy's status from vaguely remembered neighbour to 'old friend'. 'I know!' Sir George clicked his fingers. 'I don't suppose you've kept some prints of your... subjects have you?' His affected lightness of tone did nothing to disguise the malevolent glint in the rheumy pink eyes.

'Better than that - memory sticks!'

'Eh?' Sir George looked blank.

'Little gizmos to store all your pictures and data. You put them in your computer.' Bunny looked doubtfully at the tweed-encrusted figure and seeing no signs of comprehension added: 'You do have a computer don't you?'

'Of course we do.'

'Well then, no problem, you just pop it in the right dock and it downloads. Then you can view away,' he sniggered. 'And print too.'

'Print? Ah... I see.' The potential was becoming clearer. 'Umm, I suppose you wouldn't let me borrow your little stick thing, the one with the... ha, ha, ha, you know, the photos of old Donald on it?'

Bunny looked dubious. 'What, for a joke?' He sensed something was happening here but didn't quite know what.

'Ha, ha, yes, I can't wait to see his face, heh heh heh.' The laugh, forced way too far, had become more of a death rattle and it was unsettling Bunny.

'Well I suppose ... they're quite expensive actually.'

Sir George smelt blood and moved in for the kill. 'Of course I would expect to pay you for it. I tell you what, I'll buy it from you and then you needn't worry about it again. What shall we say... twenty pounds?'

Bunny hesitated and studied his camera.

'Why my dear fellow,' continued Sir George, 'I was forgetting, of course we must put a price on your time, not to mention your patience and... er, special talents.' The country gent bonhomie stopped abruptly and Sir George's voice hardened, 'Shall we say fifty?' It was not an offer it was a snapped command. Something not lost on Bunny.

'Done,' said Bunny.

Simon had slipped round the end of Sid's bar and found a spare stool from where he could see the whole tent and most of its occupants. At the opposite end of the counter was slumped a drunk and wholly ignored Mickey Moyst, his spiked hair crest-fallen, sunglasses twisted and knees muddied after repeated falls from his stool. He'd acquired a guitar from somewhere and occasionally twanged one of the remaining four strings. Simon watched him for a minute before catching Sid's eye. Sid grinned back, mouthed the word 'wanker' and charged down the bar to fill another impatient order.

Level with Simon's knees and sitting at a small metal table were the Aaright pair, temporarily uprooted from the bar of The Smuggler's they'd adopted their familiar head-to-head pose and as ever the levels in their glasses were identical. Simon hadn't yet heard either of them utter a word but a sharp rumble of thunder seemed to prompt a sudden sage exchange:

'It's gonna kick off.'

'Aar.'

There was a synchronised sip.

'Right.'

Simon looked around the heaving marquee to see what had prompted this observation and realised that the Aarights were right; there was a palpable tension in the air and not a smiling face to be seen. The weather reflected the mood. The dripping canvas of the giant tent slapped back and forth, poles shuddered and creaked and, unnoticed, stakes were dislodged and guy ropes slackened. Another resounding crack of thunder prompted an involuntary wince by everyone. Simon heard a gleeful cackle from Sid who'd taken advantage of the distraction to duck below the bar and re-chalk his price board before appearing to announce to no one in particular:

'Fucking grand!'

Sid was not the only one capitalising on the mood and weather. With increasingly slimy stock still to shift the hot dog concessionary had taken advantage of the largely deserted site and lack of officialdom to re-position his van immediately adjacent to the beer tent's only entrance/exit. He called this his '*National Trust* gift-shop strategy' and as the smell of freshly frying onions filled the marquee he waited confidently for the flood of departing drinkers who'd be forced to pass within irresistible feet of his hot plates and ketchup squeezers.

Simon's nose was twitching but he was saved from a particularly nasty strain of *e-coli* by the appearance of Bunny. Simon recognised him immediately, the soaking combat jacket incongruous amongst the optimistic summer outfits and more pragmatic anoraks. As Bunny wandered towards one of the larger crowds a pleasant looking dark-haired woman, smartly dressed in frock and matching jacket, detached herself from the edge of the group and to Simon's surprise greeted the slightly unsteady urban guerrilla with a peck on the cheek. Presumably his wife, not what Simon had expected at all. Bunny was quickly absorbed into the group, which immediately became more animated. It was like pushing a stick into a wasp's nest Simon thought and wondered whether he should be making a few journalistic notes.

Cockburn was confused. He'd started purposefully down the terrace steps to mingle happily with his constituents but had been taken aback, alarmed even, by the chilled response his platitudes had received. He'd delivered a few dud speeches in his time, and a few crackers too that for whatever reason had not gone down well. But he'd thought this afternoon's effort was one of his better ones, and yet the proverbial lead balloon couldn't have gone down quicker. Surely the announcement of the wind farm couldn't be the problem; Hallibut had assured him that an extrapolation of the (admittedly limited) *Scoping Consultation* had indicated strong support for the scheme amongst the villagers, so that clearly wasn't the issue. No it was probably the council tax thing, which hadn't been going down well in other parts of the county either. Probably shouldn't have mentioned it. He shrugged with the indifference of a seasoned thick-skinned politician and decided to try one last canvas. There were bound to be a few gullible yokels left in the beer tent. Turning up his collar against the rain and wrinkling his nose in disgust he hurried towards the hot dog van.

Simon happened to be looking at the flapping entrance as Cockburn was hit in the back by a particularly strong sqall and shot into the marquee before slithering to an uncertain halt. It was clear he hadn't anticipated the scene that now met him, and even the dimmest most optimistic canvasser would have realised that this was not a receptive electorate. Their anger was visible and audible.

The general volume had been increasing in the last few minutes largely due to the group that had absorbed Bunny, which had been swollen by several gangs of lively lager-fuelled youngsters. This crowd was rapidly taking on the identity of a mob but elsewhere around the marquee there was no doubting the anger of the more level-headed villagers. As Cockburn moved hesitantly towards the centre of the tent voices of dissent were clearly audible above the howling weather:

'...a wind farm vicar! That does sound dreadful. What *are* we to do?' This in a despairing tone from just over Cockburn's left shoulder.

'...of course the *damn* things don't work. Nuclear, that's the way.

Plenty of room in Kent, build 'em over there...' This, a strident boom from a distant flapping corner.

'...bomb the bastards,' that's what *I* say. Blow them to...' The rest was lost in the rising roar of voices and storm.

The vicar, Richard Devine, recently combat-tested, eyed the scene warily.

'Is there going to be a fight, daddy?' The child's eyes gleamed in excited anticipation.

Richard Devine sighed heavily, just one year at secondary school and he hardly recognised his eldest son. 'I *do* hope not,' he said, an image of Mrs Sponge's pulverised nose flashing before him. 'I really think perhaps the children should be going home, dear.'

'Do you think so?'

'Yes I do.'

There was a burst of expletives from the mob.

'Paul, John, go with your mother. Home! Now!'

'Oh, Daddy!'

Richard Devine became aware of Cockburn moving dangerously close to the seething mass at the centre of the tent. 'Right, off you go... quickly. I'll see you later, dear.' He watched fondly as his gently smiling wife ushered the children towards the smell of frying onions, nodding demurely to the various groups she passed on the way. Richard Devine turned reluctantly back to the central scene. Cockburn had stopped, hesitating, head up like an animal sniffing the air as if sensing danger - and if he had, he was right.

The mob had become the sole centre of attention, Bunny's voice clearly and angrily distinct above the background noise. Suddenly with a feral roar he burst flailing from the huddle.

'Oy! You! I wanna word with you!'

Cockburn had picked up the warning signals a few seconds too late. He'd already been on his way back towards the entrance but now turned to face his aggressor, instinctively backing up against the marquee's vibrating central pole.

Bunny closed in, shoulders hunched aggressively, his right hand fidgeting under the left armpit of his combat jacket. 'You the council bloke?'

Cockburn tried a confident smile and thrust out his hand. All Bunny saw was a superior smirk - he ignored the outstretched hand and kept his own firmly out of sight under the jacket. Cockburn's smile slipped slightly. 'I am the *leader* of the council, yes.' He withdrew the redundant hand. 'Pleased to meet you.'

'What's all this about then?'

'You'll have to be a little more specific, ha ha.' The jovial tone and simpering smile were a mistake.

'You know what I mean,' Bunny snapped, 'this fucking wind farm.'

The expletive caused a ripple around the tent. A few people tutted disapproval and glanced at their vicar, others chuckled in anticipation. Linda Warren quietly made her way to the entrance and slipped away unnoticed, even by Simon who'd been watching events with amused anticipation ever since the councillor had been propelled into the tent.

Cockburn ignored the obscenity but his lips thinned and his eyes hardened. 'Yes well, the council are keen to listen to all ideas. It is after all, all our responsibilities to do our bit for the planet. Sir George Hoggit's scheme will be duly considered once all...'

'A fucking wind farm!'

Cockburn couldn't help but wince. There was a little whoop of approval from Bunny's posse who'd moved up closer behind him.

'Er, yes, that is what's being mooted.'

'Mooted! Never mind fucking mooted! Are we going to get a wind farm on Spout Hill, yes or no?'

The first part of the reply was drowned out by deafening creaks and slapping as the whole giant tent shivered violently. People started glancing nervously at the sagging canvas and some were even reluctantly dragging themselves away from the developing drama and heading for the flaps.

'As I say,' Cockburn persisted, nearly shouting now, 'the council are keen and the government has indicated that renewable energy is something we should all...' The rest of his words were lost to the storm

82

and increased rumblings from the steadily advancing mob, but a sudden lull in both allowed a concluding, '...so yes, a wind farm on Spout Hill is being mooted.'

Encouraged by the animal growls from close behind him and incensed at Cockburn's increasing evasiveness Bunny gave his final judgement:

'I'll fucking moot you!' he roared, and although he'd had no intention of backing it up with physical action a phalanx of the drunker and wilder youngsters, whooping and bellowing, heaved forward until Bunny found himself pinned chest to chest with the startled councillor.

'God!' Cockburn groaned, and then struggling to catch his breath nearly gagged as he caught a ripe blast of Bunny's.

His lager forgotten, Simon watched fascinated as the mêlée was joined by two community police officers and, to his surprise, the vicar. The addition of uniformed bodies to the scrum encouraged yet more of Bunny's excitable supporters to join in, and as most were playing members of the local rugby club rucking came naturally to them, as did the odd surreptitious punch and knee. As the squeeze increased Bunny became aware of Cockburn wriggling frantically against his stomach and then watched in amazement as the puce, pop-eyed councillor squirmed his way down the green-painted pole and, as far as Bunny could tell, disappeared between Bunny's own legs. The void was immediately and involuntarily filled ... by Bunny, as he was slammed forward by the combined weight of Plompley's first XV and various other assorted thugs. There was a resounding crack.

Simon hesitated for a moment mesmerised by the slow motion flop of the huge dripping canopy, the cartwheeling lengths of jagged tent pole and other tumbling and flailing spars and ropes. There was an ominous whoosh, the sound of a large quantity of water on the move, and the bellied canvas above the bar suddenly dipped and twisted to create a spectacular waterfall. Sid appeared soaked and gasping from behind the bar.

'Fuckin' 'ell!' he spluttered, and Simon realised to his amazement that Sid was almost helpless with laughter.

The rest of the marquee was now collapsing fold by dripping fold.

There were screams and bellows from all corners. Some people had been knocked to their knees by the lashing sodden canvas, others had dropped to all fours as a precaution and were slithering desperately towards the lingering smell of frying onions - the hot-dog entrepreneur, sensing imminent disaster, had already relocated to the front of the St John Ambulance tent. There was another apocalyptic crash of thunder.

'Blow wind, crack your cheeks...' Simon muttered and with a last glance at the chaos slipped nimbly through an unlaced flap. Taking shelter under the partially collapsed awning of the abandoned hook-a-duck stall he sipped his lager and wondered what to call his next article for *The Bugle*; 'Fete Day Massacre' was a thought - maybe a bit over the top. 'Wind Farm Riot' - no one could argue with that he decided cheerfully, surveying the mass of cursing, wriggling canvas and listening to the thuds and screams coming from its muddy folds. Sid suddenly appeared, soaked to the skin and dishevelled but still inexplicably chuckling.

'Oh, bloody 'ell! I 'aven't 'ad a laugh like that since Aunt Mabel got 'er tits caught in the mangle,' he gasped, snatching Simon's lager bottle and taking a long gulp. 'Ta.'

'What are you so cheerful about?' Simon reclaimed what was left of his drink.

'Never 'ad one like it,' Sid said, patting a large linen bag tucked securely under his arm.

'What's that?'

Sid looked at him pityingly. 'Fuckin' till, that's what.'

'Aah.'

'Not a drop left in there, sold the lot, five quid a pint by the end. Four for one of them,' he said nodding at the lager bottle, which Simon hastily put behind his back. Sid grinned.

'Anyone hurt?' Simon asked with professional interest.

'Dunno. Don't reckon that DJ pratt'll play the guitar again for a while though.'

'He couldn't in the first place. Dead d'you think then?'

Sid looked a bit shocked, 'Callous bastard, aren't you? No, shouldn't think so, just a bit knocked about, there were poles flying round like bleedin' javelins in there. F... f... flip, 'ere's the vicar.'

Richard Devine, minus his dog collar and with mud-smeared knees, appeared calmly from under a dripping fold of canvas leading a wild-eyed and visibly shaking Cockburn.

'You should be all right now, councillor,' he said gently, 'probably best to get on home. Have a hot bath that might help some of the bruises. And perhaps a change of clothes,' he added with no apparent irony. Cockburn's sharp political outfit of a few hours earlier was unrecognisable. One shoe was missing, an arm had been torn almost right off his suit jacket, the original colour of his shirt was indiscernible through the mud and it appeared that someone had chewed his tie in half. The flamboyant matching-purple handkerchief had completely disappeared - it was later found by bemused paramedics attached to Bunny's flies, presumably snagged as Cockburn had slithered to safety.

'Are you all right getting to your car? Happy to drive, yes?'

Cockburn nodded vaguely, looked in nervous disbelief at the ruins of the beer tent and hurried away mumbling incoherently.

'You'd better call an ambulance, Sid.' Richard Devine used the same calm tone he had with the shell-shocked councillor, and Sid, who hadn't even realised the vicar knew his name, reacted unquestioningly to the quiet authority in the voice. He held out his hand to Simon who wordlessly handed over his mobile phone. Richard Devine puffed his cheeks and with a weary sigh stooped back under the folds of canvas. Sid was still waiting for the operator to answer when the vicar's head reappeared, 'Better ask them to send two, Sid.'

CHAPTER SIX

Linda Warren sipped at the tepid coffee without enthusiasm. She'd hoped to be on her way home by now. The doctors had already said that Bunny could leave; it was apparently quite a nasty concussion but he needn't spend another night in the hospital. But now they couldn't find his clothes - there was always something with Bunny - and now, although still naked except for the buttonless A&E smock, the police were insisting on talking to him. Something about carrying a concealed weapon. Linda waited patiently and watched as the little *Friend's* shop and cafe steadily filled up. There was the usual hospital bustle of anxious relatives clutching magazines and brown paper bags of fruit, pretty, tired-looking nurses smelling of recently smoked cigarettes and self-important young men in white coats juggling mobile phones, stethoscopes and pagers. One by one the other chairs at Linda's table had been whisked away until just one was left.

'Do you mind if I sit here?'

Linda looked up with a start, 'No, of course not. I mean yes, um, please do.' She stumbled over the courtesies confused by a vague recognition.

Lady Arabella nodded her thanks, sat down and looked frankly at Linda. 'I know you. Now remind me ...'

'Um, Warren, Linda Warren, I live in Plompley.'

'Of course you do.' Lady Arabella clicked her fingers gently and smiled at Linda with satisfaction. 'I knew I recognised you. Visiting?'

'More collecting really.'

'Oh well that sounds like good news then. Nothing too serious,' she concluded brightly.

'A bit of concussion ... my husband ... a clonk on the head. He's a bit accident prone,' Linda added with a sigh.

'I wish mine was.'

'I've lost count of the hours I've spent in this place over the years.'

Linda glanced around the bustling shop.

'Has he got a dangerous job?'

'No!' Linda snorted. 'We have the caravan site in Plompley. Tents too sometimes.' She paused, clearly making her mind up about something. 'Actually,' she said with a nervous laugh, 'it was a tent that put Bunny in here this time.'

'Bunny?'

'My husband.'

'Oh. How can you hurt yourself with a tent?'

'Bunny could hurt himself with anything, even a drinking straw once. It fell on him.'

Lady Arabella looked confused, 'A drinking straw fell on him?'

'Oh no. No, that went up his nose. The *tent* fell on him.'

'Aah, it must have been a big...' Lady Arabella's voice tailed off and she stared intently at Linda who nodded and smiled wryly.

'Yes it *was* a big tent; it was the marquee at your fete. When the big pole in the middle broke it clonked Bunny on the head. An awful storm wasn't it.'

Lady Arabella leant back in her chair. 'Do you mean the weather or that... that riot?' She almost spat the last word.

'Both I suppose,' Linda said, not taking her eyes off Lady Arabella's.

'I suppose your husband was in the middle of it?'

'I expect so,' Linda sighed, 'I'm afraid he's easily led on. People wind him up, even the Scouts for goodness sake ... and he certainly wasn't very happy about this wind farm thing.'

'He wasn't the only one!' Lady Arabella said bitterly. 'The first I knew of it was when that slimy little politician got up on his hind legs and started gushing about me and George. *Lord* Hoggit my arse!'

Linda laughed at the unexpected crudity and Lady Arabella quickly joined in. It seemed she wasn't going to hold Linda responsible for Bunny's part in destroying her fete. 'So are *you* visiting someone?' Linda asked, 'or do you actually work here?' She glanced at the leather briefcase on the table.

'Well, work I suppose, in a way, I sit on the *Friends* committee. In fact I'm the chairwoman for my sins. I agreed to do it as long as they didn't call me 'Chair'! I told 'em, "I'm not a piece of bloody furniture!" Oh Lord, and I'm going to be late.' She jumped to her feet and snatched up her bag. 'I'm glad we met.' She paused and looked down at Linda thoughtfully. 'Do you ride?'

Linda was caught by surprise, 'Um... well I used to. I loved it, but finding time and the cost of...'

'Come up to the house sometime... anytime. I'm usually around the stables somewhere. We'll have a hack. Yes?'

Linda smiled up into the grey eyes but didn't have a chance to reply.

'Good, lovely. Soon yes?' Lady Arabella hurried off towards the teeming main corridor.

Linda was still re-running the conversation through her head when Bunny appeared. His head was swathed in crisp white bandages from the eyebrows up and ended neatly in a little topknot, like a sanitary onion. The rest of him was clad in an astonishing collection loaned by lost property: a crumpled pink-and-blue striped shirt, impossibly tight grey shorts, presumably removed from some unfortunate schoolboy, and lace-less plimsolls. His arm was firmly held by a stern looking policeman wearing a holstered sidearm.

Bunny smiled at Linda sheepishly. 'They wanted a statement.' He held up the empty sheath and shoulder harness for his favourite commando knife by way of explanation.

Linda sighed and picked up the car keys.

The council leader's untypical political *faux pas* at the Hoggit fete and the publication of Simon's heavily edited but sensationalist article about the wind farm - splashed across the front page of *The Bartford Bugle* and hammered home by three inch headlines - ensured that the whole of Plompley now knew of the part they were expected to play in the fight against global warming - like it or not. They'd also been left in little doubt where their council, as represented by Claude Cockburn, stood on the matter.

Simon's 'scoop' had appeared anonymously, which although initially disappointing he now realised was in fact an advantage as it allowed him to move anonymously around the village listening quietly to the debates, threats or howls of protest, all depending on which faction he was eavesdropping on at the time.

By far the loosest and most placid group Simon had nicknamed *The Handwringers*, who had at their core, reluctantly, the vicar. There were no formal meetings but the post-Communion tea-sippers would cluster anxiously round Richard Devine every Sunday morning, clucking and bleating anxiously whilst he gave reassurances that he didn't really believe himself. In fact, he didn't really know what he was meant to think - or say.

'Do you think I should be speaking out on this wind farm thing?'

George put her book down on the eiderdown and eased her glasses down her nose. 'Do *you* think you should?' she asked gently.

'I really don't know, we don't seem to be allowed opinions on very much these days. The bishop has got quite fierce about it recently. I think he was a bit upset by that thing Harry wrote in *The Guardian* on the possible benefits of cannibalism in the Third World.'

'I think this is a little different, dear.'

'Yes, I dare say, but it does seem to be an issue that divides opinion.'

'Not in Plompley it doesn't, I haven't heard a single word in favour. In fact it even seems to have brought some of the community closer together... at least for the moment. Mrs Sponge has even dropped her grievous bodily harm case against the *WT*.'

They sat propped against their pillows in silence for a moment.

'You're right, I haven't heard a single person speak *for* the damn things either. But it won't last,' Richard Devine sighed wearily. 'Once these wind farm people start their bullying and propaganda... divide and rule that's how they operate ... they'll have this community tearing itself apart. I've seen it happen again and...'

'Richard...' It was unusual for George to interrupt him, '...I think you should do what *you* think is right. It's clear what our friends, your flock...' she smiled gently, '... what they think. And it's quite clear, at least to me, that they expect your comfort and support. And your strength,' she added firmly. 'Does that fit in with your own thoughts on these wretched things? It does doesn't it?'

'Oh yes, no doubt of that. I think the whole idea's appalling, destructive, divisive, a travesty. And there's something a bit ... I don't quite know, a bit... *funny* about the whole thing.'

'Well then, I'm sure you'll do what you think is right, dear.' She picked up the little *Anais Nin* book and started to read.

Simon's second village group and by far the most entertaining was more of a mob really. He'd labelled them *The Headbangers*. Their natural habitat was the old bar end of the Smuggler's Finger and they naturally attracted some of the younger groups from around the village, including the rugby team and the Young Farmers. There was no attempt to organise or co-ordinate, it was a wholly anarchic group whose suggestions for 'direct action' and sabotage became increasingly violent and unlawful as the evenings went on - and as the consumption of lager went up. Most schemes were completely forgotten by the next morning and none, at least so far, had been put into action. Simon hadn't been surprised to see Bunny Warren very much at the heart of things and towards the end of most evenings unsteadily on his feet proposing one of the blood-thirstier actions. So extreme in fact that even the first XV's front row would often shout his excesses down. Sometimes Bunny's surprisingly attractive wife would hover loyally at the edge of the unruly crowd but once Bunny got to the gizzard-ripping stage she would smile politely at those nearest and slip away. After a few weeks of this, clearly feeling unappreciated, Bunny had stormed from the pub one night muttering about 'lone wolves' and was never seen with the Headbangers again.

Meanwhile at the other end of the room in the 'lounge', Simon's *Moderate*s would gather. This was predominantly the early-doors crowd, retirees having a pre-dinner drink and commuters treating themselves on the way home. These gatherings were also informal; the real business took place secretively behind closed doors and curtains in various drawing rooms and dining rooms around the village. From what Simon could gather, at the beginning there had been one group in the village, which showed promise as a well-organised and cohesive campaign, but it had quickly collapsed under the weight of individual prejudices, feuds and egos. What resulted was a splintered collection of mutually suspicious rival committees, each with its own hierarchy of self-important officers and complicated constitution. Their tactics varied subtly but were generally based on campaigns of letter writing, political lobbying and gaining a sympathetic press.

The one campaign idea all the groups had hit on was the unoriginal idea of displaying protest signs and posters. Even some of the Handwringers had timidly slipped A4 sheets under the net curtains of street-front windows bearing the polite legend: 'No Wind Farm - Thank you.' The Moderates had all managed to agree on a rather more strident message, but stamped their individuality by using different coloured backgrounds. So: 'NO WIND FARM HERE!' duly appeared on fluorescent orange, green or fuchsia throughout the village, the coloured clusters indicating committee allegiance. Meanwhile the Headbangers had drunkenly come up with any number of choice phrases ranging from the threatening to the outright obscene, but no posters had ever been produced and like the rest of their lager-fuelled ideas it had all been forgotten by the next morning. Except by Bunny - who'd been well on with his eight-by-four-foot: 'FUCK THE WIND FARM!' before Linda quietly negotiated a compromise and in due course a rather lame red and white: 'BAN WIND FARMS' had appeared on the verge at the entrance to the caravan site.

Sir George Hoggit was swivelling gently to and fro in the leather chair and eyeing the whisky decanter that beckoned seductively from the sideboard. Nearly quarter to ten, they'd be here soon, better leave it. He glanced nervously at the door of the study. Sir George was still in the habit of locking it, even though he'd only seen Lady Arabella once since the fete.

On that chilling occasion he'd been caught out by the politeness of the knock at the door, which at his unsuspecting invitation had been thrust open to reveal, to his ill-disguised horror, his wife. Not deigning to venture beyond the threshold she'd curtly informed him that 'some of the girls' had helped her move into the old chauffeur's flat and she would shortly be going down to the Tuscan house with a friend for a week or so. Sir George had been left visibly shaken by the encounter. After a week of nerve-shredding silence he'd found her steely calmness and studied politeness far more threatening than the long-anticipated explosion of fury.

Shuddering at the memory he heaved himself to his feet, moved stiffly across to unlock the door and went to stand by the long windows. Plans for the wind farm were going well, and with a fickle government being shamed, bullied and lobbied into promising ever-more generous subsidies, apparently in perpetuity, his financial future looked very rosy indeed. The thought cheered him and he was just contemplating a congratulatory snort when Hallibut was shown in. He was early, damn him. Sir George dragged his eyes away from the sideboard and scowled at the planning officer.

''Morning Sir George.' Hallibut sounded more cheerful than he felt. He was nervous; he'd never been to Hoggit Hall before and although curious felt uncomfortable being so openly associated with his dubious benefactor. He'd have far preferred the sordid discreetness of the grotty Bartford pub.

'You're early.'

'Sorry, is that a problem?' Hallibut glanced at his watch. It was two minutes to ten.

Sir George gave the whisky decanter a last wistful look and waved a podgy hand. 'Well sit down then. I wanted a quiet word anyway. Now, what about *Cock*burn?'

'It's *Co*burn Sir George, I think it would probably help if...' He was stopped by the expression on the mottled face.

'Have you had any feedback?' Sir George demanded. 'I've only dealt through his office, some electoral agent or something. We've made our... contribution, as agreed, and he got his bloody speech. God, did he get his bloody speech! Why didn't someone tell me?' He slapped the desk and winced. 'What possessed him to let it out like that?'

'I thought you'd told him to,' Hallibut lied.

Sir George gave him a withering look. 'Bollocks!'

'I thought Lady Hoggit looked a bit surprised.'

'Surprised? Of course she was fucking surprised, I hadn't told her!'

'Ah. Is she OK about it now? None of my business of course,' Hallibut added hurriedly.

'No it's bloody not. Who knows, she's in Italy.'

'Ah.' Hallibut understood the choice of meeting place now and felt slightly more relaxed about being in the house.

'So, *prospective* Parliamentary Candidate *Co*burn,' Sir George said nastily, 'can we now take it that we've got his unstinting and unquestioning support?'

'Well, I gather he's still a bit shaken up, but...'

'Look! He's had my money and I gave him his chance to sound off - as agreed.' The pink watery eyes locked onto Hallibut's. 'He's mine now, too.'

Hallibut shivered. 'I'm not sure he picked up many votes though,' he said dryly.

'It's not my fault he started a bloody riot... got his name in the press didn't it?'

'I'm not sure that was quite the coverage he was hoping for, but anyway... I understand another call to his electoral agent may help to, er... settle things down.' He glanced nervously at Sir George who leaned back in his chair and sighed heavily.

'I see.'

There was a discreet tap at the door prompting a snarled: 'Come in!' Terse introductions followed.

'So Wormold, where are we? Geology fixed? Environment fixed? Those letters of support all rubber-stamped and ready to go?'

'Um, I'd rather we didn't use the word "fixed", Sir George...' Wormold was perched nervously on the edge of a chair with a laptop balanced on a pile of plans and coloured files, which in turn were balanced on his knees. His ill-fitting glasses were too near the end of his nose and he spoke in a nasal whine, '... but we do seem just about ready now to make our application.' He glanced uncertainly at Hallibut who was studying his fingernails. 'We have the data we need and have, er... presented it in a way that I'm sure will appeal to ... well, *satisfy* all interested parties,' he said carefully.

'I doubt it. Have you had a chance to go through it, Maxwell?' Sir George turned to the fourth person in the room, who to Sir George's irritation had quietly let himself into the study and without acknowledging the other occupants taken up a pose with his back to the room in front of the long windows. He now turned towards Sir George's desk, his air of cultivated superiority emphasised by a flamboyant bowtie and arrogantly unfashionable moustache.

'Of course.' The voice was smooth, oily. 'I assume we can speak freely?' He looked pointedly at the planning officer.

'Yes, yes, of course,' Sir George snapped. Hallibut shifted uncomfortably in his chair.

'Well, from Ref Watt's point of view it seems to tick all our boxes. The formatting and presentation is what we would expect and follows a pattern that we have used successfully for other schemes where we've had an exceptionally constructive level of officer and political input at local level.' He glanced meaningfully at Hallibut again, who refused to meet his eye. 'An open-minded approach and the unquestioning acceptance of our data tends to ensure a smoother process - which is of course to everyone's advantage.' He smiled thinly and turned again to look out of the window. 'We might have to do a little work on the geological reports though.' He turned back to the room. 'Some of the geophysics isn't particularly..., helpful, but I'm sure it's something we can soon get on top of, so to speak.' He smiled coldly at Wormold who started tapping frantically at his computer. 'Now...' Maxwell continued, '...the next thing is to open the *PR* front. Regardless of the help we're getting from our technical friends...' he nodded towards Hallibut, '... and of course our, shall we say, political advantage, we've found in the past that if we at least go through the motions of a local consultation, what we bill "a robust and open public debate", it helps gives us a distinct advantage in claiming the moral high ground.'

Hallibut suppressed a snort.

Sir George shifted uneasily. 'What sort of debate?'

'Oh quite straightforward. We usually take over a venue in the village, the parish hall or somewhere like that, pop up a few pretty posters - lots of cuddly endangered species that sort of thing - make up a few computer enhanced landscape images (you can do wonders with those these days), lots of stats that no one understands and then some blurb about the number of homes we'll be powering. Or could with a fair wind, ha ha ha ... my little joke. And then we give everyone a free light bulb - low energy of course.'

Sir George looked dubious.

'Then there's normally some sort of meeting,' Maxwell continued. 'The parish council often get involved and they normally let me have a say. You probably could too...'

'Good God, no!'

Maxwell looked at the scowling porcine face. 'No, perhaps not... probably for the best... and then there's normally a question and answer session, whether you want it or not,' he chuckled. 'That can get quite frisky.'

Wormold looked up from his laptop. 'Yes, I can see your point on the *geophys*, some of the old radar imaging seems to suggest that just about where...'

'Right!' Maxwell clapped his hands together loudly and beamed around the room until he reached Wormold... then the smile froze and a penetrating stare locked onto the smeared glasses. 'That will be dealt with...' he said quietly, '...later.' Wormold shrivelled and Maxwell turned back to Sir George. 'If you want to leave the local meeting for my people to organise then that's OK; we have our own way with these things.' He was completely in control again. 'I presume you have some sort of ... influence with the parish council?'

Sir George struggled to catch up. God, he needed a drink. 'Er, yes... yes of course.' He brightened and looked cunning. 'The chairman is currently under the impression that I'm going to ... well he's hoping that ... well lets just say he'll be helpful anyway.'

'Splendid, half the battle, buy him lunch or something like that.'

'Yes, something like that.' Sir George muttered.

With that the meeting broke up. Hallibut escaped as quickly as possible but found himself following Maxwell's logo-bearing Range Rover down the drive. He didn't relax until the association had been broken when they turned in opposite directions on reaching the road.

'Er, Sir George...'

'I'm not interested, Wormold, too busy.' Sir George looked hungrily towards the sideboard. 'You and Maxwell can sort out your geo ... whatever.'

'No it's not that, Sir George, there's one other thing we haven't quite sorted out and I really need to before we put the planning application in. It's a question of notices you see, whether it's a Certificate A or...'

'Well, what is it?'

'Well it's the access. It really is very important, you see it's a question of...'

'Ah yes, the access, the famous *green road*.'

'Yes, quite.'

'Don't worry, Wormold, we shall have our access. I imagine I'll be able to confirm the details for you once the post has been delivered tomorrow morning.'

By the time a puzzled Wormold had bundled together his paraphernalia, Sir George was back in his chair clutching a brimming glass and smirking happily to himself.

Donald McCruddy hated porridge and even the thought of a kipper, at least for breakfast, was equally revolting. His tenuous Highland heritage didn't reach as far as matters culinary and he loathed haggis. Burn's Night was always a trial. No, strong black coffee and a large plate of eggs and bacon were the only things for the first meal of the day. Sitting at the large scarred pine table, corduroys and brogues below the waist frayed towelling robe above, McCruddy contentedly pushed the greasy plate away and reached for the coffee pot. It was a little ritual he had, first a coffee, then the fry-up, then a second coffee, and then, and only then, the post. There were rarely any surprises. The bulk of it was bulging envelopes from various government departments containing incomprehensible forms with nonsensical explanatory notes, which were simply passed on to the part-time farm manager, as was the large pile of catalogues offering ever more desperate discounts on everything from castration rings to combine harvesters. Envelopes clearly marked from his bank, the Inland Revenue or VAT office were filtered out and put in a separate pile to be forwarded to his accountants. A small local firm who were as imaginative as they were discreet. This left any personal correspondence, which was rare. He'd not yet managed to convert his sister to e-mail so there was an occasional letter from her full of the usual dull family news and invariably ending with hints that he should be doing more for his nephews - particularly financially. He usually sent back a one-sentence greeting and begrudgingly enclosed two ten-pound notes. The stiffened hand-addressed envelope that slipped from the pile this morning was therefore unusual, and got his attention first. He took a sip of the stewed coffee, neatly slit the flap and tipped a jumble of glossy photographs onto the table. The subject matter was immediately obvious and a slight smile appeared on McCruddy's face. He was amused but puzzled; why should anyone, unsolicited on this occasion, send him a collection of fairly hard-core porn? He fanned out the photos... and froze.

The accompanying note simply and politely suggested that he should call a given telephone number. This turned out to be the private line of a partner in a small but efficiently amoral London law firm, who explained the situation: *no* he could not reveal the identity of his client; *yes* he did have full authority to act; *no* there was no room for negotiation; *yes* he was in possession of a memory stick containing certain photographs and he could confirm that he had detailed instructions as to its disposal or publication; *no* Mr McCruddy did not appear to have much choice; and finally, *yes*, he agreed, blackmail was 'an ugly business'. Apparently all the necessary paperwork granting the required easements and rights-of-way had already been prepared and it was agreed that Mr McCruddy would attend the solicitor's offices within the next few days to sign it. Donald McCruddy decided he'd do it on his way to Gatwick - just in case.

'Come on in, Mattie, 'What's the news?' It was an old but now largely discarded 'in' office joke.

'Don't ask me you're the editor,' she replied sourly.

'I wasn't trying to be funny. What's going on then, better?'

'They're not going to shoot Rebecca.'

'Oh.' He sounded disappointed. 'Not guilty then?'

'Oh yes, guilty as hell apparently, just they don't shoot male prisoners in Thailand - they hang them.'

'How's that affect Rebecca?'

'You mean Bernard.'

Jordan looked up sharply and slowly took off his glasses. 'What! You mean Rebecca isn't a... you mean...' He flopped back in his chair, '... you mean *she's* a... *he*... a *Bernard*?'

'Yep.' Mattie was enjoying herself. 'They spotted it in the Bangkok prison.'

'I bet they did,' Jordan grimaced. 'But how come we didn't, after what, three years?'

'Don't know, Rob, maybe you'd better bring in full body searches for all new members of staff from now on. Either that or check them out personally at the Christmas party.'

Rob Jordan narrowed his eyes and silently waved Mattie to a chair. She wondered whether she might have gone a bit far. Jordan was after all her boss. They both knew what she'd been referring to and Jordan was still regularly reminded of it on *You Tube*. Reason enough for him to have forbidden his children access to social networking sites, or so he thought. The incident had occurred in the latter stages of the office Christmas party a few years before. The drink had been flowing and the

98

photocopier suggestion, an ambitious development of the 'bottom-print', had, appropriately enough, come from the pictures' editor. She was an attractive girl with a good figure in a Marilyn Monroe sort of way and ten years younger than Jordan. He'd been flattered.

At the actual point of collapse the photocopier, set to 150% enlargement and colour, was still gamely printing. But distracted by cramp and their joint efforts to keep her breasts out of the paper-feed Jordan and his new friend had missed the warning signs of imminent structural failure. The crash and scream had brought would-be rescuers rushing, the scene of tangled twisted metal and naked limbs initially provoking a stunned silence, which was soon broken by the clicking of mobile phones and subordinate sniggering. No Christmas since had passed in the offices of *The Bugle* without the episode being gleefully recounted. It came out every year with the decorations, the plastic tree and *Slade*.

'So...' Jordan smiled thinly, '...Rebecca, *Bernard*, I presume we're following it up?'

'Yeah, Michael's on it. He's working on the family but they're not very happy, not very cooperative,' she sniffed. 'He's trying to dig up old school friends, boys, girls or whatever and apparently can do something clever on the computer to get into medical records to see if anything's been chopped off or stuck on.'

'Fine. Any date for the execution?'

'Oh it could be years, all sorts of appeals to go through. The Foreign Office usually gets involved somewhere along the line, which always confuses things, so no, nothing's going to happen in a hurry.'

'Ah well, shame, but perhaps we can make something of the he/she thing for the time being, keep the story alive. Those medical records would be handy. D'you reckon they'll include photos?'

'What, sort of: The Chop - before and after?'

'Yeah, exactly.' Mattie wrinkled her nose in disgust but Jordan ignored her. 'Lets see how Mike gets on,' he said. 'Right, now closer to home, actually a bit too bloody close for my liking.' The Jordan family had just a year before broken free of Bartford suburbia and now, mortgaged to the hilt, were settled in previously desirable Plompley. 'This wind farm story, your re-write certainly seems to have got them going, a bloody riot by all accounts. Excellent!'

'Actually, we can't take credit for that - wrong timing.'

'Eh?'

'The riot was in full swing by the time *The Bugle* came out that afternoon. Haven't you read *Mr Countryman's* epistle?' She nodded at the dog-eared pile of paper on his blotter.

'Not in detail, no. Is it any good?'

'No, but it does seem to cover everything. Apparently it was the speech by Claude Co'burn, the council leader that got them going. No one had a clue about the wind farm except the land owner and one or two people at the council, including Co'burn obviously, and he seemed to expect everyone to love the idea!'

'Stinks a bit doesn't it?'

'Yes, to high heaven. Anyway the whole fete thing was a bit of a wash out. Pissed down all afternoon. Apparently there was quite a gathering in the beer tent, nothing else to do, so too much booze all round and a few hot heads were up for it. Then in struts Co'burn to do a bit of flesh-pressing and expecting a warm welcome!'

'Sounds like he got one.'

'Yeah, carnage. Especially when the marquee collapsed,' Mattie giggled.

'What, really? It just gets better!'

'Oh there's more, Co'burn gets beaten up, two ambulances called...'

'Two?'

'Yep, Mickey Moyst, you know, *Radio Bartford*, he's hospitalised. Stomach pump amongst other things.'

'Excellent.' Jordan thrust the bundle of paper across the desk. 'Right, this is what I want: we'll definitely run with this, too late for today so you've got until eleven tomorrow and I want to use this Cassady bloke's piece...' He riffled the wad of papers. '...but for God's sake shorten it, make it punchy, noisy, let's go tabloid. You know the sort of thing.'

'D'you want real interviews and quotes or make-ups?'

'Hmm, best go and speak to a few people I think. From what I hear this Co'burn's not a character to be messed with and we don't want that DJ pratt slagging us off on air. In fact go gentle on him, maybe try and make him out a bit of a hero or something, we might get a couple of decent plugs. While you're at it talk to the advertising people and see if they can get *Radio Bartford* to take a bit more space. Once you've done your "Hero DJ" piece of course.'

'What about Cassady?'

'I think start with him. He may not be able to write but he obviously knows what's going on. Tell him he's a *source*, the amateurs always like that, makes them feel involved, relevant. Maybe lead him on a bit... use your womanly wiles... whatever they are.'

Mattie looked at him coldly but it was wasted, the glasses were back in place and Jordan was already reaching for one of several phones on his desk. She left the room unnoticed.

Simon was getting bored sitting in the bar by himself, the notebook he now habitually carried sat blankly and accusingly on the sticky table in front of him, and he started thinking about the vicar's wife. The sudden unexpected shrilling of his mobile phone brought him out of his sexual reverie and with a guilty start he had to fidget himself comfortable before he could answer. The conversation was short and to the point: *The Bugle* wanted him as *a source* and was sending out one of its senior staff reporters to interview him... now, if convenient. Simon readily agreed and went looking for someone to tell.

He found Sid in an overgrown corner of the car park swathed in dark grey smoke and scowling at a huge pile of cardboard boxes.

'God, are you burning plastic?'

'Fuckin' dustmen won't take it.'

'Stinks.'

'You can take it down the tip if you want.'

Simon edged up-wind and took a swig from his lager bottle. 'No it's

OK, I'll just stay here and watch you getting kippered.'

A string of expletives was abruptly choked off by another acrid cloud. Sid eventually emerged, eyes streaming, and gasping for breath. 'Give us a hand,' he wheezed, and headed for a ramshackle corrugated iron shed.

'Ah, the old sign you were telling me about.'

'Yeah, can't be arsed to break it up for the burner, I'm gonna bung it on the fire. Come on.' Between them they half carried, half dragged the warped and peeling board out into the smoky daylight. It was much as Sid had once described it, clearly some sort of smuggling scenario but curiously understated, almost artistic. Simon also thought it was strangely familiar in an old-family-photograph sort of way and he tried to remember whether it had still been hanging outside the pub when he'd first come to the village. They tumbled it onto the fire, which effectively smothered it.

Arriving in Plompley earlier than she'd expected and finding the pub devoid of customers or staff it was beside the remains of the bonfire that Mattie found her *source* ten minutes later. Sid was cursing and stabbing at the smouldering pile with a fork whilst Simon lolled against the remains of a stone wall sucking at his lager and offering advice:

'... I tell you, it'll get it going.'

'Going! It'll likely blow me fucking 'ead off! *You* chuck petrol on it.'

'It's your fire... and your head. Why don't you... oh hello.' Simon straightened up from the wall and walked across the pitted tarmac towards the slim young woman who'd appeared uncertainly round the corner.

'There doesn't appear to be anyone inside,' Mattie said apologetically, 'I'm due to meet someone...'

'Yes, probably me.' Simon smiled and glanced at his watch.

'I'm a bit early. It's not as far as I remember. Mattie James.'

'Simon Cassady. No problem, lets go inside.'

'Where is everyone?'

'Well that's the landlord...' Simon nodded towards the muttering Sid, '...and I'm the customer, and that's about it.' He glanced at his wrist again, 'Aaright will be in soon.'

102

'Ah, right,' Mattie said hesitantly.

Whilst Simon busied himself behind the bar Mattie glanced around; she vaguely remembered coming in here as a teenager. She carefully inspected her *source*. He seemed more normal than *The Countryman's Musings* had suggested, certainly younger, maybe about thirty. He was clean-shaven and conventionally dressed in jeans and trainers, although there was perhaps a hint of eccentricity in the longish brown hair and waistcoat. He seemed confident and ironic but on the whole, she decided with relief, definitely *normal*.

'Do 'elp yourself then,' Sid said sarcastically.

'I have thanks.'

'That's 'er then?'

'Yes it is, now sod off we've got business to discuss.'

'Charming!'

Simon ensconced Mattie in his snug. He placed a large glass of white wine in front of her and pulled out Sid's usual stool for himself. 'So what happens now?'

'I want you to tell me all about this,' she smiled and patted the crumpled typewritten A4 sheets, 'blow by lurid blow.'

CHAPTER SEVEN

Bunny kept the revs low trying to mute the irregular growl from the ancient un-muffled engine. The overloaded sidecar creaked and groaned in protest, every rut or stone prompting ominous cracks from the connecting brackets. He wished he could turn the headlight on but up on the exposed ridge he knew he'd be seen for miles, which was the last thing he wanted. At least if he *was* spotted his unorthodox choice of transport should confuse any observer - his Land Rover would have been perfect for this off-road mission but he couldn't risk the locally familiar vehicle being spotted in the vicinity - so he'd rummaged around at the back of the barn until he'd uncovered the almost forgotten and rusting motorbike combination. It was of an uncertain vintage, an obscure East European model acquired by his father at the height of the cold war and even in his father's day it had never been road-legal. But Bunny was sure that at least no one could associate him with it. It hadn't occurred to him that the motorbike combination itself might attract attention, grinding along under its enormous load of sand bags and gas cylinders with Bunny hunched over the handlebars in huge goggles and a Nazi storm trooper's helmet - another of his father's unexplained acquisitions.

Through the murk Bunny suddenly became aware of the skeletal mast immediately in his path. He braked violently causing the combination to slew through ninety degrees and the two heavy cylinders spilled out of the sidecar unbalancing the whole thing and sending Bunny flying off into the darkness. The stalled bike settled into the mud and hissed gently and so did Bunny. He lay stretched on his back dazed and winded just a few feet from the mast and tried to correct his double vision by focusing on the algae-glow of the digital read-out just visible through the gloom.

The whole idea had come to him whilst watching a television news report of a huge factory fire somewhere in the Midlands. The TV coverage seemed to show the fire being allowed to burn un-checked whilst firemen stood around drinking mugs of tea. But the commentator had explained that they couldn't yet get close enough to fight the fire because of the large number of gas cylinders on the site - apparently if over-heated they would go off like bombs. Bunny had already decided that it was time for some *direct action*. Whilst the rest of the village held their secretive meetings and re-shuffled their committees he would strike a blow that would make them all sit up and take notice. He took measurements, made sketches, filled pages with obscure acronyms and meaningless formulas and pored over maps. Then he carefully burned them all. The plan was actually simplicity itself: place a couple of big gas cylinders at the base of the mast, build a wall of sandbags around them to direct the blast upwards, and get them to the critical temperature with a strategically placed camping stove. The necessary component parts were easily available and their purchase would raise no suspicions. Even so, he decided to keep away from local suppliers, pay cash and be careful not to draw attention to himself.

'Look!' Bunny bellowed, 'All I'm asking for is a few bags of bloody sand. You're a DIY shop, how hard can it be?'

'Waiting for a delivery.'

'I don't care, have you got *any* here? Now!'

'What?'

'Sand! Bloody sand!'

Curious heads appeared around the end of aisles and stared. The other customers in Bunny's queue puffed and tutted and a security guard appeared from a back office, adjusted his cap and scowled at Bunny suspiciously.

The polo-shirted assistant at the till used one finger to tap at a computer keyboard. 'We've got two.'

'Two what?'

'Two bags.'

'Of sand?'

The assistant looked at him pityingly, '*Of course*, sand.'

'I need eight.'

The assistant shrugged.

Bunny had a thought. 'What about gravel?'

There was some more single-digit tapping. 'Pea shingle.'

'What's that?' Bunny's voice was rising again and the security guard fidgeted.

'Gravel.'

A few minutes later the till assistant, security guard and other customers all pretended not to watch while Bunny tried repeatedly to negotiate the automatic doors with his over-loaded trolley, ramming displays, cracking his shins and eventually running over his own foot.

Acquiring the gas cylinders had been less confrontational. Bunny had calculated that two should provide the necessary blast and had decided to buy them separately. The first one he'd spotted in a dubious back-street yard that appeared to operate as some sort of engineering and car repair business. The tank had felt suspiciously light but Bunny was assured that it was newly filled and he hadn't felt inclined to argue with the large tattooed proprietor - or his chained dog. The second cylinder had come from a camping shop on the by-pass where he'd also bought the small cooker, but had to spend ten bad-tempered minutes loudly assuring the earnest young assistant that he fully understood he couldn't use the huge 15kg gas tank with the tiny device.

The sidecar seemed to groan with relief as Bunny dragged out the sacks of sand and gravel and hauled them to the base of the mast. He paused to take a breather and peered up at the vertical struts disappearing into the dark, surprised not to see any sort of light on top to warn off unwary aircraft. (There should have been one but Sir George had balked at the cost and, declaring it 'a load of bollocks' had ignored Wormold's protestations.) Having arranged the wriggling bags satisfactorily Bunny turned his attention to the gas cylinders. One was definitely heavier than the other and he cursed and muttered as he fumbled it through the mud and the dark.

There was no moon, he'd checked the calendar to make sure of that, and with Linda away the timing was perfect. Bunny had been surprised by his wife's quiet announcement that she was going to Italy with a friend from the village for two weeks holiday - and during their busiest period - but it had fitted in well with his plans and spared him any awkward questions.

Bunny sneezed loudly as a jet of gas shot up his left nostril and a third match fluttered and died. Bloody wind. He slashed away at the matchbox several more times before at last there was a roar and an intense blue cone of flame leapt from the little burner. Bunny grunted in satisfaction and nervously screwed it into the mud beneath one of the cylinders. Straightening stiffly he backed hurriedly away, stumbled straight into the sidecar, cursed, slipped and sat down abruptly in the mud. Bloody Hell! Bloody bike! Christ, he'd left it stalled as well and it was a sod to start at the best of times. Bunny glanced back towards the faint blue glow at the base of the mast and hurriedly threw a leg over where he thought the saddle was ... and found the petrol tank. He yelped as his testicles crunched against the filler cap, then gasped as the cold metal of the tank forced mud through the seat of his trousers. Still fumbling with the various levers and taps that had to be set in just the right positions to have any hope of starting the machine, he started kicking frantically at the starter lever prompting wet slapping noises from the engine and a gurgle from where the exhaust pipe used to be. Suddenly from behind him there was an enormous bang and a jet of orange flame. Bunny hurled himself off the bike, headfirst into the sidecar, and was still trying to clamber out when he realised that it was only the ancient engine that had erupted into life. Remounting he almost stalled again in his panic to put distance between himself and the ominous blue glow. The wheels eventually broke free of the mud and the combination careered away along where Bunny thought the track was. He didn't slow down until the bike suddenly tipped forward down a steep bank and brought itself to a slithering halt. A flash of the headlight revealed that he was in one of the curious bowl-shaped depressions that occurred on some parts of the hillside. Bunny reckoned he was at least a hundred metres away from the mast and as long as he kept his head down the depression ought to provide adequate cover. The question now was whether to wait and see the results of his sabotage, which was tempting, or whether it was best to get well clear. He peered over the lip of the depression. The blue glow was just discernible and he decided to wait, just for a while. Bunny clutched his filthy jacket around him and pulling the tin helmet firmly over his ears settled down into the sidecar and yawned.

He woke with a start, bewildered, cold and stiff. The cold reminded him where he was and he realised with disappointment that there was no way he could have slept through the expected explosion - his device had failed. Standing up in the wobbling sidecar he squinted blearily into the murk. Was there still a blue glow there? No - damn! Bunny clambered out of the hollow and trudged back across the muddy grass. After a moment he could make out the ghostly outline of the mast but it was some way off to his left, he'd been looking and walking in the wrong direction. Then it started to rain. Bloody weather! He put his head down, changed course and trudged on. He'd have to dismantle the whole thing now. Sod it! Looking up to check his bearings he found he'd almost reached the pile of sand bags, which from this distance appeared to be curiously illuminated, the clear plastic reflecting a warm orange glow. The aura was explained a moment later when he peered over the little rampart and found both gas tanks glowing rosily, spitting and hissing in the rain. Bunny gasped, half delighted, half terrified and tearing his fascinated eyes from the iridescent metal turned quickly and walked as fast as the mud would allow back the way he'd come. Instinctively he hunched his shoulders, forcing the coal scuttle helmet down over his eyes, and was still fumbling blindly with the strap when there was a faint pop from behind him. He broke into a shambling run.

Bunny woke up lying on his front, his face awkwardly forced to one side on the stiff white pillow. He blinked his one exposed eye in the bright daylight, wrinkled his nose at vaguely familiar smells and felt dizzy and sick. He thought he heard a door open and became aware of voices.

'What's that?' giggled a young female voice.

'An arse.'

'I know that, I'm a highly trained medical practitioner I'll have you know!' She giggled again, 'I've never seen one like that before, though.'

'Good isn't it?' said the other voice, with obvious professional pride.

'What's all that... stuff?'

Bunny thought he felt something touch his backside.

'Pea shingle, apparently.'

'What's that?'

'Gravel,' Bunny mumbled through the half of his mouth not buried in the pillow.

'Oh Mr Warren, you're awake. How are you feeling? Do you know where you are?' The voice expressed professional concern but there was a suppressed snigger from further back in the room.

'Uh uh'

'Was that a no?'

'Uh, yes,' Bunny groaned. He was sure he was dribbling.

'You're in Bartford General. You've had a bit of an accident.'

There was a snort from over by the door.

Bunny tried to cock a furious eye over his shoulder and groaned again.

'Don't try and turn over for the moment; you may find it a bit painful...' There was a long pause, '...you've rather hurt your bottom,' the nurse finished in a gasping rush.

Bunny could imagine the hand clasped to the mouth. He'd already started to draw his own conclusions as he struggled to piece together the events of what was presumably the night before but thought he'd ask anyway. 'What happened?' he eventually mumbled.

'Well, you've had a bit of an accident,' the voice repeated, now back under control, 'but if you want to know all about it and feel up to it, there are two policemen outside the door who'd like to speak to you. They've been waiting half the night,' she added.

Bunny's groan turned into a resigned sigh.

'We'll just cover you up then.'

Mattie was at the office very early the next morning. The odd bleary night-worker was still drifting zombie-like around the wood-chipped corridors counting down the last minutes of their shift, but blinds had been drawn and an occasional phone could be heard ringing as the newspaper started shaking off the night. Mattie knew that Rob Jordan would already be at his desk and she was ready for him. Her draft was already polished and she'd comfortably meet her deadline. But whilst interviewing Simon Cassady it had become obvious to her that there was more to this story than just a disrupted village fete - all she had to do now was convince her editor.

'How did it go?'

'Well. Very well actually.'

Rob Jordan quickly removed his glasses, a sure sign that his attention had been caught, and looked closely at her. 'Go on.'

'I've got a piece on the fete incident.' She held up a sheaf of papers.

'Riot.'

'OK, one woman's incident is another man's riot, but I think it's better than that. It's the whole wind farm thing, there's definitely something going on here, Rob. Simon...' Jordan noted the familiarity but shrewdly didn't interrupt. '...he thinks the council and this Sir George Hoggit have already done some sort of a deal. And this Co'burn, the council leader ... he's hoping to run for parliament incidentally ... he's right in the middle of it all. Clearly no one in the village had a clue about the scheme, not even Lady Hoggit Simon reckons. Apparently she looked stunned when it came out in Co'burn's speech. There's something going on here, Rob, I'm sure of it. By the way, I've asked around, have you any idea how much money these things can be worth to the landowner?'

'I've got a shrewd idea.'

'We're talking bloody millions! And I don't understand it fully yet, but from what I gather it doesn't even matter whether they work or not, it's all about subsidies apparently. Even if there's no electricity old Sir Whatsisname still gets his millions - bloody madness!' She shook her head in disbelief. 'No wonder there are strings being pulled.'

'Are there, can we be sure of that? More to the point, can we print it, preferably without getting our arses sued off?'

'I think we can, Rob. I'd like to go and talk to a few of the people involved, see what's there, see if anything slips out. Simon and I are sure...'

'So you said,' Jordan interrupted quickly, 'and as it happens I agree.'

'You do?' Mattie sat down for the first time.

'Yep. I think you're right. While you've been busy snuggling up to your *Countryman,* things have been occurring.' He ignored Mattie's indignant snort. 'Firstly, news has reached your editor's shell-like ear that there's to be an *extraordinary* parish council meeting, which apparently is being set up as a bit of a shop window for the wind farm people. No doubt it'll be a complete PR whitewash... but be there.' Mattie scowled, she'd spent too many cub-reporter evenings in draughty village halls with pencil sharpened but mind blunted by endless sub-committee reports. 'And, and...' Jordan continued, '...you're gonna like this, there's been a sodding great explosion! Guess where?' Jordan was enjoying himself and didn't give Mattie a chance to reply. 'Spout Hill is where. Some bright spark tried to blow up your friend Cassady's mast thing last night. Big, big bang! Lots of damage, especially to the lunatic involved ... much speculation, outrage and all the usual good juicy stuff. And most of all, Mattie, a fucking great story!'

'Wow.'

'Wow indeed. Now here's the plan. Polish up your bit on the fete riot - by eleven, yeah...?'

'Done.'

'OK, great, we'll get that in tonight and use it as a holding story on the wind farm. I'll knock out a "Stop Press" bit on the big bang and you get to work on pulling all these stories together. I'm thinking of a special "Insight" piece for Saturday, OK? Like you said, get out and talk to some of the parties. Hoggit's reaction to the explosion should be good. Try and get to what's left of the bomber, neighbours, the police, and especially anyone from the council. Try the planning people; you might trip someone up there, more chance than with the politicians, especially this eel Co'burn.'

'We've got a few other ideas too.'

'Mattie, I can't help noticing this constant 'we' thing. Anything I should know here?'

Mattie ignored the mock paternalism. 'Look, I think you're right about Simon, he almost certainly can't write, but he does seem to have picked up on something here. He's got his ear to the ground around the place, seems to know people too, people involved. As it turns out I think he probably *is* a source. I thought he could tag along with me, make a few introductions, fill in a few local gaps maybe. It won't cost the paper anything,' she added hastily.

'No, you're right it won't. It'll be a bit intimidating though won't it, the two of you crashing around like bloody Starsky and Hutch or something?'

'We will not be "crashing around,"' Mattie sniffed, 'and anyway I've thought of that. He'll be my photographer.'

'Will he indeed? Thought of everything haven't you?'

'It'll explain his presence, and anyway I think it might actually loosen up a few people, get them to open up. The politicians always want a photo and that DJ's got an ego like, like... Madonna.'

'Madonna?'

Mattie shook her head and tutted impatiently. 'It's all I could think of, but you know what I mean. A photographer hanging around could actually help us to get more out of some of these people.'

Jordan looked thoughtful. 'OK, I buy it.'

'Great.' Mattie jumped to her feet and was half way to the door.

'Whoa, one more thing, *you* can explain to Jeremy why he's not your photographer of choice on this one, I can't stand another one of his artistic hissy fits.'

'OK, OK.'

'Hang on a minute... weren't Jeremy and Rebecca, er... Bernard... special friends?' He removed his glasses. 'Christ! You don't think...?'

Mattie shrugged, 'Who knows, why don't you ask him... or her,' she grinned.

CHAPTER EIGHT

Mattie and Simon had spent twenty fidgeting minutes sitting in the goldfish bowl reception area drinking cardboard coffee from Styrofoam beakers and watching the comings and goings of a provincial radio station. The woman who now approached them had the disapproving air of an old-fashioned hospital matron and was the oldest person they'd seen since entering the building.

'Miss James?' She ignored Simon who sat at the other end of the couch from Mattie fiddling with an ancient Pentax camera. 'Mickey is free now and happy to see you. He's just come off air and you'll find him a bit frazzled. Up since four, poor lamb.' She rolled her eyes at Mattie in a shared gesture of female disdain. 'He always likes to see the press though - even if they don't always like to see him. She finally acknowledged Simon. 'Don't even think about using that thing unless he says so,' she snapped, nodding at the camera.

They were shown into a glass kiosk cluttered with electronic gadgetry and lined with signed and framed photographs of long forgotten presenters.

'Whoa, way to go! Mickey Moyst! What can I do to help my friends from the *Bungle*?' Simon looked blank but Mattie managed to force a hearty chuckle at the hackneyed slur. The diminutive DJ was almost swamped by the huge chair, which he spun away from the littered desk. He was made to look even tinier by the bulbous headphones artfully arranged around his neck and the outsized sunglasses. Introductions were made and Mattie half-heartedly made the promised sales pitch for *The Bugle's* advertising people before bringing up the subject of the fete. She quickly made it clear that as far as the paper were concerned Mickey Moyst had been the star turn at the fete, also a hero-rescuer during the disaster and subsequently an injured victim. Mickey happily adopted these fictions and warmed to his stories, unashamedly building up his multiple roles whilst

Mattie fed him his lines, hung onto his every word and made a great show of transcribing them into her notebook. She laughed uproariously at his jokes and simpered at his inanities.

Simon was taken aback by her professional seduction but amused by the adopted estuary twang, her use of street colloquialisms and the occasional obscenity. She was laddish, matey and leading Mickey Moyst and his ego to commit ever more indiscretions. Mickey got onto the speeches and clearly wasn't happy at nearly being upstaged at the last minute by '...a fuckin' politician," who, according to "Lady A." was there at the insistence of "'is fuckin' lordship'". Mickey clearly didn't know any more about the Sir George/Councillor Cockburn relationship so Mattie decided to have some fun:

'Of course you ended up in hospital yourself didn't you, Mickey?'

'Yeah, get a load of this.' He whipped off the huge sunglasses to reveal both eyes puffed and mottled in shades of purple and yellow. 'Don't touch that!' he snapped at Simon, who had moved the camera in his lap. 'You can have one later... with the shades on.'

'And I gather you got some sort of bloody food poisoning too mate?' Mattie went on quickly, frowning at Simon and the camera.

'Yeah well...' Mickey put the sunglasses back on and smirked, '...lets just say I ate something that I shouldn't... and I'm not talking about the hot dogs,' he sniggered. 'Although come to think of it...'

'Yeah, right. Dodgy gear eh?' Mattie grimaced knowingly.

'Right!'

'Yeah. Some bad stuff on the streets right now, dunno who to trust.'

Simon thought perhaps she was overdoing it but Mickey Moyst didn't pause.

'I mean the little sod was even in uniform.'

'Right, er... those bloody St John Ambulance!' Mattie tutted.

'Nah, the fucking Scouts!'

'Yeah, yeah of course, them too. Never been sure about their stuff either.'

Mickey slumped back in the enormous chair. 'Last time I buy any 'E' off them. Little bastards! And the leader's no better either from what I hear. St John Ambulance you say? Anyone in particular I...'

'The Scout leader,' Mattie interrupted quickly, 'what's he been up to this time? Same old tricks I suppose?'

Mickey Moyst shook his head and suddenly looked bored. 'No, I think it's just the dope these days.' He reached out a hand, flicked a switch and something started to hum. 'I don't think he's been at the other stuff since he was defrocked ... well, he hasn't been caught anyhow.'

'Defrocked?'

'Yeah.'

'What did he do?'

'Oh, the usual.'

Mattie considered a moment. 'Boys... girls?'

'Both, the whole flock ... literally sometimes, they say. Baaa!'

'Charming!'

'Well he obviously thought so,' Simon muttered, earning another frown.

The humming machine suddenly shot out a blast of pumping, rasping noise. Mickey flipped his enormous leatherette ears into place and the interview was over.

'Where next? We didn't exactly learn much from that big-headed little pratt.' Simon turned up his collar against the rain as he and Mattie hurried along the greasy pavement.

'Oh I don't know, we know the Scoutmaster's a defrocked vicar, a sexual deviant and a drug dealer.'

'Well that's really made my day. Nothing much about Hoggit and Co'burn and the wind farm though, that's what I meant.'

'I'm not so sure. Our Mickey confirmed what you thought; no one had a clue what was coming at the fete apart from Sir George and Co'burn, which was interesting. And also Co'burn was only brought in to do his party piece at the last minute, and it would seem at the personal insistence of Sir George - that gives us a connection.'

'Hmm, I suppose so,' Simon said.

'Apart from that though, as little Mickey was clearly out of his tree most the afternoon I presume everything else he said back there was a figment of his imagination?'

'A pack of lies? Yes.'

'Oh well, let's see if we get any more truth out of Councillor Co'burn.'

'Dream on.'

Mattie ignored him. 'We've got an appointment at ten, fifteen minutes of the great man's time if we're lucky my office said. Come on, we can just make it, no point moving the car. Bloody rain! What happened to the summer?'

Yet again, Simon and Mattie found themselves in limbo as they were made to wait the prescribed fifteen power minutes after the appointed time. At ten fifteen exactly a women strangely similar to the fierce matron at Radio Bartford approached them across the bland carpet tiles of the Bartford council offices. Mattie and Simon exchanged a glance and trotted obediently after her down a stark corridor. Simon cleared his throat. 'You don't have a sister working in local radio do you?' he asked, prompting a snort from Mattie. The answer was a curt 'No.'

The secretary stopped at a pair of huge oak doors, incongruous in their otherwise modernistic surroundings. She knocked, paused and threw one half open. 'Councillor Co'burn will see you now,' she said.

Having imposed a Stalinist concrete edifice on the rest of the appalled population of Bartford, Claude Cockburn had chosen for his own enormous office the décor and trappings of a Victorian squire's study: deep rugs, a certain amount of wood panelling, sooty oil portraits of no one in particular and a reproduction Adam fireplace. The 'squire' himself sat at a huge dark-wood desk in the middle of the room, backlit by the incongruously modern picture window. He ignored them for several more minutes before eventually putting down his pen and looking up from the papers he'd been pretending to annotate.

'Good morning, you're from the, er...' He consulted an appointments pad, '...er, *The Guardian* yes?' he said, knowing full well they weren't.

'No, *The Bugle*,' Mattie said firmly.

'Ah, *The Bugle*, the local... sheet.'

'Yes, that's right. My... our office fixed the appointment, an interview.'
Cockburn made a show of consulting his diary again, 'I can spare you
ten minutes. You're late.'

Simon clenched his jaw and Mattie swallowed. 'It's good of you to
spare the time to see us,' she managed.

Cockburn nodded, glanced at Simon's camera and tentatively stroked
his face. The effects of the fete were not as spectacular as those on Mickey
Moyst but there were undoubted signs of rough treatment on the carefully
shaved face, particularly around the eyes.

'So what is it I can help you with?' He waved expansively at a leather
Chesterfield in front of the huge desk where once seated they would be at
least a foot below him.

Mattie produced a pad and a pen and snapped off a quick shot: 'How
well do you know Sir George Hoggit?'

Cockburn's expression didn't change but his body stiffened almost
imperceptibly and the opulent office seemed to suddenly darken and take
on an air of menace.

'In what context?' Cockburn's eyes never left Mattie's.

'We're interested in Sir George Hoggit's plans for a wind farm on his
land. It's caused quite a stir locally and...'

'Yes indeed. The Hoggit's Green-energy plans.' Cockburn leant
forward with exaggerated sincerity. 'And of course you and your readers
would like to know where the council stand on this issue, and quite rightly
so.' Mattie opened her mouth to speak but got no further - Cockburn
had long since mastered the steamroller interview technique as a way of
avoiding awkward questions. He powered on: 'Following clarification
by our senior planning officers of central government policies on Green
energy generation - you'll forgive me if I can't remember the exact policy
reference off the top of my head - the council is keen, nay duty-bound,
to do its part locally in the fight against the very real threat of global

warming and the carbon pollution... er, emissions problem. We must all do our bit and we here at the council are therefore taking a positive view of any proposal that may help us to meet these obligations.' Without pausing long enough for the fidgeting Mattie to interrupt he leant back in a pose of relaxed confidence. 'As I say, we must all do our bit and Lord and Lady Hoggit are leading the way. Allowing their land to be used for a significant Green energy development sets a fine example and where they and the Spout Hill wind farm lead, others will follow.'

It was his speech from the afternoon of the fete, delivered almost verbatim, even down to the stumble over carbon pollution and emissions and the accidental elevation of Sir George Hoggit to the Lords. Simon half expected him to finish with, '...and I now declare this fete open!'

Mattie hadn't bothered to hide her frustration during the evasive monologue. 'Will you, the council that is, benefit financially if this wind farm goes ahead?' she asked.

Cockburn looked at her coldly. 'There will be many who benefit from this scheme. The community as a whole... mankind as a whole.'

'Mankind didn't seem too keen on the idea when you announced it at the Hoggit Hall fete. Could you tell us exactly what happened there? It sounds like some sort of riot. You were injured weren't you? Do you think it was your fault that it started? Why did you choose to make the wind farm public there? Did Lady Hoggit know about it? How much...'

Cockburn stood up and snapped up a hand as if stopping traffic. 'An important county event and charity fund-raiser was unfortunately disrupted by a... an element. As ever it was a small minority, some of whom had clearly had too much to drink, who spoiled it for everyone.' He cleared his throat. 'That and global warming.'

'Global warming?' It was Simon who'd spoken but Cockburn still addressed his answer to Mattie, or at least to her notebook:

'An extreme weather event, a shocking storm for this time of year. Most unusual.' He gesticulated towards the huge window, which was opaque with splashes and rivulets. 'Appalling weather, climate change you see - global warming.' He looked at his watch, 'Now if you'll excuse me.'

'What a load of crap!'

'Yep, but what did you expect, he's a politician? One in a hurry too I'd say - but with a limited repertoire,' Simon chuckled. 'That little speech in there, it was word for word what he said at the fete you know.'

Mattie was not amused. 'That man's dangerous,' she said, 'a really nasty piece of work.'

'Yeah, I've met the type. I bet he's a bastard to work for.'

'Well, lets go and find out shall we? May as well try and see someone in the planning department while we're in the building, see if anyone can be persuaded to spill a few beans.' She grinned wolfishly.

'God! How on earth do people ever get here?'

'Beats me,' Simon panted.

'What language was that guy at the information desk speaking?'

'Polish I think.'

'But he was Asian.'

'You must get Asian Poles - or maybe he thought we were Polish and was trying to be helpful.'

Mattie gave him a withering look, 'Yeah sure.' She studied the illuminated *Outreach And Public Engagement Servery* sign. 'What on earth...?'

The counter was unattended and there were no signs of life down the avenues of partitioning that separated the honeycomb of workstations.

'No one about,' Mattie muttered, drumming her fingers impatiently on the counter. 'Hellooo, anybody in? SHOP!'

'Simon started. 'Christ! That should go down well, nothing like waking up a civil servant mid-tea-break to guarantee their co-operation.'

'Be right with you,' a disconnected voice called hoarsely from somewhere within the beige maze.

Mattie smirked at Simon and a few moments later a shambling figure partially emerged from behind one of the partitions like a Hobbit from its hole. It was wearing a shapeless dandruff-flecked cardigan, an unlit cigarette dangled from under a ragged grey-yellow moustache and it seemed not to have noticed them. After a few seconds of rubbing vigorously against the screen and breaking wind loudly it slouched over to the counter.

'Can I help you?'

Simon recovered first. 'We'd like to speak to a planning officer.'

'Yes, can I help?'

Simon looked doubtful. 'Oh, right. Well, we'd like to talk to someone about the Spout Hill wind farm. Please,' he added.

The cigarette waggled, 'Ah, you really need to speak to Clive Hallibut, he's the one setting that up but he's not in this morning. Site meeting I think. Somewhere,' the Hobbit finished vaguely.

'"Setting up?" What do you mean, "setting up"?'

The Hobbit looked at Mattie with a sort of sly respect. He'd chosen his words carefully and they'd obviously hit their mark. 'Just a figure of speech, dear.'

Simon grinned, knowing Mattie would be bristling at the patronising brush off.

'Mr Hallibut's the case officer for Spout Hill,' continued the Hobbit, 'he's done all the policy interpretation...'

'"Interpretation?"'

The cigarette waggled again, 'Yes, you know, made it work, picked out the right pieces of policy and got them to fit the application. Sort of tailored it - "interpretation".'

'So the council want to make it work then, they support it?'

'Ah, you'd have to ask Mr Hallibut that, it's his case, but he always does his best for the applicants.' The Hobbit looked sly again. 'Perhaps more for some than others... he does have his *special* ones.' He'd produced a disposable lighter and was absent-mindedly flicking it ever nearer the tip of the drooping cigarette. 'Got to be done properly of course, the politicians insist on that. Must comply with policy see? It's all a matter of...'

'Interpretation, we know.' Mattie was openly scathing. 'We'd like to speak to this Mr Hallibut.'

The Hobbit's lips twisted into a smile of satisfied spite, 'You may find him at home of course,' he said quietly.

'Where?'

'Oh, I couldn't tell you that.' He accidentally singed the end of the cigarette. 'But personally, if I'd had a bit of luck, you know like a few *special* cases... well I'd be on the move. Always fancied a place on the Copthorn Park myself,' and with that he dived into a convenient lift.

'This would be a millionaire's row in London.'

'It's not far off round here,' Mattie sniffed.

Copthorn Park was a fairly typical example of one of the *executive* developments that had been slotted into previously undeveloped enclaves on the leafy edges of Bartford. Typically, having chosen one of the developer's two or three standard designs new residents had then set about stamping some sort of individuality on their chosen model. Those on modest budgets settled for a couple of extra flowering cherries or a row of fast-growing hedging - depending on how well they expected to get on with their neighbours - whilst those with unspent mortgage funds summoned one of the circling builders and commissioned ambitious extensions, conservatories and brick sets by the acre. Copthorn Park was about fifteen years old. Time enough for lumpen turf to have become velvety lawns, smudged pointing on cowboy extensions to have blurred and for several acrimonious leylandii disputes to be well under way. 'The Park', as the resident's association headed their newsletter, had matured and mellowed and was now smugly 'exclusive'.

A quick inspection of the electoral role had revealed two occupants of voting age called Hallibut (Clive and Maxine) registered at number eighteen, also known as The Beeches. All the houses on the development had been given names, much to the irritation of the Post Office. Some had sought originality but mostly they were the usual collection of the nostalgic, rurally wistful and whimsical. The Hallibuts had considered copying their neighbours and naming number eighteen by combining parts of their names, but 'Maxcli' sounded like an obscure Roman emperor and 'Climax' was out of the question, so 'The Beeches' it was.

Simon and Mattie pulled up outside 'Rupau' and between bleary swishes of the windscreen wipers watched the activity at number eighteen. There were several small vans at the kerbside and a large white sign-written van, back doors gaping, on the cement-smeared brick sets that used to be the Hallibut's executive drive.

'Got the builders in.'

'Hmm. Money to spend.'

'Nothing wrong with that is there?' Simon was starting to find Mattie's professional cynicism a bit wearing.

'Well you said it: "Millionaires Row". Not the sort of place you'd usually expect to find a middle-ranking town hall employee, and with extensive building work going on. And a Mercedes I think, and a...' she craned her neck, '...yes, an Audi. Both this year's plate too. *And*, if I'm not mistaken, a swimming pool out back as well.'

'Eh, how do you know that?'

'Well look! In the garage behind the van, the two of them, top of the range, silver...'

'No, not the cars, the pool.'

'Look down the side, over the gate, you can see the top of a slide. You can bet your budgie smugglers there's a lovely sparkly blue pool at the bottom of that - or at least there would be if it would stop bloody raining. There's money here, and more being spent.'

'OK, I take your point. So what next?'

'Lets go see who's spending it. Come on.'

The front door was slightly ajar and a faintly audible one-sided conversation suggested that someone inside was on the telephone. Mattie rang the bell and after a minute the door was yanked open.

'What is it now? Oh sorry, I thought you were the bloody builders.' She was a tall figure in designer jeans and a figure-hugging rugby shirt that hadn't been designed for any pitch. Her feet were bare and the long dark hair had been carefully tousled. The apologetic smile swiftly disappeared and she eyed them suspiciously, 'Look, if it's about Jesus, then yes, I think he was a great guy, sorry about the church thing and I'm busy so...'

'Mrs Hallibut?' Mattie cut across the flow and put a confident hand on the door.

'Ye-ees,' the tone was more wary, 'you're not the police are you?'

'Why, were you expecting them?'

'No, but... now look, who are you, and what do you want?' The builder-bashing confidence was back now.

'We're from *The Bugle*.'

'The what?'

'*The Bugle,* the local paper,' Mattie said. Simon smiled and flourished the ancient Pentax, like diplomatic credentials. 'We were hoping to speak to your husband. We're doing a piece on the role of civil servants in our everyday lives and the positive contribution they make to their community,' Mattie lied smoothly.

'Well he's not here.' Maxine Hallibut was not impressed. 'Why don't you speak to him at the office?'

'He's not there.'

'Oh.' She obviously wasn't particularly surprised.

Mattie thought she'd stir things up: 'Do you know Sir George Hoggit?'

At last, Maxine Hallibut looked carefully at Mattie then glanced at Simon's camera. 'You sure you're not police?'

'Why would we be?'

'Look, exactly what is it you want? That bloody business-park stuff is over and done with.'

Simon stepped forward. His mouth already forming a question when there was a huge crash from inside the house.

'Oh Christ! Bloody builders!' Maxine Hallibut turned back into the hallway and Simon heard her mutter something about a 'fucking snooker table'. She returned, clearly distracted. 'Look...'

'Like I said,' Mattie continued cheerfully, 'we're just trying to get an insight into the lives and workings of council officers.'

Maxine Hallibut looked sceptical,' Sounds pretty bloody boring to me.'

'Well you married him.'

'Right, that's it! Now piss off or I'll call the police!'

Screaming could be heard from behind the slammed door and Simon felt quite sorry for the hapless builders. Mattie looked pleased with herself. 'Silly bitch,' she muttered as they trotted back to the car.

'Well that went well,' Simon said dryly. 'Is that what they call "doorstepping"? You turn up at someone's place pretending to be someone you're not, doing something you're not and then insult them until they throw you out or slam the door in your face? That's a real insight into investigative journalism!'

Mattie looked at him quizzically. 'Look, if you'd rather not be here...'

'No, no, it's fine. It's just ... well it's pretty unsubtle isn't it?'

'Yeah, usually,' she agreed cheerfully, 'but it works. Actually, that *did* go pretty well.' She bent forward, partly disappearing under the dashboard and started to wring her hair out in the footwell.

Simon waited until he could see her face again. 'So come on then, how did that go well? What did your nasty tabloid mind pick up that I missed?'

'We-ell, we have a business park to look into...'

'Yeah, I picked up on that.'

'It was obviously something Hallibut was involved in and sounds like the police might have been involved. Someone back in the office is bound to know something, I just hope it's not Rebecca... or Bernard,' she muttered to herself.

'Eh?'

'Nothing, I'll tell you later. Anyway, the other thing is... I know how much that building work is costing, and probably how much they spent on the other stuff, the pool and things. And quite probably... where the money's coming from.'

Simon looked at her sceptically. 'How could you know all that - already?'

'Well I *almost* do ... one phone call. To my dad.'

'Your *dad*?'

'Yep. Did you notice the builder's van on the drive? "Ben Dover", well he's best mates with my dad. I've known him since I was a kid - Uncle Benny - he'd do anything for me. He's helped me out before, and like I say, one phone call. Impressed?'

Simon smiled. 'So you got lucky.'

'Yep.' Mattie grinned back at him. 'Let's go and have some fun.'

'Where next?'

'Plompley Caravan and Camping Park. Proprietor, one Godfrey Warren, he's our man.'

'Bunny?'

'You know him?'

'Well not exactly, we've met though. What do we want him for?'

'He was in court this morning, apparently with half a sack of gravel up his arse. Your Bunny is the Spout Hill bomber!'

'Bloody Hell!'

Bunny was sitting in the garden shed that served as the caravan site's reception office. He'd perched himself gingerly on a pile of cushions stacked on a fraying typist's chair and was gazing moodily down the rain-swept field. Several other caravans had left early, one without paying. Bunny sighed heavily. Linda would be home within a few hours, which would normally have cheered him up but he knew on this occasion he was going to have a bit of explaining to do. And the court hearing had not gone well.

In fairness to Bunny he'd been unlucky. Justice of the Peace Sir Edmund Croak rarely sat on the bench these days... for good reason. His encroaching deafness and unapologetic bigotry meant a fair hearing, on whatever charge, was a rare thing in his court. An apparent terrorist, even if experiencing extreme discomfort in his nether regions, was never likely to elicit much sympathy from the deaf old fascist. Furthermore, and unfortunately for Bunny, Sir Edmund was in a particularly foul mood following the latest in a series of port-fuelled rows at his club the night before. The bone of contention, as usual, being Croak's ancestry, which he stubbornly claimed could be traced back without interruption to the court of Queen Elizabeth I. The claim was dubious to say the least, particularly following a well documented disruption to the lineage in the mid 18th century when an Italian footman had managed to introduce himself into the Croak household and thence into Lady Constance Croak's entourage and eventually into Lady Constance herself... repeatedly... and with a remarkably high degree of reproductive success. But this inconvenient bit of genealogy hadn't stopped Sir Edmund from persisting in his claims to ancestral purity, attracting widespread scepticism and derision from other club members, particularly those with bloodlines untainted by Neapolitan domestic servants.

'You may sit down,' Sir Edmund snarled.

'Er, I'd rather not,' Bunny said. 'Sir,' he added.

'Sit down!'

Bunny squirmed. 'It's rather difficult, sir.'

Sir Edmund looked at him with distaste, moustachioed lip curling. 'Why, what's wrong with your ar... backside, then? Here, you're not one of those...' He was interrupted by a clerk hurriedly leaning forward to mutter in his ear. 'Eh? He's got what... pea shingle... what the Devil's that?'

'Gravel,' Bunny said helpfully.

'Be quiet!'

From then on it had all been down hill. The police statement had made a big thing of the storm trooper's helmet and its Nazi associations, which if anything Sir Edmund might have accepted in mitigation, but he clearly had no idea what a wind turbine was, let alone an anemometer, and with the mention of caravans had immediately concluded that the defendant was a traveller. A homosexual gypsy terrorist, no matter how right wing, was never going to get much sympathy from Sir Edmund Croak. Bunny's only bit of luck had been Sir Edmund mishearing his clerk and accidentally granting bail.

Balanced on his foam-rubber stack Bunny was still brooding on his time in court when Simon and Mattie squeezed into his 'office' later that morning. Despite recognising Simon, Bunny was not receptive. He said

126

he'd been 'bound over', which he didn't quite understand, he was worried about how Linda was going to react and he was 'pissed off' that the police had been more amused by his shredded arse than concerned about his defiant act of civil disobedience. 'Fucking pea-shingle!' he said bitterly.

'What's that?' Mattie asked.

Bunny wriggled uncomfortably on his cushions. 'Don't you bloody start,' he muttered and changed the subject to the caravan site. He bemoaned the weather, the lack of bookings, the scars left on his turf by disposable barbecues, dog mess, footballing children and people sneaking away without paying. He was seriously thinking of selling up, he said. He'd be talking to Linda, his wife, when she got back from holiday but he was worried that the wind farm would make the business un-saleable. Simon and Mattie sympathised but Mattie was getting restless, she'd hoped for more gory details about the 'attack' but Bunny wouldn't be drawn.

'Time we were off I think, thanks for your time Mr Warren. Good luck,' she added, getting to her feet and opening the flimsy door.

'I should never have given him those photos.'

Mattie stopped, forced the door shut against the wind and waited.

'I reckon he used them somehow,' Bunny said. 'Mr McCruddy would never have let him use his land otherwise and Hoggit can't build those bloody things without it, without that track. They hate each other those two, but all of a sudden Hoggit gets McCruddy's road and McCruddy disappears. Spain they reckon down the pub.'

Mattie glared a warning at Simon not to interrupt.

'Said he was going to play a joke,' Bunny went on, 'dirty photos, just a joke. Well the bloody joke's on me now. Fifty lousy quid! Bastard!'

Bit by bit, expletive by expletive, Mattie teased the story out of the miserable Bunny. He explained the geography of the area and the significance of the green road, reminding Simon of their first encounter. Then he gave them a brief history of the bitter Hoggit/McCruddy feud, described bumping into Sir George at the fete, and admitted he'd been "a bit out of it." - he blamed the Scouts. Simon and Mattie exchanged glances. Bunny then explained the deal with Sir George, casually brushing over the exact reasons for having taken the photos in the first place, but left Simon and Mattie in no doubt about the contents of the memory stick and Donald McCruddy's starring role. Curiously the identity of the other party was not revealed and for some reason neither of them thought to ask.

Bunny had suddenly had enough. He suspected he'd said too much and Linda could be home any minute. He stood up abruptly and without thinking scratched his backside prompting a yelp of pain.

Mattie took the hint. 'We'll get out of your way, thanks for everything.' She opened the door again, wincing at the driving rain.

Simon glanced back over his shoulder as he followed her out into the rain. 'Not got any other operations lined up Bunny? No work for the Silent Killer?'

Bunny shook his head. 'Longbow, that's what it needs. More power, longer range.' He waved two forked fingers at them in the familiar sign used by motorists the world over. 'Agincourt, see?'

'What a can of worms.' Simon smeared the condensation off the side window. 'It all makes sense though doesn't it, seems to fit together?'

Mattie looked thoughtful for a moment. 'Who, or what, in God's name, is "the Silent Killer"?'

'A crossbow.'

'God, that's worrying!'

As they made the short drive to Hoggit Hall the rain was unrelenting, driving almost horizontally through the occasional gaps in the roadside hedges with puddles rapidly becoming ponds and shredded foliage littering the lane. They drove in thoughtful silence, each trying to work out the relevance of the jigsaw pieces of information they'd collected and how, if at all, they fitted together. Mattie had had a cheerful and jokey telephone conversation with her father.

'No problem,' she said, fiddling with the buttons on the tiny phone, 'Dad 'll get Ben on his mobile and then get straight back to me.' She sat back happily.

'You get on well?'

'What with Dad? Yeah, sure.' She looked at him curiously, surprised by the question.

As they passed through the grand gates and started to wind up the long drive Simon couldn't help glancing through the rhododendrons towards the area of woods where he thought the secluded hollow of his previous visit lay. Mattie peered impatiently ahead until the grand facade of the house appeared through the trees.

'Wow, quite a pad, I've never been here before.'

Even through the sheets of slanting rain and despite a backdrop of tumbling dark grey clouds the honey stone of Hoggit Hall emanated a mellow and timeless grandeur.

Simon grunted an acknowledgement and looked apprehensively up the sweeping flight of steps to the huge black-painted front door. Although his only experience of Sir George and Lady Arabella had been from a distance at the fete he had a shrewd idea what sort of reception they were likely to get. 'After you,' he said gallantly.

The door was answered by a stooped middle-aged woman in a stained housecoat who appeared to be some sort of domestic or cleaner. She let them in and then left them to wander at will while she went off in search of 'someone'.

In due course the unmistakeable figure of Sir George Hoggit bristled into sight at the far end of the chequered hall and lumbered aggressively towards them like a bad-tempered bear roused from hibernation.

'Who are you?' he demanded.

Mattie introduced them and since Sir George clearly had no intention of returning the courtesy she hurried on with her story. She explained that *The Bugle* was preparing a series of articles on a Green theme and were keen to report on the wind farm proposal - any casual listener would definitely have got the impression that the piece was to be positive and supportive. Again Simon was impressed and slightly disconcerted by Mattie's casual disregard for the truth and her disingenuous wordplay. But Sir George remained wary, and most of Mattie's innocuous questions received a monosyllabic answer delivered with barely concealed impatience. Simon thought he looked unwell.

Mattie softened her approach, tried a bit of flattery and fed Sir George a few lines. He responded immediately:

'Aah yes, sense of community y' know? Social and economical responsibility ... must do our bit ... taking the lead locally in the very real fight against the threat of... er, you know, global warming and carbon whatsits... ejections, and so forth. Very real y' know?'

Mattie let him go on for a few minutes, scribbling attentively as he gabbled and misquoted the speech they'd already heard that morning in Claude Cockburn's office, until with an apologetic smile she lifted her pencil in polite interruption.

'Yes, m'dear?'

'Do you have any business links with Councillor Co'burn or any of the Bartfordshire planning officers?'

Sir George blinked rapidly several times. His mottled cheeks turned predominantly purple, his breathing rasped and the piggy pink eyes moistened. 'That's all I've got to say,' he snarled, 'if you want any more speak to the RefWatt people.' He turned away.

'Do you own a business park, Sir George?'

The bulging tweed back froze.

'This... interview... is... at an... END!' The words were spat out one at a time towards the far end of the hall, followed by the lumbering figure of Sir George who disappeared without another word. Less than three minutes later he was slumped behind his desk, the door to the study firmly locked, and a brimming glass of whiskey clutched in both hands. Sweat ran from his indistinct hairline.

'Did you see that reaction?' Mattie jumped gleefully down the last three stone steps and spun round to Simon who was taking them one at a time. 'I knew there was something in it! That Hallibut woman gave it away. There really is something going on here, Simon. We're onto something.'

'I think there are a few more questions we need to ask.' For some reason Simon wanted to deflate her; he didn't know why but her exuberance annoyed him and he was tired of playing the role of hapless assistant, the bumbling Watson to her brilliant Holmes... and he wanted some lunch.

'Yes, yes of course,' Mattie dismissed his scepticism.

'Let's get some lunch, I could do with a beer.'

'Let's just have a quick look round, come on, while we're here.' She brushed the rain off her nose and eyebrows and without waiting for an answer set off round the corner of the house. Simon glanced at the steamed-up car and sulkily followed her.

The stable yard was surprisingly busy. Despite the rain and swirling wind there was an industrious milling of shiny dripping figures plying shovels, brooms and buckets. By the time Simon caught up with Mattie she'd installed herself under a convenient overhanging roof and was engaged in an animated conversation with a plump blonde girl. Simon held back and watched as the young women collapsed in girlish giggles; Mattie was back to work, no doubt lying through her teeth he thought, but picking up the staff gossip and scandal, most of which presumably involved the occupants of the grand house. At last the plump girl replaced the hood of her anorak, picked up a bucket and with a sisterly pat from Mattie disappeared inside the nearest loose box.

'Lots of girly giggles,' Simon said sourly.

'Yes,' Mattie laughed, 'the cat's been away so the mice have been playing - pretty hard too by all accounts. Lots of scrumpy in the hayloft and it sounds like those bloody Boy Scouts have been around too, and not just to peddle a bit of dope by the sound of it.' She laughed again. 'Anyway, apart from their own fun and games all the yard gossip and giggles are about her ladyship, Lady Arabella. Apparently she's been away on holiday in Italy with a friend, a *special* friend, and she doesn't care who knows it either. She's moved out of the big house into a flat over there.' Mattie nodded across the yard, 'and they reckon she's barely spoken to Sir George since the fete.'

'Yeah that figures,' Simon said, involved again despite himself.

'She and the friend are due back today, that's why all this lot are rushing around in the rain like blue-arsed flies. They've got a bit of catching up to do and...' Mattie broke off and waved cheerily as the blonde girl reappeared from the stables, her bucket brimming and steaming. 'Right, come on that'll do.'

'Pub?'

'Yeah, sure, we can go over what we've got.'

'Not until I've had a beer.'

Simon had swung the little car round the gravelled circle in front of the grand house and was heading back up the main drive towards the gated entrance. Mattie had just answered her phone, the caller clearly her father, and Simon was wiping condensation from the windscreen with his sleeve when suddenly the bulk of a large dark car, headlights blazing, loomed up like a ship in the fog. Simon stamped on the brakes and felt the car skid on the loose surface, the back end swinging neatly into the path of the oncoming behemoth. He took his foot of the locked brakes, frantically spun the steering wheel and stamped again sending the rear of the car obligingly back the way it had come, just in time to allow the speeding Range Rover to squeeze past them. In that freeze frame moment Simon just had time to glimpse two faces peering down on him, one a snarling blonde rictus, the other dark-framed and hollow-mouthed with fright.

'Christ! What happened?' Mattie's voice was angry with shock and Simon could hear an anxious warble coming from the mobile phone clutched in her lap. He was prickly with relief.

'Near miss.'

'Bloody right! Fucking maniac!' There was an extra-distressed warble from the phone. 'Yeah, sorry Dad. No, no we're fine.'

Mattie had hesitated over her choice of drink before finally taking the alcoholic option and ordering a white wine but Simon had had no such reservations and was in no mood for affected rural niceties - he ordered himself a lager and ignored Sid's sneer. Finding the pub unusually busy and his usual alcove occupied by a couple of bored visitors silently nursing glasses of flat coke Simon and Mattie settled in a window seat near the unlit log-burner.

'Quite a morning.' said Mattie

'Yeah.'

Mattie took a sip from her glass. 'Where are you?' she asked after a moment.

Simon turned from the rain-streaked window and stroked the beads of condensation down the sides of his fluted glass.

'Are you ok? That was a near thing, bit of a shock, I'm still shaking...'

'Yeah, yeah no problem,' Simon flicked his hand dismissively. 'D'you know, I'm pretty sure I know who was in that car.'

'Well Mrs... I mean *Lady* Hoggit I presume.'

'And her friend.'

'Yes, and her friend. It looked like another woman though, what little I could make out.'

'It was,' Simon said. 'It was Mrs Warren ... Bunny's wife.'

'Her *special* friend.' Mattie nodded to herself. 'That explains it!'

'Explains what?'

'Oh it was something I was picking up in the stable yard, vibes if you like, a few things that girl Becky was saying, or not saying. It makes sense now.'

'So Lady Arabella Hoggit, darling of the county set, has a girl friend, she's a dy... a lesbian. Bloody hell, you couldn't make it up could you... the whole thing? It would make a great book.'

'It had crossed my mind,' Mattie said. 'Anyway, let's get down to business.' She spread her notebook on the sticky table. 'We need to get this lot into some sort of order, try and make sense of it. And Dad, or at least dear old Benny has come up trumps as well, I knew he would.'

Simon sat back, happy to sip at his lager while Mattie scribbled in her pad, summarising the morning's events and occasionally using the other end of the pencil to distractedly untangle her damp hair. Simon mainly just listened, his irritability from the morning neutralised by the effects of alcohol and one of Sid's fresher ham baguettes. At the end of half an hour they were both satisfied that they'd unravelled the tangle of facts as far as they could; they'd identified the key players and established the links between them, however unlikely, picked over any indiscretions and eliminated the coincidences. Although far from verifiable they had pieced together a reasonably plausible conspiracy theory and, remarkably, it was surprisingly close to the truth.

'Pretty good eh?'

'Do you think so? Do you reckon your editor, what's his name, will go with it?'

'Rob, Rob Jordan, yes I'm sure. It's a *story*.' Mattie scowled at her notebook. 'I guess the lawyers will have to have a look at it. We'll have to see.'

She stood up and headed across the room, to the ladies Simon assumed. From the back her bra straps were visible through the white blouse and the regulation young businesswoman's black trousers were stretched damp and taut over her shapely bottom. Simon thought of George. He contemplated another beer but a glance towards the bar showed that Sid was struggling to cope with a sudden flurry and getting increasingly ill-humoured. Simon watched in amusement as the scowling landlord summarily dismissed an apologetic little man apparently sent to chase up his lunch. He was promptly replaced by his tweedy wife who was twice her husband's size, deeper voiced and an altogether more promising opponent for Sid. But after just a few moments of verbal sparring she too was dispatched with an impatient: 'Oh, get stuffed!' To her credit the woman recovered quickly and managed to bellow back: 'That's precisely what I'm trying to do, you wretched little man!' but Sid was already gone.

Sid's withdrawal from the field finished the fun and Simon turned back to the window. There was little to be seen through the streaks and rivulets and his attention drifted to the murmur of the Aarights.

'Gonna build up on Spout 'ill.'

'Aar. What?'

'Them big windy mills.'

'Oh, aar.' The contents of glasses were examined. 'Aar, they don't wanna go an' do that.'

'Right.'

There was a synchronised sip and once the glasses were safely back on the table both old men started cackling with demonic delight.

Simon watched and listened almost fondly, like a besotted parent listening in to the earnest conversation of a couple of toddlers.

'I've got you another beer.'

Simon started. 'Oh, thanks,' he glanced at the abandoned bar, 'how did you manage that?'

'I found Sid skulking out the back and gave him one of my smiles.' Mattie leered grotesquely and laughed, 'He's quite sweet really.'

Simon snorted.

'So anyway, you never told me what your dad had to say.'

'Ah ha, the clincher. I was saving the best 'til last.' She glanced at the rustics and Simon felt her warm breath on his face as she lent towards him. 'Ben *has* done most of that work for the Hallibuts, and I was right about a pool too. Mostly it's been cash...'

'Nothing surprising there.'

'Lots of cash, lots and lots of it. Ben loves them... well their money anyway. The pool alone was over thirty grand.'

Simon sat back and looked thoughtful. 'Where does a...'

'There's more. Twice Ben was paid by cheque, big amounts, but they weren't from the Hallibut's bank, they were in this company's name...' she stabbed at her notebook, '...and the account is with a bank in the Isle of Man of all places.'

Simon turned the notebook round and looked at the scrawled name. It wasn't familiar.

'It's got to be dodgy hasn't it, a council worker with pots and pots of cash and a corporate account in a tax haven?' Mattie pulled a wry face. 'Trouble is I can't really see how we can take this much further, local builders are about my level, I'm afraid my contacts don't include many international off-shore bankers.' She laughed self-depreciatingly.

'Nor me either,' Simon said quietly, 'but I know one or two people who's do. Give me an hour or two.'

The editor of the *The Bugle* had his mind on other things when Mattie charged into his office, not least the ever-present cash flow problems of the paper and the unrealistic expectations of its owners. Rob Jordan was distracted and bad-tempered and not in the mood for an excitable sub-editor peddling wild conspiracy theories. His own attempt to pitch the wind farm corruption story to the powers-that-be had been met with withering horror and firm instructions that this sort of story was to be left to the well-funded national tabloids and their libel lawyers. There was some questioning of his personal judgement for even suggesting they run the story and even mutterings about the board exercising more editorial control in the future ... and why hadn't he hit their advertising target? In fact the meeting couldn't have gone worse. It had been a bloody disaster.

For the first few minutes in the office Mattie had been far too excited to notice her boss's dire mood, her enthusiasm boosted by a phone call from Simon minutes before, who, through one of his unidentified contacts had discovered that the name on Hallibut's cheques wasn't that of a company but a trust. And among the listed trustees, Simon thought she 'might be interested to know', was one Sir George Hoggit. It was Mattie's eureka moment - or so she thought.

A few minutes later Mattie sat slumped and stunned in her chair as Rob Jordan bad-temperedly and ruthlessly, point by point demolished her case:

Firstly, the rumours swirling around Hoggit's business park were well known and well documented. Yes, the police had been involved, and yes, *The Bugle* had taken an interest. In fact Rebecca, or Bernard, or whatever his bloody name was ('I wish they'd get on and shoot the bastard.') had done a bit of digging but nothing was ever going to stick.

Secondly, there was no reason why the payments to Hallibut couldn't be explained by private consultancy work, the fact that some came from the Isle of Man meant nothing. Furthermore, if Mattie bothered to read her own paper's obituary column she would have noted the recent death of Clive Hallibut's father - no doubt there had been a legacy. It was not illegal or newsworthy for a council employee to be independently wealthy, and frankly Rob Jordan wasn't surprised that Mrs Hallibut was pissed off at being hassled again when the whole thing was history.

Next, Mattie was reading too much into Councillor Cockburn's response to her questioning. Rob Jordan was not at all surprised she'd got 'an odd reaction' at the mention of the Hoggit name, the poor sod had nearly been murdered at their bloody fete.

As for Donald McCruddy being blackmailed; he'd obviously done a deal with Hoggit for the access and buggered off to Spain to enjoy the proceeds. ('Don't blame him,' he'd added gloomily.) She, Mattie, had no proof, none of the famous photos and was relying on the word of some homicidal nutter with an arse full of gravel and a chip on his shoulder. And as for trying to read anything into Mickey Moyst's account, that really was scraping the barrel, the little pratt was a walking ego and too out of his tree to know what day of the week it was most of the time - and by the way had she softened him up about more advertising?

Rob Jordan delivered this diatribe pacing round the office stabbing the air for emphasis and occasionally slapping his desk. He flopped back down into his chair. 'It's not bloody Watergate is it?' he said, peering over the accumulated clutter on his desk at the stunned Mattie. After a few moments awkward silence he sighed wearily and ran a hand through his hair. 'Look, I'm sorry, but we can't do anything with this stuff, the lawyers would rip us apart. And even if it's true - and I'm not saying it isn't - no one cares. Council corruption, a few people taking the odd back-hander, rich men buying their own way, it's always been there, always will. It was news once, it's not anymore, at least not for us ... we can't afford it.'

'So why did you send me and Si... me, all round the place interviewing these people? Why, when...?'

'Why? I'll tell you why! Did I say: "Go dig up some dirt, go root out a bit of council corruption...?" alleged,' he added out of habit. 'Did I? No!'

'Well yes actually...'

'What I wanted was some good old-fashioned local reporting! Not

Poulson, not Profumo, not bloody ... bloody ... Watergate!'

'So you said,' Mattie muttered, 'and yes you did,' she added furiously.

Rob Jordan ignored her, 'Look, I want to read something like: "Wind Farm destroys landscape!" ... or go for a different angle, some people might even think they're a good idea, get both sides for a change. Or I want to read: "Riot at village fete" ... who started it and why? Who were the heroes and who were the villains? I want to read about nutters with home-made bombs and an arseful of gravel! Well come on, make up your own headline for that one, it's a bloody gift!' He was on his feet again and glowering down at her. 'Local stories, that's why I sent you and your boyfriend out and about, sweetheart.'

Mattie leapt to her feet too and only anger held back the tears, 'He is NOT my boyfriend,' she snarled, 'and yes you did...'

'Whatever. If you want to take something out of this whole bloody mess you'll make sure you get to that parish council meeting, with or without lover-boy, and do a bit of good old-fashioned reporting. Who knows, maybe they'll even lay on another riot for you.'

CHAPTER NINE

'Cheers.'

'Up yours.' Bunny raised a cloudy glass of cider to his lips. 'So, how've you been, Filch?'

'Oh, mustn't complain. Met a few old mates and it was only six months this time.'

Bunny nodded an acknowledgement and studied the small greying man for any obvious changes during his recent absence. Finding none he nodded again.

'Well it was only a spot of shoplifting this time, hardly worth the effort,' the little man explained without bitterness.

'Six months sounds a lot.'

'Well... it was a big TV.'

Bunny nodded sympathetically. He was one of the few people left in Plompley who would speak to Filch - short for Filcher, a corruption of Fletcher, the name he was known by at his regular court appearances. These in recent years had more often than not led to prison, something Filch seemed to accept with equanimity. His criminal incompetence was largely due to his having the lowest IQ that prison psychiatrists had ever tried to record, but in fairness he'd also had his share of bad luck; a misguided attempt to burgle a property guarded by the only mute pit bull terrier anyone had ever heard of - or rather hadn't - had been a disaster on several levels. As he explained to a sympathetic arresting officer: 'Never 'eard the bugger coming. First thing I knew 'e 'ad me by the knackers!' This encounter had unnerved Filch and was largely what had prompted him to abandon housebreaking, his crime of choice, and diversify into shoplifting.

He and Bunny had an arrangement; between stays in Brixton and Wandsworth, or his favourite on the Isle of Wight, Filch would slip back to the only home he knew, his elderly father's council house on the edge of Plompley, and in due course quietly appear at the caravan site. Bunny would put the petty-cash tin out of sight and set Filch to work on the jobs he hadn't much fancied himself and been putting off since he knew Filch was up for parole. Anything involving the septic tank or high gutters would be top of the list and then there was always litter and dog mess to be collected. At the moment, while the last of the pea-shingle worked its way out of Bunny's posterior he was also happy to entrust Filch with the sit-on mower.

Filch had never heard of the minimum wage, never complained and on the rare occasions when his pitiful wages were handed over he happily accepted that he was expected to accompany Bunny to the pub and spend them buying his employer drinks, crisps and cigars for the evening. It was a symbiotic arrangement that seemed to work for both parties.

'So you going to the meeting?'

'What meeting?'

Bunny tutted impatiently. '*The* meeting, the meeting at the school.'

'No, I don't think so. What's it about then?'

'The bleedin' wind farm of course!'

'Oh that. No, don't bother me.'

'Well it bloody bothers me.' Bunny took another sip and sat back in his chair. 'But I've got a plan.'

'Oh yeah.'

Bunny waved his empty glass under Filch's nose.

The little thief was no more popular with Sid than anyone else in Plompley and it took him a while to get served. Bunny passed the time gazing around the pub; clearly many of the other customers were also waiting for the wind farm meeting at the school. Bunny's thoughts turned to home, not just the business but Linda. She was in a very funny mood, had been since she got back from the unexplained holiday and he didn't know what to make of it. In fairness, he supposed, returning to find your husband had blown himself up, had multiple injuries to his arse and was on police bail would have come as a bit of a shock to most wives... but there was something else, he was sure. She'd seemed more amused than cross and he'd been quite hurt.

'Right,' said Bunny, once he'd taken a long pull from the fresh murky glass. 'Listen up.' He'd heard the expression used repeatedly in a Vietnam War film and liked it. 'What do you think of this?'

Filch looked around guiltily, 'What?'

Bunny looked at him blankly, 'Eh? No, listen. I want run this by you.' He glared and waited for a response.

'Oh yeah, right.'

'Right! You know the fairy tale with the princess, the one who's been stuck up in this tower and can't get down?'

'Eh?'

'You remember. When you were a kid. She's up in this tower and a prince comes along and is going to rescue 'er.'

'Is he 'andsome?'

Bunny was caught by surprise. 'Well, yeah, yeah of course, they always are, it's...'

'And she's dead pretty?'

'Yes of course, but...'

Filch obviously felt involved now. 'So who put her in the tower then, not nice is it?'

'Well you should bleedin' know,' Bunny said spitefully. He was starting to lose control of this conversation. 'Look it doesn't matter, a wicked step-mother or something.'

'Aah,' Filch smiled knowingly.

'So the prince has got a plan to get her down see? And this is the plan I'm going to use.'

'Do you reckon he'll give her one?'

'What?'

'You know, when he gets her down from that tower, 'im 'andsome and 'er pretty... and grateful too,' he sniggered, 'you know...'

'Christ!' Bunny was shocked and rather repulsed by the idea of fairy tale heroes and heroines actually indulging in something as worldly as sex. Like most people he'd never considered that aspect of 'living happily ever after'. 'Look, maybe, it doesn't matter right now...'

'Might to them.'

'Not now!' Bunny almost shouted. 'He's got to get her down first and if you'd shut up I'll tell you how!'

Filch looked sulky and hid behind his pint glass. Bunny risked a quick sip.

'No stairs then?'

'No! No fucking stairs!' Bunny spluttered. 'Now listen...' he slammed down his glass and rushed on with his explanation before Filch had a chance to interrupt. 'So the prince wants to get a big rope up to the tower so he can climb up to the princess... *and rescue her.* Not...' he couldn't bring himself to use even a euphemism for the sexual act, let alone one of his usual casual obscenities, '...so he gets a bow and arrow. A long bow,' he added reverentially, 'and he can't get a *big* rope up there because it's too heavy, so what he does is...'

'What if he hits 'er?'

'Eh?'

'What if the arrow hits 'er?'

'Well it won't.'

'It might.'

'Look! He's a brilliant shot, ok?' Bunny snarled, '...like Robin Hood. So he ties some silk to his arrow...'

'Might,' Filch muttered.

Bunny ignored him, '...and then he ties some cord to the silk, and he ties the heavy rope to the cord and he fires the arrow through the window ... *missing her by a mile* ... and she pulls up the silk, which pulls up the cord, which pulls up the rope and the prince climbs up and rescues her. And they live happily ever after.' He looked at Filch's sulky face and sighed. 'Yeah, well maybe they have a quick one. Anyway...' he glanced at his watch, '... I've got to go, see you in here later. I'll look after this for you.' He swept up the little plastic bank bag that contained the remains of Filch's wages and fished out a crumpled five-pound note. 'Here, get yourself a drink.'

The red brick Victorian schoolhouse had long been a source of pride in the village. Built as a guilty vanity by a long-forgotten local industrialist it was disproportionately large for the immediate population but this meant that it alone had survived the numerous cuts and 'rationalisations' of recent decades as it absorbed displaced pupils from its smaller satellites. The buildings boasted the classic ceilingless high-gabled rooms, towering ill-fitting single-glazed sash windows, concrete granolith floors and obsolete plumbing. All of which made it a caretaker's nightmare to heat and maintain. The fabric only survived in its present condition and complied with modern health & safety regulations (just) thanks to generations of tenacious PTA committees and their fund-raising efforts. The evolution of these moneymaking activities was a social history in itself; tea dances had given way to the Saturday night hop, and eventually the disco; the whist drives and bingo had steadily been replaced by casino and race nights, and fish and chip suppers, after some resistance, had made way for the appalling cheese & wine party and eventually the curry night. Throughout this evolutionary process committee members, supporters and volunteers had shed blood, sweat and tears - and during a period in the early seventies when the committee had been dominated by a cabal of enthusiastic swingers various other bodily fluids - all to ensure that Plompley Primary continued to carry the educational banner in their corner of Bartfordshire.

It was in the lofty main assembly hall with its stripped wooded floors, large stage and sagging blue velvet curtains that the parish council had decided to hold their extraordinary public meeting and where Ref Watt had been invited to set up their travelling exhibition. The main body of the hall was ranked with coloured plastic chairs, whilst the councilor's ancient oak table dominated centre stage. Various bright display panels, cheerful posters and tables covered in glossy pamphlets had been dotted around at the front of the hall. Immediately in front of the stage, flanked by two huge landscape photographs showing rows of computer-faded wind turbines blending unrealistically into their backgrounds, an attractive young woman with a professional smile stood behind a cloth-covered table greeting everyone with a shiny booklet, a mechanical, 'How are you today?' and a cheap low-energy light bulb.

Maxwell stood confidently at the front edge of the stage nodding and smiling at the trickle of dripping, wind-swept villagers who were shyly making their ways to the front of the hall to peer suspiciously at the various display panels. Maxwell was pleased with the appalling weather - it would keep the attendance down and the questions short. He decided it was time to work the crowd and looking around selected a stooped gentle-looking couple, probably in their early seventies, greying and shabbily formal in their dress. They were carefully studying the huge coloured maps of the area on which Maxwell's staff had very faintly marked the proposed positions of the giant turbines. Maxwell was confident that they had no idea what they were looking at. Harmless, he decided, and bounded down the steps at the side of the stage, smile widening hand out-thrust.

'How good of you to come. Fascinating isn't it?' he said gazing admiringly at the map as if it was a piece of fine art. The old couple smiled vaguely and their slight air of bewilderment encouraged Maxwell. 'Absolutely fascinating,' he reaffirmed, 'the way modern science and engineers have found a way to harness nature to work for us, eh? With no carbon, no noise, no unsightly chimneys, no pollution and *no fuss!*'

'That's our house.' The old man's finger rested lightly on a small, pink 'L' shaped box near the middle of the map. 'Not very far from your windmills is it? Let's see...' he bent down to look at the bottom edge of the map, '... scale, yes, right. Let's see now, yes about five hundred yards I'd say.' He straightened up and looked directly into Maxwell's startled eyes. 'Now that *is* close isn't it?'

'No, no I think you'll find...'

'They'll be very noisy being that close,' the old lady said quietly.

'They will I'm afraid my dear.'

'We've lived there for over forty years,' the old lady said addressing Maxwell. 'All the children were raised there.'

'Ah, I think you'll find that with modern engineering the noise issue has been effectively dealt with and at five hundred yards...' (The old man's estimate had been unerringly accurate.) '... and once we've planted...'

'That's not what they say in *The Telegraph*,' the man said.

'Well, you can't believe...'

'Or *The Mail*.'

Maxwell gave a superior smirk. 'Yes, well, what do you expect from...'

'*Sunday Times* too,' the old man said looking at his wife for confirmation.

She nodded emphatically and added, 'And *Saga Magazine* says...'

'Saga, for goodness sake!' Maxwell spluttered.

The old man tapped him lightly on the arm. 'And the latest paper released by WHO - that's The World Health Organisation...' he explained helpfully.

But Maxwell had heard enough. He didn't repeat the handshakes, noddded a curt goodbye and hurriedly remounted the stage. The old couple looked after him, unperturbed and apparently unsurprised by the rudeness and with a quiet dignity went to claim their free light bulb.

During Maxwell's brief absence others had gathered on the stage and several androgynous be-tweeded individuals were now seated at the huge table. Amongst them the clerk fidgeted with piles of agendas and minute books, occasionally looking up, spaniel-like, at the chairman who stood behind the table. The chairman was ignoring all around him, especially Sir George Hoggit skulking in the wings, and had fixed a magisterial gaze on the back wall of the hall and was distractedly humming a little Elgar to himself.

Sir George was staying deliberately under cover, using the moth eaten curtains as protection from the gathering villagers, but failing to attract Maxwell's attention he was eventually forced to risk exposure and stepped out onto the stage careful to keep a large panel of photographs between himself and the main body of the hall.

'I don't see why you need me here,' he snarled. His usual early evening whiskey consumption had been curtailed by Maxwell's insistence that he put in an appearance and it had done nothing for his mood.

'Well this is *a partnership* if you remember, between responsible business... that's us,' Maxwell tapped himself on the chest, 'and the community, as represented by...' he started to reach a pointed finger towards Sir George's straining waistcoat but thought better of it '... you.' he concluded.

'Load of bollocks!' Sir George barked.

And they both knew it was. But with the promise of a new children's playground and a commitment to 'civic involvement', *Community Partnership* had become the mantra and appeasement the strategy - at least for the moment. Every display, poster and pamphlet in the hall bore a photograph of happy smiling children under the promising heading: *YOUR Community Partnership.*

Sir George remained stubbornly off message. 'This lot will do what they're bloody told - or else,' he muttered, glowering at the profile of the council chairman, who continued to ignore him. 'And the Bartford lot have as good as said yes. Don't see the bloody point of all this!' He flapped contemptuously at the hall. Then suddenly bending forward he peered closely at the nearest photo display. 'What the hell is that?'

'A polar bear, Sir George.'

'I know it's a bloody polar bear but what's it doing there?'

'It's about global warming...'

'What is?'

Maxwell was starting to wonder whether insisting on Sir George's presence had been such a good idea after all. He sighed, lifted his eyes to the ceiling and started the address he usually reserved for primary school audiences. 'We need wind farms because of global warming; global warming is melting all the ice caps; the ice caps are where polar bears live; with less ice to hunt on the polar bears are starving...'

Sir George looked at him incredulously. 'I'm not a bloody child,' he snarled and stabbed at the panel, 'and anyway that damned thing doesn't look very hungry to me.'

It was true. The huge animal in the photograph was a fine example of the species; plump and sleek with heavy sleepy eyelids, the hint of a smile and apparently quite content with the small iceberg it was lazily draped over. This was an issue Maxwell had repeatedly raised with his publicity department. 'For God's sake, can't you get a skinny one? Or at least get one that looks a bit miserable,' he'd pleaded. 'Maybe one with a bit of mange or whatever it is polar bears get. What about a starving cub or two? Or even better, a dead one. There's got to be a Chinese zoo somewhere you could get a few shots.' But for the moment Maxwell was stuck with this annoyingly healthy specimen with its swollen belly and mockingly happy expression. 'Well, that's what we'd *like* them all to look like,' he mumbled.

Sir George snorted.

More and more people were appearing in the hall and coagulating into familiar groups and cliques. A pattern of behaviour soon emerged; after individual members of a group had made a careful inspection of the various displays there would be a whispered discussion at the edge of the hall, then a delegation would revisit the display or map in question for verification of whatever point was in dispute before reporting back. This process might be repeated several times before the group was satisfied. It would then splinter and individuals would move on to scoop up the literature and leaflets and their low-energy dog-turd-shaped freebie - a reward for their anticipated gullibility.

Sir George had slipped away, exiting *stage right,* and a relieved Maxwell resumed his position front and centre. From there he had a fine view of the light-bulb dispenser's cleavage and looked forward to a more thorough investigation later. She looked up, caught his eye and gave him a slow wink and her only genuine smile of the evening - and a little wiggle. Maxwell felt back in control.

Suddenly there were raised voices from the back corner of the hall, then frantic yelping and a crash as Bunny came stumbling head first through the double doors. He wasn't exactly drunk but three pints of scrumpy, four chain-smoked Castellas and only a packet of pickled-onion crisps for his tea had left him light headed and a bit unsteady. The low-energy lighting in the corridor hadn't helped and once the pinioned dachshund had started to wriggle under his foot he'd quickly lost his balance and found himself propelled through the swing doors.

Ignoring the stares and nervous smiles of welcome from Maxwell and his mistress he made his way to the front of the hall and pretended to study the displays. Those on the stage relaxed while more dripping anoraks bustled in to re-animate the crowd and more low-energy light bulbs were dispensed.

Maxwell was collared by the parish council chairman, who having finished humming the first movement of Elgar's cello concerto decided to enlighten the Ref Watt man with a potted history of the school, its dubious founder and mediocre alumni. Bunny's presence on the stage therefore went unnoticed until he pushed his way between the two men, and ignoring the chairman who was currently addressing the ceiling, thrust himself at Maxwell.

'What about compensation then?'

'I beg your pardon.'

'So you bloody should! But what about compensation? You build those bloody things and what's it going to do to our properties, eh? House prices, eh? Our businesses...?'

Maxwell was on familiar and well practiced territory here. He squared his shoulders and straightened his bowtie. 'You will find that all the industry research indicates that wind farms do not have a detrimental effect on property values. There is absolutely no evidence...'

'Bugger "industry research"! What about what my estate agent tells me? Reckons he couldn't sell at any price at the moment. And when those things get built...' Bunny had moved to the edge of the stage and waved a dismissive arm at the exhibition at his feet. He was momentarily distracted by the nervous smile and swelling breasts of the light bulb dispenser. '...er, when they get built... well God help us! I'm in the tourist industry,' he announced. 'How many tourists are we going to get round here with those things up there?'

'There's no evidence that tourism is effected in anyway. Indeed industry research has shown that some visitors will go out of their way...'

'Yeah, to avoid the fucking things!'

'Now I think we need to calm down...'

'Calm down! Calm down! You knock thousands off my property, bugger up my business, give me a fucking light bulb as compensation and then tell me to "calm down"!'

There was a muted cheer and an unexpected smattering of applause, which caught both protagonists by surprise. Bunny turned and grinned at the hall. The light-bulb girl smiled nervously back then moved quickly away to the side of the stage.

'Does that thing go round in the wind then?' Bunny suddenly demanded.

'I beg your pardon. What thing?'

'Your own little wind turbine there,' Bunny reached forward and flicked the ends of Maxwell's flamboyant bowtie. 'How much wind does that need then?'

There were a few sniggers from the body of the hall, which only encouraged Bunny. 'What's it take to get it spinning then?' He reached forward again.

Maxwell slapped his hand away. 'Look I really think that...'

Bunny produced his free light bulb like a magician with an egg and thrust it under Maxwell's nose, 'I'll tell you what *I* think.' He turned with a smirk to the hall. 'What *I* think is, we get that thing...' he lunged forward and managed to tweak the bowtie before darting back to the edge of the stage, '...we get it spinning good and fast and then we take this...' he brandished the bulb, '...and we stick it up your arse and see if it lights up!' On delivery of the punch line he turned with a triumphant grin to the audience. Apart from the odd embarrassed cough the only sounds were the wind and rain tearing round the building.

'Right, well that was all very... interesting. Illuminating even, ha ha!' There were a few polite laughs and Maxwell looked relieved. 'Moving on ladies and gentleman. Shortly your councillors will be...'

'Hang on! I'm not bloody finished!'

'Oh, I think you are Mr... sir,' Maxwell said firmly, 'and I really think you should move away from...' He reached out a guiding hand towards Bunny.

'Don't you bloody push me around you smarmy bast... aahh!'

There was a chorus of little screams and gasps as Bunny did his best to defy gravity; he teetered, then flailed, then flapped and eventually plummeted, landing neatly backside first in the still half-full box of light bulbs six foot below. The flaccid crump of collapsing cardboard was accompanied by a series of loud pops and then a curious crackling sound. Bunny was strangely silent for a moment but as he tentatively moved in an attempt to get out of the box the popping and crackling intensified and he let out a long groan. And then, as if talking to himself:

'Ow, my arse! Bloody hell my arse!'

Maxwell peered over the edge of the stage. 'Er, you all right?'

'No I'm fucking not! Get an ambulance. God, my arse!'

'You'll have to pay for those you know.'

Bunny looked up at him with a look of pure hatred. There were two more pops and a slight crackle. 'Aaah! Just get that fucking ambulance,' he hissed between gritted teeth, trying desperately not to move.

Maxwell bent lower. 'You will let me know if any light up won't you?' he whispered.

'Just get that fu....'

'Right oh!'

Trudging through the rain towards The Smuggler's Finger Simon still wasn't quite sure why he'd agreed to accompany Mattie to the parish council meeting. He'd already decided that his final contribution to the investigation was providing the insider banking information, and having done that he hadn't really expected to hear from her again. It hadn't worried him. It was curious his lack of interest in Mattie, she was after all a very attractive, bright and apparently available young woman. Perhaps it was her rather masculine authority and the casual amorality she employed in her work that were a turn off.

He'd been sitting at the blank screen of his laptop waiting for inspiration, or distraction, when she'd called. Her mood seemed to have changed. The confident exuberance of earlier had been replaced by flat almost weary tones. It was not the voice of a ruthless reporter on the brink of her first scoop. They arranged to meet at the pub.

Arriving at the Smuggler's Finger first Simon was surprised to find it shut. He spotted a disconsolate Filch sitting hunched under a dripping parasol at one of the garden benches and learnt to his further surprise that Sid had suddenly decided to go to 'some meetin' down the school.'

As Mattie pulled up Simon sprinted from the cover of the parasol and bundled into the passenger seat of the steamy little car.

'They're shut. Sid's gone to the meeting apparently. Didn't think he'd be interested.' There was no immediate reaction from Mattie. 'Are you all right?'

'Bloody fed up!'

'What's happened?'

Mattie gripped the steering wheel tightly in both hands. 'Rob bloody Jordan, that's what's happened. Bastard!' She lapsed into silence.

Simon was taken back by the vehemence. He drew dribbly spirals in the condensation on the side window and waited patiently for her to continue. 'Well go on then,' he said eventually, 'tell all!'

'It's not funny.'

'I'm sure it's not.' He went back to his doodling, the silence only broken by the rattle of rain on the roof.

Mattie sniffed and swallowed hard and Simon thought she was going to cry.

'Come on, what's going on?' he prompted gently.

Mattie sighed heavily, glared at the opaque windscreen and started to describe her early morning meeting in the editor's office. Simon listened carefully and without interruption.

'That's rough,' he said, 'and it doesn't sound like your friend Rob was too gentle in letting you down either. But you've still got a story here, several in fact. Good ones too; the wind farm is controversial - and it's *your* exclusive - there's still more fun to be had out of the fete riot and God knows what Bunny Warren might do next.' He turned to look at her. 'Maybe we did get a bit carried away...' He was careful to use the inclusive plural. 'It probably was all a bit far fetched; conspiracies, bribery and corruption and all that, but...'

'No! That's the point, that's the worst of it!' Mattie snapped. 'Rob more or less admitted we'd probably got it right, but the owners are terrified of being sued. Can't have that, it might *impact* their precious advertising revenue, and anyway apparently everyone's at it, corruption's so commonplace these days it's not even bloody news. Jesus!' She lapsed into a moody silence.

Simon allowed her a few moments. 'Come on!' He slapped the dashboard, 'We've still got work to do.'

As they hurried across the rain-swept playground an ambulance was just pulling out of the staff car park.

'The riot must have started without us,' Simon joked.

Mattie grimaced. 'Looks like another story I've missed. Better go and find out what's going on I suppose.'

They had no problem getting an eyewitness account. Sid had just arrived at the back of the hall when Bunny launched his attack on the Ref Watt executive and had watched the whole episode with vindictive delight.

'Right on his arse, like something out of a fuckin' circus it was!' Sid enthused. He was delighted to give Mattie a full account, ignored Simon and insisted they inspect the ominously large bloodstain on the floor in front of the stage. The caretaker had already been summoned to remove the blood-soaked box, Sid explained regretfully.

A sort of order was at last starting to take shape in the hall. Some of the better organised cliques had staked claims to strategically positioned blocks of seating whilst other groups hurried to fill any prominent gaps where they might have a chance of catching the chairman's eye. Any remaining seats were being filled by unaffiliated couples and individuals and several gangs of lively youngsters were ranked along the back wall. The assembled councillors shuffled self-consciously behind their committee table. Their parochial discussions were rarely witnessed by more than a bored local reporter or a hopeful householder seeking planning permission, so a hall full of parishioners keen to express their views was a new and intimidating experience. For the serious business of the evening the distractions of the display panels had been removed, as had the low-energy light-bulb stall. The semi-hysterical light-bulb girl had point-blank refused to handle the remaining intact but bloodied stock, so Maxwell with the plea '... not to let this spoil things,' had kindly sent her back to their hotel.

The parish council chairman decided to lighten the mood, or at least his own, and paced up and down at the back of the stage, eyes lifted, loudly humming tunes from *South Pacific*. Without any preamble or apparent reference to a watch he suddenly stopped mid *Happy Talk*, marched to the table and with eyes still lifted to the ceiling rapped repeatedly with a small gavel. The startled clerk gave a little shriek and dropped his glasses. The hall slowly quietened and the chairman lowered his eyes, cleared his throat ostentatiously and boomed: 'This meeting is now called to order! There are agendas on your seats but Mr Pecking, our clerk...' he gestured to the seat on his right '...will now outline the *extraordinary* format for this meeting.' He returned to his pacing, 'Mr Pecking.'

'Yes chairman, um, right with you.' The flustered little man fumbled with his pile of papers and re-arranged his twisted spectacles. 'Umm...'

The agenda was explained in pedantic detail. The only parts remotely of interest to anyone in the hall were *Item 8: An informed and balanced address by a respected expert on wind energy* and *Item 9: A limited number of questions will be accepted from the floor - at the chairman's discretion.*

'Thank you Mr Pecking.' The chairman was back behind the committee table, eyes apparently fixed on the highest point of the far gable wall. 'There can be no doubt that the need for small wind farms in rural areas has been irrefutably proven...' There were murmurs in some parts of the hall. '... but as a council mindful of our responsibility to inform and guide parishioners we felt it was important that, although unarguable, the precise benefits of wind power should be explained by an acknowledged authority. We are therefore most grateful to have Mr Maxwell with us - he will be addressing us shortly.'

As the murmurs in the hall rose to a rumble Simon whispered, 'This is going to be a stitch up - and not a very subtle one!'

Mattie didn't look up from her notebook but nodded. They'd found two seats at the end of a row at the opposite end to the doors and near the back of the hall. Sid had sat down immediately behind them. He leant forward. 'Done deal I reckon,' he grinned.

A tall suited figure had risen from the centre of a group near the stage prompting a silence that caused the chairman to reluctantly lower his gaze. 'We will be taking *some* questions later. Item... er, nine, now...'

'This is not a question, chairman; it's a point of order.'

The chairman hesitated and looked enquiringly at the clerk. Neither of them was quite sure what a point of order was but since the spokesman from the floor was surrounded by some of the more affluent and influential members of the village and the clerk thought that he might be a lawyer of some sort he nodded gravely up at the chairman.

'Very well Mr...?'

'Vincent-Townend. *Doctor* Vincent-Townend.'

'Yes, very well Dr Townend.'

'Vincent-Townend, there's a hyphen. Just for the minutes.'

'Yes yes, very well.'

'Also for the minutes, I am the chairman of PAWs OFF.'

The clerk scribbled frantically, glancing up at his chairman for any sort of guidance.

'Paws off?'

'Plompley Against Wind farms, it's an acronym.'

The clerk tugged at the chairman's cuff and whispered, 'What's the "OFF"?'

'What does the O, F, F stand for?'

'Well... off. It's a word, "off". That bit's not an acronym.'

'A bit confusing isn't it?'

'It may be to you sir but I assure you our message is not!'

Maxwell, watching from the wings, didn't like the way things were going. The idiot chairman was losing control and this Dr Vincent-Townend had definitely taken the initiative.

'It is clear from the printed agenda and your opening remarks that we are this evening to hear an address very much in favour of wind power. I, we, assume that your Mr Maxwell represents a wind power or turbine company?' Vincent-Townend paused and getting no answer continued, 'Yes, I thought so.' A growl went round the hall. Sweeping an arm around him Vincent-Townend continued. 'Most of us here have turned out on this foul evening hoping to find our *elected* parish council supporting us, or at the very least we expected a balanced debate. I see no mention here...' he slapped the agenda, '... of a speaker *against* wind power.'

The earlier growl became a rumble of assent, a few people clapped and there was the odd 'hear, hear!' A single piercing whistle came from the back wall. The chairman raised his hands to calm the swell and said firmly: 'That would not have been appropriate.'

The swell became a roar and in the wings Maxwell put his head in his hands.

A few rows in front of Simon and Mattie an anorak-clad figure rose and stood calmly looking towards the stage.

'A relieved bellow came from the chairman, 'Yes vicar!' and with the exception of one isolated and repeated shout of 'shame!' the words worked like biblical oil on troubled waters.

'Mr Chairman, if I may respectfully suggest to you, and indeed everyone present, that we now let Mr Maxwell give us his address...' The vicar raised a hand as if conferring a blessing to quell the rising groans, '... and that you, Mr Chairman, in the absence of a speaker to make a formal reply then let the people of this community ask their questions and make their own reply.' Richard Devine remained standing and after the briefest of pauses there was loud applause. No shouting, no whistling or cheering, just a dignified uniform clapping around the hall.

The chairman had no choice and he knew it. He nodded his assent and summoned a slightly alarmed Maxwell from the wings. 'Mr Maxwell of...' he consulted his notes, '...Ref Watt Green Energy.' There was a handful of claps and one ironic whistle.

Maxwell beamed at the hall and tried to exude a confidence that for once he didn't feel. 'The very real threat of global warming and carbon pollution... er, emissions...' he corrected himself and settled into the mantra.

'Recognise it?' Simon whispered to Mattie. She nodded and continued writing. Looking over he could see she'd written 'REFWATT' in large capital letters followed by a series of question marks.

At first Maxwell's audience was held by the quiet authority of the vicar's reasonableness and listened politely, but attentions soon wandered. Elected group spokesmen mentally honed their pre-prepared questions, others tried to think of something pithy to throw at the stage and whispered conversations, mostly unrelated to the matter at hand, sprang up all round the room.

Simon was bored stiff, he'd heard all this drivel at least twice before. He glanced across at the pad on Mattie's lap. She'd been doodling, the loop of the R and the triangle of the A in REFWATT had been filled in and the two Ts had acquired little hats. He studied the doodle for a minute but couldn't see any further potential for embellishment. The letters danced meaninglessly in front of his eye ... when suddenly there was a cerebral flash, a brainwave, that sensation familiar to regular crossword doers. Simon snorted loudly. Mattie gave him a quizzical look and Sid prodded him in the back thinking he was snoring. Chuckling quietly to himself Simon leant across and took the pad from Mattie's lap; he turned to a fresh page and started to write. After a moment, grinning happily, he ripped out the page, tore it neatly in half and passed one half over his shoulder to Sid and slipped the other to a bemused Mattie. On both pieces he'd written:

'REFWATT GREEN ENERGY   =   WET FART GREEN ENERGY!!!!!!'

Simon was rewarded by a loud and appreciative snigger from behind him and a pitying shake of the head and a half smile from Mattie. It was the first time she'd smiled all evening and Simon smiled back encouragingly.

Sid gleefully passed his slip of paper onto his neighbour who appeared to think that he in turn was expected to pass it on. Its progress around the room could be tracked by a ripple of suppressed giggles and sniggers and the odd disgusted snort. The loudest of these came from the opposite corner when eventually the crumpled slip was thrust into the podgy hand of Sir George. He'd slipped into the room whilst everyone's attention was on the stage and wedged himself into the shadowy corner beside the double doors from where he was grimly watching the proceedings. Simon's note went no further.

The chairman was back on his feet - and so were at least twenty people in the main body of the hall. Some stood calmly just expecting to be called, others waved a frantic hand or damp agenda and the general volume was rising. Gently flapping a pacifying left hand the chairman arched his right arm and pointed towards the far left hand corner. 'Yes sir, you sir in the black jacket.' The crowd twisted in their seats to see who'd been chosen while many of the disappointed questioners remained on their feet, frowning impatiently. The chairman's choice only now stood up, hesitant but aggressive - it was the same man who'd slipped from his seat earlier to pass Simon's note to Sir George - shaven-headed, ear-ringed and wearing a short black jacket zipped to the throat.

'Yeah, well, it sounds good to me. Er... we all gotta do our bit 'aven't we?'

There were bemused angry murmurs from those around him and the speaker became more aggressive, the unmistakable London accent even more pronounced.

'What about the kiddies eh? What about them... and our grandkids?' He glanced at a piece of paper in his hand. 'And polar bears. Wind turbines will make it safe for them. Er...' He looked down again and said woodenly: '...it will guarantee their future on this planet.' He stuffed the bit of paper into a pocket and glowered around. 'We need 'em, that's what I say. Get on and build 'em up there on... er, Teapot 'ill. 'Many as they can and sooner the better.' He snarled round at the rising chorus of furious disbelief and abruptly sat down.

'Yeah, wind power's what we need, 'specially round 'ere.'

On the opposite side of the hall a figure clad in a quilted tartan lumberjack's shirt had suddenly jumped to his feet. There were shouts of protest from a score of disenfranchised questioners but the chairman, eyes fixed on the exposed roof structure and determinedly humming Beethoven's *Choral*, flapped impatiently with his left hand and pointed in the vague direction of the new speaker with his right.

'Yeah right, well I think Mar... that bloke's right, and 'im...' he gestured towards the smirking Maxwell on the stage. 'Wind power is the answer, right? Good for the kids, good for the polar bears. Whotsit hill is just right for them. They won't do no 'arm up there and this place... er, the village, it'll be doing it's bit. Only right isn't it?'

There was uproar. More people were now on their feet than sitting, many gesticulating towards the stage. There were howls of protest.

'VICAR!'

The single desperate word boomed around the hall but the effect wasn't as immediate as it had been earlier. Richard Devine climbed up onto his chair and silently raised both arms towards the mass of the hall. The silence was quickly and almost miraculously complete.

'Shame I say!'

'Sshhh.'

'Vicar.' The chairman repeated.

Taking George's proffered hand, Richard carefully climbed down from his chair.

'Mr Chairman, we have now heard several opinions ... from one side of the argument. I have been doing a little layman's reading on this subject and wondered whether Mr Maxwell would be kind enough to answer a few questions for me. Many of them, I know, are on the minds of a lot of the people here and I'm sure that clear and straightforward answers will go a long way towards satisfying and reassuring our community.'

There was some restlessness in the hall, not everyone wanted to be satisfied or reassured at this early stage of the proceedings and without having had their own say.

But Maxwell liked the sound this. 'By all means, I'd be delighted,' he enthused and walked to the front of the stage.

The chairman gesticulated vaguely at the vicar and retired behind the committee table where his council colleagues sat woodenly, democratically elected gargoyles gazing blankly into the hall.

'Thank you Mr chairman. Mr Maxwell, I gather that the Spout Hill wind farm will provide enough power for ten thousand homes.'

'Indeed, indeed!' Maxwell lightly clapped his hands together delightedly.

'However, I understand that many wind turbines only operate for twenty five percent of the time, or even less. Is that the case?'

'Oh, we have much higher productivity expectations than that from Spout Hill. It really is a most promising site,' Maxwell beamed.

'Exactly what level of productivity can the community expect from its wind farm, Mr Maxwell?' Richard Devine asked innocently.

Maxwell nodded studiously. 'Ah, well, the calculations for productivity are not straightforward. They can of course be tabulated using several different criteria which will vary...'

'I'm sorry to interrupt but I understand that to gain *accurate* figures the wind speed and direction must be monitored over an extended period and in all weather conditions. That is right isn't it?'

'Yes, well...'

'Good, I thought so. Your meteorological mast has only been up on Spout Hill for a matter of weeks, and it was out of action for some of that time...' There were knowing chuckles in some parts of the hall, '...so exactly what are you basing your productivity figures on?'

'Yes, well, the data we *have* collected has proved most valuable and by using extrapolated computer modeling...'

'I'm sorry to interrupt you again, Mr Maxwell'

Maxwell smiled indulgently and shook his head to indicate that it was no problem at all. Richard Devine smiled back and nodded his thanks. No one was anticipating what came next, least of all Maxwell.

'So, it would be fair to say that your company is proposing to inflict on our community a scheme for a massively intrusive, noisy and wholly unwanted industrial development, which at best offers questionable benefits that have been calculated using incomplete data and little more than computer aided *guesswork*. Is that right, Mr Maxwell?'

The gently quizzical, almost apologetic tone of a few minutes before had been replaced by a harshness that surprised even George, sitting quietly and smiling up at her husband. There was a ripple of excitement as the hall sensed a shift in the mood.

Maxwell held his smile and wagging a knowing finger to buy time, mentally ran through his list of practised replies - he was too slow.

'I also understand, Mr Maxwell, that as your turbines will only work for relatively little of the time - and we've established that you've no idea just how much in the case of Spout Hill - then someone somewhere has to carry on burning coal or gas or creating nuclear power anyway, just in case the wind stops blowing. It's illogical isn't it, Mr Maxwell? Wasteful. Ludicrous. You can surely see why people are reluctant to sacrifice their landscapes and communities for something so... half-baked, can't you, Mr Maxwell?'

There was a momentary awed silence, which then gave way to a storm of delighted applause, hoots and whistles. As the commotion died down there was a single shout of, 'Go Ringo!' followed by laughter round the hall. Richard looked around, confused. George reached up and squeezed his hand.

Although he'd heard all the arguments before, Maxwell was unsettled by the exchange; perhaps it was having to argue the toss with a vicar. The bloody man had certainly stirred them up. It was time to move it on:

'Are there any *other* questions?'

Richard Devine was still standing.

'Let the vicar finish!'

'I think someone else should be given the opportunity,' Richard Devine said in his more familiar voice, 'but perhaps one last point if I may.'

Maxwell shrugged nervously.

'It's my understanding, Mr Maxwell, that as far as the wind farm operators are concerned, and the landowners...' he paused to glance around the hall and Sir George shrunk further back into his corner, '... it doesn't really matter whether the wind blows or not, or indeed how much electricity is generated because they get paid anyway - a great deal of money - *regardless* of their productivity.' There were mutterings of disbelief in the hall at this. 'That is the case isn't it, Mr Maxwell?'

'Well... er, it's not quite as... but what needs to be understood is that the levels of investment required and...'

'We'll take that as a "yes" then.' There was no apology for this interruption. 'So Mr Maxwell, since you can't tell us how much electricity will be created by your scheme perhaps since we're your *Community Partners* you could tell us exactly how much money is going to be made from it.'

There was a rumble of approval from the crowd, some sarcastic laughter and calls of: 'Come on then!' 'Well go on!' and more bluntly, 'How much?'

Maxwell scowled down from the stage and shuffled defensively back from the edge.

'Well, Mr Maxwell?' Richard Devine had to almost shout.

'That, Reverend, is commercially sensitive information and not...'

He didn't get to finish, or if he did no one heard because a vast cynical roar of disapproval drowned him out. Richard Devine sat down.

The chairman, who had paused in his humming and pacing at the back of the stage, started to take a guilty interest when the question of money was mentioned and now looked nervously towards the back corner of the hall, his face contorting in an effort to communicate. He needn't have bothered, Sir George had already made his mind up and was transmitting his own facial messages.

Suddenly in the back row a huge bearded figure leapt to his feet and pointing aggressively towards where Richard Devine had just sat down started bellowing.

'Bloody disgrace! Stupid questions that make no sense. None of our business how much money they makes. People gotta make a profit. We need these wind farms, they're good for all of us and we've gotta expect to pay. Bloody Nimbys!'

The two earlier enthusiasts were also on their feet now, both bellowing Green clichés and sound bites, while shouts of 'Shut up!' and 'Sit down!' came from all other areas of the hall.

'Who are these people?' Simon shouted over his shoulder.

'Dunno, never seen 'em before. They've never been in the pub, sounds like they come from my old manor though,' Sid grinned. 'There's gonna be a bleedin' ruck, you watch,' he added gleefully.

There was no attempt from the stage to control the situation. The chairman had already slunk out through the kitchens humming *The Ride of The Valkyries* and the other councillors, abandoned and leaderless, were nervously stacking their papers ready to slip away. Maxwell, having assured himself that order was never going to be restored and confident he could claim to have 'consulted the community' was looking for the nearest exit.

Next there was a scream, and then a crash from the back of the hall, quickly followed by a string of bellowed expletives and more clattering and squeals as chairs were toppled and sent skidding over the polished floor. As Mattie discovered later, there was some uncertainty as to exactly how it started but it seemed probable that a few of the local likely lads had tried to encourage the bearded giant to shut up with a couple of hefty shoves in the back - to which he had predictably and satisfyingly reacted. Most of the groups from the back wall had then gleefully pitched in to join the resulting mêlée concentrated on the huge figure. Arms and legs whirled and flailed and meaty thuds were clearly audible. More screams, oaths and sounds of violence came from the other areas of the hall where black jacket and lumberjack shirt were both trying to force their ways over and through the crowded seating to provide support for their comrade. They were both soon embroiled in their own battles as incensed locals defended their male pride and womenfolk.

As soon as the two secondary skirmishes had started, grimly satisfied that the democratic process had been successfully stopped in its tracks, Sir George slipped out the double doors and hurried to the car park. Other non-combatants were also heading for the available exits, including the fire doors to the sides of the stage, which was where Simon, Mattie and Sid found themselves in a crush with the vicar and his wife. Simon looked down shyly at George who responded with her usual enigmatic smile.

'No need for ambulances today, Sid,' Richard Devine said. 'At least not yet, but I think you'd be doing everyone a great service if you opened the pub, don't you?'

Seemingly for the first time in weeks it had stopped raining. Richard and Georgiana Devine walked hand in hand, as was their habit, up School Lane towards the heart of the village and The Smuggler's Finger. The lane was littered with leafy debris and large puddles straddled the road in places. Nervous weather agencies were issuing their complicated codes of warnings for flooding and threatening more to come. It was apparently the wettest summer since sometime in the 1970s... or the 50s... or this century, depending on which newspaper you read. The lane was crowded with excited villagers. Nearly everyone who'd been in the school hall was heading towards the pub, reluctant to leave behind the drama of the evening and determined not to miss out on the post-mortem. As they hurried past some glanced curiously at their 'new' vicar, the unsuspected champion who had appeared in their midst. Eventually the Devines found themselves more or less alone in the darkening lane.

'Good Lord, what is this village coming to?' It wasn't clear whether the question was rhetorical or a direct appeal to the Almighty. George didn't say anything. 'I never expected to see such levels of violence, not in a village like this. First Arabella Hoggit's fete and now this ... and in the school! I mean it was different when we were at the hostel in Peckham but here...'

'You did your best, dear.'

'I don't know, I can't help thinking I may have been partly responsible.'

'Nonsense,' George said, 'those things needed to be said. People were encouraged and... well, comforted by your involvement. It was the right thing to do.'

'Thank you, dear, that's a comfort to me.'

They walked on in silence for a few yards before Richard burst out again, 'It's so damned divisive! Destructive! And I don't just mean the landscape, look what it's doing to people, ordinary decent people who'd never normally dream of behaving like that; it's setting them at each other's throats - literally!' He shook his head in despair.

They reached the war memorial and as usual stood silently together looking at the heroic list of local names above the flaking stone steps still littered with the sad remains of last November's poppies.

'Sometimes it's difficult to keep things in perspective,' Richard Devine said quietly. George squeezed his hand and after a few moments they walked away.

'People will be looking to you more than ever now,' George said suddenly. 'I think you might find you've become a bit of a local hero,' she laughed.

'Nonsense!'

'What, after your performance this evening?' she chuckled, 'single handedly taking on big business, the Goliaths ... well the *big* bullies anyway. I bet the collection's good on Sunday!'

Despite himself Richard Devine laughed too. 'Every cloud I suppose...' He pondered his new status, 'By the way, who or what is Ringo?'

She looked up at him shyly. 'You are, dear.'

'Me?'

George nodded. 'He was one of *The Beatles*.'

Richard looked blank. '*The Beatles*? But I've never even been to Liverpool and I certainly can't play the guitar.'

'He was the drummer dear.'

'Well I've never played the drums either.'

'It's a nickname, Richard, an affectionate one. I think it was started by someone in the choir, most things like that are,' she laughed.

'Oh well, I've been called worse.' Richard grimaced thinking of theological college where he was known as 'Di', short for 'Devine intervention' and the Peckham bail hostel where he'd pretended not to know his unprintable nickname. 'But I still don't understand. Do I look like him?'

'It's our names, dear.'

'Our names?'

'Yes, the family, we've got a John and a Paul, and I know you don't like it, but people call me George. So you're Ringo, Richard was his real name, you see? The four *Beatles*.'

Richard Devine considered this for a moment; he'd always rather liked the biblical association of his son's names. They'd both been George's suggestions, which he'd readily accepted unaware that her John and Paul had nothing to do with the Scriptures but were in fact messrs Travolta and Newman, who had respectively, at least in George's imagination, been present at their children's conceptions. Richard Devine wasn't sure how he felt about his family being named after a bunch of pop stars.

'Oh well, at least it's not *The Rolling Stones*,' he said.

It had started to rain again and they quickened their pace, soon reaching the now well-lit pub. Richard held the door open for his wife. 'Perhaps I ought to take up the drums.'

'I don't think so, dear.'

'No, you're probably right.'

CHAPTER TEN

Most of the villagers who'd been at the meeting and subsequent riot at the school hall had gathered in The Smuggler's Finger. People who had not set foot in the place for years, some because of their own private demons others because they didn't like its abrasive landlord, had given in to the post-traumatic herd instinct and followed the crowd.

All were now crammed into the pub. The bar was heaving and Sid was at his offensive best. He hadn't needed any encouragement from the vicar to rush back and get the doors open. Although he'd already anticipated a surge in business at the end of the evening the early disintegration of the meeting had been an unexpected bonus and one that Sid was now happily exploiting - he'd rounded-up all his prices ('...no bleedin' change mate.') and was cheerily dispensing drinks, insults and obscenities along the full length of the bar.

Telepathy or patience had ensured that Aaright had been waiting on the doorstep for Sid's return and despite the overcrowding they'd managed to claim their usual table and adopted their customary positions. Amidst the general roar of discussion their conversation was even more limited than usual but from time-to-time one or other of them would shake his head in amused disbelief and cackle delightedly.

Simon had also managed to claim his usual corner for himself and Mattie, but for the moment sat alone, watching and listening. Mattie had left her glass untouched and reluctantly taken her notebook in hand before setting off around the room to try to get some memorable quotes to pad out her article. He watched as she moved towards the vicar and his wife. George turned to meet Mattie and over her shoulder seemed to catch Simon's eye. She smiled although Simon wasn't quite sure whether the smile was for him or Mattie. He smiled back anyway.

Even some of the vestry Handwringers, alarmed and bewildered by the mayhem and violence at the school and in need of the reassuring presence of their vicar, had slipped shyly into the lounge end of the bar and now huddled in a tight little group around Richard Devine. Sid had never sold so much sweet sherry or pineapple juice.

Mattie didn't spend long amongst the vicar's little band of nervous disciples and soon moved on down to the other end of the bar where she was readily absorbed by the large and raucous Headbanger crowd. Various assorted hangers-on and opportunist thugs from around the area had reinforced the usual rugby players and Young Farmers and the group was still growing as bloodied stragglers who'd managed to dodge the police or convince them of their non-involvement made their way from school to pub. Bruises and grazed knuckles were proudly compared and the lager-fuelled bragging grew louder and more implausible. If even half of the violent episodes described had actually occurred Plompley Primary should have been a scene of utter carnage littered with the dead and dying.

The arrival of a real reporter, female, attractive and apparently credulous, amongst this volatile and drunken crowd predictably caused an increase in volume and male posturing. All expected to be quoted and: '... and spell the bloody name right!' was considered the height of original wit. Mattie, through gritted teeth, duly played her part, flattering and flirting and scribbling encouragingly in her notebook. Eventually, amongst all the outrageous stories one incident cropped up often enough that she thought there might actually be some truth in it; apparently the ultimate act of anarchy and highlight of the evening had been the setting off of a foam fire extinguisher in an unattended police car, with at least half of those present claiming responsibility for this act of hilarious daring. Tired of the beery breath, BO and bullshit Mattie decided that a luridly written account of this gem of un-attributable vandalism would be sufficiently shocking to catch the eye of *The Bugle*'s readers and she could now move on. The largely male group, however, was leeringly reluctant to let her go and Simon watched in amusement as she was forced to wriggle her way out of the mêlée. She'd reached the edge of the group and almost fought her way clear when he saw her whip round with a last snarl. A pinched bottom, Simon guessed.

'Having fun?'

'Bloody animals. Prats! They think they're so bloody clever, just because they filled up some poor sod of a policeman's car with bloody foam. Half of them didn't even know what the meeting was about, still don't, they were only there for a punch up! Apparently one of the rugby club knows the brother, or cousin, or something of that second guy in the hall tonight, the one in the checked shirt, so he tipped off a few mates and they thought they'd come along for a laugh!' She paused to sip her wine. 'Apparently those guys doing all the talking were meant to come along and stir things up a bit.'

'Well that certainly seemed to work.'

Mattie took another sip, 'Yeah, well, what's more they were paid to be there.'

'Naturally.'

'Guess who.'

Simon made a show of pretending to think, he raised his eyes to the beamed ceiling and exaggeratedly rubbed his chin, 'Now let me think...'

'Yeah, you've got it, the charming Sir George Hoggit. Makes it stink even more doesn't it?'

'Not surprising really. Anyway it doesn't really matter does it? Remember what your editor said, the story is the wind farm... and the riot... well, *riots* now. And of course Bunny Warren's arse, that certainly deserves a place back in the headlines after his efforts tonight. Forget all the dodgy conspiracy stuff, Mattie. Remember?'

Mattie scowled and banged her glass down. 'I'm going to see if I can get any sense out of doctor hyphenated,' she said, 'at least he doesn't look like the arse-pinching type.'

She'd probably have stalked if there'd been the room but instead Mattie was forced to weave and thread her way back towards the lounge end of the bar, where as well as the little vicarage clique the usual crowd had gathered, their numbers swollen by other groups who'd marched up from the school all determined that someone should hear their voices of outrage - even if it was only each other. The PAWs Off group seemed to have positioned itself at the centre of proceedings both physically and influentially, the tall lank figure of Dr Vincent-Townend providing a natural rallying totem. He was currently holding forth, his cultured and authoritative tones easily discernible above the general roar, whilst his skinny tousled wife, Guinness glass in hand, chivvied and marshalled strays around the edges of their group.

Left alone again Simon sipped at his flat beer and looked around. He tried to observe as he imagined a journalist or commentator might observe, noting the various groups, cliquey and disparate and all engrossed in their own debates and arguments. It was hard to believe that they had any common cause. The paradox acted as a sort of catalyst and an idea that had been tucked away somewhere in a neglected creative recess of his mind started to take form; here was the start of a plot, a story. Memorable phrases and streams of imagined dialogue started to occur to him and short scenarios enacted themselves in his mind's eye; the idea was becoming a possibility.

'Well that was interesting.'

Simon started.

'What were you smiling at?' Mattie looked at him curiously, her mood seemed to have lightened.

'Oh I was just thinking, bit of an idea I've had.'

'Oh, right. That Dr...' She checked her notebook, '...Vincent-Townend, had lots to say. Interesting bloke. He's not a *doctor* doctor, you know medicine, he's a doctor of history. He teaches at some university, lectures on the history of nutrition or something like that, and get this, his special interest is *cannibalism!*'

'Nice, pick up any recipes?'

'His wife's a doctor too. She runs some sort of centre providing re-hab, booze and drugs, you know.' Mattie flipped a sheet of her notebook, '... does voluntary stuff with the local Scouts too.'

Simon looked at her over his glass and raised a quizzical eyebrow.

'Anyway,' Mattie continued, 'between them they're really getting this PAWs Off lot well organised. He's convinced, well everyone is, that the village is being stitched up, even by its own parish council, and definitely by the Bartford planning people. The vicar thinks so too. He's pretty switched on actually. His wife's a funny little thing isn't she, do you think she's all there?'

'Oh yes, I think so.'

Mattie swivelled on her stool and looked round the bustling room.

'Well that's it for the moment I suppose.' She turned back to Simon. 'I've got what Rob wants, like you said: two riots for the price of one and now a trashed police car. He'll love that. I suppose I'd better go and see your Bunny and get his side of the story.'

'Hmm, yes, ok.'

'Well... I've enjoyed us, um, being... well, working together. A good team eh?' She immediately regretted the hearty games-mistress cliché.

Simon gave her a wry smile, 'Yes,' he said slowly, 'it's been interesting, an insight.'

She looked at him for a moment. 'Simon, I've decided I'm not going to let this thing go, this corruption story, it stinks, the whole Hallibut, Hoggit, council thing. They've obviously done a deal and they shouldn't be allowed to get away with it. Even if this sort of thing is going on all over the place and no one cares - and I don't believe that - it should be exposed. If I can write it someone will have the guts to print it. I don't care what Rob bloody Jordan says, I'm going to see it's bloody published!'

'And be damned presumably,' Simon smiled.

Mattie snorted and stood up.

'OK, OK, I believe you,' Simon lifted both hands in submission, 'but it doesn't sound like you'll change Jordan's mind.'

'Oh forget *The Bartford Bugle*!'

Simon nodded. 'Well, good luck with it then.'

'Yes, well, thanks, I thought you'd like to know.'

'Fine.'

Mattie looked down at him and after an awkward hesitation put out her hand. Taken by surprise, Simon shook it rather limply and then watched her thread her way back across the room. In a gesture he himself

170

didn't quite understand he picked up the half finished glass of wine and raised it to her retreating bottom.

For the rest of the evening The Smuggler's Finger became temporary campaign headquarters for the villagers. Strategy and tactics were discussed and seasoned lobbyists from previous protests as diverse as saving the whale to the restoration of hanging, dusted off their militant skills. Early on it had generally been agreed that village unity was the key, but as the evening went on and drink was taken earlier promising attempts at inter-group co-operation broke down in acrimony and heated personal exchanges. The Aarights happily cackled their way through the evening and Simon watched it all fascinated; he couldn't make out many individual conversations through the wall of sound but it was easy to interpret the protagonist's expressions and gesticulations and his imagination did the rest. He was absorbed.

'I didn't feel like going home.' Suddenly Mattie was standing over him, she had an unopened bottle of white wine in one hand and two glasses cupped in the other. 'Do you feel like getting drunk?'

'Hello Godfrey.'

'Eh?'

'It's me, Linda. How are you feeling?'

Even through the pain Bunny noted the use of his despised given name.

'Oh, could be worse.' He managed a nervous little laugh and craned his head round on the pillow. His wife stood near the foot of the bed and he could only see her head and shoulders above the pink-blanketed frame they'd erected over him. She moved to the side and Bunny lowered his cheek back onto the pillow, peering at her with his one available eye. She looked nice, smart, quite posh really, he couldn't remember seeing any of the clothes she was wearing before.

'Sorry about this, love,' he mumbled. It was more a whine than an apology and Linda ignored it.

'Does it hurt much?'

'Uh huh.'

'They're worried about the gas...' Bunny stiffened. '... the stuff they put in those light bulbs. No one here is quite sure what it is but they think it might be corrosive or poisonous or something. They're going to check.'

Bunny groaned.

'How are your... bits?'

Bunny lifted his head off the pillow. 'Bits? Oh them.' He lowered his head, 'I don't know... they won't let me look.'

Linda nodded. 'I've brought you some Liquorice Allsorts.'

'Thanks.'

'I've taken out all the pink bobbly ones.'

'Thanks.'

There was a long visiting-time silence.

'I was pushed you know, it wasn't...'

'Have the police been yet?'

Bunny sighed heavily. 'They came with me in the ambulance, took a statement. They say there shouldn't be any charges.'

Linda nodded again.

'They seemed to think it was all so very bloody funny...' Bunny burst out angrily, '... said they'd, "get to the bottom of it," thought it was a great joke. It's all very well but my arse has become a fucking laughing stock in this...'

'Don't swear, Godfrey!'

Bunny was shocked into silence, Linda never spoke to him like that. Something was definitely not right, the use of his Christian name was worrying in itself but this hardness, the apparent lack of sympathy, it just wasn't like her. Apart from the Liquorice Allsorts she just didn't seem that bothered about him. Bunny was hurt and confused.

'You look nice,' he said eventually.

'Thank you.' She looked down at herself critically and used both hands to smooth the silk blouse over her breasts, then with a glance towards the bed quickly fastened an extra button.

Bunny thought he could make out her nipples but wasn't sure. He switched his gaze to the unfamiliar pendant that glistened expensively on the exposed area of her chest.

'You're going to be here for a few days,' Linda said abruptly. 'They think some of the glass will come out by itself but they want to remove two more of the metal fittings ... apparently the screw ones are easy but the bayonet ones can be a bit tricky.'

Bunny's exposed eye opened further in horror and he groaned again.

'They may want to keep an eye on you for a little while. Anyway I probably won't be here when you get out. I've been asked away by a friend and I don't want to let her down.'

Bunny lay quite still, his confusion and hurt complete.

'Another holiday?' he managed to mumble.

'Well... yes.'

'For how long?' he said miserably.

Linda walked to the end of the bed out of Bunny's immediate line of sight. 'I'm not quite sure at the moment.'

As the expensive car swished its way through the rain and gathering gloom towards Bartford, Maxwell cheerfully tapped his fingertips on the steering wheel keeping time with the music from the radio. Over all, he decided, now it was over, the evening couldn't really have gone much better. That irritating old couple with their passive stoicism had left him strangely unsettled and that bloody vicar had managed to land a few blows, but Hoggit's hired thugs had certainly done their bit. Admittedly their attempts at reasoned pro-wind arguments had been risible but their disruptive qualities, as promised, had proved excellent and the intervention by the local yobbos had been an unexpected bonus. No, on the whole the evening had gone well... and it was still young! He grinned happily to himself at the thought of the delightful big-bosomed Chloe Jellaby waiting at the hotel. Hopefully by now she'd have recovered from the fit of hysteria prompted by witnessing the whimpering Bunny and his bloodied backside being rolled onto a stretcher. Maxwell strode confidently into the hotel lounge and any worries about his secretary's emotional state were soon dispelled. A scandalised shriek from a small huddle at the far end of the bar suggested that Chloe Jellaby might still be hysterical but she certainly wasn't in shock.

Walking into the lounge two hours earlier, alone and clearly shaken, Chloe had attracted the attention of two middle-aged men wedged into white leatherette stools at the far end of the bar. They were suited but tieless and turned out to be 'Senior Field Marketing Executives' peddling a revolution in carbon-fibre toilet seats. They'd hit their targets early in the day and were now relaxing with their expense accounts. Chloe allowed herself to be befriended, was talked out of her usual Babycham and found that she quite liked Cognac and Crème de Menthe - shaken together with crushed ice and drunk through a straw. The barman knew what was going on but he also knew that his passport was a very poor forgery and he needed this job, so triple Cognacs for the lady it was. Names were exchanged and backgrounds explained - Chloe Jellaby's at least were real. Things got predictably boisterous; the men's jokes got more risqué, the double entendres less subtle and a contrived reference to in-room hotel television had introduced the subject of sex. Having established that Chloe didn't have a friend who could join them the two men moved on from sly breast fondling to overtly stroking the top of a thigh each and started hinting at a threesome. Chloe, squirming and giggling drunkenly was too busy trying to keep her skirt below her crotch to get the point.

'Chloe. Miss Jellaby!'

'Piss off mate, three's company, four's a crowd.'

'Miss Jellaby, Chloe, are you...'

'Look mate, I told you...'

'Hello Maxie. 'S is my boss,' she slurred.

The party broke up after that, the toilet seat executives sulkily withdrawing, each accusing the other of not 'closing the deal' quickly enough.

The hotel was typical of the by-pass type of motel, modular in an open-plan way, anonymous, sterile and 're-launched' every two years. The donkey grey/muddy brown interior design team had swept through

Bartford the year before and the 'Inn' was now indistinguishable from numerous other hotels within about two hundred miles of London - the designers' murky wave was still rippling out over the rest of the country. The effect was a bleak but reliable uniformity. Bartford's motel, however, was different in one respect; it could boast an excellent restaurant. The décor was as to be expected but there was crisp white linen to soften the brown plastic upholstery, the menu and wine list were imaginative and the chef exceptional. Any trendy mid-city eatery would have snapped him up, but having arrived in the back of the same lorry as the barman and with equally dubious credentials he'd been shrewd enough to suppress his chef's ego and keep a low profile in the provinces - at least for the time being.

The growing reputation of the restaurant was the only reason Maxwell deigned to stay in the otherwise dreary hotel and he'd been looking forward to impressing Chloe Jellaby with his epicurean sophistication. He sat looking warily at her across the table and poured her another glass of mineral water. She'd obviously had far too much to drink and he'd had to practically carry her into the restaurant before bundling her into a corner booth. When the waiter appeared she'd snatched the proffered bread roll, hacked it in two, smeared both halves with a thick layer of butter and devoured it in seconds. To Maxwell's relief this seemed to have a slight sobering effect. Her voice became less slurred, her eyes more focused and he was gratified to find her interested in the menu and receptive to his guidance. He was starting to enjoy himself and ordered champagne.

Chloe giggled happily at the 'pop!', downed half a flute and picked a few random dishes from the extensive menu. She clearly had no idea what moules, or 'mules' as she insisted on calling them, were, but seemed delighted when they arrived. She looked owlishly at the finger bowl with its floating lemon slice.

'You don't drink it!' she eventually exclaimed.

'No.'

Maxwell poured more champagne and watched as Chloe demolished the garlic bread that had accompanied her mussels. Licking crumbs from her fingers she eyed the mound of steaming shells then turned back to the finger bowl, 'Wassit for then?'

He explained and then watched as she clumsily set about the shellfish, slurping down the residual liquor and swigging the Moet as quickly as he dared pour it. All of a sudden she gave him an uncertain smile, swallowed hard several times and crumpled back into her corner. Thanks to the combined attentions of the toilet seat reps and his own man-handlings the voluptuous Chloe now had one breast fully exposed and Maxwell realised that the evening probably wasn't going to progress as he'd hoped.

'Those are Miss Jellaby's,' he snarled five minutes later as he stalked through reception and tossed a set of keys onto the desk, 'you'll find her in the restaurant trying to extinguish your head waiter.'

It was unfortunate that Chloe's sudden unsteady dash for the ladies had coincided with the waiter at the next table tipping the warmed brandy into the flambé pan. Maxwell had watched in fascinated horror as the floored man had flailed around in dignified silence, his shirt front a mass of blue and orange flame, before being doused by the contents of Chloe's finger bowl... and then her stomach.

'Hello George.'

The chillingly familiar voice made Sir George jump in the big leather chair and he felt a deep icy stab somewhere in his enormous belly and a momentary slackening of his bowels. He cursed his recent tardiness in not locking the study door and slammed down the telephone. The chairman of the parish council, mid-sentence at the other end, was startled but not particularly surprised. Sir George could be abrupt. But at least he'd confirmed that following this evening's meeting the chairman's tenancy of the West Lodge would be renewed.

'George you look dreadful,' Lady Arabella said cheerfully, and was right. Sir George did not look at all well. He seemed to have swelled up inside his already tight clothing and any exposed flesh was mottled puce and grey. Blue veins stood out on his glistening forehead and his eyes were almost lost between sagging brows and puffy bags. And the deterioration was not all outward: his joints had swollen, his head ached permanently despite handfuls of pills, the slightest exertion made him wheeze and his breath was foul.

'I'm quite sure Mrs Bridges is looking after you so it must be self inflicted.' Lady Arabella looked pointedly at the half-full tumbler in her husband's hand and snorted her contempt. 'Right, George,' she continued briskly, 'there are one or two things I want to sort out. It won't take long, there's won't be any discussion but I don't want any misunderstandings later on. Is that clear?'

Sir George nodded cautiously. He hadn't said a word since his wife had appeared in his sanctuary and even if he'd known what to say he wasn't sure he'd recovered sufficiently to speak. God he needed a sip from that glass! He waved vaguely and belatedly towards the Chesterfield sofa.

'I won't sit down, *thank you*. I'm going to Sorento, George, to the house. I've informed the Carinis and they're expecting me. They'll continue to keep house and look after the garden and vines - and you will continue to pay them. I'll let you know when there are any other expenses as and when they occur. Oh, and I intend to have the pool enlarged.'

The flesh around Sir George's eyes stretched slightly and he gulped noisily. It was the only reaction he dared.

'I don't know how long I'll be there. You of course will not be welcome,' Lady Arabella said without any real enmity, 'and I shall be taking a friend.'

Sir George's mouth worked flabbily as if he possibly intended to speak but his priority at the moment was the contents of the glass in front of him and as his wife turned to survey the books and paintings of the panelled room, as if for the last time, he clumsily slopped half of it into his grateful mouth.

'I shall take the Range Rover of course and...' She took a step towards the desk, fixing steely eyes on where she knew her husband's were, '...I shall require an increase in my allowance, twenty-five percent will do for the moment.' She skewered Sir George with her stare until he nodded reluctant agreement. Lady Arabella nodded and turned away. A sigh from Sir George turned into a fit of coughing as he tried to expel air and swallow whiskey at the same time. His wife looked down at him for a moment, her face an ugly mask of contempt, disgust and anger.

'You're upsetting a great many people in this village, George, my village. You're making decent people very unhappy, ruining lives, do you realise that? You and your cronies on the council and your slimy little 'yes' men with their phoney reports, and your offshore bankers and your bullying and cheating and lying and greed and that bloody ego. You disgust me, all of you...'

Sir George stared fixedly ahead.

'There was a meeting at the school this evening...' Lady Arabella continued, '...about your bloody wind farm. It turned into a riot - oh yes I've heard, George - and I wonder whose fault that was! The police were called. People got hurt, George.'

He managed to stop himself shrugging and remained motionless like a child under the blankets who hears a noise in the night. This wouldn't go on much longer. Lady Arabella gave a last equine snort and turned towards the door. His hand was already on the decanter when she suddenly turned back.

'I almost forgot; the stables, don't interfere with my yard, George. I've got it all organised, everyone knows what they've got to do and the girls will keep me up to date and let me know about any problems.'

This aspect of a prolonged absence by his wife hadn't occurred to Sir George and he was considerably cheered by the thought of the carnal opportunities the un-chaperoned stable yard could present. His flush of anticipation was, however, short lived.

'Oh, and by the way, George go gently on little Becky... she's in foal. I thought you'd like to know, better make sure you've got some DNA spare.'

In the pub the evening had reached the point where even the most opinionated groups found they were just making the same points and repeating the same opinions as they had been an hour or two before. The futility of wind power had been established, the natural beauty of Spout Hill reaffirmed, the greed of many (but not all) landowners condemned and anyone holding public office, at any level, had been accused of everything from indifference to corruption. Nothing much else was going to happen tonight; everyone was tired, many were bored and *Newsnight* was about to start. People began to drift off home.

Richard Devine had long been ready to leave. His earlier performance in the school hall had left him drained, the subsequent violence had depressed him and he was struggling not to show his irritation at the constant bleating of the Handwringers. He muttered a few quiet words to George, smiled reassurances to his huddle of remaining disciples and moved quickly towards the door. Here, in a carefully orchestrated ambush he was intercepted by the chairman of PAWs Off who'd earmarked the vicar as a potentially valuable new recruit. Richard Devine, however, had had enough - *damn wind farms and all those involved with them* - it was time to go home, home to his raggedy old dressing gown, a glass of last year's elderberry and a taped episode of *Father Ted*. Curtly he explained that he didn't think it would be appropriate for him to be associated with any particular group and giving his anorak a vigorous matador's shake neatly disappeared behind it and out the door.

A bit abrupt, Gordon Vincent-Townend thought but it had been worth a try. He hurried back to his now-shrinking group and noted the fresh pint of Guinness in his wife's hand. 'We *do* have an early start, Lucy,' he hissed.

'And a late finish!' Lucy roared happily, blowing the foamy head off the beer at him. 'Bloody good!' she hiccupped half a pint later, foamily mustachioed.

'Lets talk about anything except wind farms.'

Richard and George Devine, ignoring the steady rain, were walking slowly towards the vicarage. Neither had said anything for a few moments, the rain rattling on their hoods.

'This weather is dreadful,' Richard said at last. 'It must be one of the worst summers for years.'

George murmured her agreement.

'Some sunshine would be nice wouldn't it?' Richard added wistfully. They walked on.

'Actually I've been invited to sunny Italy.'

'Oh that's nice, dear, do you think you'll go?'

George thought for a moment. 'I don't think so, there's so much to do here: the mother's group is having a bit of a crisis and of course there's the boys.'

'Oh I'm sure us chaps could cope for a few days... you know, on prayer and Pot Noodles,' Richard laughed.

'I know you could.' She squeezed his hand.

'Who's the invite from by the way?'

'Arabella Hoggit and Linda Warren.'

'Oh yes, they're lesbians now, I gather.'

'Yes, that's right.'

'Not really your thing is it, dear?'

'No, not really.'

The condition of his exuberant wife was not the chairman of PAWs Off's only worry. During his brief absence there'd been an attempted coup. While he'd been distracted trying to woo the vicar, and Lucy had obviously been busy at the bar, that bloody Scott Driver had seen his chance and started banging on again about the committee using his and Nicole's place for meetings, or more specifically the appalling art-deco-themed conservatory they'd recently added to The Old Manse. Gordon Vincent-Townend knew that this arrangement would be the thin end of the wedge; the ambitious newcomers would have gained another foothold close to the heart of village affairs and next it would be the committees and chairmanships that controlled them - *his* committees and chairmanships. He rejoined the group, had a few quick words with some of the more prominent members, loudly announced that he looked forward to seeing everyone at 7.30 on Wednesday evening '... *at our place*,' bade an abrupt 'good night' and dashed for the door propelling his startled wife before him. They didn't stop for several hundred yards, not until Gordon

Vincent-Townend felt well clear of any possible dissent, and it was only now, as he fumbled with the zip of his anorak, that he noticed Lucy was still clutching her pint glass.

'Oh God!' he sighed.

'What happened there?'

'We left.'

'So I see!' She took a sip from her glass. 'Why?'

'We've got an early start. And anyway the bloody Drivers were starting to get uppity again and...'

'Aah, of course! So what happened then?'

'What do you mean, "...what happened..."?'

'Well I wasn't paying much attenshun, so who won?' She swung unsteadily around, glass held aloft, and addressed the shadows: 'where will the heart of our fine village beat henceforth? Will it be the humble doctor's cobwebby dining room or is it to be that... that temple of hedonishm, the Gatsby knocking shop?' She chuckled into the foamy glass.

'It's not funny, Lucy. But anyway, as you obviously weren't listening, *we're* having the usual meeting on Wednesday.'

'Oh goodie.' She tossed her empty glass over a garden wall.

'Bloody incomers,' he muttered.

'I thought we were bloody incomers.'

'Yes, but not in the same way.'

'Oh I see.'

He gave her a sour look.

'No one's fooled by that donation to the cricket club,' he said suddenly. 'It was blatant, a couple of new side screens and he thinks he owns the place. Bats anywhere in the order he fancies and straight onto the pavilion committee ... everyone knows he wants the chair ... it's only a matter of buying a few more bloody votes. Money talks,' he added in jealous disgust.

'I wonder if he'd do something with the Scouts.'

'I shouldn't be at all surprised.'

'Gordon!' She gave him a playful shove and as he struggled to keep his feet let out a delighted shriek, galloped forward a few yards and landed squarely feet together in a large greasy puddle. 'Oooh, I'm singing in the rain, just singing in the rain...' she warbled.

'Oh God, Lucy, not now please'

The barrage of noise from the bar end of the room had finally persuaded the rest of Sid's customers, even the charming Drivers and their growing band of supporters, that it was time to leave. Having checked that the Vincent-Townends were out of sight this group guiltily trouped off towards the controversial conservatory, curious for a taste of the jazz age and more to the point some of Scotts's famous Armagnac. Meanwhile Sid decided it was time to sort out the Headbangers. Apart from Simon and his reporter lady, who, Sid was amused to note, had spent the evening ignoring the rest of the pub and working their way through three bottles of his over-priced Pinot Grigio, the only customers he had left were the rowdy gang of rugby playing young farmers. The noise and bad language was one thing, but Sid knew it was only a matter of time before tempers were lost, fists started to fly and something, and probably someone, got broken. Sid also knew that when they did leave it wouldn't be quietly, so the earlier the better. He certainly didn't want trouble with the neighbours or the licensing people just at the moment. Years of bitter and sometimes painful experience had taught him that to wade straight into an over-excited, late-evening crowd and try to exert control through reason or authority could be near suicidal. It was a matter of suggestion and psychology, or put another way: disingenuity and animal cunning.

Even Simon and Mattie looked up at the sudden bellows of masculine laughter, foul-mouthed shouts of approval and shrill female whoops of encouragement. They watched in bemusement as a grinning Sid emerged from the heart of the Headbanger mob accompanied by hearty slaps on the back and handshakes. One enormous very drunk front row even ruffled his hair. Sid ducked beneath the bar and disappeared, there was no question of last orders and he obviously expected the mob to just move on, which to Simon and Mattie's amazement was exactly what they did. As the main door shut for the last time Sid shot out from behind the bar, dropped the latch, slammed a couple of bolts across and flicked a bank of switches putting most of the pub into darkness. He looked over towards Simon and Mattie and grinned.

'How did you manage that, Sid, without getting your head kicked in?'

Sid kicked his usual stool into place and slumped down on it wearily. The inevitable half-pint glass had somehow appeared in his hand and he looked archly at Simon. 'Psychology, mate.'

Simon looked blank but Mattie nodded knowingly with the wisdom of the drunk.

'Well bullshit really,' Sid admitted. 'You've got to distract 'em... give 'em something more interesting to do, see? Anyway hang on a tick I've got to call the old bill.' He stood up and moved towards the bar.

'Why, what's happened?' Simon called after him, looking blearily around for some previously unnoticed criminal act taking place in a shadowy corner.

'Nothing yet, but any minute now their motor is gonna be bobbing down the Bart. Thought I ought to let 'em know, that's all.' He disappeared behind the bar.

'Could be a story in that,' Mattie said carefully.

Simon eyed her sceptically while he tried to make out what Sid was saying on the telephone. It was a short call and Sid was soon back at their table, the half-pint pot full and clutching two opened bottles of lager.

'Here you go, my children, something to flush through the kidneys. Not driving are you? No, thought not.' He looked from one to the other and grinned.

'What did the police say, Sid?'

Sid sipped an inch of his bitter. 'Very grateful they were,' he said smugly, 'shame more landlords don't behave so responsible, that sort of thing.' He took a large self-congratulatory swig.

Mattie pecked gingerly at the neck of her lager bottle. 'How do you know the police car is going to float down the River Bart, Sid?'

'Cos it's full of foam, bound to.'

' No, I mean how do you know it's in the river?'

'Because about now that lot that's just gone screamin' outta here will be busy bunging it in, that's how.'

Simon and Mattie both stared at the smirking landlord.

'Now I wonder where they got that idea from,' Simon mused.

'I wonder,' Sid acknowledged.

Mattie looked from one to the other and gasped 'Sid! You...!'

CHAPTER ELEVEN

'**D**id you know your garden's under water?'

Simon started and smelled coffee. The bed heaved and a cool draft slipped under the duvet accompanied by a body. He let out a small involuntary groan and turned towards the voice feeling strangely shy and for some reason a bit sheepish.

'Morning.' It was all he could think of to say.

Mattie smiled down at him. She looked remarkably fresh and appeared to be naked, at least from the waist up. Simon lifted a knee, carefully adjusted his own nakedness and shut his eyes again.

'Have you ever done that before?'

'Eh?' his eyes snapped open. 'What? Oh I see what you mean... er, no... well not quite like that anyway.'

'No, me neither.' It was said with obvious satisfaction as if a long held ambition had been achieved. 'Have you got a cigarette?'

Simon heaved himself to a sitting position and confirmed that Mattie was indeed half naked. 'I don't smoke.'

'Not even after sex?'

'I don't know - I've never looked.'

She gave him a withering look. 'That's not original, clever or funny,' she said, but was smiling as she handed him a mug of coffee. It was black without sugar - he liked it white with two when he was hung over but he sipped at it anyway. They sat, knees up, nursing the coffee mugs as the brightness that had filled the small, beamed room steadily dimmed and rain started to splatter against the little window.

Mattie looked at the streaked glass. 'Your garden's flooded.'

'I know. There's a little stream behind the hedge at the back, well not so little at the moment, it comes down off the hill...'

'Spout Hill?'

185

'Yes, I suppose so. It comes out of the hillside about half way up, like a spring or underground stream or something. It burst its banks weeks ago and every time it rains I lose a bit more garden. Saves mowing I suppose.' He sipped his coffee and grimaced. 'Breakfast?'

The ordered domesticity of Simon's kitchen surprised Mattie. They sat at a small table under the window and fed their hangovers orange juice and bacon sandwiches. The kitchen smelled faintly of oil from the Aga, fresh coffee and the bacon, the homeliness emphasised by the foul weather thrashing outside. Mattie insisted on washing up and stood looking down the garden over the chipped old butler's sink. Simon had been surprised and amused at her child-like delight when a pair of mallards suddenly appeared through the hedge and up-ended their way across the flooded lawn.

'What'll you do if it reaches the door?' Mattie asked.

Simon thought for a moment. 'Go to the pub.'

Mattie gave him a wry grin and dried her hands. 'Just what I was thinking.'

'Bit early isn't it?'

'My car, remember? Some of us have to get to work.'

'Ah yes. So what are you going to do now?'

'What do you mean, "do"?'

'Well the paper, or at least your editor, wants one thing but from what you were saying last night you've got other ideas. The corruption thing - how are you going to work it?'

Mattie sat down again. 'Do both,' she said. 'I'll go in now and write a lurid account of last night's little fracas, exaggerate the bloodshed, beef up a few quotes and basically feed Rob's nasty tabloid tastes and then as the in-house expert on Plompley, I'll offer to follow up the wind farm story. I can cover all the boring planning and technical stuff and so on, which will give me the perfect excuse to keep a private eye on any dodgy goings on round here and the dodgy characters doing them. Beyond that what I do in my own time is my business, I've got a few ideas to move things on. I've asked Uncle Benny - the builder, you remember - to keep his eyes and ears open round the Hallibut's place and I've already done a bit more sniffing around at the council. You and I both know there's something going on here, it's just a matter of filling in a few gaps ... proof really I suppose ... and then finding someone with the balls to publish it.' Mattie flicked a crumb off the table. 'So what about you?'

'What do you mean?'

'Well, when I walked in last night, the second time...' she added with a little smile, '...you were miles away, something about an idea or something. More writing?'

'Yes,' Simon said slowly, 'It's just a thought at the moment but...'

'More revelations from a musing countryman perhaps,' she laughed, 'Stop Press! ... "Frogspawn discovered growing legs! Salmon seen jumping! Cuckoos heard in spring!" Simon dismissed the sarcasm with a slightly raised eyebrow. Mattie grinned back, 'Yeah all right, sorry but seriously I'd like to know.'

Simon hesitated for a moment. 'I've had an idea for a book,' he said. 'It came to me in the pub after the meeting... or riot if you prefer. Take this whole small community thing; there's your ready-made cast of weird and wonderful characters, all sparking off each other one minute and taking chunks out of each other the next. And then the plot; well there's this corrupt threat they've all got to fight, which somehow seems to unite them and right in the middle of it all I thought I'd have an investigative journalist.'

"I'll sue.'

'Mine's a rugged, intrepid *him*.'

'OK, I'll call off the lawyers ... not autobiographical then?'

'Thanks. Anyway, just an idea at the moment. Right I think it's eased off a bit, I'll walk up to the pub with you. Fend off Sid.'

Mattie was pulling on her coat. 'Oh Sid's quite sweet really.'

'So you said last night. I put it down to the Pinot.'

There was no sign of Sid when they reached the pub. Mattie had left her car round the back in the potholed car park where they'd first met and as she dug out her keys Simon glanced across to the soggy bonfire pile and the old pub sign, partially charred but still recognisable.

'What are you looking at?' It was starting to rain heavily again and Mattie had the car door open.

'Just the old sign over there on the bonfire. Do you know it's funny, somehow there's something familiar about it. Weird.'

'Do you want a lift back down the hill?'

He said he'd walk, clear his head, and Mattie drove away, any awkward goodbyes conveniently curtailed by the weather.

Brimming with outraged fervour they may have been but over the next few weeks it slowly occurred to the protesting residents of Plompley that at this stage they didn't have anything to protest against. The planning application had yet to be submitted to Bartford Council and until such time as it was the local people, frustratingly, weren't involved. After a meeting or two with nothing much to discuss, and some naïve optimists even claiming that the strength of feeling shown at the parish council meeting had frightened the developers away, most groups were quietly dissolved, or at least put in suspension.

On the other side of the fight, however, the activity was frenetic. At the centre of the web was Sir George, who despite regular and detailed briefings had convinced himself that he was being kept in ignorance regarding progress. The problem was that he rarely listened properly to the answers to his snapped questions and when he did, being semi-coherently drunk, he forgot them immediately. If Sir George *had* stopped to listen he'd have learnt that the plans for his wind farm were making very sound progress and by the usual standards of such large and controversial developments remarkably quickly.

The key to the expediency was the level of collusion that had been established between Hallibut, Maxwell and Wormold to ensure the planning application in its final form contained only opinions, data and conclusions that were irrefutably supportive. If 'case officer' Hallibut identified an unhelpful section in a report or submission it would be discreetly highlighted and then passed back to Maxwell at Ref Watt, who would draft an amendment and pass it on to Wormold and his laptop, whose job it was to make any changes appear technically plausible by amending the data and field records as necessary. It would then be returned to Maxwell for a final spin and polish before being re-submitted to Hallibut who would place it on the file having removed and destroyed the inconvenient original. During this process the council experienced repeated and inexplicable IT problems; the planning department's website in particular seemed to be gremlin-prone, whilst planning officer Hallibut was rarely at his desk, his diary apparently filled with back-to-back meetings. In effect, there was really no way for a member of the public or the press to get any idea of what was going on with the proposed Spout Hill wind farm.

At the discreetly luxurious business park offices of RefWatt Green Energy plc Maxwell was absent-mindedly fondling Chloe Jellaby's bottom and admiring Wormold's latest work of fiction, a screen full of curves and tiny coloured crosses that supposedly proved that not a single resident would hear a single whisper of noise from the giant Spout Hill wind turbines. Maxwell had been down this route many times before; he felt confident and in control and was almost ready to launch the next phase of the operation. This would start with a potent mixture of alarmist misinformation and Green mumbo-jumbo, which would bombard the hapless residents, who in due course would be pilloried with accusations of selfish ignorance and Nimbyism before finally being bullied and shamed into accepting the inevitability of a wind farm in their landscape. Press releases to counter every possible argument from residents were already drafted and ready to send at the push of a button, including several lightly veiled attacks on the characters of likely prominent protesters. Sheaves of ambiguous pro-forma letters of support were ready to be topped and tailed, usually by unsuspecting shoppers cornered by earnest young 'researchers' on the high streets of towns miles from the wind farm site, or if time and resources were short, RefWatt employees using the phone directory and varying handwriting styles. Usually this same group would also be instructed to take to the local streets and lanes to steal or vandalise the more vulnerable of the resident's protest signs, although on this occasion Sir George had said he would provide the necessary yobs and on the evidence of the riot at the school hall no one had argued. Maxwell sighed contentedly and suddenly aware of the firm plumpness in his left hand, squeezed. His right hand reached out to click 'send'.

Hallibut was not so happy. Admittedly the wind farm application was coming together well; it was easy tailoring Maxwell's and Wormold's data to fit ambiguous council policies and he had no doubt that Cockburn would ensure that members of the appropriate committees would toe the line. But Hallibut was nervous, he knew his contribution to the successful outcome of this development was in a different league to previous 'co-operations' and the unexplained arrival of journalists at his home had rattled him. It hadn't done anything to improve the humour of his wife either, who was not enjoying the wet school holidays in the company of bored children and muddy builders. It also seemed to Hallibut that colleagues were looking at him differently, especially the revolting Radar whose knack of disappearing into the office maze and silently materialising within earshot was particularly unnerving at the moment. The frequency of phone calls from Sir George was also attracting comment and the summons to see the head of Human Resources had been particularly worrying. Supposedly the meeting was to inform Hallibut that several switchboard operators had complained about Sir George Hoggit's behaviour on the telephone when asking for Hallibut, which he invariably did. Sir George was unacceptably rude and aggressive it seemed. All through the interview Hallibut had the feeling that there was something else that really interested Human Resources and this 'advisory briefing' was just an excuse to probe. The manager had seemed more interested in the content and frequency of Sir George's calls than their tone, and the implacable stare and hanging silence that followed each question left Hallibut with the feeling that he was being interrogated rather than briefed. He'd returned nervously to his office, got a knowing wink from Radar and found two more telephone messages from Sir George.

Claude Cockburn was also facing some unexpected challenges. For once, he wasn't getting all his own way - and he didn't like it. Several recent by-elections had inconveniently allowed in a couple of free spirits whom he hadn't yet had time to bully, bribe or blackmail into line. Even more worrying, they were having a disruptive influence on some of the other usually pliable councillors who were threatening to disrupt the council leader's personal agenda by brazenly voting the *wrong* way. Decisive action was needed to regain control, but probably a case for cunning and carrot rather than threats and stick he decided ... at least for the moment. He authorised a 'conference away-day'. The single topic would be: *To make members and officers aware of the need for consensual accord and collective responsibility within council committees and other working bodies.* The new freethinkers were top of the delegate's list, followed by the recent voting rebels and then by those showing early signs of disloyalty or independence. Non-attendance was not an option. Aware of the diverse tastes and interests of his colleagues, Cockburn insisted that the event should be held in Brighton and involve an overnight stay. To ensure sufficient numbers and to emphasise the democratic and inclusive character of his administration he insisted that the number of elected delegates should be matched by a similar number of council employees. Attendance for this group had of course been optional but it was well known that careers could be made... or broken, at such gatherings. On the whole the event had proved a success, at least for Cockburn; he'd acquired some startling new material on several key committee members and certain waverers had inadvertently dropped their guards, knew it, and would soon be back in line. Best of all, it turned out that one of the awkward newcomers who Cockburn had already established was married, a sidesman at his local evangelical church and chaired the Police Liaison Committee, had some peculiarly revolting vices - tastes that even freewheeling Brighton and half a dozen of its gay community had struggled to satisfy. The new member also seemed unaware that mobile phones came with cameras these days.

That was the plus side. There had, however, been some unfortunate fall out. The expense to start with. He'd specifically instructed that individual mini-bars should be well stocked and put no restrictions on the use of the hotel's restaurants and bars. The drinks bill on its own had been phenomenal and stories of individual profligacy were legion. Amongst the more lurid reports it was rumoured that the chair of the Women's Interests Committee had instructed her spa-bath be filled with champagne, which she had then shared with two six-formers from Roedean and a bemused but delighted bellboy, apparently invited to provide 'socio-economic balance'. Aware of his class-warrior colleague's tastes, both epicurean and sexual, Cockburn was quite prepared to believe the account. The group membership of the hotel spa had also been ludicrously expensive but fruitful, with both the Jacuzzi and steam room being put to a variety of imaginative uses. The resulting photographic images were steamy but the subjects, on the whole, recognisable. On balance, Cockburn decided, although the excercise had been expensive both in terms of cash and criticism if it helped to re-establish his authority it would have been worth it. And anyway he'd soon arrange for the cost to be buried amongst much larger examples of council profligacy and it would soon be forgotten. The complaints of sexual harassment, however, might need a more considered response. He knew it was important that he adopt the politically correct stance of paternal concern and shocked outrage and be seen to be taking his staff's concerns seriously. He decided to jump on the issue and let it be known that he was keen for a meeting with the head of Human Resources and the union representatives in order to address the matter as soon as possible. They responded as anticipated.

On this occasion Cockburn waived the usual fifteen-minute 'stewing time' but was surprised when it was only the head of HR who was ushered into the office. He knew little about this relatively new employee beyond his surname, Moody, and that he'd had an unremarkable police career. Moody walked briskly across the office and ignoring the low sofa pulled up a high-backed chair, sat down uninvited and fixed Cockburn with a confident and expectant stare. There was something about the stillness, the unblinking eyes, a feeling that Mood somehow ... knew, that Cockburn found unsettling.

'Er, on your own? I thought the union people were attending. I was keen to hear their views,' Cockburn said ingratiatingly.

Moody looked at him steadily for a moment. 'They're happy for me to represent them and their members on this occasion.'

Cockburn was impressed. It wasn't like the bolshie union reps to give up the chance for a dreary Trot rant and a bit of management and councillor bashing. He'd expected them to really get their teeth into a tasty bit of sexual harassment.

'Right, yes. Well this is all most regrettable, such a successful bonding weekend too in every other way. Er, I suppose these people, the complainants, they haven't changed their minds? You know, for the sake of colleague solidarity or something?' He looked at the implacable face across the desk. 'No, no, I suppose not. So what's to be done?'

Moody, without notes and in a steady voice, listed the names of the four claimants: three were female, one possibly Asian, the last clearly male.

'Er, nothing racist being suggested is there?' Cockburn whispered.

Moody ignored him. 'They all allege that during the council-organised bonding weekend they were harassed, had their private space invaded and to one extent or another, were effectively abused. Alcohol seems to have been a common factor and all the alleged offences were of a sexual nature... involving extreme perversion in the last case.'

This was worse than Cockburn had thought, and he still couldn't quite get the niggle out of his mind that a member of an ethnic minority might have been involved. 'Um, what would you suggest?' he asked warily.

Moody considered him coldly. 'A clean settlement,' he said, 'draw a line under the matter.'

'Oh yes!' Cockburn breathed fervently.

'Well there must have been *some* bonding going on over the weekend,' Moody said, 'apart from the obvious... because none of the claimants feel inclined to press any sort of charge or accusation against specific colleagues - or elected members.' He let the accusation hang for a moment. 'They're not looking for revenge or to cause any embarrassment to the council.'

Cockburn brightened. 'Well that's remarkably...'

'But,' Moody snapped, 'they do expect their ordeals to be acknowledged and to receive some form of compensation, both emotional and financial.'

Cockburn looked wary again. 'What do they have in mind?'

'In order to have the time and space to fully recover, for the emotional scars to heal, they are each to be granted a months leave... on full pay. And each is to receive ten thousand pounds.'

Cockburn winced and tried to work out how that could be lost in the accounts without attracting comment.

Moody knew exactly what he was thinking. 'The funds can be provided from the Hardship Fund,' he added. 'There'll be no awkward questions, no one knows what it's for anyway.'

He was right, no one was quite sure why this murky pool of money existed and an appropriate use for it had never been clearly defined so its appearance in the accounts was always unquestioned and vague. A precise description of the proposed four transactions would not be required.

Cockburn couldn't believe his luck. At the very least he'd been anticipating demands for tribunals, sackings, and even worse, six-figure compensation. Not to mention the attentions of the press. 'So,' he said, 'if that can be agreed no more will be said about the matter, is that right?'

Moody nodded. 'The individuals concerned have already signed agreements to that effect and as long as they're happy so is the union.'

'No talking to the press?'

Moody shook his head, 'No.'

'Done!' Cockburn leapt to his feet, his hand thrust eagerly across the enormous desk.

Moody didn't move, or even blink. 'You're acquainted with Sir George Hoggit I understand,' he said.

Cockburn froze.

'Are you aware of how close one of your planning officers is working with Hoggit on a particularly controversial development that Hoggit is proposing?'

Cockburn found the edge of his chair, he sat down and took a deep breath.

'I'm aware that Sir George and Lady Hoggit are proposing to build a very welcome Green energy generator, a wind farm, on their land,' he said coldly, 'and that they're consulting with our officers to make sure that proper procedures are followed and that the proposal is given due and fair consideration.'

'Quite so,' Moody murmured, 'however, it's been brought to my attention that in this case the officer, a Clive Hallibut, seems to be taking what could be deemed an inappropriate interest. There's even a suggestion that it's him who's preparing this application - clearly a potential conflict of interest.' Cockburn opened his mouth to speak but Moody quickly carried on. 'It seems that Hallibut and Hoggit meet regularly, in work hours and socially. To some people it might appear that *our* planning officer was actually working for this applicant ... which would, of course, raise the question of *payment.*'

'I think at this point I should make it clear that I too have had contact with Sir George and Lady Hoggit,' Cockburn said quickly. 'They did me the honour of asking me to open their garden fete, you may have seen it in the paper, and naturally we socialised at the event. So I too have had contact with these landowners,' he gave a little laugh, 'but I certainly don't work for them.'

'I hardly think that's relevant.'

Moody's apparent lack of interest restored some of Cockburn's confidence, 'As a matter of fact,' he continued, 'I had a brief meeting with Hallibut and Tom Gander, the senior planning officer, about this very scheme. It could be a very important development for the county, and it's something I think this council could support as a matter of fact.'

Moody nodded slightly. 'I believe this officer, Hallibut, has been involved in a little controversy before, a business park that floods I gather. This, I understand, also involved Sir George Hoggit... and the police.'

It was Cockburn's turn to be dismissive. 'That was all dealt with some time ago quite satisfactorily. If you think this officer is acting in any way inappropriately then by all means lay the facts before me but really you should speak to his line manager, and he'll no doubt mention it to the Chief Executive ... lines of command, you were a policeman, you'll know all about them.' He picked up his glasses and a pen and pulled a file towards him. The meeting was over.

Moody remained seated and quite still for some moments. Finally he rose to his feet, looked thoughtfully round the opulent office and turned towards the door.

Cockburn glanced up at his retreating back. 'By the way, exactly who is it that thinks this...' he pretended to forget the name, '...this whatsisname, Haddock, who is it that thinks he's on the take?' He immediately regretted the question, and the flippant reference to corruption.

The corners of Moody's mouth twitched. 'Just something I heard,' he said.

This was literally true; some days before Moody had come across two figures huddled suspiciously in a corner of the underground carpark. The old copper's instincts had kicked in and naturally he'd wanted to hear what was being said and by whom. He'd edged himself close enough to hear most of the conversation and to see that it was between an attractive young woman and a grubby old man in a revolting cardigan, who, Moody thought, he'd seen around the offices. Both were smoking and to his mind made a suspiciously unlikely pair. The young woman was doing most of the talking and asking a lot of questions. Both Hallibut and Hoggit's names came up regularly, there had been the odd reference to Claude Cockburn and Moody definitely caught the words 'wind farm'. He decided the young woman was probably a journalist. Moody was well aware of rumours concerning Hallibut's probity from his earlier enquiry, the enquiry that had damned Hallibut's promotion, but it was the mention of Cockburn's name that kept him listening. As the pair finished their cigarettes and ground out the stubs Moody slipped away to make some notes.

Cockburn, of course, knew of none of this, but once the office door had clicked securely shut he slumped back in his chair with a nervous sigh. This he did not need, especially at this point in the electoral cycle.

Could he somehow get Moody moved ... or sacked ... promoted even? He reached for his private line and stabbed '1'.

'Rennie?' The question was unnecessary, the phone at the other end was always picked up immediately and only ever by one person, his formidable electoral agent. 'Those two large donations we got recently,' said Cockburn, 'there's a couple of things I want you to double check...' He explained his reasons and then listened intently for a few minutes. When Rennie had finished Cockburn gently replaced the receiver and nodded in satisfaction; if anyone was going to come unstuck over this bloody wind farm it was not going to be Prospective Parliamentary Candidate Claude Cockburn.

CHAPTER TWELVE

The phoney war continued through the second half of the sodden summer. The sun was lower, the days were shorter and there'd even been the odd foggy evening by the time Hallibut was satisfied that his planning application and all the supporting reports, statistics and environmental assessments fully complied with council policy - or that council policy now fully complied with the reports, statistics and environmental assessments. The enormous bundle was formally submitted and registered and in due course, in line with their legal obligations the council, with ill-concealed reluctance, advertised the fact that the application had been received and started going through the motions of consulting near neighbours and residents. The process was, to say the least, half hearted; the statutory announcement in the local press was minute and mysteriously appeared in the lonely hearts column; flimsy paper notices were loosely pinned to remote telegraph poles and soon blew away or were attacked by curious crows; the letters sent to individual residents were all dispatched second class, hilariously misaddressed and inexplicably bearing Glasgow post codes - most never arrived.

But with the submission of the application the phoney war was definitely over and hostilities could commence. Protest meetings were convened, committees re-appointed and fundraising started. Those who had drifted away during the hiatus became re-engaged swelling the numbers of protesters until almost every one in Plompley was involved at some level. Attempts were again made by the more tactically astute to try and persuade all the groups to unite, to campaign under one outraged umbrella and to pool resources. But minor feuds and major egos remained stumbling blocks and it was a motley and disparate collection of groups and individuals who set out to fight their own lonely battles against the combined forces of Maxwell's RefWatt organization, Sir George Hoggit's thugs and a biased and corrupt council.

The first to come out fighting were some of the bigger and wealthier local landowners. The area was peppered with ancient titles, estates and families and most, even the post 17th century *new money*, were one way or another well-connected; some through political friends and affiliations, others with the press, the judiciary or the City - and in one case organised crime. Letters started to appear in the quality papers one or two of which also ran brief supportive articles or commentaries. Maxwell had anticipated this well-heeled assault and immediately mobilised his usual stable of influential and financially motivated letter-writing supporters, who obligingly bombarded their left wing media outlet of choice with glib praise for Maxwell's latest project whilst condemning the 'selfish ignorance' of any who dared resist. Even Sir George, unbeknownst to him, had a letter published in *The Guardian*, which obligingly followed it up with a laughably biased editorial. Having effecively neutralised the first wave of protest Maxwell moved on to engage with the next group of protesters.

The Handwringers were never going to pose a major threat on their own but Maxwell was wary of the vicar so the activities of the little group of church-going tea drinkers were discreetly monitored. It was noted that their numbers had grown slightly, more little protest signs had appeared in cottage windows throughout the village and they'd taken on a new stridency. The Sunday after the church organist had spotted the planning notice in *The Bugle's* lonely-hearts column the post-communion gathering in the vestry had decided by a slim majority that their original signs were too timid. 'No Wind Farm - Thank You' was deemed too polite and it was proposed, and duly seconded, that the 'Thank You' should be dropped. The debate was at times quite heated and as tea went cold and biscuits uneaten there were accusations of intolerance and, unthinkably, even rudeness. Several compromises were explored; a replacement 'Thanks' was considered to be informal but still adequately polite by some and the replacement of 'Thank You' by 'Please' had its supporters. But after lengthy negotiations, during which an exasperated Richard Devine had made his excuses, it was finally decided that a blunt 'No Wind Farm' would be The Handwringer's message. Although there were still dissenters, old-fashioned, independent-minded and above all polite, who insisted on retaining the original wording.

Richard Devine had taken his frustrations into the vicarage kitchen where George was preparing Sunday lunch.

'Bloody meetings!'

'Not a good service, dear?'

'No... I mean yes... the service was fine, it was the tea-drinking club in the vestry afterwards and this damned wind farm.'

'Oh dear. Do you want horse-radish?'

'Er... yes, thank you.' Richard Devine paced round the room several times before pouring himself a small glass of wine from an open bottle on the battered pine table. 'It's about the community above all else isn't it?' he suddenly demanded. 'What I hate is what these things seem to do to communities, what they're doing to *this* community, *our* community. It's changing the people, you know; I barely recognise some of them.' He sipped his wine moodily. George silently handed him the carving knife and steel. He put down the glass and slashed the two lengths of metal angrily together. 'There's a balance,' he continued, 'an equilibrium, a harmony even that a little community like ours can achieve. As long as there's give and take...' He stabbed the long knife into the beef joint oozing on its platter, '...and as long as we can keep the greed and corruption out. Once that creeps in... well, then it's just the few who do all the taking and the rest of us are expected to do all the giving. So then you have *in*-balance and *dis*-harmony and a community tearing itself apart.' He picked up his wine and moodily watched his wife putting the last touches to their lunch. 'Right!' he said, 'I'm going to write one letter, just one, and it's going to be about the damage these wind farm developments do to real people and their communities.' He made it sound like the subject of his next sermon. 'I'll circulate it round the village and send it to every newspaper I can think of, and the radio people... and television! Why not?' He was interrupted by his two sons lured by the cooking smells tumbling into the kitchen.

Maxwell had been expecting something of the sort from Richard Devine, in fact after the vicar's performance at the parish council meeting he'd expected a lot more. But what he hadn't expected was the thrust of the attack, the emphasis on community and *real* people, as Devine insisted on calling his troublesome parishioners. This was something more nebulous than the usual arguments, something almost spiritual and therefore virtually impossible to counter. Maxwell knew the industry's fatuous claims of community involvement didn't stand up to scrutiny and even he had to admit that in this day and age a new see-saw for the village kids was unlikely to cut much ice. Richard Devine's letter was a superbly crafted piece. It was well argued and well informed, emotive without being sentimental and very, very persuasive. Local papers across the county had published it, and to Maxwell's surprise so had several of the nationals, some of them following it up with editorials and special investigations - none of which were helpful. The sudden upsurge in unfriendly attention had not gone unnoticed by Prospective Parliamentary Candidate Claude Cockburn either. Hallibut was summoned and left in no doubt that Cockburn expected action to change the public agenda, and quickly, before the next election campaign started. What was needed, he demanded, was something that would neutralise the vicar's arguments, a demonstration of public support that could be used to vindicate the council's pro-development decision when the time came. Hallibut knew how fragile Claude Cockburn's support was, especially if he thought votes were at stake. After some thought, reluctantly, he telephoned Hoggit Hall. Hallibut had timed the call hoping for maximum sobriety, or at least minimum inebriation, and was relieved to hear Sir George's voice, hoarse but lucid.

'So, any ideas, Sir George?' Hallibut hazarded.

There was a long silence then a bark erupted from the earpiece: 'Parish council! Did they ever write anything?'

'Well, no. After the... er, meeting, the matter seemed to be dropped but...'

'Would a letter help?'

'Well it would depend what it said,' Hallibut said warily. After the reaction of the villagers in the school hall that evening he couldn't imagine how the parish council could possibly put their name to anything helpful to the wind farm cause, at least not without running the risk of prompting another riot and possibly lynchings.

'Leave it with me.' The phone went dead.

Ten minutes later Hallibut's phone buzzed and a sulky receptionist announced that she had Sir George Hoggit on the line... again.

'The parish council are strongly in favour of my ... of the Spout Hill wind farm and will give whatever support they can,' Sir George growled. 'You draft what you want and you'll get it back on council paper signed by the chairman. And the clerk too if you want.'

'That's great, Sir George but won't there be some...'

'I've discussed it with the chairman. He and the clerk speak for the whole council and agree that on a fundamental democratic basis that meeting was *in favour* of my... the wind farm; there were two speakers against and three in favour, a clear majority, motion carried. Plompley Parish Council supports the Spout Hill wind farm and they're prepared to say so.' He rang off.

The Chairman of the parish council had been polishing his spoon collection and humming *Tea For Two* when the phone rang. Five minutes later he was left considering his immediate future and in particular his personal safety. Sir George had pointed out the 'simple majority,' which had carried the extraordinary meeting in the school hall and had made clear that the parish council *would* be supporting the wind farm planning application and that the chairman *would* be putting his name to a letter saying so. Both the lease renewal of West Lodge and the clerk's frequent overnight stays there were mentioned in passing.

'But... but, you've already renewed the lease,' the chairman stuttered.

'Have I?' Sir George hissed.

The Chairman didn't bother to reach for the stiff brown envelope of un-checked documents on his desk. He knew he was beaten and miserably started humming Barber's *Adagio For Strings*.

'Right, that's better,' Sir George said. 'You don't need to worry about composing the letter, I'll let you have a draft shortly for typing and signatures. And I'm sure we can rely on the co-operation of Mr Clerk,' he added nastily.

Back at the council offices Hallibut thoughtfully replaced the receiver, and reflected that when sober, Sir George Hoggit was quite an impressive operator. He made a mental note to always ring him at 8.00 am.

At 9.00 Hallibut rang Maxwell, who was delighted with the proposal and immediately agreed to take over the letter drafting. He summoned a fresh coffee and Chloe Jellaby; he'd had some of his best ideas whilst kneading her generous buttocks, curiously the left one seemed particularly inspirational, and he now sipped, kneaded and thought. A letter from the vicar's own parish council worded as Maxwell was already envisaging would not just negate Richard Devine's 'broken community' arguments, it would flatten them. And if the letter sparked a bitter civil war within the ranks of residents and protesters, as he suspected it would, and a few parish councillors ended up hanging by their heels from Plompley lampposts then so much the better. Maxwell un-handed the sqirming Chloe Jellaby and started tapping furiously at a keyboard.

The Devine family was doing their best to ignore the wind farm battle raging around them and get on with their normal village and parochial life. George was pleased she hadn't accepted the invitation to Tuscany; in some well-thumbed magazines accidentally discovered under her eldest son's mattress she'd found some graphically illustrated examples of Sapphic lovemaking techniques and none of them had appealed much. It was also a good thing that she'd been on hand for a series of crises at the Mother's Group; a batch of new 'arrivals', all of mixed race, remarkably similar physiognomically and born to three different mothers in the space of a month, had created considerable domestic turmoil within the village. Richard Devine had been dispatched to have a pastoral word with the young West Indian tyre fitter at the local garage whilst George had provided comfort, reassurance and in one case sanctuary, for the women involved. Apart from this, George had drifted through the sodden summer in her usual dream-like state, continuing her bicycle-bound meanderings around the lanes and hedgerows foraging and harvesting whatever fruits the maturing seasons offered. Amongst other things she'd harvested Oliver Le Rolms. He was the newly appointed manager of the absent Donald McCruddy's farm and a personable young man who despite his teaseable name and exposure to the usual attendant vices at agricultural college was still sweetly naïve in many ways - he'd been disarmed to a state of near paralysis when George had first made love to him amongst the sodden ferns that fringed the green road.

Richard Devine had found it harder to dodge the wind farm maelstrom. Satisfied he'd made his personal contribution to the debate with the writing and distribution of his letter he'd been happy to settle back and resume his pastoral duties. But he'd underestimated the power of his carefully chosen words and with growing alarm realised that his letter was starting to attract widespread interest and media attention. To the disappointed of his excited sons he'd point-blank refused to appear on several 'phone-in' radio shows, which in his opinion were just designed to attract the bigoted and ill informed, and he hadn't even told the boys about the calls from the local television people. He had, however, allowed himself to be interviewed over the telephone by a couple of the more persistent newspapers and on several occasions found himself talking face-to-face with the young woman reporter from *The Bartford Bugle*. Richard Devine remembered Mattie from the night of the parish council meeting and found her open and pleasant, unlike some of her aggressive national counterparts. The encounters in the village were un-planned, at least by him, and it was during one of these impromptu interviews that they'd been spotted by Scott Driver. He'd hurried across the road attracted moth-like to any good-looking woman and was delighted to find that Mattie was also a journalist. She was wary of his superficial charm but had found herself readily accepted into the inner circle of the anti-wind farm activists and with an invite to attend an upcoming PAWs OFF meeting. Against his better judgment Richard Devine also reluctantly agreed to attend.

There had recently been an outbreak of unity in Plompley with villagers at last rallying to the PAWs Off standard, largely due to a nosy curiosity prompted by the relocation of the group's headquarters to the glitzy conservatory at The Manse. The Vincent-Townend's opposition to the move had finally been undermined, not by village politics or even the charms and liqueurs of the Drivers, but by a rampant outbreak of cat-piss-induced dry rot, which had left their heavily timbered dining room largely floor-less. Reluctantly they'd had to bow to the inevitable. Confident in his own art-deco environment Scott Driver had from the first slipped smoothly into the role of *de facto* chairman. He'd successfully completed the coup after just a couple of meetings by innocently suggesting that the group should have an Honorary President. Dr Gordon Vincent-Townend was of course the only suitable candidate, and was duly elected, thereby neatly drawing any remaining teeth the hapless cannibal expert might have had.

PAWs Off flourished during the next few months and under its umbrella the village conducted a well-organised and relatively concerted campaign. But despite this new-found spirit of co-operation it soon became clear that the protest movement had just about run its course - the protesters had run out of ideas. Every conventional campaigning tool had been utilised: carefully tailored letters had been sent to an enormous number of people of influence, from Prince Charles to the Dalai Lama by way of Nigel Farage and David Beckham - who had at least sent back a signed photograph with the message: 'Good luck for the new season' - councillors had been repeatedly lobbied by letter, e-mail and telephone until some had complained of harassment, and at huge cost to a few altruistic villagers an enormous file of critical reports from respected experts in acoustics, hydrology, landscape architecture and wildlife had been compiled. This had been solemnly submitted to Bartfordshire Council where it now lay dead, buried and unread somewhere in Hallibut's chaotic workstation and with no chance of rebirth.

A small band of the more able-bodied activists was kept employed replacing and maintaining the stolen and vandalised protest signs. Village unity had brought a uniform livery of red and white, with one corner of the signs painted a suitably doom-laden black. The signs now appeared throughout the area, peeping from hedges and gardens, wired to farm gates and boldly (and probably illegally) propped on roadside verges. Some landowners had even painted the sides of outbuildings and old trailers, which were then parked prominently in outlying fields. The maintenance gang was kept busy. Whilst the sign-written barns and trailers were more or less safe from interference the more modest signs and boards were only too vulnerable, and most, at one time or another, were stolen, defaced or smashed. Half an hour or so after closing time on Friday and Saturday nights was when most of the damage was done, and in the early stages of the campaign the losses had been near total. A couple of sarcastic letters to *The Bugle* questioning the specific and targeted nature of the vandalism and a commendable interest from the local bobby on his fortnightly beat had some slight effect, but the real break-through came when some of the Headbangers on their way home from a Young Farmer's barn dance came across a couple of Sir George's hired vandals at work ... and gleefully beat them to a pulp. Word got round that there was sport to be had, and whilst the harvest and the approaching new rugby season took up most of their daylight hours, the weekend evenings were for drinking and fighting. The Headbangers happily took to their role as vigilantes. Fired up by a tough old-fashioned loyalty to their community and industrial quantities of lager, they would set up ambushes behind hedges and parked cars and await their prey, passing the time with belching and peeing-up-the-wall competitions. They invariably emerged victorious but eventually became victims of their own success and the attacks and sport tailed off, the only damage inflicted on the signs now by the elements.

For the more peaceable residents of Plompley there seemed little more to be done, but a general feeling that doing nothing was not an option prompted the more restless residents to look round for new fronts to open and new ways to fight the battle. There must be *something* more they could do. It was decided that the next PAWs Off meeting wouldn't have an agenda; after the usual formalities it was to be a brainstorming session, an open forum where any ideas to keep the campaign alive and prominent would be welcomed and discussed.

The architecturally ambiguous conservatory was huge but close to capacity with PAWs Off supporters squeezed into, onto and between an extraordinary collection of mismatched furniture, pert-breasted statuary and overflowing jardinières. Some of the assorted artefacts were genuine, most were reproduction, and all were carefully arranged under overlapping arcs of kaleidoscopic lights and had been chosen to reflect the age, the jazz age, although the effect was somewhat blurred by the presence of *objets* that appeared to date from anywhere between the early years of the First World War to the latter years of the Second. With a background tattoo of rain on the clear roof and even the quietest voice echoing up into the lofty void of the barn-like atrium the noise was deafening.

'Didn't expect to see you here.'

'Christ! You made me jump.'

'I seem to have made a habit of that,' Mattie said. 'Move over.'

Simon, now a veteran of these meetings, had arrived early to claim one of the more comfortable chairs (woolly brown velour, deep, soft and armed), which was placed where he could observe the whole room and everyone in it. He shuffled to one side and Mattie squeezed her hips into the gap.

'So what are *you* doing here?'

'I'm a journalist, remember? This is news ... or it might be.' She looked round the heaving room and grinned. 'They don't look much like a rioting bunch though. Which one's Gatsby?'

'He doesn't usually show at his own parties.'

'Oh.'

'I'm surprised they let you in, grubby press. This lot can be a bit cagey, you know about their cunning plans, they like to play their cards close to their chests.'

'Mr Driver invited me, in fact he almost insisted.'

'Ah, the charming Mr Driver, our Scotty.'

Mattie grunted non-committally. 'So how are you?'

'Fine thanks, you?'

'Yeah, fine. Are you under water yet, at the cottage I mean?'

Simon laughed. 'Not quite, but it's got closer. The ducks have taken up permanent residence, I was thinking of charging them rent but I'm not allowed to sub-let. They send their love.'

Mattie gave a little smile at the memory and wriggled deeper into the chair, pleased that they both seemed equally relaxed about their night of casual sex and the subsequent lack of contact.

'So how's it going then, the journalism I mean? I presume you're still with *The Bugle*, still running around looking for riots.'

'Yeah, yes I am, it's not too bad. How about you?' She nodded at the red exercise book held firmly closed on Simon's lap.

'Oh, it's coming on.' He twisted awkwardly to look at her. 'I think I've got the plot worked out. And look at the characters I've got to play with...' he flicked a hand at the eclectic crowd, '...and the set! I've started chapter four now.'

'I'd like to hear more about it.' There was a stirring across the room. 'I've got lots to tell you too, if you're interested, about Hoggit and...' The rest was lost in a sudden hubbub of chair scraping and hurried greetings as seats were found and glasses filled. During the expectant hush that followed Simon leant into Mattie's hair and whispered: 'Let's get together next week, I'll come into Bartford.'

Mattie nodded without looking at him. She could still feel him in her hair and wasn't sure whether it was his breath or his lips on her neck. 'I'm only staying an hour, I'll give you a call,' she whispered back.

The minutes of the previous meeting were read, approved and sulkily signed by the Honorary President - one of the few responsibilities Gordon Vincent-Townend still had. Scott Driver resumed his seat, glanced round to make sure everyone had a glass and something in it, and spread his hands.

'Well, fire away,' he smiled.

There was an uncomfortable silence and some fidgeting. Eventually: 'Yes, Mrs... er, sorry I mean, *Dr* Vincent-Townend... Lucy. Yes?'

'Scouts! My Scouts!'

Scott Driver paused uncertainly. 'Yes... well, I think getting the youngsters involved could perhaps have some... merit,' he finished doubtfully. 'But...'

'Tie 'em in knots!'

'Um, who?'

'Them! The enemy! Sheepshanks, bowlines, round turn and two half hitches, smack 'em where it hurts with a monkey's fist. Worked with the bloody Zulus!' She chuckled happily and ducked back behind a curtain of frizzy hair and into a huge, brimming glass of red wine. There was an uncertain silence for a few seconds interrupted only by a deep sigh from the Honorary President.

Curiously this bizarre outburst seemed to break the ice. The usually vociferous found their voices, the reliably opinionated opined and even a few of the more timid fringe members contributed. In fact theirs were probably the most reasoned suggestions - unfortunately they were also the dullest and least imaginative. Yet another letter-writing campaign was wearily dismissed - there was no one left to write to - collecting a Downing Street petition requiring 100,000 signatures was deemed unachievable in a village with a population of under 3,000, and the old idea of floating a blimp over Spout Hill was yet again shot down, not only for reasons of expense and health and safety but also on the practical grounds that there would be nothing to tether it to that didn't belong to Sir George Hoggit. It seemed that at the moment he not only held most of the cards but also all the secure anchoring points.

Scott Driver discreetly took a large sip of nearly neat gin and resumed control. 'Publicity!' He slapped the arm of his chair. 'That's what we need, some way of showing people beyond the village, beyond the county, how beautiful our countryside is and what will be lost if Hoggit and co. get their way. We need to catch people's imagination, take it to an even bigger audience.' He glanced towards Richard Devine, sitting uncomfortably upright in a curious hooded wicker creation that resembled an aroused peacock and threw intriguing shadows over his face. Everyone in the room knew that of any of them it was the village vicar who had single-handedly generated more attention and positive publicity for their cause and given the wind farm developers most headaches. There was an expectant silence broken only by the interminable clattering of rain on the polymer roof panels.

Richard Devine had listened politely to all the discussions and been glad his face was in the shadows. He'd insisted on a tonic water on his arrival and now wished he'd accepted the proffered red wine. It was clear he was expected to speak.

'I've had one thought,' he said quietly. 'Marches used to be all the thing in my youth, you know, Grosvenor Square, Aldermarston and all that.'

There was a stirring in one part of the room where an older, reactionary clique had collected and a muttered but clearly audible 'Bloody CND!'

Richard Devine ignored it. 'I'm not suggesting we march on Parliament or even Bartford Town Hall, in fact to take our protests into an urban setting would rather seem to counter our own arguments.' He leant forward out of the shadows. 'I thought some sort of peaceful, family-orientated procession here in Plompley, perhaps to the top of Spout Hill, maybe even by torch light. I thought that might catch people's imagination.' He paused and looked at Scott Driver and then around the rest of the room. There were a few thoughtful nods and approving whispers. Then, unwittingly, Richard Devine played a trump card: 'And the television people would like it,' he said. The whispers grew in volume and an excited ripple spread round the room. Scott Driver, glass in hand, moved quickly across the room to confer.

Gordon Vincent-Townend, the deposed chairman, smiled rigidly at the enthusiasm of his neighbours: why the bloody hell couldn't this of happened on his watch? He took his frustration out on his wife who had somehow managed to refill her glass and was repeating her 'bloody good' mantra over and over to herself. 'For God's sake, Lucy, shut up!' he snarled, and decided to try and re-establish a bit of his authority by joining the vicar and Scott Driver in conference. But he was too late, before he could unravel his lanky frame from the low chair Scott Driver had moved back across the room, positioned himself carefully on a spot where several angled lights shone kindly on his slightly puffy features and held up his hands for quiet.

The debate that followed was lively and optimistic. The campaigners, re-invigorated by Richard's intervention, bombarded their chairman with ideas and suggestions. It was decided that it would be a *procession* not a march, which was considered too militant, and it would take place in two weeks' time on the Friday evening when there would be a full moon, the harvest moon. They wanted a big family crowd of all ages, especially children; grannies and dogs would also be welcome and everyone was to gather in the lay-by at the bottom of the green road at dusk. Flaming torches would be carried by some for effect, and electric torches by the rest for practicality. The half-joking suggestion that pitchforks and the odd scythe should be carried was nervously dismissed but it was agreed that there would be banners - but no chanting. One of the more militant contributors argued belligerently for the hackneyed chorus of: 'What Do We Want?' But it was pointed out that the responses were less obvious; 'No wind farm!' seemed reasonable enough but then things got a bit confusing with the: 'and when do we want it?' and the concluding 'now!' The exchange would not only be ambiguous but also grammatically suspect, which some cynical commentator - perhaps on *the television -* could make mischief with. Alternatives were explored; changing the last response to 'never!' appeared to create a double negative, which itself could be negated by dropping the 'no' from the first response, but shouting *for* a wind farm felt all wrong. The debate made for an enjoyable twenty minutes for the pedants but attentions started to drift and patience wore thin. Finally it was decided to rule out *any* chanting, grammatically correct or not. Since no one could remember the words to *We Shall Overcome* or *My Land is Your Land* the idea of protests songs was also dropped, but it was decided that the children should be encouraged to sing and *All Things*

Bright and Beautiful was deemed appropriate. The idea of a hilltop bonfire was keenly supported but apparently any scorch mark would probably constitute a trespass and no one was in any doubt that Sir George would take vindictive action so this was also ruled out. Instead it was decided that those bearing flaming torches would spread out along the ridge to emphasise the linear scale of the development and the meteorology mast would be illuminated with electric torches to give some idea of the vertical impact. It was assumed that the vicar would persuade his media friends to obligingly focus their cameras and microphones accordingly. By then Richard Devine was no longer there to disillusion anyone having long since made his apologies and hurried home to his customary glass of elderberry and episode of *Father Ted*.

Once Dr Lucy had stopped mumbling 'bloody good' to herself and lapsed into a brooding silence the Vincent-Townends had also left. Gordon Vincent-Townend made their usual excuses and assured an indifferent Scott Driver that he'd return alone shortly ... something that was not to be.

Frustrated by his wife's staggering progress and determined to miss as little of the meeting as possible, half way up their drive Gordon Vincent-Townend had in desperation bundled Lucy over his shoulder in a poor imitation of a fireman's lift before tottering on towards the house. Stumbling across the threshold with Lucy still limp and giggling round his neck their combined weight had proved too much for the ancient hall-floor timbers where another feline *pissoir* had been surreptitiously operating for years, nurturing more of the pernicious dry rot. Gordon just had time to register a tortured groan from beneath his feet before he lunged forward and disappeared abruptly through the floor, leaving his unsupported wife to sail on down the hall. Dr Lucy had a relatively soft landing ending up sprawled comfortably on the stained Persian runner at the far end of the hall where she lay nibbling the threadbare pile and mumbling happily to herself. Her husband had not fared so well. He was now a twisted figure lying motionless amongst a pile of splintered smelly timbers in the basement. The brain-searing flash of pain from the double fracture to his left leg, sustained on impact, added to the excruciating agony of testicles crushed against one of the more resistant joists during his descent, had rendered him unconscious.

He wasn't missed. By the time Scott Driver, ever the impeccable host, had indicated that the evening was coming to an end by replacing his gin tumbler with a brandy balloon and producing a bottle of his legendary Armagnac, all the necessary details for the *Procession* had been agreed - without need for further reference to the Honorary President.

CHAPTER THIRTEEN

Despite the amalgamation of most of Plompley's protesters and their disparate groups under the PAWs Off umbrella there still remained a few independent types and rogue operators within the community. Most were quiet souls who simply preferred their own methods, often thoughtful, always peaceful and frequently eccentric. But Godfrey 'Bunny' Warren was in a different league; despite the painful hospitalisations, numerous police interviews and recent court appearances he was determined not to change or compromise his anarchic methods. Bunny's latest stay in Bartford General hadn't lasted as long as predicted and he'd been released before the liquorice allsorts ran out, although not in time to see Linda before she left for Tuscany. Discharged from one institution the hapless Bunny had promptly found himself in another, namely Bartford Magistrate's Court. After his previous hearing before the deaf and deranged Sir Edmund Croak there had been considerable confusion over Bunny's release and bail conditions. This time the police were insisting on an unequivocal nod from a higher authority, higher that is than Sir Edmund, before they released a potentially homicidal maniac back into the community.

'Don't worry, mate you've got a pussy cat today.' The uniformed policeman patted Bunny kindly on the knee.

They were in the back of a police car somewhere between the hospital and the court. The plump rather fatherly policeman was slouched comfortably over two thirds of the lumpy back seat while Bunny, arched on shoulders and heels, tried to keep his damaged backside off the remaining third.

'Nice as pie Mrs Jeffries is,' the policeman continued. 'They got rid of that mad bastard Croak and not before time either, mad as a March hare 'e was.' He chuckled amiably. 'In the nut house now they say... probably just as well.'

The policeman was factually, if not politically, correct. Sir Edmund's port-fuelled behaviour at his club, always eccentric and frequently offensive, had finally descended into violence after the appointment of a new steward of Italian descent. After subjecting the poor man to several weeks of racial and personal abuse, including accusing him of raping his great (to the power of eight) grandmother, Sir Edmund had ambushed the steward in the senior member's dining room, braining him with the dinner gong and threatening to castrate him with a broken bottle of the club claret. For the first time in the club's history the police had to be allowed access to its hallowed halls, although they were first made to remove their helmets and boots. As well as the usual pepper spray and tazers the officers came equipped with a straitjacket, and after a brief pursuit with much Keystone-Cop slithering around the highly polished floors the surprisingly nimble Sir Edmund was cornered, captured and duly sectioned. His relieved family chose a discreetly secure establishment on the edge of the New Forest where, once his medication had been balanced, he spent his days cheating at Scrabble with Lord Lucan and two Napoleons.

The friendly policeman had also been right about the kindly nature of Sir Edmund's replacement; The Honorable Judith Jeffries JP was, as her husband put it, of 'the bleeding heart tendency'. After asking Bunny a few gentle questions, and ignoring frantic notes from her clerk, she concluded the hearing by enquiring about the state of the defendant's 'bot bot' and instructed that a police car should be dispatched to take him safely home.

For the longer drive back to Plompley Bunny was granted the whole of the back seat, where he crouched head down, arse up, rocking jerkily on knees and elbows.

'Told you so,' said the fat policeman from the front passenger seat, addressing the swaying backside behind him.

As Bunny crawled backwards out of the police car and straightened up, the first thing he noticed was that his huge anti-wind farm sign was not where he'd left it. He spotted it in the ditch on the opposite side of the lane lying muddied, face down and apparently in two pieces. 'Bastards,' he muttered and tottered stiff-legged towards his 'office'. The second thing he noticed was that the caravan park seemed to have been doing extraordinarily good business in his absence, in fact astonishingly good business since the main season was now over and it still hadn't stopped raining. The amount of mud and the depth of the ruts along the park's access drive confirmed an exceptional level of traffic.

To Bunny's surprise he found Filch in the shed. Filch was surprised too. He'd been dreamlessly dozing in an old camping chair and partially sedated by the fumes from a wheezing Calor gas heater had more or less forgotten that Bunny existed.

'What are you doing here?' Bunny demanded.

'Thought I'd keep an eye on things for you.' Filch tried to sound hurt.

'Any money left?' Bunny asked nastily, looking pointedly at the drawer where the cash tin was kept.

'Loads,' Filch said proudly. 'Paid in advance, see?' He reached for the usually locked drawer, which opened with suspicious ease and thrust the old grey tin into Bunny's hands. Bunny flipped open the lid and was immediately hit by the pungent smell of horse. Recoiling slightly he peered into the tin and was startled to see a large sheaf of crumpled notes, many of which appeared to be fifties. He snapped the lid down and tucked the tin protectively under his arm.

'Where did they come from?'

Filch shrugged.

'How many are there?'

'Not sure.'

'Not sure! What d'you mean, "not sure"? How did you know what to charge? How d'you know some didn't get in for free?'

Filch fidgeted and the ancient canvas chair groaned and creaked in sympathy. 'Well, they all come together ... and *they* kinda told *me* how much they were gonna pay.'

Bunny looked at him incredulously. 'They told you...' He stopped suddenly and looked down at Filch. 'They all came together? All of them?'

Filch nodded, hoping to please, and Bunny looked out of the streaked window and down the rutted track towards the collection of caravans.

Some of them were huge double-axle jobs, all were immaculate, chrome shiny, and many had smoke flicking off the top of little chimney pipes. The towing vehicles were a mixture of vans and trucks, scruffy and disreputable besides the gleaming caravans, and a collection of giant, nearly new and mainly black SUVs. There was no sign of the usual family estates and Chelsea tractors. A number of bored looking children and dogs of all ages, sizes and indeterminate breeds mooched aimlessly in the rain amongst outsized gas cylinders and piles of black bags. Bunny rubbed at the steamed glass for a clearer view attracting the attention of one of the smaller children who cheerfully raised two fingers in greeting. Bunny jumped back and sat down heavily on the old typist's chair

'Ow!' Once he'd regained his breath he said: 'You know what we've got here don't you?'

Filch's face lit up and he beamed at Bunny's left armpit, 'Two thousand, six hundred and thirty-four quid!'

Bunny just looked at him. 'Travellers,' he said, 'that's what we've got, travellers.'

Filch didn't know how he was expected to react so he stayed silent and watched Bunny carefully for a lead. There was just the flicker of what could have been a wry smile and Filch decided to try his luck. 'Er... I s'pose there wouldn't be a bit of commission, like owing, would there?'

'Nope.'

'Fair enough.'

Bunny entrusted the precious tin to his desktop for a moment and patted it. 'How much did you say?'

'Two thousand, six hundred and thirty-four quid.'

Bunny nodded. 'Uh huh... how long's that for then?'

'Eh?'

'For how long? How long have they paid for?'

'Oh.' Filch brightened, then clouded again. 'Dunno.'

'Bloody Hell! I'll go and ask them...'

'You don't wanna do that,' Filch said quickly, a look of genuine alarm on his face as he struggled out of the sagging chair. 'They don't like visitors, they told me that, made sure like. And you gotta watch them dogs...' He looked out of the window, '...and them fuckin' kids!'

Bunny glanced at the streaming window and nodded. 'Ok,' he said slowly, 'we'll see how it goes.' He cuddled the tin again. 'Anyway I've got a few other things to think about. Remember what we were talking about in the pub the other night, before... well, before?' He looked at Filch for a second. 'No of course you don't, well never mind I'll tell you all over again... in the pub.'

'Does that mean I get me wages?' Filch asked eagerly.

'Of course,' Bunny said, heading for the door. 'Come on.'

Yet again Simon failed to notice Mattie's approach. As she clicked across the slate-effect floor to where he sat nursing a bottle of lager she could see he was preoccupied by the other occupants of the echoey, over-lit pizzeria; in particular a nearby crowd of loudly confident young women. They'd pushed two tables roughly together, encircled them wagon-train style with bag-slung buggies and were busily stacking the tables with baby paraphernalia. Two of the mothers had already produced plump, pink-nippled breasts, one of them, almost stripped to the waist, still defiantly sipping her coffee whilst her unattached baby howled its impatience. As Simon watched, others started to unbutton. Several toddlers were crawling and tottering outside the defensive circle, spreading out to disappear amongst the legs of other tables and their occupants, followed by the unnecessarily loud shouts of proud mothers unconvincingly pleading with them to return... but actually delighting in the precocious mobility and confidence of their offspring and determined to bring them to the attention of the rest of the restaurant.

'Hi, getting broody?' Mattie grinned.

'Bloody kids.' Simon looked at his bottle as if just remembering it and took a swig. 'Actually it's not the kids is it, it's the bloody mothers, the kids can't help it, I suppose.'

Mattie looked around. 'Hmm, not quite what I'd expected. It's a new place, thought you'd feel at home, it's meant to be *metropolitan*.' She looked doubtfully at the bared breasts and they both watched as a young waitress tripped over a particularly adventurous crawler who had almost made it to the kitchens. The outraged wails of both child and mother were now added to the cacophony.

'Shall we move on?' Mattie bellowed.

'Any ideas? You know the town better than me.'

Mattie helped herself to his beer. 'I've got an idea; it'll be a bit more expensive...'

'Don't worry about it, my treat,' he held up a warning hand, 'unless, that is there's a single nursing mother or child under fourteen in the place, in which case you're paying!'

'No problem, you'll love it - the Bilge Rat.'

'The what?'

'Bilge Rat,' she shouted. 'I'll just check it's there.' She produced a mobile phone.

The noise went up a notch as the young Polish waitress, berated in a language she barely understood by the trampled toddler's mother, also started to howl. Mattie waved the phone at Simon and indicated the door.

'What did you mean "...check it's there"?'

Mattie had finished her phone call and set off down the street. 'You'll see.'

To Simon's delight the Bilge Rat turned out to be a disreputable-looking narrowboat tenuously moored on the fast-flowing and close-to-bank-bursting River Bart. It was held in place by a cat's cradle of straining chains and scraps of multi-coloured ropes attached in turn to various handy trees and fence posts. The interior had been crudely converted to a sort of tubular restaurant; on the right, the starboard side, diner-style benched booths had been built in, each capable of seating four at a pinch and each booth with its own window looking onto the wildly eddying river. On the left, the port side, the dripping vegetation on the bank largely obscured the windows and there was a narrow walkway where staff and customers squeezed past each other with unavoidable intimacy. There was a slight smell of diesel and muddy damp throughout. The theme was predictably nautical, with a collection of chipped canal-bilia and faded photos of over-laden barges, straining horses and gurning, pipe-smoking bargees scattered along the length of the boat. The staff were all young and uniformed in flip-flops, torn tee shirts and stubble.

'You *were* joking about it not always being here, weren't you?' They'd been pointed towards a vacant booth, drinks and menus had appeared and Simon was now looking around curiously.

'No, it regularly sets sail, usually with no one on board and with the help of the local yobs. The authorities have been trying to get rid of it for years, say it's a navigational hazard, but somehow it keeps going. The floods always give them a problem,' she nodded at the rain-streaked window, 'this won't be helping.'

'I think it's great. And no tits or tots yet so it looks like I'm paying.'

Mattie laughed and sipped her wine. 'I'm glad you like it. Better make the most of it while it's here though. Last time they lost her she went miles and nearly didn't make it back. A load of drunken stag idiots dressed as Elvis in pink jump suits managed to release her with half of them still onboard. They were completely out of it, three of them ended up in hospital and they thought they'd lost one altogether. He turned up days later and couldn't remember a thing. And the poor old Bilge Rat carried on downstream and nearly took out Overbart Bridge, even Oliver Cromwell didn't manage that apparently. Another trip like that and I think that might be it.'

They both gazed out of the large window, eyes drawn to the moving water.

'Ducks,' Simon said suddenly, 'friends of yours?'

'No, and they're moorhens.'

'Whatever! This countryman's done musing. I don't care if they're bloody dodos!'

'They're extinct,' Mattie said seriously.

'Are they? First I've heard, no one tells me anything.' He tossed a balled paper napkin at her. 'Don't take the piss! Lets eat.'

Simon decided first. He put down the stained piece of paper that passed as a menu and turned sideways on his bench. 'Actually, I've stopped trying to write the country notes things.'

'I thought so. Rob Jordan said he hadn't heard from you for a while.' 'How are things with him these days?'

'Not too bad. He's calmed down a bit, I think advertising must be up and the owners are probably leaving him alone, and the Thailand situation seems to have sorted itself out.'

'Oh yes, your religious correspondent wasn't it?' Simon chuckled. 'What's happened there, I haven't seen anything in *The Bugle* for a while? Did they ever shoot him... or her... or whatever?'

'No, Rob never got his execution. It seems that Rebecca... or rather Bernard, was quite a hit in the Bangkok jail. She got befriended by the governor who passed her around a bit and now she's the chief of police's number one ladyboy. Kept in quite some style apparently.'

'Good God! Couldn't make it up could you? Mind you...'

'So that was that,' Mattie continued. 'Funnily enough, what's getting to Rob most at the moment is our wind farm. He overstretched himself buying a place in Plompley, he's got a mortgage bigger than the national debt of a small African country and needs to sell. Problem is the estate agents reckon the wind farm has knocked about a third off the value. Poor old Rob's got negative equity so he's a bit stuck.'

Simon nodded sympathetically, 'Yeah, that's rough, I bet he's not the only one either. I'm glad my place is rented.'

'Still above water?'

'Only just.' He poured them both some more wine. 'Right come on then, never mind Rob Jordan and *The Bugle*, you've been humming like a top since you walked into *Pizzahell*, or whatever it's called, you're bursting about something. What's going on?'

'What's going on...?' Mattie mused with eyes flashing. She leant forward over the table, '...well, I did what I said I was going to do... did a load more digging around, got a bit more gossip about the Hallibuts, and some really good stuff from the council. I've found myself a source, a spy in the camp, a real gold-plated mole!'

'And?'

'And everything I've found out confirms what we thought, what we put together. In fact it more than confirms it, I think it proves it. And...' she took her time sipping the wine, '...and I've written up the whole story, a real professional job. It's edited, referenced and everything and...' she took another sip.

Simon was happy to let her have her moment and feed her her lines, 'And?'

'And ... well, it's top secret, you mustn't say a word, OK?'

Simon nodded.

'Well, it's all going to be published... in *The Sunday Telegraph*!' The words tumbled out, loud and triumphant. 'They loved it!' A few heads in other booths turned in their direction.

'Wow! That's quite something, Mattie, seriously impressive. When's it coming out?'

'Soon, very soon, say they don't want to miss the moment, want to blow the whistle before the planning is passed. They've even put a team of their own onto it, you know to make a few extra enquiries. I think it's the libel thing. But apart from that they've taken *my* piece as it is... and they're going to print it... in *The Sunday Telegraph*. And my name will be on it.' There was that childlike quality about her again that Simon had glimpsed before.

'So this "mole,"' he said, 'sounds like he's pretty key. Where'd you get him from?'

'You've met him actually.'

'I have?'

'D'you remember when we were at the council at that planning desk and that funny little bloke with the cardi and the fag and the dandruff?'

'The Hobbit?'

'That's him.'

'Really?'

'Gold-plated! Pure luck of course, these things usually are.'

Simon smiled slightly at her newly assumed role of veteran investigative hack.

'I bumped into him in the underground car park at the council,' Mattie said, 'He was sneaking a ciggie. Anyway he remembered me, I think it was giving away Hallibut's address that clicked with him, so we got chatting, had a smoke...'

'Hang on, I thought you only smoked after sex,' Simon feigned shock, 'you didn't...?'

'Don't be revolting, don't even think... ugh!' she shuddered. 'Anyway, as I was saying, we got chatting and what that guy doesn't know about what's happening in that building isn't worth knowing. He's got all the dirt, doesn't like *anyone*, but seems to have a particular downer on Clive Hallibut. I'm not sure why. Apparently Hallibut calls him "Radar", but actually I think he secretly quite likes that.'

The food arrived. Mattie just played with hers, poking it around the plate.

'Come on, eat,' Simon chivvied, 'It's really good. You can talk while you eat, I don't mind...' he glanced around the other customers, '... and I don't think anyone else is likely to object if you talk with your mouth full.'

Mattie obeyed and between sips and bites described the regular subterranean meetings with Radar and how, bit by malicious bit, he'd given her the details of numerous eavesdropped phone calls. Initially, she explained, it had been those between Hallibut and Sir George Hoggit that were particularly informative because Radar could hear both ends of the conversation. Then at their second meeting he'd told her about Hallibut's contacts with Maxwell and someone called Wormold. The next meeting was the first time she heard the name of Moody, the head of Human Resources. Radar hadn't yet managed to hear enough to work out where Moody fitted in, or even whether he was there to smell out rats or smelt of them, but having helped himself to another one of Mattie's cigarettes, which he clipped behind his ear, Radar wandered off promising to find out more.

'Did you pay him for any of this?'

'Nope, not a penny.'

Simon shook his head in bewilderment. 'And we've got your word for it that you didn't sleep with him,' he grinned. 'So ... social conscience?'

Mattie shrugged. 'I think he's just naturally vindictive. But anyway that's just about it, basically we were right; Hallibut has effectively been working for Hoggit and Ref Watt to get this wind farm built, and along the way it looks like he's fiddled the data and tech stuff to make it all fit. According to Radar he's even mucked about with council policy, or at least *interpreted* it (remember that word?) in a helpful way. They're all in on it, including Councillor Co'burn, I'm sure, and there's no doubt that Hallibut's getting paid for it... and thanks to you we know how.' She picked up her glass.

You said, "*just about*", that that was "...*just* about it".

Mattie's eyes flashed at him over the rim of her glass. 'I did, didn't I?'

'Well?'

'I saw Radar again this morning.'

'I thought you smelt of smoke, I assumed you'd been...'

Mattie ignored him. 'Not to put too fine a point on it I think the shit has hit the fan. According to Radar, Hallibut got a call on Friday that seriously rattled him. I haven't checked yet but I'm guessing it might have been my *Telegraph* people sniffing around. Anyway, I don't know what they said to him but he didn't handle it very well by the sound of it. Fairly panicked apparently, got straight on the phone to Hoggit and Maxwell and got a bollocking from both of them. Radar says they've arranged an emergency meeting for later in the week for all of them. Then there's this mysterious Moody, we still can't quite work out where he stands in all this but he seems as thick as thieves with Co'burn, and all on the quiet... off the record. Radar's sure that somehow Moody knows something's going to blow in the press and he reckons there might be some sort of political damage-limitation going on. What I can't work out is how Moody knows... and how much. My people at the paper won't have spoken to him because I've never even mentioned his name.'

Simon puffed out his cheeks and exhaled slowly. 'Christ, Mattie, you've really stirred it up haven't you? A right hornet's nest... or can of worms.'

'Call it what you like, as long as I get my byline in *The Sunday Telegraph* and a few of these greedy bastards get their comeuppances.' She looked out of the window thoughtfully. 'It'd be good if the wind farm never happens too.'

'Yeah, I'm with you on that. So what's next?'

Mattie thought for a moment: 'How about a pudding and another glass?'

They ate and drank and watched the moorhens through the steamy window, easy in each other's company.

'So how's chapter four?' Mattie asked after a while.

'Fine. It's happening... it's coming.'

So what are you actually writing about?'

'Exactly the same as you.'

Mattie stiffened.

Simon smiled reassuringly, 'Exactly the same as you... except yours is fact and going to be published... and mine is fictional rubbish and almost certainly won't be.' He grinned and raised his glass in salute. 'Here's to *your* scoop.'

While they were waiting for the bill the conversation drifted back to Plompley and Spout Hill.

'So will you be covering the march, sorry I mean the *procession*, for *The Bugle* then?'

'Naturally, wouldn't miss it for the world,' Mattie grimaced. 'Who else would they send? I'm Plompley's very own special correspondent. God, I hope it doesn't bloody rain.'

'Bound to. Fancy sharing a brolly?'

Mattie smiled and nodded.

'Going to bring a toothbrush?' Simon added casually.

It was a typically quiet mid-week lunchtime in The Smuggler's and Bunny and Filch had their choice of tables. Sid scowled at Filch as they entered but apart from that seemed in uncharacteristically good humour.

This seemed to be happening more often of late, he could still trot out the usual expletive-strewn insults but there was almost a cheery edge to them these days and some performances weren't altogether convincing. The only other customers were the Aarights, neither listening to the other nor anyone else, but Bunny still chose a table as far away from them as possible.

'Right, you remember that fairy tale we were talking about?'

Filch looked blank and his mouth sagged.

'Bow, arrow, thread, cord, rope ... rescue! Remember?'

The mouth snapped shut. 'Oh yeah, yeah. I've been thinking about that.'

For a moment Bunny thought their earlier conversation might just have registered. Then Filch continued: 'Yeah, this princess, couldn't she just let all her hair down like?'

Bunny looked at him in disbelief. 'That's a different bloody story!'

'Oh.'

'Bow, arrow, thread, cord, rope,' Bunny said quickly, 'got it?'

Filch hesitated. 'Yeah,' he lied, more worried about what was left of his dwindling pay packet.

Bunny looked at him sceptically but decided it was worth carrying on. 'So, that's how I'm going to launch my attack,' he said, as if that explained everything.

'Who on?'

'Not who... what! The bloody wind turbines of course.'

'Ah,' Filch nodded and took a packet of crisps from the pile on the table. 'But they 'aven't built them yet.'

'No, that's true, well spotted. This is going to be a trial run, a practise. I'm gonna have a go at one of those over near Bogdownton up on Motley Common.'

'Yeah they've got some there,' Filch confirmed. 'Like a practise then?' he repeated.

'Yesss, that's it. Then I'll be ready.'

Filch nodded knowingly and up-ended his crisp packet aiming a stream of crumbs at his mouth and missing. 'Ready for what?' he coughed.

'Oh Christ! The real thing! The *Spout Hill* wind turbines, our own bloody wind farm!' Once they've built it,' Bunny added quickly. 'I'll have a method worked out, a *modem operatic*, all tried and tested and ready to go. *Sabotage!*' he whispered.

For a moment Filch looked impressed but then his brows furrowed over the rim of his glass. 'But them windymills never go round.'

'They must do sometimes,' Bunny snapped, 'or they wouldn't have built them.'

'Don't know about that, but they don't get much wind over Bogdownton way... never 'ave. And when they do they always 'ave to shut the windymills down because it's blowin' too bleedin' hard.' He chuckled.

'I'll pick me time,' Bunny sniffed. 'They must go round sometime.'

There was a pause while stocks were replenished and Filch's wages were further depleted.

'So 'ows it going to work then?' Filch eventually asked, after Bunny had made it clear he expected further interest.

Bunny squinted furtively over his shoulder at the nearly empty pub and quickly dipped in and out of his cloudy pint glass. 'Well... the arrow goes over the top, through the blades, which are *turning* ... see?'

'Right,' Filch said brightly.

'Shhh,' Bunny hissed, glancing over his other shoulder.

'I only said, "Right".'

'Well don't. So it goes through the blades, like I said, and the arrow's got this fishing line tied to it and that gets all tangled in the blades... see?'

Filch looked worried and sucked his teeth noisily. 'Don't see it meself.'

'What?'

'Well them's big sods them windymills, powerful like, fishing line'll be nothing to 'em.' With that, Filch dismissed the subject and looked towards the bar hoping against the odds for a friendly face and perhaps a different conversation.

'No, listen you pratt, that's not it. Remember the princess in the tower?'

Filch thought for a moment. 'Nope.'

'Oh Christ!' Bunny gave himself a harder than intended slap on the forehead and turned it into a rub. 'Yes you do! We were just talking about it... the one in the tower... where the silk's tied to the string and the string's tied to some rope and all that... nothing to do with fucking hair!'

'Oh yeah, *that* princess.'

'Yeesss, *that* princess. Right, so my fishing line is like her silk, yeah? So tied to that is a nice strong bit of nylon cord, like sailors use...' He made the mistake of pausing to light a cigar.

'What for?'

'What do you mean, "What for?"?'

'What do sailors do with it?' Filch liked boats, he'd seen lots of pictures and had the occasional glimpse of a real one on the way to the Isle of Wight.

'It doesn't matter.'

Filch looked sulky.

Bunny sighed. 'OK, for pulling up sails and things, all right?'

Filch brightened and nodded.

'So the sailor's cord is tied to some much thicker rope and...' Bunny held up a restraining hand as he saw Filch's mouth twitch, '... and that's tied to some heavy duty towing chain and the whole lot gets pulled up and then it gets wrapped and wrapped and tangled and tangled until it's all up in the working bits, right in the hub - that'll fuck it!' He rocked back in his chair for a triumphant puff of cigar.

Filch frothed his beer up with a dirty finger. 'Don't reckon it'll be enough meself,' he muttered.

'What, a hundred yards of towing chain wrapped round its bits? Come on!'

Filch took a sip and tried to look sage. 'You wants a weight, a bleedin' great lump of something on the end of that chain. That'd do it.' Satisfied with his contribution he helped himself to another packet of crisps and copied Bunny's lolling pose, balancing his half-empty glass on the sponsor's logo stretched over his Premiership belly.

The logistics for Bunny's latest attack were relatively simple to arrange, certainly simpler than his ill-fated assault on the Spout Hill meteorology mast, but there were other factors that to one extent or another were beyond his control. By avoiding sudden movements and with regular applications of chilled Vaseline he had some influence over the healing rate of his lacerated backside and genitalia but there was nothing he could do about the series of autumnal high-pressure systems, which persisted in slipping down from Scandinavia depriving most of the country, including Motley Common, of even a breath of wind. The targets simply wouldn't move.

While Bunny waited he sorted out the usual seasonal jobs around the caravan site, gingerly practised with his long bow and got used to living the life of a single man. The hurt of Linda's apparent desertion, like his buttocks and scrotal sack, was slowly healing. He'd had one letter, cordial but cold, that gave him an address in Italy but no phone number and no real clue to his wife's new domestic arrangements... or proclivities. Filch drifted onto the caravan park most days and with a bit of bullying made himself useful. He seemed curiously reluctant to return to his usual life of crime, something his newly qualified parole officer proudly ascribed to her talents, which in a way was true. Certainly Filch fancied her, but more importantly her encyclopedic knowledge of the benefit system meant he was now receiving more money from the state than he'd ever made through thieving. And with her encouragement, he'd been taken on by the local Citizen's Advice as a mentor to young offenders, many of whom he already knew professionally. Filch was very much enjoying his new status. On the face of it he was a living endorsement of the penal system, a resounding success for the parole service and a fine example of how the welfare state's 'safety net' should work - although there were some lingering questions over the whereabouts of the Bartford CAB's petty-cash tin.

Whilst going about his site chores Bunny was careful to work around the traveller group, especially the children, but via Filch he'd opened up a line of communication. Bunny still had no idea how many caravans or vehicles there were on his site, let alone the number of people, but a reasonable monthly rate had been agreed and was paid punctually in horse-scented cash. Bunny also had no idea how long they intended to stay, probably for the winter he decided, but in the meantime he was happy with his monthly wad ... whilst other negotiations continued.

Like many local residents, the Warren's Spout Hill wind farm consultation letter from the council hadn't arrived (it was in fact on the mantle shelf of a bemused pensioner in the Gorbals), but Bunny knew that the planning application for the wind farm had now been lodged with the council and was aware from pub and post office gossip of a coordinated campaign of protest in the village. The campaign of protest was of no interest to him; he'd grown to despise his neighbours and they in turn treated him as a laughing stock, encouraged by the *Bartford Bugle's* wry coverage of his regular court appearances and hospital stays. Bunny didn't care, he was his own man and ready to take direct action... once his arse had healed. However, news of the proposed march rather forced his hand. He'd been looking forward to the publicity, notoriety even, that his latest action was sure to attract, albeit anonymously. He'd even toyed with the idea of releasing an al Qaeda style video of himself, balaclava-ed and cradling the Silent Killer, but now, he suspected, his thunder would be stolen by the torch-lit Plompley Procession. It was sure to make the front pages and if it got the rumoured TV coverage then it was bound to relegate his own story to the inside pages, the cutting-room floor and obscurity. If he was to grab the headlines he needed to get on with it, and soon. His arse could cope he decided but he needed the wind.

It was Filch who had brought news of the procession and to Bunny's surprise announced that he'd be participating.

'You?'

'Yeah, why not?'

'Thought you weren't interested.'

Bunny was right to be suspicious. Rather than developing a sudden interest in local affairs Filch had been learning new skills from some of his mentees, including a worldly fourteen-year-old from Bucharest who'd taught him the rudiments of picking pockets. It was, the youngster stressed, essential to operate within crowds, and Filch had decided that the Plompley Procession would provide his first crowd, and the start of a new pit-bull and store-detective-free career. 'Thought I'd lend a hand,' Filch muttered, with unintended irony.

Bunny snorted his disbelief but since Filch was there he got him to lend a hand loading a huge coil of chain into the back of the old Land Rover. Best start getting ready.

'What's all this for then?' Filch panted.

'Motley Common, remember?' Filch's mouth slackened and both eyes started to drift towards his nose - he was thinking. Bunny decided it was probably best the idiot couldn't remember, he knew Filch told his father just about everything and the old man was a notorious gossip.

Filch started suddenly as if given an electric shock, 'You got that lump of weight sorted yet?'

In the following days Bunny scoured the weather forecasts and his outhouses looking for signs of wind and something heavy. By the weekend things started to look more promising. If the little girl on the TV was right, then by the middle of the following week the isobars on her chart should be close enough together to turn at least some of the Motley Common wind turbines, and in the same barn that had yielded up his father's vintage motorbike Bunny had found another relic from the same era, which could easily be adapted for his purpose.

Bunny had once again got his inspiration from a television programme; he'd been intrigued by a modern-day reconstruction of the inspired attempt by prisoners of war incarcerated in Colditz Castle to build and launch their own glider, probably the most audacious escape attempt of World War II. Having to rely on materials to hand, for obvious reasons, and requiring a heavy weight to drop off a roof to catapult their creation into the air, the ever-ingenious prisoners had latched onto the idea of a concrete filled, cast iron bathtub. Bunny remembered seeing something very similar in his barn and set to work.

The forecasters proved to be right and sure enough during Tuesday of the following week several of the huge turbines on Motley Moor creaked obligingly into life. Bunny decided that Wednesday night would be perfect for his attack, this would give the press the Thursday to investigate and time to put their stories together for the Friday editions, the day of the Plompley Procession. Wednesday would be D-Day: his arse had healed, the concrete had set and the wind continued to blow. A near-full moon was a nuisance but he'd keep to the back roads and smear the number plates of the Land Rover with mud before setting out. Bunny spent a restless Wednesday. Towards dusk he got dressed in black, strung and re-strung his bow nervously and waited impatiently for darkness to fall. Once underway the journey was slow and nerve wracking. It was soon clear that the bathtub had been a step too far, the suspension protested alarmingly and the sagging Land Rover could only creep along as Bunny rode the clutch and cursed Filch and his bright ideas. Eventually, somehow, and exceeding the manufacturer's wildest claims for ruggedness he brought the car to a shuddering halt in the moon-flecked shadows of one of the working turbines. After a struggle with the over-loaded and unassisted steering he then managed to back up to within a few yards of the enormous pylon.

It was time to put his plan into action. He had a quick look round, ducking instinctively as the huge blades swished past way above his head, then with a last glance up at the target he reached into the car for the long bow. Three arrows later and to Bunny's considerable surprise it worked, almost exactly as he'd planned... up to a point.

As soon as the third arrow had disappeared into the darkness between the blades and Bunny had felt the nylon line tauten he'd dashed for the cab of the car, slamming the door shut just as the hissing of the rapidly disappearing rope changed to the rattling roar of uncoiling chain, spinning and flailing out of the tailgate. History doesn't record whether the Colditz bath had large protruding lion's claws feet, but if it did, the would-be escapers would no doubt have removed them, or at least worked out how to prevent them snagging when their bath was released. Bunny had done neither, and as the last of the chain rattled deafeningly out the back of the old Land Rover the whole car gave just the briefest shudder of warning and then shot violently backwards. Bunny's unrestrained torso was slammed into the steering wheel cutting of his startled scream, which as his face was smeared across the windscreen became a whimper and eventually a wheezy sigh as he slipped into unconsciousness.

The litter of full ashtrays and half-drunk cups of cold tea were evidence of a quiet and lethargic mid-week evening in Bartford Police Station. No one was in a hurry to lower their stockinged feet or interrupt an article or crossword when the phone rang. Apart from anything else even answering the phone these days involved having to write some sort of report - even for a wrong number. Eventually, with a resigned sigh, the least senior PC folded down the corner of his *Beano* and picked up the receiver.

'Oh, hello, mate, thought you were off tonight.' He listened for several moments. 'That's one for the brigade isn't it? Have you rung them?' He listened again. 'There's a *what*?'

A couple of his colleagues lifted their eyes from their magazines and papers and the duty sergeant put his *Mirror* down and picked up his boots. Something was up. 'Who is it?' he mouthed at the young PC.

'Hang on a sec, mate, Sarge wants me.' The young PC put his hand over the mouthpiece.

'Who is it,' the sergeant asked again.

'Mike Pratt.'

'What's going on?'

'One of those wind turbines up on Motley Common is on fire and...'

'Well put it through to the fire brigade then.'

'There's a bit more to it, Sarge... um... there's a car hanging off the thing, about half way up apparently.'

No one in the room was reading now.

'A what?'

'A car, a Land Rover he thinks... sort of... dangling.'

'Is he on the piss, or just taking it?' There were sniggers around the room.

'Don't think so, Sarge. Shall I ask him?'

'No!' The sergeant bent down to lace his boots. 'What's he doing up there at this time of night anyway?'

'Dunno. Bird watching?'

'*Bird* watching? It's the middle of the fucking night!'

The PC shrugged. 'Owls?' he ventured.

'Give him to me.' The sergeant snatched the receiver. 'Pratt? What the bloody hell's going on?'

PC Mike Pratt had been on one of his regular nocturnal cycle rides. These invariably took in the old quarry; a huge jagged bowl hacked out of the side of Motley Common sometime in the early years of the Industrial Revolution but long since abandoned and now a favourite spot with lovers and doggers. The off-duty policeman always tried to make it there on Wednesday nights, more often than not an ever-changing group of swingers from Bartford would be there and they always put on an enthusiastic show in the back of their specially equipped Transit van. That night PC Pratt had got himself to the front of the little audience and could feel the tight, excited press of other voyeurs against him. Some were even women. In the back of the brightly lit van amongst crumpled layers of duvets and piles of Laura Ashley cushions an indistinguishable number of naked bodies squirmed, writhed and contorted. This evening's efforts were particularly imaginative and an accurate head count was almost impossible, even when several did pop up simultaneously to swig from a wine bottle or puff a circulating joint. PC Pratt thought there were probably five women - he'd counted nine different breasts, two of which were definitely a pair, they were black - and possibly four men - he'd definitely seen four erect members but might have double counted. Erotic tattoos and unusual piercings were much in evidence and the happy owner of a multiply pierced foreskin was definitely the star of this evening's show and getting most of the attention from participants of both sexes. PC Pratt was enjoying himself. Bulging but restrained in his Lycra cycling outfit (worn next to the skin), crushed between like-minded enthusiasts and within touching distance of the mass of sweating and smeared bodies he was in his kinky element. There was, however, an unspoken etiquette on these occasions and it was time for him to move over and allow someone else a ringside position. He eased to one side and a couple of dumpy lesbians he'd met before smiled and squeezed gratefully into his space just as the ringed and studded penis disappeared, prompting a delighted squeal, possibly from the black girl whose position made her the likeliest recipient.

Despite the chill of the evening PC Pratt was hot. He reached behind him to the belted pouch he wore in the small of his back, fumbled out a bottle of water and looked around the shadowy quarry to see if there were any other shows tonight. But apart from two silhouetted figures of indeterminate sex bent over the bonnet of a Volkswagen Beetle the Bartford swingers seemed to have a monopoly. It was the sudden appearance of the moon from behind a cloud and the resultant stroboscopic flickering of blue light through the blades of the distant wind turbines that made the policeman look up towards Motley Common. His startled eyes were immediately drawn to a livid horizontal plume of orange and green flames streaming from the hub of one of the stationery turbines. As he watched the moon was blotted out and the tips of the blades and the turbine's mast were almost lost in the darkness, but the torpedo-shaped pod flamed brighter than ever like a tethered comet. PC Pratt realised he had to do something: a quick triple '9' for the fire brigade should do it and then he could get back to the now swaying Transit. As he dialled the moon reappeared. He glanced up at the stricken turbine and his finger froze, poised over the pad, and he screwed up his eyes in a long blink before looking again. There was no mistake, a car or small van was suspended from the mast, bonnet down, about thirty foot above the ground, whilst way above it the flames, orange and sooty in the bright moonlight still flared out on the wind. Nobody else in the quarry seemed to have noticed the bizarre scene, which was explained a moment later by an orgasmic roar from the back of the Transit van followed by a sighing groan from the crowd. PC Pratt groaned too; he might be a voyeur, and arguably a pervert, and he was certainly confused about his own sexuality but first and foremost he was a copper, and duty came before pleasure - he dialled the direct line for Bartford Police Station.

Alerted by the sirens and blue flashing lights of all three emergency services the dogging enthusiasts at last became aware of the flaming turbine and its curious dangling appendage and dispersed. By the time the fire brigade, police, ambulance service and local mountain rescue team had stopped bickering and found Bunny, PC Pratt was also long gone and was now otherwise engaged. Heading reluctantly for home he'd made a last hopeful detour to the Riverside car park where he'd encountered a solitary exhibitionist couple who'd invited him to watch them perform in the back of their Skoda estate over which he was now happily masturbating.

'That's Mr Warren isn't it?'
'Yep.'
'He's the right way up.'
'I know.'
'Nothing wrong with his arse then?'
'Don't know, we haven't looked yet, we're concentrating on his nose and ribs for the moment. Oh yes, and his spleen. Perhaps we'll look at his arse later, what's left of it, it's always good for a giggle.'

Both nurses did.

'Fugg off.'

'Ah, Mr Warren, welcome back, I expect you know where you are. Try not to move too much you've been involved in a... well... a sort of car accident.'

'What's "a sort of car accident"?' her colleague whispered.

'I'll tell you on the break, it might take a while.'

CHAPTER FOURTEEN

'A snooker table! What the hell's a snooker table got to do with it?'

'Friend Hallibut,' Moody said patiently, 'as we've already established, is on the take. It's not the first time and on this occasion his... reward, seems to involve an improvement to his property, including a snooker room... to house a snooker table.'

Cockburn snorted impatiently to cover his nervousness. He might be the one behind the enormous desk but in recent weeks after a series of private meetings demanded at short notice by the head of Human Resources he'd been left feeling increasingly powerless. And why did the man always sound like he was giving evidence?

'How do you know all this?'

It wasn't the first time Cockburn had posed the question over the last few weeks. Bit-by-bit, meeting by meeting, Moody had laid bare the plot involving Hallibut, Ref Watt and Sir George Hoggit. Cockburn's own financial involvement had only been referred to obliquely but it was clear that somehow Moody knew about that too and now apparently the Sunday newspapers were onto it. Cockburn knew it was imperative, not least for his political ambitions, that no connection should be made or even suspected between him and the conspirators and it would seem, for reasons that weren't yet clear, that this man Moody had taken it upon himself to ensure this.

'But how do you know all this?' Cockburn repeated.

Moody had no intention of revealing his sources. That was his business, and his strength. In fact, unbeknownst to her, most of his information had come from Mattie. An ex-colleague of Moody's in London who regularly swapped triple Scotches and gossip with an investigative journalist on one of the Sunday nationals had picked up on the name *Bartford* during one their furtive conversations. It had rung a bell with the CID man and he'd thoughtfully contacted his old mate and fellow lodge member to pass on what he knew. At Moody's request a copy of the whole file, including Mattie's draft article and list of sources had followed.

'As we've already agreed, it's important that the council as a body is seen to be detached from any wrong doing by any individual officer.'

Cockburn nodded sternly.

'And we're also agreed that it's vital that no blame or whiff of corruption be allowed to be attached to the body politic... or any senior policy maker,' Moody added dryly. 'I take it that following our earlier discussions you've now ensured that your own situation is... shall we say, covered?'

Cockburn nodded emphatically. His nervous calls to Rennie had been met with an almost contemptuous dismissal as the electoral agent had impatiently explained, once again, his uniquely impenetrable system for disguising and redistributing political donations; they were 'untraceable' Cockburn had been assured, but if there was a glitch the system was set up to pin any scandal automatically on the Tories - 'credible and fool proof'.

'Right,' said Moody, 'you realise this thing is coming to a head now? It's not going to go away by itself and we need to be proactive.'

Cockburn was uncomfortably aware that Moody had again taken the initiative.

'We ignore the papers for the moment,' said Moody. '*We* need to set the agenda, it's time to get my old mob involved.'

'Your mob... the police do you mean?' Cockburn shifted uneasily in the huge chair.

'*You,* a vigilant, responsible and concerned local politician will contact them as leader of the council. This sordid affair has come to your attention and you're determined to act boldly and decisively to root out any bad apples and to safeguard your constituents interests.' It could have been Rennie speaking, Cockburn thought, his political antennae starting to twitch. But Moody was ahead of him: 'You might even pick up a few extra votes,' he sneered. 'It needs to be the Bartford Police not my lot but I've arranged that they'll have some... *influence,* shall we say, on the direction the investigation takes. The papers will follow the police investigation - they always do - and that way we can make sure they focus on the areas we want them to.'

'What areas?'

'Hallibut and Hoggit of course,' Moody snapped. 'And we'll make sure they're reminded of that business-park fiddle again, it might make a helpful additional distraction.'

'And you can actually do this? You have this... er, influence?'

'Yes,' Moody said simply, 'if I'm incentivised.'

Cockburn let out a long breath; he'd been expecting something like this. 'What exactly do you want?' he asked carefully.

Moody began giving evidence again. 'What this cock up has shown is that there's a need within this organisation for some form of internal monitoring and surveillance. What's required is the appointment of an experienced *internal security operative*.' He paused for this to sink in.

Cockburn looked alarmed. 'You won't have to carry a gun will you? I'm not sure I could get that past ways and means.'

Moody ignored the idiotic question but did note that the appointment had already been made. 'The position would justify a salary of... shall we say £150,000? And to attract the right candidate from a very limited pool it would be necessary to offer a 'golden hello'... shall we say, £100,000? The position would involve a certain amount of foreign travel for research and technique comparisons with other security experts. To avoid misunderstandings it may be prudent for Bartford to be twinned with some of these destinations, I would suggest Las Vegas and Antigua for a start. There will also be considerable travel within the UK and suitable transport will need to be provided for that, probably a Jaguar, possibly a high number BMW. A council credit card will be required... there will be other expenses of course.'

'Of course,' Cockburn echoed.

'The council budget need not be affected adversely.'

'I was wondering,' Cockburn muttered. 'Don't tell me, the Hardship Fund...'

'Can be raided... utilised, for any initial capital expenditure. The ongoing cost will be covered by the saving of Hallibut's salary...' Moody held up his hand as Cockburn was about to interject, '... topped up by the salary saved by dumping his line manager. Gander isn't it? Clearly not up to the job: eye off the ball, corruption on his watch and so on. He's tainted.'

Cockburn leant back in his chair and tugged thoughtfully at his upper lip. 'You seem to have it all worked out.'

Moody had got to his feet. 'Phone the police,' he said, 'they're expecting the call. You know what to say, you're a politician. Oh yes, and I presume I don't have to tell you: you *will* make sure the wind farm gets turned down won't you? That's tainted too, lose it and you'll lose the attention.' He set off across the office.

Cockburn watched the retreating back. 'And what do I get from this?' he blurted petulantly.

Moody turned from the door and stared at him in cold disbelief.

'What do *you* get?' He walked back across the plush rug until his thighs were touching the desk edge. 'What *you* get,' he flicked a contemptuous hand round the ostentatious office, 'is to keep your position here. What *you* get, is to keep your reputation. What *you* get, is to keep your chance of a parliamentary seat. And what *you* get... what *you* get... is to stay out of prison!'

Plompley was buzzing with anticipation. Richard Devine's spurning of the television company's earlier approaches had only increased their interest in him, so when he suddenly telephoned, not only agreeing to an interview but also with details of the torch-lit procession they hadn't hesitated. A camera crew fronted by an impatient and heavily made-up reporter had been in the village since late morning 'doing background', charming and annoying residents in equal measure. Most of those chosen to be interviewed, with the exception of Richard Devine, had been charmed, but those ignored, forced off the pavement or shooed out of shot by the bossy peroxide reporter were less enamoured. Despite being the supposed star the reporters were frustrated by the vicar's quiet and measured tones and quickly moved on hoping for something or someone a bit more animated, angry or outrageous. When it started raining again the soundman suggested they duck into the church to get some 'historical perspective'. Once inside, and more out of curiosity than in hope, they followed the sound of voices to the vestry - and immediately regretted it. The ambush was genteel but effective; the door was firmly shut behind them, chairs were provided and it was obvious they weren't going to get away without drinking at least one cup of tea. The Handwringers explained that this was their regular Thursday morning Pray & Sip coffee morning - except, of course, today was Friday and they'd run out of coffee, so they were drinking tea, which most of them preferred anyway because it was gentler on older bladders. But anyway, they'd moved their usual meeting so they could all prepare for that evening's procession - 'So exciting!' The media team was shown the rack of loaned coats and macs that had been assembled to fit out those who didn't own outdoor clothing suitable for climbing wet mountains in the dark. Chuckling delightedly the chief outfitter explained that the tangle of mismatched Wellingtons and walking sticks over in the corner was their 'stick 'n' welly library' - 'People are so kind.' In an effort to move the conversation on from the relative merits of zips versus Velcro the reporter decided to try out a few provocative questions about the wind farm.

Reactions were predictably negative but on the whole unspecific: 'quite disgraceful!' 'shocking!' 'so upsetting' and what's more it had brought 'a nasty element' into the village. This last claim neatly led the Handwringers into one of their favourite stories, one that perfectly exemplified the 'wickedness' of the wind farm developers, if ever one was needed. A diminutive but confident little grey-haired lady was gently pushed forward, obviously the storyteller, and the reporter dutifully nodded to the cameraman. By way of background the old lady explained that she was one of the leading flower arrangers at the church, she lived in a small cottage on the High Street and had done so for many years since 'poor Wilf' was sectioned. On the day in question she'd gone into the front parlour to change a vase of flowers: '... the water gets so smelly you know,' and there it was, a hand, in a black glove.' The old lady paused for a moment and the reporter had a sudden gruesome image of detached body parts scattered around amongst the chintz and lace of the old dear's front room.

'Through the window you see.'

'Ahh.'

Apparently a be-gloved hand, obviously still attached but with its owner out of sight, had been squeezed through a gap in an open window and when the old lady had entered the room it was busy tearing down her polite little protest poster. 'So what do you think of that?' she demanded.

The Handwringers tutted their outrage but the reporter, clearly unimpressed, just muttered polite shock and was about to give the 'cut' signal to the crew when...

'And the blood was awful, everywhere, and I'd only cleaned the windows the day before.'

The reporter stared at her.

'And of course the booties.' The fluffy grey head shook sadly. 'Such a shame ... for my sixth grandchild ... due at Christmas.' She brightened, 'I like to have some booties ready for them. Lemon of course, you just know if you knit blue ones it'll be a girl and if you choose pink it will be a little boy,' she chuckled. 'So the first pair is always lemon, and they were so nearly finished too, but I would never be able to get the blood out and anyway it wouldn't be quite...'

'Yes, yes, look, am I missing something here? Where did the blood come from?'

'My knitting.'

'Yes you've just said, but...'

'Well it was handy you see. I always keep it on the little table by my chair with the remote control and my spare teeth. Near the window you see, so it was handy.'

'Yes, but...'

'So I stabbed him. Well more skewered really I suppose, I think they went all the way through.'

There were more sympathetic clucks from the circle of grey and balding heads and a gulp from the cameraman whose hangover had reached the nauseous stage. The reporter declined offers of yet more tea and home-made macaroons and with her make-up in urgent need of repair and the cameraman visibly shaking they beat a hasty retreat in search of a mirror and a Bloody Mary.

Sid almost managed a civil welcome when the TV people came bundling wetly into The Smugglers bringing a crowd of casually disinterested villagers in their wake. Anticipating the media people being on expenses and used to London rates he'd adjusted his prices accordingly, ignoring the outraged regulars. Business was good and with the procession that evening it was going to get better. And what with the two phone calls earlier, one from London the other from Blackpool, he was having a good day, a very good day. The TV crew stayed in the pub long enough for the cameraman's tremors to stop, then on Sid's advice they headed for the post office and its gossip-in-chief mistress, where they were surprised and pleased to find a large and animated crowd squeezed into the little shop. There were even a few promising raised voices. From what the team could gather it seemed that out of the blue and against the wishes of just about every one of their parishioners Plompley Parish Council had written a widely circulated letter addressed to the Bartford planners *supporting* the Spout Hill wind farm. Residents were incensed and the mood of anger and suspicion had been compounded after a furious delegation found the council chairman's house mysteriously curtained and deserted with no indication of where he'd gone or when he was likely to be back. A search for the parish clerk had been no more successful. His elderly mother, with whom he lived, was clearly bemused by her middle-aged son's sudden absence but vaguely thought he might be away with a friend on holiday - she wasn't sure where but she knew he was fond of Tenby... or was it Abergavenny? The TV crew, needling and provoking, filmed interviews with a couple of the more outraged and confident villagers while the freshly made-up reporter, her ambition sharpened by three double gins, snapped interruptions mid-sentence in true *Newsnight* style.

Tipped off by the post-mistress, the reporter then marched her crew off to the school. The children of Plompley Primary had effectively been given the day off and under the supervision of teachers and volunteer parents were gathered in the school hall busy designing and painting banners and placards for the evening's procession. The headmistress, whose childhood home was amongst the closest to the wind farm and whose elderly parents had been literally worried sick, loathed the proposal. She'd had no compunction in suspending the National Curriculum for the day and was in no mood for a debate on its educational merits. If any stray Ofsted Inspector had happened by and queried the relaxed timetabling he or she would have been told that the children were involved in 'project work', including elements of art and design, handicraft, humanities and environmental studies - and then he or she would be told to 'fuck off!'

The arrival of a television camera team in the hall caused inevitable excitement amongst the children, and a few of the adults, with some of the pushier parents jostling for a position in front of the camera for themselves and their simpering offspring. The teachers tried to keep some form of order but disruption was inevitable and during the distraction an industrious group of unsupervised eight year olds managed to produce a series of rainbow-lettered banners demanding 'NO WIND *TURDINES* HERE'. To the dismay of the responsible adults these immediately caught the attention of the media crew who gleefully recorded the unfortunate slip for a sniggering early evening audience, before retiring once more to the pub. Happily ensconced at their earlier table and waited on by Sid they'd watched disinterestedly as a fire engine rushed through the village, thus missing probably one of the more dramatically newsworthy incidents of the day. In a workshop behind what was once the village smithy the redundant PAWs Off sign repairers had turned their ingenuity and practical skills to making the flaming torches for the evening's procession. Broom handles and oil-soaked rags were the main components but unfortunately one short-sighted helper had confused his cans and whilst testing a ragged torch accidentally soaked in petrol managed to blow most of the roof off the ancient building. Miraculously, apart from some singed fringes, eyebrows and one moustache, no one was hurt, but production was brought to an abrupt halt. .

Meanwhile Scott Driver was at a loose end. He'd taken the day off work to act as 'coordinator' but now found himself frustratingly under-employed with nothing and no one to co-ordinate. Lonely amongst the palms and aspidistras he mixed himself a livening mid-morning Martini and passed the time in making a series of unnecessary phone calls to people who had better things to do. He managed to confirm that the Boy Scouts would be 'parading' that evening in uniform, and was told that a contingent from the rugby club and Young Farmers would be attending in some yet to be confirmed role. This left him slightly uneasy.

There might have been tension around the village but on the whole it was a positive tension reflecting a communal mood of determined anticipation. The same could not be said for the atmosphere at Hoggit Hall. In one of his more lucid moments Sir George had decided that with the planning application at a critical stage and some nerves fraying, particularly Hallibut's, it would be prudent to bring together all the main protagonists for one last 'review meeting'. He wanted to ensure that nothing had been overlooked: that every report had been doctored, every graph tweaked, every helpful box ticked and unhelpful one discarded. As for Hallibut, there was no doubting Sir George had the man by the short and curlies but if the planning officer panicked ... well, it would inevitably feed through to Claude Cockburn and Sir George was under no illusions how the council leader would react. The loss of Cockburn's support at this stage could prove fatal to the whole scheme. A panic-stricken phone call from Hallibut had introduced him to another unwelcome element - Sir George had not anticipated serious interest from the *national* press and nor, he was sure, had Maxwell. With such additional scrutiny it was vital that they all 'sang from the same hymn sheet' - or preferably didn't sing at all.

One by one and with varying degrees of reluctance and furtiveness the plotters presented themselves at the Hoggit residence. Maxwell arrived first, sweeping his new executive car confidently round the drive and squirting Cotswold gravel onto the manicured grass. Chloe Jellaby was beside him and had amused herself on the drive over by plucking hairs from the back of Maxwell's gear-changing hand before 'kissing it better' and placing it firmly on the exposed flesh above her stocking tops. Maxwell automatically started to knead, not that he was particularly in need of inspiration. As far as he was concerned his job was done and this meeting was an unnecessary nuisance, although it did at least give him an opportunity to visit a newly Michelin-starred restaurant (with rooms) recently opened nearby. He let his fingers brush the taut gusset of Chloe Jellaby's underwear, re-tuned the car radio to a pop channel and strode towards the pillared entrance of Hoggit Hall.

Wormold arrived next in a lop-sided and steaming taxi that he'd found round the corner from the station. Neither it nor its stubbled driver had the necessary licence to operate but Wormold had other things on his mind. He wasn't quite sure what this meeting was about or what more he could do or say; the levels of data manipulation required to make the scheme even vaguely plausible were already unprecedented, even by his creative standards, and this knowledge made him even more nervous than usual. The wolfish smile Maxwell gave him as he entered Hoggit's study didn't help. Wormold sat down quickly, arranged various bags and files around his chair and balanced his open laptop on his knees.

Clive Hallibut was the last and most furtive to arrive having slipped through the back lanes in his rusting old Vauxhall - his usual mode of transport as far as the council tax-paying public of Bartfordshire were concerned. With the press sniffing around he'd rather not have been there at all but the Hallibuts urgently needed money; the next stage payment for the builders was well overdue with the most recent account from Ben Dover now outstanding for some weeks. And Mattie's Uncle Benny wasn't quite so 'cuddly' with people who owed him money. Hallibut left the Vauxhall at the far side of the circular drive partly concealed by clumps of dripping rhododendrons and dashed across the rain-washed gravel to the imposing portico.

Having shooed Mrs Bridges away to a distant part of the house Sir George greeted each of the arrivals personally, treating each to a tailored degree of rudeness and a blast of whiskey-laced halitosis. In contrast to the house and grounds, which, thanks to the small army of groundsmen and gardeners loyal to Lady Arabella looked stunning in their autumnal livery, Sir George, despite his loyal housekeeper's best efforts, looked a wreck. He'd continued to swell within his already tight clothes some streaked with the unidentifiable remains of past meals and he needed a haircut and a decent shave. An unpleasantly sour odour hung around him, not dissimilar to that found in the stairwells of multi-storey car parks, and he breathed in a series of irregular wheezes punctuated by gurgling coughing fits. Sir George had long given up worrying where the sun was in relation to a yardarm, or any other such quaint conventions; his whiskey consumption had become arbitrary and largely uninterrupted making him ever more irascible. A letter recently received from a top firm of London divorce lawyers and containing a twelve-page catalogue of his 'unreasonable behaviour' and an invoice from Italy for several tens of thousands of euros that he didn't fully understand, but obviously had something to do with a swimming pool, hadn't improved his mood either.

Sir George slumped heavily in his office chair. Without saying a word he emptied and refilled his cut glass tumbler and through puffed eyes studied the other people in the room. He at last collected himself, straightened in the chair and placing both hands firmly on the desk before him spoke steadily, lucidly and persuasively for nearly ten minutes. The transformation was astonishing. No one else spoke, there were a few nods, Hallibut's expression lost some of its strain and even Wormold dared to look up at one point. The gist of Sir George's address was simple: the job was done, the application with every 'i' dotted and 't' crossed had been accepted by the council, case officer Hallibut had duly prepared his report, unequivocally but not unreasonably recommending that the scheme should be approved, and this had been accepted, quite properly, by his immediate superior and in turn endorsed by the council leadership. The protesters were running out of steam and local opposition had largely been neutralised helped by the recent contribution from the parish council. The silly little 'procession' planned for that evening would amount to nothing, a pathetic publicity stunt and certain to be a damp squib, particularly in view of the weather forecast. What's more, Sir George assured the plotters, any press interest would not last beyond the weekend, including any nonsense from the dirt-digging Sundays. He'd glowered at Hallibut at this point before finishing calmly: 'So, gentlemen, we are there, all we have to do is hold our nerve and allow the democratic process to follow its course, and...' there was a grimace, which might have been a smile, '...and we shall have our wind farm!'

He stood up with an effort, raised his glass in mock salute and drained it. Then watched with a strange detached bewilderment as it slipped from his hand and bounced off the desk. The look of surprise remained while a dark stain spread down the left leg of his corduroy trousers and yellow bubbles started to froth from his lips.

'Is he breathing?'

'God! Can't you hear him?'

'Shouldn't we loosen something?'

The three men looked down at the mountainous body with shocked revulsion, Wormold still from a sitting position as Sir George had crashed to the floor at his feet, Maxwell and Hallibut from opposite ends of the huge desk.

'He doesn't look well.'

'No.'

'We ought to do *something*.'

'He's just drunk.'

'Didn't sound very drunk a minute ago.'

'He can switch it on and off.' It was the first time Wormold had spoken. He was ashen.

'Looks like he's switched it off for the moment.'

'Look, I really ought to go. I shouldn't be here, this isn't...' Hallibut started towards the door but was stopped by Wormold's hoarse whisper.

'I think he's stopped breathing.'

'Ambulance do you think?'

'It's either that or the kiss of...'

'Good Heavens!' No one had noticed the intuitive housekeeper enter the room. She took in the scene at a glance and to the astonishment of the three men hurled herself on top of her employer and started thrusting vigorously at his chest.

'CPR,' she puffed.

Sir George gurgled encouragingly.

'Well don't just stand there you damn fools, call a bloody ambulance!'

Less than half an hour later the ambulance crunched away down the drive between the dripping rhododendrons, the paramedics muttering uncharitably about the carelessness of Plompley residents. 'At least it's not that bloke's arse again,' the driver sniffed.

Hallibut, Wormold and Maxwell stood in a loose group at the foot of the grand entrance steps and watched the ambulance out of sight. The front door banged shut making Wormold jump and they all looked round.

'Well, that's a turn up.' Maxwell sounded calmer than he felt. From the minute the ambulance had been called his brain had been frantically computing the likely implications of Sir George's condition. 'We'll need to talk soon... once we know if Hoggit's... well, you know...' They all understood what he meant.

Maxwell stalked towards his car where Chloe Jellaby had spent the last twenty minutes unsuccessfully trying to remove half a bottle of nail varnish from the tan leather interior of her boss's car - the sudden arrival of the ambulance had startled her, she explained. Maxwell grunted his displeasure and sprayed more gravel as he left.

Wormold looked at Hallibut then at the firmly closed front door. 'My lap top...' he said suddenly, 'and the other things.'

'You'd better get them,' Hallibut said. 'I'll wait for you.'

'No, don't worry, Mrs Bridges knows me, I'll sort it out.' It was a surprisingly confident statement from Wormold, particularly in the circumstances.

'You sure?' Hallibut sounded doubtful but Wormold was already on his way back up the steps. The door opened almost immediately and after a few muttered words he was readmitted.

Hallibut shrugged and trudged back to his car trying to work out where this left him, and more to the point how the hell he was going to pay his increasingly aggressive builders. Oh God, and explain to Maxine. Driving reluctantly towards his partially completed home he was preoccupied with these thoughts when his mobile phone suddenly trilled. He ignored it; apart from anything else the last thing he needed at the moment was a sixty-quid fine.

It had taken over an hour to reach the restaurant (with rooms), during which time Maxwell had come to terms with the altered state of his upholstery and fondled his thoughts into some sort of order. Sir George's illness was clearly serious and would inevitably cause delay and attract yet more attention to the scheme, during which time Maxwell could very well see Hallibut losing his nerve. The planning officer was in too deep to do much damage but his political boss, Cockburn, could walk away from the deal without seriously compromising himself and Maxwell had little doubt that at the first sign of trouble that's exactly what he'd do. In which case the deal could, and probably would, quickly start to unravel. Maxwell was nothing if not a realist. The forgiven Chloe Jellaby purred happily as he massaged his thoughts to some sort of conclusion: on the up-side, well RefWatt were never going to build the things anyway, they would probably have flogged the whole scheme on to the French or the Danes; Hoggit had picked up most of the fees so there was no great financial loss, and if any mud did get thrown about in the press, well most of it would stick elsewhere. It could all have been worse. Maxwell put both hands back on the steering wheel and mentally moved on to the next deal. Early days but it was already coming together very nicely, an interesting part of the world, plenty of decent restaurants, granite bedrock and a completely unscrupulous and limitlessly rich client. God knows how a Russian gas importer had got hold of a chunk of the Lake District but apparently he had.

'As one door shuts another one opens,' Maxwell mused aloud, as he steered Chloe Jellaby and her inspirational bottom through the studded oak door of Ye Olde Leathern Codpiece.

Mrs Bridges didn't like Wormold and she knew her Ladyship didn't either but he seemed pretty harmless. It was only fair he should get his things from Sir George's study and although she wasn't quite sure what a 'backup' was - something to do with computers probably - if Sir George had asked Mr Wormold to do one, then he'd better do it. Although how he could be thinking about something like that at a time like this she really didn't know. She led Wormold as far as the study and left him to it.

Wormold glanced around the chaotic room. It looked as if there'd been a fight in there, the large leather chair was still lying on its side, the dropped whiskey tumbler had sprayed broken glass over a large area and the carpets and rugs were rucked by the paramedic's boots and stained by the contents of the overturned decanter. The room reeked of whiskey. Wormold carefully gathered his files and papers into a pile and topped it with the laptop. He then took a slim black bag, padded quietly over to the far corner of the room and knelt down by the last in a row of fitted oak-fronted cabinets. The door swung back easily to reveal a large safe. Wormold opened his case and set to work.

As Hallibut's ancient Vauxhall turned into The Park it announced his homecoming with a loud, smoky backfire and simultaneously shed the driver's-side windscreen wiper. Hallibut sighed heavily, wound down the window and stuck his head out into the rain to navigate the last few hundred yards. He regretted having taken the day off and wasn't looking forward to getting home. The kids had a day off school for some reason, meaning his wife had been obliged to take the day off work too 'in the middle of something important', and it was raining, so they'd all be bored and irritable. There'd probably be a surly builder or two about the place too and he suspected they knew he hadn't paid their boss recently ... and come to think of it he vaguely remembered mentioning to Dover that he might be in funds today, so he'd probably be waiting too. He groaned. This was not a homecoming Clive Hallibut was looking forward to.

God, there were cars everywhere! Some bloody coffee morning or ladies lunch club he supposed. He was forced to park across the end of his drive, which was full of unfamiliar cars, and... oh yes, there it was, Ben Dover's van. Shit! And the garage door had been opened for some reason, Hallibut prickled, if those bloody builders had scratched one of the cars again... the front door seemed to be open as well. And then a small group emerged from the garage, they weren't dressed like builders but Dover was with them. So was Maxine, looking furious. Hallibut was alarmed now, something wasn't right; he scrambled out of the car and set off up the drive, vaguely aware that other car doors were opening and slamming along the kerbside. His children appeared at the front door and stared past him. Alarmed and confused now, he paused on the cement-splattered brick sets to look round and found several large cameras pointed at him. Then he felt a hand on his shoulder.

'Are you Mr Clive Hallibut, Mr Clive Aloysius Spencer Hallibut?'

'Um...'

'Of course he fucking is!'

Clive Hallibut gave his wife a hurt look.

Sir George's arrival at Bartford General had not been auspicious. The paramedics had found a slot in the corridor to park his trolley, quickly passed their scribbled notes to a passing orderly and gone off shift. The unwilling orderly worked the same shift, she was already late and in danger of missing her bus, and she thrust Sir George's pink file at a junior doctor who was staggering in the opposite direction. He hadn't slept since Wednesday and after looking blankly at its cover added it to a pile of green files stacked on a trolley by the nurse's station. And there it sat until a sharp-eyed filing clerk noticed the colour discrepancy and transferred it to another trolley, where it sat again, until later that afternoon a porter trundled the trolley into a lift and down to the hospital incinerator.

In the meantime, and perhaps fortunately for him, the curious noises and smells emanating from Sir George's trolley attracted attention. He was pronounced 'paralytically inebriate', blood tests were taken to establish the level of alcohol poisoning and the anonymous and presumably vagrant drunk was reluctantly allocated a bed, there to regain consciousness and sober up.

Bunny had long got used to the hospital-morning routine: the ludicrously early wake-up call, the inedible breakfast, the buttock-clenching wait for a bedpan and odorous delay until any offering was removed, and then possibly a nod, a prod and a few muttered remarks from a white coat before a pre-lunch nap. But today this routine was interrupted and his nap was disturbed by the familiar swish of curtains, not his but those round the next bed. Unusually, it had been empty for some hours, in fact since the previous evening when there'd been a bit of a commotion followed by a brief high-pitched whine and then an ominous silence. It would seem that Bunny now had a new neighbour, and from the sound of it one who was already unpopular with the nursing staff.

'God, he stinks! Can you roll him this way? Ugh!'

'Pissed as a newt.'

'Dunno why they let them in. I'll clear up the top end, you get on with the other.'

'Oh no you don't. I did that junkie's shitty arse yesterday. I'll do his face, you get down to his... yugh!' There then followed a series of groans and grunts accompanied by gasps and exclamations of disgust.

'Big bugger isn't he?' one of the nurses panted.

'Not down here he's not.'

'Oh please!'

And so it went on. Bunny got bored and put his headphones on. He'd put in a request to the hospital radio's morning show for the old Black Sabbath favourite, *Paranoid*. Not *Sunbeam Radio's* usual thing but you never knew - he was a regular now.

CHAPTER FIFTEEN

By half past six at least half the population of Plompley had gathered in the litter-strewn lay-by at the bottom of the sunken green road. Despite the light drizzle and doom-laden forecast there was a carnival atmosphere amongst the villagers, neighbours gossiped and bitched happily, their children chased around between the parked cars flicking discarded condoms at each other and dogs sniffed and yapped excitedly. There was much for the adults to gossip about; most of the village had received their evening paper before leaving home and the front page had spectacular photographs of the flaming turbine on Motley Common, complete with dangling Land Rover. Bunny's injuries were described with gruesome relish and had been so exaggerated that readers were left in no doubt that his death was imminent. Rob Jordan had texted Mattie to ask whether she thought Bunny warranted some sort of an obituary, and if so, whether she could cobble one together - quickly. There was also a rumour doing the rounds that Sir George Hoggit had been taken ill. No one was sure whether it was true, nor indeed how the story had started, but a regular flow of ambulances to and from Plompley in the last few days added plausibility to the rumour.

Near a lop-sided litterbin oozing fast-food detritus a fan of gravel and dead leaves washed down from the hillside marked the start of the track. It was from here that Scott Driver intended to marshal his troops, waving a shiny new clipboard to semaphore meaningless signals to new arrivals and anyone else who met his eye. Some of those who'd partaken of the Driver's late-night hospitality felt obliged to wave back but mostly he was ignored. The usual greasy mobile-fast-food purveyor had arrived early, picked his pitch carefully and was now smothering Scott Driver in a cloud of fatty steam with every new batch of Budget Bigga Burgas that hit the hot plates. Following an outbreak of hotdog-related food poisonings, including that at the Hoggit Hall fete, the fast-food purveyor had changed his culinary emphasis and re-branded. He'd had the van cheaply re-sprayed and by his own sign-writing efforts managed to distort HAPPY DOGS into HARRYsBUGRERS and was back in business. No one was fooled, least of all the local environmental health officer, but business was brisk and the smell of over-fried onions and processed offal now drifted across the lay-by.

Watching the chaos, the Reverend Richard Devine stood miserably with his family under a dripping ash tree. They were surrounded by nervously twittering Handwringers, most of them clad in unfamiliar, ill-fitting outdoor clothing and fiddling with borrowed walking sticks. Oh good Lord! What had he started? George intuitively squeezed his hand.

Scott Driver came marching across the tarmac, clipboard tucked under his arm like an officer's swagger stick, and appeared to come to attention in front of Richard Devine. He barked out a situation report - or 'Sit Rep' as he'd probably call it - the impression of a keen young officer fresh from the mess reinforced by the breathy blasts of gin that accompanied his comments.

'Splendid turn out vicar... and still more to come. The Scouts are on their way with the Vincent-Townends, as long as Dr Lucy can keep that old minibus on the road,' he chuckled. 'Bit worried about the old chap though, that was a nasty fall. In a wheelchair I gather. Never mind, they should be here any minute.'

'Lucy Vincent-Townend?' Richard Devine looked worried. 'I thought Malcolm had banned her from driving the boys around in that thing. Isn't he coming?'

'Not available,' Scott Driver said briskly. The vicar obviously hadn't heard the most recent rumours about the Scout leader. 'Had to go away on business ... at *very* short notice.' The extended pause between the two statements was heavy with meaning. 'A bit of a misunderstanding, well, two really, with Cecil Pearce down at Bridge Farm ... thought he'd caught Malcolm rustling lambs.'

'Rustling! Malcolm?'

'Well, that was the first misunderstanding.'

Richard Devine looked at him warily. 'And the second?'

'Well... then Owen found his trousers, Malcolm's that is, hanging on a stile, and his...'

'Yes, yes OK.' Richard held up a hand, 'I'm sure there will be a... you know... a logical explanation.'

Scott Driver raised his eyebrows. 'Of course vicar.'

Meanwhile the First Plompley Scout Troop and its assistant leader were closer than everyone realised. Having spotted the congestion in the lay-by, and never quite sure of the dimensions of the ancient van, Lucy Vincent-Townend had decided to park on the grass verge, which had promptly collapsed sending the minibus slithering into a brimming ditch. For several minutes the frightened giggles of the scouts and muffled cries of Gordon Vincent-Townend were drowned out by Lucy Vincent-Townend's attempts to extricate them as the engine screamed and the spinning wheels sent great fans of mud and other autumnal debris arcing down the road. Eventually she had to admit defeat and an orderly evacuation was effected via the driver's door. Two of the older boys were left behind to extricate the cursing Gordon Vincent-Townend and his wheel chair, both of which they abandoned at the first opportunity on reaching the edge of the crowded lay-by.

'So what d'you think, Vicar? Got the lads here on time, eh?' Lucy Vincent-Townend had clearly surprised herself with this achievement.

'Yes, that's wonderful Lucy,' Richard Devine said. 'All present and correct eh?' he added with a forced heartiness that awkwardly tried to match her mood.

'Well not quite, young Archie Nicholls hasn't made it. One of our Ventures ... bit Tom 'n' Dick.'

'Oh, I'm sorry...'

'Oh, don't be.' She leant forward in an attempt at discretion but carried on at the same volume: 'Says it's the flu but its not, he's picked up a dose. Ha! Bloody jamborees!'

Richard glanced at George then down at his wide-eyed children.

'Isn't that your husband waving over there, Lucy?' George asked gently, gesturing over the crowd toward the flickering shadows. Richard nodded to his wife gratefully.

Lucy Vincent-Townend spun round. 'Gordon! Yoo-hoo!' She waved wildly. 'Do you want another pill dear?' She set off across the tarmac. 'It's for his nuts not his leg,' she shouted back cheerfully.

Scott Driver, who'd feigned disinterest during this exchange, scratched away importantly at his clipboard. 'So the Scouts are here,' he said unnecessarily, making an exaggerated tick on his pad.

A few stragglers still drifted along the road from the village but the flow was dwindling as the appointed hour approached. The torch makers started to move amongst the crowd eager to distribute their oily bundles although word of the earlier accident, now wildly exaggerated, had spread and there was an understandable reluctance amongst some villagers to expose their families to a potentially lethal device. As one wag put it: 'Illumination not immolation!' Sid hadn't helped either; during the early evening session at the pub he'd gleefully described the owner of the singed moustache (now sitting at home with a pair of tweezers and a bottle of camomile), as a veritable human torch and had nickamed him *Flambe Phil*. Those persuaded to accept a torch gave them a good sniff and then waited nervously for someone else to light theirs first. Non-torchbearers were less hesitant and many were now unfurling their banners and hoisting their placards. Rainbow signs, paint and ink already running, started to sprout from the field of glistening umbrellas lending an air of celebration rather than militancy. And then it started to rain in earnest.

Simon and Mattie had met at the pub and been greeted by a Sid who was positively bubbly.

'Nice to see you two together again,' he leered. 'You awright love?'

'Yes, fine thank you, Sid,' Mattie said coyly, before whispering to Simon, 'Told you he was sweet.'

Apart from the Aarights they had the pub, and a chatty Sid, to themselves and were both relieved when some of the early-doors crowd came in and demanded the landlords attention.

'Right,' Mattie said, looking after Sid, 'do you want the latest?'

'Of course.'

'It's all going to kick off on Sunday! They're going to run it *this* Sunday, two whole pages.' She could hardly contain her excitement. 'It's a broadsheet too!'

Simon smiled. 'I know.'

Mattie ignored him. 'They've asked me, *me*, to report on tonight's thing. Just to round the whole article off ... 'strength of feeling of decent local people', that sort of thing. It's to make all the corruption bits look even shittier. Clever eh? They want it by the morning... I'm going to be up all night I reckon.' She hugged herself happily.

Keen not to miss a moment of her assignment Mattie refused a second drink and hustled a reluctant Simon out of the pub and on to the Procession's rallying point. A small bank at the edge of the lay-by gave them a handy if slippery vantage point from where they could look out over the heads of the surprisingly large and glistening multi-coloured crowd.

'So what do you think?'

'Chapter Eight, that's what I think,' Simon said.

Mattie grunted and started scribbling notes.

Simon watched her for a moment. 'Has your friend Jordan got any idea you're doing this?' he asked.

'Nope, not a clue, serves him right. He texted me earlier, wants an obituary for your friend Bunny,' she snorted.

'Bunny Warren? An obituary! Christ, has he died?'

'Good as.'

Simon stared at her, not sure if he was more shocked by the news or Mattie's callousness. 'Poor old Bunny, what happened?'

'Haven't you seen *The Bugle*? Oh, it's a good one,' Mattie crowed, 'even by your Bunny's standards. Silly bugger went and tied himself - or at least his car with him in it - to one of those bloody great turbines on Motley Common. It was actually going round at the time and seems it took your loony friend with it... multiple injuries.'

'Oh bloody hell, what a shame.' Simon looked across to where he knew the start of the sunken road was and remembered his first meeting with Bunny. 'Looks like this thing's claimed its first victim then.'

'I hadn't though of that, good point.' Mattie scribbled something in her crumpled pad.

Simon looked away, slightly revolted, and moved the shared umbrella a bit more over himself.

'Who's that little guy?' Mattie asked suddenly.

'Who, where? You may have to be a bit more specific, I reckon I can see about five hundred people at the moment.'

'There, with the vicar's little flock. He doesn't look like the rest of them, just keeps hovering round the edge, weaselly little bloke in the hoodie. See him?'

'Oh yeah, but I don't know him. I've seen him in the pub sometimes, he's a friend of Bunny Warrens I think - or was.'

They stood in silence for a few moments surveying different sections of the gathering crowd.

'No one's lit their torch yet.'

Simon was reminded of an impatient child waiting for the first firework on Guy Fawkes Night. 'Can't say I blame them, no one's quite sure what those things have been dipped in, they say you can still smell burning flesh if you stick your head into the Old Smithy.'

'Urrg.' Mattie gave a giggle. 'Who called him *Flambe Phil*?'

'Sid, who'd you think?'

There was a sudden oily flash, a whoosh and a chorus of exclamations. One brave soul, having removed his family to a safe distance, had risked lighting his torch and was now brandishing the flaming broom handle, his face a mixture of relief and bravado in the flickering orange light.

'Well there's one.'

Both watched the torchbearer. 'Was that guy really called Phil?' Mattie asked suddenly.

'Could be, some people are ... I don't think he's called Flambe though.'

Mattie elbowed him gently in the ribs.

There was a swirl in the crowd at the far end of the lay-by.

'Hang on, looks like things are happening,' Simon said, '... aah'

'What?' Mattie peered through the darkness.

'It's those TV people, looks like half of Plompley are trying to get their fifteen minutes of fame and our Scotty's right in there with them.'

The camera crew was indeed on the move, threading their way between curious groups of villagers and their badly parked cars. The female reporter led the way, the sodden faux-fur-fringed hood of her parka re-arranging her make-up with every turn of the head. Her attempt to head off a post-lunchtime hangover with Jack Daniels and a suspiciously long visit to the ladies had failed, as had her repeated calls to the office begging to be allowed to return to 'civilisation' and her warm, dry editing suite. She was cold, miserable, foul-tempered and didn't care who knew it. The large group of children, naturally drawn to a vaguely-recognised celebrity, suddenly scattered, rushing squealing back to parents: 'Mummy, that lady who does the weather on television just told Emma Harris to "fuck off".' And another piping voice: 'Daddy, Daddy, the TV lady called Mr Driver a "wanker"... what's a wanker, Daddy?'

To the relief of Plompley's squirming parents the flow of shrill obscenities was interrupted by the cheerful blast of a three-tone air horn and the appearance of a battered van. It skidded to a halt in the fan of debris as a final deafening fanfare announced the arrival of the combined forces of Plompleys young farmers and the rugby club - the Headbangers had arrived.

Unsettled by his earlier phone call and still smarting from what he thought the TV presenter had called him, Scott Driver watched nervously as the van doors burst open and spilled forth the cream of Plompley's youth. The new arrivals were noisy and good-naturedly boisterous. They were also to a man - and possibly woman - dressed in the unmistakable robes and conical hoods of the Ku Klux Klan.

There was a stunned silence among the assembled crowd while the laughing youngsters piled out, milling around adjusting each other's robes and realigning eyeholes in dislodged hoods.

'For God's sake!' Richard Devine exploded.

'So they claim, I gather,' Simon muttered.

Nearly all eyes were on the ghostly flame-lit figures cavorting around the van but there was the odd curious glance in the vicar's direction.

Scott Driver emitted a groan. 'Richard, Vicar, this is your department. We can't allow this. What do they think they're playing at? Oh Christ, the TV people are onto it.'

Indeed they were. The camera hadn't stopped rolling since the battered van had shuddered to a halt and the reporter had peeled back her hood and was frantically trying to re-arrange her face in a hand mirror in preparation for a piece to camera.

There were some stirrings in the crowd and someone laughed. That anyone could find these grotesques or what they represented in any way funny riled Richard Devine into action. He was sure these ridiculous youngsters in their silly home-made outfits had no idea what they symbolised - or at least he fervently hoped they didn't. He headed over to the group, prepared to give them the benefit of the doubt but struggling to contain his distaste and anger.

'What the bloody hell do you think you're doing?' he exploded.

The tone and coarse language from a clergyman stunned the youngsters into a meek and respectful silence.

Eventually there was a polite: 'Evenin', vicar.'

'Do you lot know what you're doing? Have you any idea what all this... this...' he waved his arm at their robes, '...this crap, represents, what it means to people? Do you?'

'Just a bit of fun, vicar. People in the films in the States goes on marches in this clobber.' It was a female voice. 'Just a bit of fun,' she repeated.

'Fun!' Richard Devine struggled to contain himself. He wasn't sure whether it was their ignorance or just the suggestion that a bunch of murderous rednecks could ever be considered *fun* that incensed him more. 'For Gods sake! It is *not* about fun.' He stabbed a finger towards their van, 'I suppose you've got a cross in the back there somewhere ready to burn? Just for a giggle!'

'No we ain't vicar...' a soft rural voice muttered apologetically, '...could soon get one though if you like,' he added helpfully, to murmurs of assent.

Richard Devine regretted his sarcasm and flash of temper 'No! I don't want one. No. Now look...' He took a deep breath, '... look, do you people realise what the people who dress in this... stuff, represent. What the Ku Klux Klan actually is?'

There was sheepish silence.

'It's a hateful organisation, bigoted, sexist and above all racist, it hates black people. They carry out illegal beatings and even hangings, it's...'

'Ere, bugger that!' a deep voice rumbled from near the front of the group and a conical mask was tugged off to reveal a frowning face of undoubted West Indian origins. There was a titter of laughter from over Richard Devine's shoulder and he realised that a considerable number of the villagers had gathered behind him to watch and listen.

'You tell 'em, vicar!' a deep agricultural voice boomed anonymously from the middle of the crowd. 'Get that rubbish off you silly young sods and lets get on with this thing before we all get soaked. Bloody weather.'

There was a general muttering of assent and the crowd began to drift back towards their original groups.

Around the rear of the scruffy van the youngsters, muttering claims of innocence and bitter criticisms of their leader's ignorance, removed their hoods and robes. Another black face had appeared and joined several ruddy-faced girls in giving the rugby-team captain a particularly hard time. 'Well, how was I to know? I saw this film,' he said, '...well, a bit of it.' The girls stalked to the back of the van to disrobe in some privacy.

The only remaining member of the group still clad in white, a huge farmer's son who played in the second row, sidled up to his captain.

''Ere, mate, what am I gonna wear?' He plucked at the old bed-sheet, 'I 'aven't got anything on under 'ere.'

The captain looked at him in bemusement, 'What no jeans or anything?' He reached down to tug up the sheet.

'Gerroff! No, only me boxers and they're a bit... well... I come straight from milking.'

'You got no trousers on?' The humorous possibilities of the situation had already occurred to the captain and he'd raised his voice.

'Shhh, won't you?' The huge youth looked round, dismayed at the attention he was now attracting. 'Well, I thought it was, sort of, like the Scots, you know, under their kilts...' he whispered.

'Like the Scots! Well I dunno, mate, you'll just have to do something with that sheet. Have you got a shirt on?' This was confirmed. 'Well that's something. Here, girls, come and give this wally a hand to make some trousers or something. Anyone tie a nappy?'

Richard Devine kept a close eye on the disrobing from a distance. The encounter had left him disturbed, by his own actions and words as much as those of the naïve youngsters, but he had an idea on how to re-engage with them. He approached the captain:

'Look, I'm sorry if I was a little... abrupt, I'm afraid the outfits were something of a shock.'

'No problem, Vic.' Richard Devine's shoulder was solidly thumped. 'Our cock-up... sorry, mistake. All a bit daft really.'

'It's not that your involvement and enthusiasm aren't appreciated. Of course you're all very welcome on the procession, in fact I was wondering whether we could call on you for a little help? It's a job I think only you and your friends are really qualified for.'

The big youth pulled his shoulders back and lifted his chin slightly. 'Well, yeah of course, ask away, Vicar.'

Richard Devine explained that far more people than anticipated had turned out, they were very much of mixed abilities and the green road was going to be rough, wet and slippery. Some people were going to need support and encouragement - and 'stewarding' (he thought a title might appeal) - to get to the top of Spout Hill, and of course, safely back down again. Would the young farmers and rugby club with their supporters be prepared to take on that role for the evening?

'Stewards? You bet!'

Richard stepped back to avoid another bruising, manly bash.

'Oh, and perhaps you could give special attention to the Doctors

Vincent-Townend. You know who I mean? They're a little, er... eccentric. He's in that wheel chair but apparently is still determined to get to the top. Perhaps some of your stronger...'

'No problem, Vic, he'll be first to the top!'

Richard Devine returned to his family and George took his hand. 'Well done, dear,' she murmured.

Scott Driver had re-positioned himself strategically at the entrance to the sunken lane, and now armed with a nightstick-sized torch as well as his clipboard he tried to restrain and choreograph the crowds for the benefit of the film crew - who completely ignored him and disappeared up the track to look for a sheltered vantage point. Scott looked after them. Behind him people were getting restless, there was a hint of rebellion in the sodden air and a ragged chorus of: 'Why are we waiting?' broke out. An occasional flaming umbrella ignited by the dripping torches added to the general agitation. Scott gave a shrug, tossed his clipboard into the bushes and stood to one side.

The Plompley Procession was under way.

CHAPTER SIXTEEN

The rugby club captain had meant it when he'd promised Richard Devine that the Vincent-Townends would be the first to the top of Spout Hill but he'd underestimated the challeges of manhandling a flimsy NHS wheelchair with an unpredictable passenger and an uncontrollable plaster cast. After several abortive attempts and a lot of bad-tempered debate one of the girls took charge; what they needed, she explained like a teacher addressing a class of fractious infants, were carrying poles, it was quite simple and a couple of fallen branches would do. There was some sulky male muttering but a few minutes later Gordon Vincent-Townend and his chair were ready to be hoisted onto the shoulders of the Plompley rugby team.

While all this was going on Gordon seemed strangely detached, offering no comment and apparently disinterested. It had been noted around the village that Dr Vincent-Townend hadn't been himself recently, in fact not since his precipitous visit to his basement. This was generally put down to a mixture of pain and to the frustrations of immobility, but there were other forces at play. On his discharge from Bartford General Gordon had been provided with a month's supply of industrial-strength painkillers, which Lucy had promptly taken charge of, dispensing them haphazardly and often supplementing them with a tablet or two taken at random from the confiscated collection she kept loose in an old biscuit tin. Gordon's recollections of the last few weeks were to say the least, vague. At times he'd found himself in a state of euphoria, ecstacy even, but he'd also spent time in dark, confusing and lonely places. That evening Dr Lucy had already dosed him to the point of bewilderment in preparation for the ascent of Spout Hill, although he'd still been grateful for two unidentified pills offered him by his rescuers after he'd been extricated from the toppled mini-bus.

While the finishing touches were put to his litter there was a Buddha-like calm about Gordon Vincent-Townend. He cradled an empty plastic bottle provided by his wife - 'in case of emergencies, dear' - and caressed a long hazel stick cut for him by the scouts but seemed to have no particular interest in his immediate fate. However, when the rugby team eventually hoisted him aloft, thrusting his hooded head amongst dripping fronds of dead leaves, the reverie seemed to be broken. He looked about with a sudden awareness studying each of his porters in turn, his eyes lingering for just a moment longer on the bundle of grubby sheet gathered round the loins of the big second-row. He saw his wife hopping from foot to foot kicking at puddles and eager to go and he waved at the last few groups of passing villagers as they made their way into the entrance of the lane. Many looked up in amused astonishment as they passed. Some waved back. A group of primary aged children waving banners burst into song as they came level with him and he studied each of them intently, a greedy unseen glint in his eyes, and touched his upper lip with the tip of his tongue. Then, without any warning he flung back his hood, swished his stick in a wide arc and roared: 'Forward! Onwards to the gathering!'

''Ere steady!' The sudden movement had nearly upset the litter but the rugby team managed to hang on and obediently moved off up the path.

The Great Anaconda waited patiently but imperiously while his porters prepared the litter. He gazed indulgently at the passing train of bowed subjects, unsurprised by their deference but still occasionally acknowledging their obeisances. Bursts of song and chanting in his praise from passing groups of plump children amused him, and he nodded his approval at their waving standards and totems borne proudly aloft. He had watched as his bearers were chosen and the rest of his praetorian guard and remaining wives had been sent on with the infants to prepare the feast. He was elevated above his subjects and felt his cowled head kissed wetly by the sky. His jester pranced and capered ready to lead the procession. It was time. He removed his cowl, gestured with his staff and gave the command to proceed.

The litter swayed and bobbed up the sacred covered track towards The Chosen Place and the Great Anaconda wobbled magnificently aloft, content in his majesty. His enormous naked plumpness pronounced his wealth, the greased folds of glistening flesh, blue with myriad tattoos added by degrees since puberty, confirmed his rank. The ancient exaggerated penis gourd of office, passed for generations from father to son, affirmed his virility. But with divine perfection and sacred power came the obligation of benevolence: 'We shall feast!' he roared and was met by grateful wide-eyed glances from his stumbling servants.

The Great Anaconda sat back in his litter, benign and soothed by the hissing of the wind in the trees and the primaeval rhythms of the forest. Small yellow parrots flitted around, an occasional humming bird whirled past and he allowed huge wet-winged butterflies to brush his face.

The litter jerked and the Great Anaconda glowered his displeasure at the loincloth-clad bearer who had tripped and whose head was now bowed in contrition. He must do penance. 'Sing!' commanded the Ever-Merciful, and lazily reached up into the canopy to pluck a handful of the lush and plentiful fruits that hung there. Women's work but the effort amused him. Obediently the singing started, a homage to maidenhood he did not recognise but the words of the song distracted him from thoughts of food for a rare moment and he dwelt happily on another aspect of The Gatherings. 'Virgins!' the Great Anaconda bellowed and further exhortations to sexual excess followed, although the singing had stopped at his first lusty roar. He watched disinterestedly as his jester hopped from puddle to puddle ahead of him. The prancing fool occasionally gibbered some remark over its shoulder but he did not deign to listen - he was no longer amused. The singing had started again, a familiar war chant appropriate and suitable for the voice of a warrior chief, so the Great Anaconda sang too, and the litter moved onwards and upwards.

'Long pigs!' The sudden bellow made the litter shudder. The bearers stopped. 'Long pigs,' their chief repeated, stabbing his staff towards a group of pale and insolent peasants sheltering under a tree at the side of the track. 'Slaughter them,' he ordered.

The procession moved on, the war song ringing up the hill. In anticipation of the festivities the Great Anaconda slipped on the ancestral penis gourd prompting a collective groan and gasps of admiration from his attendants.

'Suckling, we shall have suckling,' he murmured.

.

The camera crew, wet, hung-over and miserable had gone much further up the sunken lane than they'd intended before they found a spot with half-decent shelter. It was of secondary importance that the raised bank under the dripping canopy of ash trees was also a handy vantage point from which to view the track in both directions. Whatever, they had no intention of going any further. As the cameraman pointed out: 'Even if any of the 'rustic idiots do manage to reach the top in this bloody weather it'll be 'invisible, un-recordable and anyway not news-worthy.' The team agreed. They'd stay for ten more minutes, see if there were any particularly serious injuries or especially distressed marchers to record - a decent heart attack would neatly cover both - and then head back to civilisation.

The ten minutes was nearly up when a small group suddenly appeared coming back down the path. The crew had got used to a steady flow of numbed children and battered pensioners being lead tentatively back down the hill but this appeared to be a threesome of youngish men and the one in the middle was clearly being assisted. At last, this might be the news-worthy injury to let them wrap up their coverage.

'Is he badly hurt?' the reporter called down hopefully.

It was the man on the left who replied. 'Oh no, nothing wrong with our Filch.'

'Who?'

'Filch. This 'ere is Filch,' he said, lifting the arm of the little man in the middle in involuntary greeting.

Filch peered out, Fagin-like from under his hoody.

'On the nick again,' the escort explained.

'On the what?'

'"The nick." Been pickin' pockets... or tryin' anyhow,' he snorted.

The reporter gave the cameraman a nod and the man on the right of the trio shifted uneasily and tried to move off. But the first speaker had also noted the camera.

'Got it wrong again didn't yer Filch?' he said amiably.

'Soo... you've caught this man trying to pick the pockets of members of the general public who are here to march in protest at the proposed Spout Hill wind farm. Is that right?' the reporter asked slowly, looking meaningfully at the camera.

'That's about it,' the big youth said. He looked down at Filch almost affectionately. 'Shouldn't try and turn over the local copper should yer?' he chuckled.

The right-hand half of the escort looked even more uncomfortable and tugged at the arm of the hoody.

'A policeman! You tried to pick the pocket of a policeman?' Then sudden realisation. 'Is that you, are you the policeman?'

The man on the right nodded reluctantly.

'And you didn't know?' the reporter said, turning back to Filch. 'Brilliant!'

'Oh, I knows Bob,' said Filch, 'known 'im since school. We're kinda cousins... I think.'

'And you still tried to pick his pocket?'

Filch looked sulky. 'Didn't see it was 'im in the dark ... and no uniform neither. Anyway I just found it on the ground... I was gonna give it back,' he said, quickly, remembering his defence.

The police officer decided it was time to assert his authority. 'Right that's enough, come on you, we'll talk about this at the station.'

'Yeah,' said Filch, 'I'm sayin' nothin'.' He eyed the camera. 'Trial by TV, that's what this is, I'm not sayin' nothin'. Not 'til I've seen my probation officer.'

The crew filmed the threesome as they moved off down the path and disappeared into the shadows.

'Right, that'll do it, lets get the hell out of here.'

Cables were coiled and the camera was already in its case when there was a sudden echoing bellow from down the hill. The reporter lifted a flap of her hood and listened. 'Hang on a second, stay there a minute.' Her crew groaned.

There was another raucous shout, closer now. It boomed up the tunnel of the path. Torch beams danced and flashed and other voices including a persistent feminine twittering could be heard.

The reporter peeled off her hood. 'Just one more, guys, this could be good. Get the gear out, come on. Quick!'

One deep voice rose above the hubbub. 'We shall feast!' it roared. Then other voices seemingly in reply, younger but also deep and tuneless, rang out: 'Ohh... four and twenty virgins came down from Inverness... and when the ball was over...'

'Virgins!' the first voice bellowed, 'we shall have virgins! We shall deflower! We shall feast!'

The TV crew looked at each other. They were prepared now - at least technically. Shapes took form below them amongst the trees and several flaming torches amongst the electric beams gave flickering glimpses of the approaching crowd.

'I know...' a disembodied voice suddenly shouted, 'Swing low...ow, sweet chaa...riot...' Other voices joined in enthusiastically, 'Coming for to carry me home...'

Bit by bit the caravan of apparent madmen - and women - began to emerge. It was led by a bareheaded, straggle-haired woman swathed in flapping blue nylon. She was apparently oblivious to the torrential rain and came skipping up the path happily hopping from puddle to puddle. Occasionally she'd stop to call instructions and encouragement over her shoulder: 'Sing up, Gordon! Don't fidget, dear, you'll fall off', and, 'well done lads! Soon be at the top!'

Behind her was some sort of litter precariously supporting a wheelchair in which an elderly man bounced around from side to side, the whole thing somehow balanced by four panting young men, one of whom appeared to be wearing an enormous nappy. Their wild-eyed passenger's uncovered hair was a tangle of twigs and the wet leaves that whirled around him in the squally wind. Below the neck he was a bulging crumpled mass of glistening blue nylon. A large plastic bottle was wedged upright in his crotch and he brandished a long stick still sporting a few tufts of foliage, which he swung wildly over the heads of his porters.

270

Occasionally he reached into a passing tree to pluck a handful of berries or a pine cone, which he would study carefully before thrusting into the folds of his anorak.

As the group got nearer, the prancing straggle-haired shaman character waved to the news team, made a peak with her raised hand and warbled, 'I looked across the Jordan... and what did I see...?' before turning back to the litter and shouting, 'Smile for the camera Gordon!' The old man leant dangerously from his wheelchair and stabbed aggressively towards the television team with his stick. 'Long pigs!' he bellowed, 'Slaughter the long pigs! Butcher them!' He sank back into his chair. 'Suckling, we shall have suckling,' he muttered, then inserted his penis in the plastic lemonade bottle. This prompted a few disgusted groans fom his entourage but apart from that there'd been no reaction to his murderous demands and the singing continued. As the last of the group passed, a young bearded face popped out from under its hood and nodded a casual greeting to the stunned television crew.

'Evenin',' it said.

The reporter watched speechlessly as the litter carried on into the tunnel of hawthorns, the words of the adopted spiritual slowly fading up the hill.

'That *did* happen didn't it?' she asked no one in particular.

'Mad as a box of fucking frogs,' confirmed the sound engineer.

'You did get it all didn't you?'

'Oh yes, we got it all right!' the cameraman assured her. 'Brilliant stuff ... can we go now?'

It was agreed that the last few minutes of footage had been far better than any dying pensioner or temporarily crippled schoolchild and there was nothing more to be wrung out of this story. It was time to flee Plompley and its lunatic residents.

At the top of the sunken road Scott Driver, self-appointed PAWs Off director of operations, crouched awkwardly under a dripping holly bush tolerating the occasional stab in the back in return for the limited shelter it offered. His clipboard gone, his only trapping of authority now was the enormous mace-sized torch, which he shone fussily into the startled faces of the villagers as they emerged onto the exposed hilltop.

'Over by the met mast, re-group by the mast!' he shouted at each dazzled newcomer.

Most complied and the crowd grew, startled by the ferocity of the wind and driven rain, and made nervous by the whistles and howls coming from the skeletal tower whose pathetic lee they sought. These were the survivors; the ascent had not been without incident and at various points the sodden, ferny banks of the track had been littered with wailing children, sobbing pensioners and other assorted wounded. Richard Devine was not the only one to be struck by the biblical imagery. And this, he though ruefully, was an exodus of *his* making. At least his Old Testament counterpart had had the promised land to look forward to, the best Richard Devine could hope for was a frayed dressing gown, a cloudy glass of wine and a *Father Ted* repeat. He sighed and vowed never to speak at... no, never to *attend*... a meeting of any protest group, however worthy the cause... ever again!

Simon and Mattie were amongst the first to reach the ridge. On the way up they'd squeezed past groups of puffing villagers exchanging brief comments with those with enough breath to talk, mostly about the weather or the wind farm; the former accepted with a wry stoicism the latter prompting the usual outraged concerns.

Emerging from the shelter of the path they'd hunched into the full blast of the storm and hurried across to join the gathering crowd at the base of the swaying mast. Mattie, determined to exercise her temporary national press credentials, was resorting to ever more outrageous questions in the hope of an original response or comment. She was trying to elicit some sort of reaction from a group of sceptical pensioners to claims (hers) that wind turbine vibration could disrupt pacemakers, when the ground gave a sudden shiver. Conversations stopped mid-sentence. Then there was another more distinct shudder, an unmistakable tremor, and mild confusion turned to alarm as the howls from the mast became high-pitched groans. A sudden lull in the storm only emphasised the drama, a momentary peace whilst the elements caught their breath. It was broken by shouts and screams and other sounds of panic from further along the ridge. Then these were blotted out as the storm came crashing back in.

'Come on!' Mattie shouted under Simon's hood and grabbed his hand. Moving quickly along the ridge, slithering over the wet turf, they could make out the cones of torchlights sweeping erratically skyward through driving waves of rain but the sources of the lights remained curiously invisible. Heading blindly towards the sweeping beams they suddenly found themselves teetering on the edge of a large steep-sided depression and the light sources were revealed. The hollow was crowded with several large family groups, the adults huddled protectively round their children like cornered rabbits. Mattie crouched down at the edge almost losing her footing.

'Watch it! That bit's slipped away while we've been down here,' said a male voice from behind one of the more powerful torches. 'I shouldn't come down if I were you... we're getting out. Thought we'd get the kids out of the wind down here but the bloody thing's collapsing, it's sinking.' His torchlight flashed over newly exposed layers of flaking rock strata and slashes of loose earth.

'You been down there long?' Simon asked.

There was no answer, the man had already turned to help push a small sobbing child up the muddy bank. The ground gave another jolt and further along, unnoticed in the dark, the turf of the bank tore open to expose another crumbling slab of rock.

'Did you feel that?' Simon bellowed. They edged away from the lip. 'Now what?'

Mattie peered into the darkness, reluctant to leave such a promising scene of natural and human drama. 'Where are *they* going?' she asked suddenly.

A number of groups were passing quite close to them in the dark, all moving further along the ridge and away from the mast and the top of the green road.

Simon told her about the ridge track leading to the road. 'It's the long way down,' he explained, 'but probably easier in all this. My stream starts somewhere down there too,' he added.

'What the one in your garden?'

'Probably *is* my garden by now.'

After another muddy slither they re-joined the determinedly cheerful crowd who'd gathered at the top of the green road patiently waiting their turns to start back down the hill. Torch beams flashed back and forth over the multi-coloured mass occasionally picking out Scott Driver hunched under his bush. The director of operations looked agitated; there was no sign of the TV crew, marchers were scattered willy-nilly across the hillside with a mass of early desertions, and the defiant chain of fiery torches had been reduced to piles of scorched broom handles and rags littered across the doomed landscape. The whole thing was turning into a bloody shambles. A vicious sluicing squall blew in under the holly bush. 'Bloody weather!'

Going against the flow, Richard Devine with George and the two children eventually reached the top of the green road and guessing it was Scott Driver dazzling new arrivals followed the beam of the powerful torch to the holly bush.

'Ah, vicar.'

Richard thought Scott sounded nervous. Lightning lit the scene again quickly followed by the inevitable boom.

'Is it the end of the world, Daddy?' the youngest Devine asked.

'No, no not just yet, but God does sound a bit fed up doesn't he?'

'Yeah, well pissed off,' the eldest confirmed.

'Paul!' George said quickly. 'Not in front of your father.'

Richard Devine, his mouth open ready with his own rebuke gave his wife a startled look. He turned back to the holly bush.

'Look, Scott,' he said, 'I think this has gone far enough, don't you? We've made our point. It's getting very...' he looked down at his children and caught George's eye, '...very uncomfortable up here. And is it a good idea that everyone's so close to that mast thing with all this lightning around? Who's bright idea was that? Oh...'

In fact people had started to work out the dangers for themselves and there was already a steady flow away from the swaying steel skeleton to join the crowd at head of the green road. The sound of crying children rose above the noise of the storm.

'Where on earth are those TV people?'

'Oh to hell with them, Scott!' Richard Devine snapped. 'Lets get these people off here before someone...'

There was a sudden loud commotion down the hill and a chorus of raised voices that might have been singing. Several torches swivelled towards the sound, their beams combining in time to capture the extraordinary arrival of the Vincent-Townend litter and entourage. Gasping out the final verse of *On The Good Ship Venus* the litter bearers splashed and stumbled their way triumphantly up the last few muddy yards.

'Oh my God! That's all we...' Richard's words were drowned out by another deafening peal of thunder ... and the re-awakening of Gordon Vincent-Townend.

'Bring forth the long pigs, light the fires, let the feasting begin!' the Great Anaconda bellowed at the astonished crowd, rocking wildly in his wheelchair.

''Ere steady,' one of the carriers protested, and got a swipe from the leafy end of the Great Anaconda's staff in reply. 'Bloody 'ell!'

'Oh, my good God!' Richard said. His children were fascinated.

'Hello everyone!' Lucy Vincent-Townend shouted happily. 'We're here!'

The Great Anaconda rummaged in the folds of his waterproofs and produced a mixed handful of twigs, pine cones and crushed berries, which he hurled at one of the rugby team's girlfriends.

'Oi, what's your bleedin' game?'

The Great Anaconda peered down at her for a moment, then thrust his stick vertically between his legs and roared, 'This is no maiden, bring me a virgin!'

'Bloody cheek!' The protest was hardly convincing and anyway it was too late, her slanderer had already fallen asleep again.

Simon and Mattie missed the Vincent-Townend's spectacular arrival; a few minutes earlier the met mast had emitted a particularly anguished metallic shriek and Mattie had tugged Simon away from the crowd at the top of the green road to join the remnants still clustered under the steel tower. As they approached there were several whip-cracks from somewhere up in the structure, a shower of blue sparks suddenly arced away on the wind from near the base and there were more squeals of tortured metal. Torches played over the writhing steelwork and children were whisked up into parental arms, elderly hands clutched and tugged and the terrified crowd surged backwards from the tilting mast.

'Lets get away from this thing,' Simon shouted. He found Mattie's hand and broke into a clumsy jog, only to be dragged to a slithering halt after just a few paces.

'No, come on, it's still standing, lets have a closer look.'

There was no question, the steel tower was definitely leaning and apparently unsupported; some of its anchoring cables hung redundantly swishing and twitching in the wind despite their weight, whilst others, although still attached sagged uselessly. Simon shone his torch at the huge exposed concrete slab of the base. It had tilted crazily, the mast still attached, with one side lifted clear of the ground whilst the opposite edge seemed to be sliding under the torn turf like a doomed ship slipping beneath the waves. Simon and Mattie edged closer and there was another tremor beneath their feet. More of the concrete was sucked into the ground and the whole structure shook like a wet dog.

'Time to go!' Simon shouted.

'No, lets wait to see it go.'

'No way! We don't know what's happening here. Lets get off this bloody hill.'

'So is *this* the end of the world, Daddy?'

Richard Devine didn't answer.

Gordon Vincent-Townend woke up again and opened one eye. 'No virgins then?' The eye started to close, 'The wrath of the Gods!' he mumbled, and his head fell forward onto his chest ... and stayed there.

Scott Driver flashed his mace around aimlessly.

The ground trembled and suddenly the sound of fast-flowing water could be heard coming from somewhere nearby.

Under the circumstances the evacuation of Spout Hill was relatively orderly and good-natured. Many of the villagers headed along the ridge path towards the road taking the longer route but seeking the reassurance of a man-made environment. The rest filed patiently back into the dripping tunnel of the green road. Shouted arrangements to meet in The Smuggler's Finger were made with a forced joviality and unconvincing bravado as the villagers sought to reassure each other... and themselves.

Mattie insisted that she and Simon were amongst the last to leave. She still hoped that the meteorology mast might reach the horizontal but eventually they too ducked down the lane, now ankle-deep in rushing water. Mattie was still looking for any last scraps of 'human interest' but there was nothing left apart from the exhausted Vincent-Townend entourage; the porters past caring, Lucy Vincent-Townend too tired to puddle-hop and the Great Anaconda noisily asleep.

Half way along the main road between Plompley and Bartford, in a steamed-up people carrier, the relieved television crew were congratulating themselves on a job well done. The carefully edited clips of the villagers' eccentric behaviour would lead neatly into their pre-recorded studio piece, which had already concluded, with some faux sympathy for the villagers, that their 'Nimbyism' should not be allowed to obstruct an important and much needed Green energy project. Support for wind farms had long been network policy.

CHAPTER SEVENTEEN

As the first bedraggled protestors approached their homes it became clear all was not well; blue lights were flashing and reflecting in various parts of the village and an occasional siren could be heard above the sound of the storm. Tired legs hurried on through the huge puddles and overflowing gutters their owners fearing the worst, some with justification, returning to front gardens full of sympathetic firemen stacking sandbags and uncoiling hoses. Others were luckier, the flooding limited to their sodden gardens. Most of the unlucky ones were persuaded to stay only long enough to give the firemen access to set up their pumps and were then sent off to the village hall from where the emergency was being coordinated and arrangements made for the displaced. This was the parish council's Civil Defence sub-committee's long-agreed plan for a local disaster - something eagerly looked forward to by its members - but unfortunately what they had not allowed for was both key-holders, the council chairman and clerk, simultaneously decamping to Llandudno. After ten minutes of confusion and repeated attempts to break through the vandal-proof security it was decided The Smuggler's Finger would have to provide an alternative.

Simon and Mattie stuck with the crowd, Simon not bothering to return to his cottage. Looking at the state of the rest of the semi-submerged village he knew what he'd find. They trailed through the flooded streets where torrential streams poured down side alleys and lanes to feed the fast-flowing rivers that were the main thoroughfares, Mattie all the while scribbling notes in her sodden pad and cursing the lack of a camera.

The pub was already packed with the more fortunate villagers enjoying a nightcap, smug in the knowledge they could shortly return to safe dry homes. So when the dripping crowd of homeless and dispossessed appeared even Sid had initially been taken aback. But by the time Simon and Mattie forced their way into the packed room he'd moved out from behind his bar, half pint in hand, and was holding forth.

'You're cheerful aren't you?' said Simon, nodding down at the floorboards. On the way in he and Mattie had noticed two firemen threading a hose through the hatch into the pub's flooded cellar.

'No problem, all under control,' Sid shouted. He lowered his voice, 'I moved all the stock up earlier... not that the fuckin' insurance company need to know that.'

'There's been some kind of an earthquake,' Mattie said.

'Bollocks!' Sid roared good naturedly, attracting even more of the pub's attention, 'it's the Smugglers' Fingers!'

'The what?'

'The Smugglers' Fingers. It's where the name comes from for this place. All you had to do was ask 'em.' He nodded towards the log burner where the hunched figures of the Aarights, invisible amongst a crowd of steaming homeless villagers, were presumably sitting. 'Old buggers,' Sid said, almost affectionately. 'There's caves, miles of them they reckon, running under the whole hill, your Spout 'ill. Five main ones there are, the *fingers*, see? And the smugglers used them in the old times to hide their gear. They used to bring it all up from the coast,' he waved a hand vaguely inland, '...you know, brandy, lace and stuff, and hide it up there for a while until any fuss had died down. Then they'd move it nice and quietly off east to the big cities, off to the punters.'

'Yes, OK, but what's that got to do with all *this*?' Mattie's question was clearly meant to go beyond the crowded pub to include the chaos of flooded homes and the streaming streets outside.

'Well... the biggest of the caves, it's more of a tunnel really so they say...' he nodded towards the log burner again, '...it goes right into the hill and somewhere in there is a bleedin' great lake, like a sort of reservoir, and sometimes it gets too full and... well, it's got to go somewhere,' he shrugged.

'Aah, got it,' Simon said.

'It's something to do with the type of rock,' Sid continued. 'It's really soft, porous like. I've never been up there but they say there's lots of big dips and hollows up on the top, like the ground's sunk in places, right?' Simon nodded impatiently. 'So, when there's been a lot of rain the caves and things get washed away, eroded like, and then things start collapsing and that's when you get yer holes. Then things get sort of...' The technicalities were starting to defeat Sid. '... sort of *squeezed*. And like I said it's gotta go somewhere, so out it all comes, spouting out... "Spout Hill" ...see?'

'Sid, that was it!' Simon prodded Sid's shoulder. 'The old sign, the pub sign, the one we burnt... *that* was the cave, that was the entrance.'

'That's what *they* said,' Sid confirmed, nodding towards the invisible Aarights.

'I've been there! I knew there was something about it, something familiar. It's where my stream starts...' Simon beamed like a proud parent, '...the entrance to *The Smugglers' Fingers*.'

Mattie watched him curiously for a moment while the noise of the pub swirled around them. 'I was just wondering,' she said thoughtfully, 'how the hell can they build a wind farm on a hill that sits on top of a lake and sinks a bit every time it rains hard?'

'Good point.'

Mattie wasn't the only one to have reached this conclusion and the wind farm debates still swirling around the pub became ever more optimistic despite the devastation in the streets outside. Every cloud has a silver lining, it was agreed, especially by those whose homes weren't under several feet of muddy water and raw sewage.

People were still arriving and somehow squeezing into the ridiculously overcrowded pub, amongst them the de-robed and slightly sheepish Headbanger crowd. They'd managed to reclaim the bar end of the pub and were now quietly sipping their drinks, uncertain of their reception. Richard Devine went over and made a point of thanking them loudly for their stewarding efforts and patience: '...particularly with some of the more... er, demanding participants,' he smiled wryly, earning himself a knowing wink and another bruised shoulder. The Headbangers, duly rehabilitated, soon reverted to their usual boisterous, good-natured ways.

The Great Anaconda had been carefully parked, still in his wheelchair, in the lounge area, where Dr Lucy had fed him another couple of random pills and put a large Gordons in his hand. Revived by the mixture of gin and confiscated amphetamines he'd found his mind inexplicably drifting between images of spit-roast suckling pig and scenes from an al fresco orgy. A sudden burst of laughter from the bar caught his attention and he found himself staring at the rugby club and Young Farmers crowd trying to work out where he'd seen them before. His wife bounced into his eyeline.

'Can I get you anything, Gordon dear?'

Gordon Vincent-Townend touched his upper lip with the tip of his tongue. 'I could murder some porky scratchings,' he said.

Scott Driver, not for the first time that day, was at a loose end. He'd not made the impact he'd hoped for on the evening's proceedings and now, here in an environment where the Drivers normally shone, he found himself isolated and largely ignored. He looked around hopefully.

'Ah, vicar.'

'Scott,' Richard Devine said without enthusiasm. He'd spent the last ten minutes comforting and reassuring the Handwringers, some of them too nervous to even check the state of their homes, and was now going from group to group of villagers trying to assess exactly how many were temporarily homeless and what could be done about it. He was tired and genuinely distressed at the plight of his parishioners and in no mood for the narcissistic Scott Driver, whom for some reason he couldn't help blaming for this whole situation.

'Vicar, can I have a word?'

Richard Devine gratefully turned his back on Scott to find Oliver Le Rolms, Donald McCruddy's farm agent, breathless and flushed under a battered tweed cap.

'Yes, of course, but I'm very...'

'It's important, really important. I think you ought to know. I don't know who else I should be telling really.' He glanced at Scott Driver, hovering nosily.

Richard Devine sighed.' Go on then.'

'Well, I've just met that Mrs Bridges, the housekeeper at Hoggit Hall. She's just come back from Bartford ... been to see Sir George to take him some clean pyjamas and a hip flask, she said.' Le Rolms realised part of his explanation was missing. 'He's in hospital,' he added.

'Ah, someone said he'd been taken ill.'

'Not any more... he's dead.'

Sadly Ozzy Osborne and his bat-munching pals hadn't got an airing on the Sunbeam am show that morning and Bunny had soon got bored with the bubble-gum pop and unnaturally cheerful presenters. The curtains round the neighbouring bed had long since been flung back and looking for a distraction Bunny heaved himself onto a bruised elbow to inspect his new neighbour ... and promptly ducked straight back down again. There could be no mistake: the hair was longer, the facial features more swollen and the skin an odd colour but Bunny was in no doubt, the next bed was occupied by Sir George Hoggit. He was asleep or unconscious, thank God, and didn't look at all well but even a sick Sir George was a terrifying prospect. After all a wounded animal was meant to be the most dangerous sort. Bunny knew his widely publicised attacks on Sir George's wind farm plans had made him a very nasty enemy indeed and when Sir George came round hospital life could become very unpleasant.

What to do? Bunny knew from nurse chatter that the hospital was full to capacity and they couldn't move him even if they'd wanted to. Could he leave? From what Bunny could gather he was on the mend, somehow his spleen had remained intact and although he'd cracked two ribs he was only days away from being sent home anyway. The latest white coat had said as much and said it was just a matter of the paperwork, which might take a day or two to track down. Bunny didn't care about paperwork, he was leaving, and quickly, before Sir George woke up and while no one was around. He eased himself upright and gingerly rubbed his ribs, they hurt but not unbearably. Sir George coughed wetly. There was no time to lose, rummaging in the bedside locker Bunny managed to find most of his clothes, annoyingly his underpants and one shoe were missing but his wallet and keys were there. Sir George coughed again and stirred restlessly and ominous rumbles came from his swollen middle regions. Bunny hurriedly started dressing. Bending awkwardly to lace his shoe he banged his head on the locker, swearing loudly, which prompted more stirrings in the neighbouring bed and the appearance of two podgy arms from under the covers. There was another gastric groan and Bunny watched in horror as the huge body gave a sudden heave, the head strained forward like a belligerent turtle's and with one last shudder spewed forth a copious stream of lumpy sulphurous slime. Bunny swallowed hard and turned away as Sir George, still semi-conscious, tugged a pillow from under his head and held it to his dripping mouth. There was a last dry retch then silence. Bunny risked a glance and found the massive figure had slumped back on the bed, the fouled pillow still clutched to its face. The stubby fingers slowly relaxed their grip and Bunny watched as the hands slipped down to rest on the coverlet. He sighed his relief and promptly dropped his bunch of keys, kicking them noisily under the bed as he tried to break their fall. Shit! He ducked under the bed, held his breath and waited. Still nothing. Straightening warily, stiffly, something occurred to him. With the tips of his thumb and forefinger, mouth distorted by disgust, he lifted up the pillowslip to reveal most of Sir George's face. The mottling of the skin had given way to a uniform grey, except the thin lips, which were blue, and curiously the eyes seemed wider in death than they'd been for many years in life.

Bunny shakily replaced the pillow and limped from the hospital.

By the time Richard Devine had returned to his family and told George what had happened the whole pub was buzzing. Scott Driver, seeing an opportunity to regain the centre of attention had wasted no time in spreading the news, only to be upstaged by Oliver Le Rolm's next bombshell.

'Murdered they reckon.'

'Murdered!' The word flashed round the room with delicious horror.

'They think it was that caravan site bloke,' Oliver Le Rolms continued. 'Bunny Warren!'

The next tremor shot round the pub. 'It was Bunny Warren!'

'Always knew he was a nutter...'

'How'd he do it?'

'Gone on the run they say...'

'Someone saw him in the village earlier.'

'Armed, he is...'

With all the movement in the heaving pub, Simon and Mattie saw an opportunity and slid into their usual alcove.

Simon looked at Mattie accusingly, 'Bloody Hell! I thought Bunny was dead. You said...'

'So did I! And I'd already started his obituary too.'

'There's gratitude for you! Well don't waste it, there's always Hoggit,' Simon said sourly.

'I've got to make a call,' said Mattie.

She wasn't the only one.

Amongst the first to hear of Sir George Hoggit's demise was the exiled Donald McCruddy. The croupier scowled at him as the mobile phone squawked insistently in his jacket pocket but McCruddy didn't care, he had no intention of returning to this particular table. Over the last hour or so he'd been dealt a run of marginal twist-or-stick hands, which he'd invariably 'bust', and the unpleasantly camp croupier hadn't bothered to hide his sneery satisfaction at McCruddy's losses. Puerto Banus was not what it was. Answering the phone finally, the brief conversation with his farm agent decided it; there were more important things to do than playing blackjack. Plompley gossip regularly filtered its way down to the Costa del Sol and McCruddy had followed the domestic upheavals at Hoggit Hall with spiteful interest. Now, with the death of Sir George, it seemed possible that six hundred acres of prime agricultural land and one of the finest houses in Bartfordshire could very well soon become available - and Donald McCruddy was in the market. From the steps of the casino he rang the number for Hoggit Hall. A distressed and exhausted Mrs Bridges answered and confirmed Sir George's condition, or lack of it. She gulped back tears and added that despite not knowing what to say, she really couldn't put off calling Lady Arabella in Italy with the sad news any longer. Donald McCruddy, the sympathetic neighbour, friend and Scottish gentleman comforted the distraught housekeeper and agreed, reluctantly, that yes it might be kinder for her Ladyship to hear the tragic news from an old family friend, and yes, he supposed as one of the closest friends it should be his sad duty ... if Mrs Bridges really thought that was for the best. Mrs Bridges assured him that she did and gave him the telephone number of the house in Tuscany. Her duty done, she finished another tumbler of Sir George's sherry and made her way unsteadily and sadly home.

McCruddy had already started to dial the international code for Italy before he realised he didn't know what he would say to Lady Arabella. Would it work to inform a woman of her husband's death and simultaneously invite her to enter into high-value and complicated negotiations for her family home? Doubtful. There was a deal to be done but it needed to be approached carefully and he needed time to think. The call to inform Lady Arabella Hoggit of her recent widowhood, and more importantly to open negotiations for Hoggit Hall would best be left until the morning.

Soon-to-be-ex-planning officer Clive Hallibut had spent the afternoon and evening being shuttled back and forth between a grim white-tiled cell and an equally bleak, windowless interview room - one inducing a state of solitary misery, the other a nervous tendency to disingenuity. He was in the interview room at the moment, alone briefly, when a uniformed head and shoulders leant through the door.

'Fancy a cuppa?'

Hallibut nodded.

'Dunno whether it's good news for you or not,' the policeman said, taking up his position by the door, 'but that George Hoggit, *Sir* George Hoggit, sorry, he's snuffed it. Dead. Done in at the hospital apparently.' He shook his head in amused disbelief.

Hallibut looked at the policeman blankly and tried to work out the implications of this latest development. 'Could I make another phone call?' he asked meekly.

Chloe Jellaby looked the two sardines in the eyes, or at least the upturned ones, and winked back playfully. Maxwell had insisted on ordering for her and had been about to explain the filleting technique when his mobile phone purred against his hip.

'Excuse me, my dear, I think I'd better take this.' He turned away, still in his seat and cupped a hand over his mouth, but just listened. His expression moved from concern to surprise through thoughtful concentration and eventually settled in a sort of cheerful resignation. He murmured a few words that sounded like reassurance and turned back to Chloe just in time to see the last of a sardine's tail slither out of sight between her pouting scarlet lips. He looked down at her empty plate and shook his head in disbelief.

'I've just got to make one call. Don't eat anything else till I get back,' he added.

Wormold couldn't have answered his mobile phone even if he'd wanted to, and Maxwell needn't have worried about the little man's laptop and its incriminating data either. All were now near the bottom of the English Channel somewhere vaguely west of the Isle of Wight. Once the ferry had cleared the famous Needles, the newly retired consultant had slipped a bag containing all the electronic devices from his previous life over the side of the rolling ship before hurrying back to the first class restaurant to re-join the cheery young New Zealand back-packers he'd met on deck earlier. They'd readily accepted his invitation to dinner, and he knew he'd be picking up the bill, but they seemed like nice girls and anyway money wasn't really a problem now.

Maxwell gave up trying to get a connection and returned to the table where Chloe Jellaby was picking her teeth with the butter knife.

'Everything alright, my dear?'

'Hmm.' She puffed a couple of tiny vertebrae onto her side plate and put down the knife. 'What's next?'

'The Lake District.'

'Eh?'

'As you may remember me saying earlier, my dear, as one door shuts another one opens. Well, I think we can say with some certainty that one door has just been well and truly shut, so it's a good job a new one has so promptly opened.' He raised his glass. 'Here's to Blencathra.'

'Bottoms up!' Chloe Jellaby downed half the glass. 'So who's this Ben Caster then?'

Council leader Claude Cockburn slumped exhausted behind his enormous desk nursing a glass of port that he'd shakily poured from the dusty bottle he kept in a bottom drawer. He rarely drank in the office but after being grilled for two hours solid by the ways and means committee over the need for an 'Internal Security Officer' he felt drained. Even normally compliant members had raised awkward questions, particularly about the cost, and tempers had frayed. Eventually, after the leader of the Women's Group had screamed that she could look after her own 'fucking internal security', something no one round the table doubted, the chairman had been obliged to intervene. Fortunately Cockburn held a comprehensive and graphic record of this lay preacher's predilections and the chairman's casting vote was never in doubt. The dedicated phone at the back of his desk suddenly rang, making him jump. Rennie never rang at this time of the evening, he was always at his club. Cockburn gingerly picked up the receiver and listened.

'How did you get this number?' he eventually asked.

Moody ignored the question and tersely reported on the current situation: Hoggit was dead, Spout Hill had proved geologically unstable and the wind farm was dead in the water, Hallibut would shortly be released on bail and Ref Watt had already moved on. There was political capital to be made out of the situation but that was up to Cockburn, he was the politician. Moody assumed his new appointment and terms had been agreed? Good. And by the way was the council aware of a traveller situation developing in Plompley?

Cockburn had hardly said a word and was still digesting it all when

Moody snapped: 'Got that?'

'How... how do you know all this? Its...'

'We'll speak tomorrow.'

Yards away from the council offices in a dingy wine bar a large man standing at the bar answered his mobile phone. He was dressed in a sheepskin coat and pork pie hat and had the air of a struggling bookmaker but he was in fact a solicitor, one with a particularly niche clientele. He didn't have offices and worked from the boot of an old Rolls Royce, moving from client to client, from site to site. He finished the call and with a curt 'goodbye' to his companion, left the bar and headed for his 'office'.

Aware of Bunny's hospitalisation, and like everyone else who'd read *The Bugle,* expecting his imminent death, the travellers were surprised to see lights come on in his house and Filch was dispatched to investigate. The little thief had been granted police bail pending probationary reports and had slunk back to his adoptive home at the traveller's site where for reasons of their own they'd set him up with his own scruffy little caravan and an even scruffier dog. The elders had warned the site children off him and within the camp Filch had become anonymous, untraceable and invisible to officialdom - something that suited him very well.

Filch returned to say that it *was* Bunny at home; he was in reasonable health, knew what they wanted and although surprised that it could happen at this hour would be over in half an hour or so. This had prompted the telephoned summons picked up in the Bartford wine bar.

Bunny was still shaken by his experience at the hospital and struggling with images of the dead Sir George Hoggit - particularly the colours and the smell he decided - but he'd been fascinated and strangely comforted by the warmth of the garishly religious interior of the caravan. He was greeted like an honoured guest, even the dogs hadn't barked just sniffed indifferently at his crotch, and although he couldn't help noticing the three small children at the other end of the caravan playing with a flick knife, he'd relaxed in the homely atmosphere.

The large solicitor was similarly greeted, glasses of brandy were poured, legal papers spread over the lace tablecloth for signature and a huge pile of horse-scented fifty-pound notes was counted and re-counted. The formalities were quickly over, there were smiles and handshakes all round and glasses were just being re-filled when a gentle knock announced a new arrival. It was the young man who'd been helping Sid out in The Smuggler's Finger for the evening and he brought startling news.

It hadn't occurred to Bunny that anyone could possibly think he might be involved in Sir George's death, let alone the cause of it. He stared down at the paper sandwich bag full of fifty pound notes in front of him and wondered how he should react. The travellers watched him closely, some in sceptical disbelief, some quietly impressed. Bunny looked up and round the large frilly table, he sensed some of the doubt but also the respect.

'Did yer do it then?' the solicitor asked bluntly, eyeing up a promising potential client.

Bunny lent back against the pink velour bench and studied the nails on his right hand. 'Depends,' he eventually ventured, his voice shriller than he'd hoped. There was an audible intake of breath around the caravan. Sensing his moment Bunny picked up the crystal brandy glass in front of him, swirled the contents and casually downed them in one. 'Time to go,' he growled, his voice satisfyingly roughened by the spirit.

There were handshakes all round again then one of the small children from the other end of the room shyly approached Bunny. She held the open flick knife before her face like a saluting swordsman before snapping the blade home and gently pressing the knife into Bunny's hand. 'Respec' mister,' she murmured, then returned quietly to her siblings.

By dawn Bunny was happy with his domestic arrangements. It had been a long night made more dramatic by the distant blue flashing lights and occasional siren, they were obviously hunting him. But he was away now over the ridge and running free, the lone wolf back in his element, back in the wilderness and now safe in his lair. The fire crackled and flared illuminating rows of carefully stacked tins and bottles of water and a crude rack supporting a selection of medieval weapons. The cavern, hidden amongst dense woods on the opposite slope of Spout Hill was a survivalist's Aladdin's cave, adapted, stocked and equipped over many obsessive years. Bunny threw another log on the fire, wriggled into his sleeping bag and checked that the bolt hadn't fallen out of the Silent Killer. He sighed happily and sleep came quickly.

Simon sat alone sprawled in the cramped window seat and watched the pub empty. He'd been at the bar when Mattie had taken the phone call and had returned to the table to find her already pulling on her coat.

'Got to go. They've called me in,' she said. 'The hill collapsing and now Hoggit's murder has changed everything. Now it's *really* big.'

'Oh... right, fine, of course. No need for the toothbrush then.'

She looked down at him with a slight apologetic smile, 'I didn't bring it actually.'

That was nearly an hour ago. Simon had finished his bottle of lager and was half way through the glass of too-warm wine that should have been Mattie's. He watched Sid collecting glasses. He'd had some help earlier but appeared to be on his own now. There was an extra slouch to his shoulders and he was clearly tired but still seemed remarkably cheerful, for Sid. Record takings, Simon decided. Sid caught his eye and raised a stack of dirty interlocked glasses in ironic salute. There was just the odd isolated group of villagers left in the pub, some still cheerfully boisterous - those with their own homes to go to - and others despondently finalising arrangements for somewhere to stay for the night. The village hall had eventually been breached but despite repeated assaults with a crowbar, expanding foam and an air rifle the alarm was still going off every ten minutes and the hall was clearly useless as a place for exhausted villagers seeking a place to sleep. It had been abandoned again and miserable family groups had trailed back to the pub where Richard Devine quietly took charge, organising, making introductions and generally ensuring that everybody was found shelter somewhere in the village. George, with their two over-tired children had already left, shepherding one flooded-out family, their gerbils and an antique patchwork quilt towards the vicarage. They were escorted by Oliver Le Rolms. The Headbanger crowd had also left the pub earlier than usual. Flushed with a new sense of civic responsibility they'd taken it upon themselves to help distribute the heavier luggage and valued possessions of displaced families around the village. After a curt whispered request from the vicar Scott Driver had also left, a reluctant escort to the bewildered Vincent-Townends; the taste of pork had set Gordon hallucinating again and Lucy was drunkenly incapable of managing his wheelchair.

Eventually, from where he was sitting, the only person Simon could see was Sid, back behind the bar and absent-mindedly topping up his half-pint glass. There were still a few voices from round the corner and Simon craned forward in time to see Richard Devine usher a last group out of the main door with a few tired, gentle words: 'You'll be fine now, things will look much better in the morning, and it *has* stopped raining. And thank you again Phil, Maureen, it's very kind of you. There'll be a place for you in Heaven,' he added with a shy little laugh. The latch dropped noisily on the door and Richard Devine turned towards the bar.

'Do you know, Sid, that's the best thing that's come out of this whole bloody affair.'

Sid looked up sharply and studied the vicar for a moment, then he turned to the mirrored shelves with their optics, took a small balloon glass and firmly pumped the upended neck of a clear bulbous bottle twice. 'Brandy, vicar ... double.' He pushed it across the bar. 'On the house.'

Sid thought Richard Devine looked close to tears but the vicar carried on, almost as if talking to himself: 'After all the fighting and backbiting and bitching something like this happens and... well, it makes you realise ... even the Hoggits and Ref Watts of this world with all their lies and greed, and all their money, well they still can't take away people's basic decency, that instinct that good people have to take responsibility for each other... neighbourliness, Christian charity if you will, their sense of... well, community.' He sipped at his glass. 'It was never really broken was it?'

Sid nodded in what might have been agreement and topped up his half-pint glass. 'Doesn't look like you're gonna get that fu... a flippin' wind farm now either, vicar.'

'No, Sid, you're right. There is that too.' Richard finished his drink, smiled his thanks and quietly let himself out.

Sid slumped wearily onto the stool opposite Simon. 'She's gone then, Scoop?'

'Yep. Deadlines to meet.' Simon smiled ruefully.

' For good?'

'Oh, I should think so.'

Sid sipped his beer. 'Shame.'

'Not really.' Simon twiddled the stem of Mattie's glass. 'The ducks seemed to like her though.'

'Not your type then?'

'She travelled too light.'

'Eh?'

'Never brought her toothbrush.'

'Eh?'

'Never mind. Oh, looks like they're on the move.' He nodded over Sid's left shoulder.

After the excitement of their earlier question-and-answer performance the Aarights had resumed their customary postures, reclaimed their pint glasses and got on with their normal evening routine. And now, with the last simultaneous sips of flat beer taken it was time for ''ome'.

'I'd forgotten they were there,' Sid chuckled. 'Not such daft old sods as it turned out eh? I shall quite miss 'em.'

Simon looked at him quizzically.

'Yeah, I'm off back to The Smoke. Had enough of the bleedin' countryside. Beryl's coming too.'

'Your wife?'

'Yeah, *that* Beryl. Been 'aving a bit of a break with her mother down on the coast. And a few holidays up at Blackpool too when she fancied it. She couldn't stand it 'ere, always said she'd come back... not that she really went, but anyway, she always said that if we got a place back in London we could get on with it again. Together. So I 'ave. Nice little place: freehouse, books look OK and it's in Peckham, just off the Rye. Getting quite posh round there these days, bit of money round the old manor. More foreigners too of course, quite a few of them Muslim types around the area now but the more the merrier that's what I say, all good for business.'

'I wouldn't bet on that, Sid but congratulations, I'm pleased for you, and Beryl. Good luck and all that.' Simon raised his almost empty glass, which Sid took as a hint and refilled at the bar. There was no mention of payment. Simon nodded his thanks. 'So what about this place then?'

'Sold.'

'*What?*'

'Yeah, went through this morning,' Sid beamed, 'sweet as a nut!'

'Well, well. Who to?'

'Oh, I dunno, some bloody dreamers from London, Clapham I think. Fancy a bit of the country life, you know the type, gonna make a fortune pulling pints of real ale and flogging organic ploughman's to the yokels. Got no fuckin' idea!'

'Hmm.'

Sid glanced at him suspiciously. 'So what about you then? What you up to?'

'I'll be off too. The cottage probably won't be habitable for a while and if I'm going to move I might as well get a change of scenery while I'm at it.'

Sid nodded, unsurprised. 'Any ideas?'

'Thought I'd look at The Lake District. I've got a pair of walking boots I've only worn twice. Thought I'd find a little place for the winter and get down to work.'

'Work? What work, doing what?'

'I'm writing a book.'

'Right,' Sid said slowly. Simon wasn't sure whether with doubt or respect. 'What about?'

'This,' Simon said, sweeping his arm around the pub. 'This place, everything that's been going on... and a few things that haven't,' he smiled. 'All the little dramas, the fights, the lying and cheating, the whole wind farm thing... and most of all the people, all the different personalities, the characters, the egos, the saints and the sinners, the normal and the nutters... especially the nutters. Warts and all.'

Sid thought about this for a moment. 'Yeah, well, probably best you do piss off out of it before anyone round 'ere sees that then,' he concluded.

They sat in the silent emptiness of the pub for several minutes sipping their drinks absorbed with their own thoughts and plans, until Sid stretched and got wearily to his feet. 'You're gonna need a bed,' he said gruffly.

'I suppose I am.'

'Better stay 'ere then.'

'Thanks Sid.'

Lady Arabella Hoggit walked slowly up the steps of the enormous swimming pool. She was glistening, bronzed and quite naked.

Linda Warren watched her lazily from where she lay on the huge double sunbed, propped on one elbow amongst a scattering of bright cushions. It was clear from her tan that she too rarely wore clothes in the sun.

'Do you want a rub?'

'Hmm.'

The gently kneading fingers had reached the hollow at the very base of her spine when there was a discreet warble from the thatched and tiled bar at the far end of the pool.

'Phone, Bella.'

'Hmm.' She arched her back slightly. 'Don't stop.'

The warble continued. 'Sure?'

'Hmm, it won't be anything important.

20529279R00182

Printed in Great Britain
by Amazon